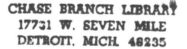

THE
DEVIL'S OWN
RAG DOLL

Mitchell Bartoy

THE DEVIL'S OWN RAG DOLL

ST. MARTIN'S MINOTAUR
New York

www.minotaurbooks.com

LIBRARY OF CONGRESS CATALOGING-IN-PUBLICATION DATA

Bartoy, Mitchell.
    The devil's own rag doll / Mitchell Bartoy.—1st ed.
    p. cm.
    ISBN 0-312-34088-5
    EAN 978-0-312-34088-9
    1. Young women—Crimes against—Fiction. 2. Police—Michigan—Detroit—Fiction. 3. Inheritance and succession—Fiction. 4. Interracial dating—Fiction. 5. Detroit (Mich.)—Fiction. 6. Race relations—Fiction. I. Title.

PS3602.A843D48 2005
813'.6—dc22

                              2005046076

First Edition: October 2005

10 9 8 7 6 5 4 3 2 1

For my mother

ACKNOWLEDGMENTS

This novel could not have been completed without the help, encouragement, and sharp criticism of dozens of people. For their enthusiasm and support and for their leap of faith on my behalf, I am deeply grateful to my agent, Andrea Somberg, and to my fine editor, Ben Sevier. Dorene O'Brien has offered years of solid friendship and keen analysis. Dr. Renata Wasserman and so many others at Wayne State University helped to make the book possible as well. I am especially indebted to Christopher Towne Leland for his boundless generosity, trenchant commentary, and simple kindness. Lastly, of course, I must thank Julie Bartoy, my patient and long-suffering wife, and my fantastic children, Jackson and Allison, who are present in every page I write.

THE
DEVIL'S OWN
RAG DOLL

CHAPTER

1

Thursday, June 10, 1943
Detroit

Bobby Swope looked over at me and grinned with smoke curling out between his long teeth. "Just remember, Pete, first thing, these niggers are always going to lie to you."

"It ain't just the niggers," I said. "Seems like nobody can talk straight anymore."

"So long as you remember," said Bobby. "You keep it at the back of your mind that he's going to be putting on a show for us, that's all."

I ran a finger around the inside of my collar. I had worn a tie just as tight and a heavier, darker shirt as a uniformed officer, but the new shirts and suit jackets I had to wear as a detective seemed to cut into me more sharply. It didn't help that June had brought thick heat so early in the year.

"Well," I told him, "I don't figure on thinking about it too much. I'll go along, just so long as you keep it simple for me."

Bobby blew more smoke through his big yellow teeth. "Okay, okay. We just go in, see what he knows, right? Not too complicated. I'll do the playacting, and you can just put that mug on him. He tells us what we need to know, we find the girl, and that's thirty-five easy simoleons for you."

"Sure," I said. "It *sounds* simple." Simple enough: Big-shot auto company man Roger Hardiman had a daughter with a taste for trouble. Young Jane Hardiman liked to run around with the shines on the dark side of town, hitting the nightspots in Paradise Valley and Black Bottom. We were to find the girl, put a scare into whoever she was with, drag her home to the mansion in Grosse Pointe, and collect the money. A little side job Bobby had cooked up. With Bobby, though, you never knew when the shit started to flow. Bobby thought he had a line on the job even before we walked into it. We had driven to the edge of Black Bottom to roust a local character named Toby Thrumm, who would tell us just where to find the girl. At least this was Bobby's expectation.

But though I had been made a detective only a little more than a month earlier, I knew from my own long time of shaky luck that nothing ever turned out to be so neat or tidy. My new badge lay heavily on the underside of my lapel as I reached in to unhook the leather strap that held my gun in the shoulder rig. I guess I took in my breath in a way that let on how it struck me.

"Hardiman's on the level?" I asked. "You're sure about it?"

"I've got a line on him," Bobby answered. He narrowed his eyes and squinted through smoke over the rounded hood of the auto. "I know him well enough, I guess. You can bet your good eye he can afford what he's paying us."

Bobby always kept so many pots simmering that I couldn't blame him for being cagey, even with me. He was so affable that you had to let it go.

Hell, I thought, *even I don't let on everything I know. That Hardiman girl…*

I could remember when Black Bottom didn't look half bad, but now it had gone to seed. Maybe the war had pulled something away. But stepping back from it, I knew it was just the way things worked. All the houses needed something: a coat of paint, a new roof, caulk on the windows. It wasn't a place where you could afford to let your guard down. But the tenants and the landlords couldn't figure out who'd pay for any repairs, and so water ripped hell out of every old building, running down and sneaking into the tiniest crack, freezing and thawing or just soaking into unprotected wood, softening and weakening. The renters couldn't see putting any money into a place that wasn't theirs, and the landlords never had a reason to set foot in such a bad part of town. If the rent didn't come, they just called in the muscle to dump the tenants, and a dozen other colored families would line up for the empty place. With the war on, nobody from the city or the department had any interest in the situation, not down in Black Bottom or Paradise Valley, where it was only colored folks piled up on top of each other.

We left the car and stepped onto the sagging porch of Toby Thrumm's place. The wood felt soft under my heavy shoes. In the colored district where Toby Thrumm rented the bottom flat of a leaning wood house, we stood out like ghosts—but Bobby preened like he was stepping onto a stage. He shook out his jacket and straightened his tie as we stood on the porch. Then he rapped a bony knuckle on the door, loud and happy like he was selling brushes. I shifted my weight back and forth behind him. The scalp on the top of his head looked pale and weak below the thin black hair. Through his clothes you could see how his bones were set, shoulders and elbows angling without any meat. I was half again as wide as he was. We kept waiting, and I kept shifting, and the loose boards under my feet creaked and pulled at their nails.

Bobby rapped again, and kept rapping until the heavy bolt rasped back.

After a moment, the handle turned and the door opened a sliver. The crack grew slowly until the blinking yellow eye of Toby Thrumm appeared. It was hard to make out any expression from just the one eye, but I saw it look sharply out, scan Bobby quickly, then flutter a little as it lit on my own dark mug. The door opened a bit more and the inside chain pulled taut. "Well," Thrumm said, "what's it all about, fellas?"

"What's with the chain, Toby? Worried about hooligans?" Bobby flicked his cigarette at the chain, dusting the threshold with gently falling ash.

"Well, it's a war on, I heard somethin' 'bout that. Maybe there's enemy agents about or—"

I slipped past Bobby and shouldered through the doorway without pulling my hands from my pockets. The chain pulled loose from its mooring in the dry wood of the doorframe, and Thrumm staggered backward with his hands fluttering up to his face. I kept moving and muscled Thrumm to a seat on the sofa. I wasn't muscling him to be hard so much as to keep things moving. Slogging through trash can easily take up a whole day, and still you end up with nothing but trash. I stood close to Thrumm for a few moments until Bobby could catch up. With the sunny windows at my back, my face lay deep in the shadow of the wide brim of my hat, and I didn't move to let Thrumm get a good look. His rheumy eyes sneaked toward Bobby a few times, and I could see that it wasn't the first time they'd been in a room together; but I kept it to myself. Thrumm's tongue darted over his shipwrecked lower teeth to wet his lips.

Bobby nudged a bit of splintered wood aside so he could close the front door and then moved slowly toward Thrumm. He pulled off his hat and glanced about for a clean place to put it down. Finding none, he held it by the brim and tapped it lightly against his leg.

He said, "We'd like to ask you a few questions, Toby. Is that all right?"

"Well," said Thrumm, "you—you all know me—they know me down to the station. I'm always willing to help out—"

"Save all that malarkey." Bobby kept his usual grin but squinted at Thrumm. "We're not selling tickets to the policemen's ball."

I hovered nearby until it was clear that Thrumm would offer no resistance. Then I stepped away and started to form a picture of the dim little flat. My anger eased and my attention spread out, and I noticed that the place reeked of sour milk, smoke, and salami. I kept quiet, and I suppose that was why Thrumm kept glancing at me, stealing looks at the black patch over what used to be my eye.

"Like I say, fellas…don't I know you from somewhere?" Thrumm tried to compose himself. He tried to sit up, but the sofa was too soft. Then he tugged vainly at his open fly, crossed his legs, and said, "I don't guess you got some badges you could show, right? Everybody got some kind of badges these days, don't they?" His eyes skated about, never meeting Bobby's for any time, now and again darting to the telephone table near the kitchen. I picked up on Thrumm's nervous concern and let myself drift that way.

Bobby hiked up his foot to the arm of the sofa and pretended to wipe a smudge off the shiny leather of the lighter part of his two-tones. You could see the well-worn leather sap tucked into his garter and the top of his sock, as well as a good portion of white skin, blue veins, and patchy black hair.

"Just one thing to get straight, boy," Bobby said. "We don't like having to deal with all the backwoods country shit that's been coming up here lately. Especially criminal trash like yourself. If you want to leave Grandmaw down on the farm in Shitville, Mississippi, and come up here sniffing for work, we can't stop you. It's still a free country, so they say. But while you're here, you'll do things our way, right?" Bobby scratched up and down his shin. "We're all set up here to take away everything you ever thought you had in this world. We do it every day to folks better made than you. It's like a system, the way we do it. Try to think about how it might be if we locked you up for a few days and you came out to find your stuff all gone and somebody else living in your house—and if you found yourself blackballed at all the factories."

"Oh, yassuh. *Yassuh.*"

Bobby looked at him sharply, then softened his expression, leaned close, and grinned. He dropped his foot to the floor and began to show a little drawl in his speech. "Let's not be funny, Toby. You can see that my partner here, Detective Caudill, is an unhappy man. You can see how his face hangs. I've tried to get him to look to the brighter side of things, but he just doesn't seem to lean that way. I don't think he likes niggers as much as I do. He doesn't like anybody, as far as I can tell. I guess he'd just like to get out of this stinking hole as soon as he can. So you can see that he'd appreciate it if you'd answer the few simple questions we have just as fast as your little brain can start to turn over."

"I see how it is," said Thrumm, giving me the eyeball. When he saw me turning toward him with some heat, he quickly looked away. "Seem like that's the way it always is."

I turned away and pretended an interest in the decor. I was afraid that my cheek might start twitching, because I always got tickled when Bobby started in with a spiel. Whether or not Bobby's act was effective, it was always good for a laugh. Bobby's ridiculous tough-guy routine wasn't all that different from the slick, breezy attitude he used in dealing with people with money or position. Maybe it was because I knew him, but neither routine seemed convincing. It was like he learned his words from watching movies, and he was willing to try anything out, even if it couldn't fairly sit on his jumbled bones and his weasel face. Somehow he got by, though. With me it was easier and duller: I treated everybody the same kind of bad, and I didn't care that nobody liked me.

While Bobby worked Thrumm over with talk, I let my mind bring another thing forward. I had caught a whiff when I busted in: opium, probably, or some kind of doctored marijuana. Thrumm looked half gone with it right now. From the way his eyes jittered, I could see that he was plenty spooked, but I couldn't tell exactly where the stash would be. Next to the telephone table there was a battered china cabinet with no glass in the doors and a collection of knickknacks arranged on the shelves. I pulled my right hand from my pocket and picked up the salt-and-pepper sets one by one, tipping them over, pretending to read the bottoms. Every one of them had at least some remnant of salt or pepper inside. Judging from Thrumm's lack of reaction, I knew the china cabinet held nothing of interest.

"We need to find Donny Pease," said Bobby. "We're told you know where he stays."

"Fellas, I ain't seen Donny Pease in six month. 'Tha's the God's truth."

Even with only one eye, I could see that he was lying. When I heard Thrumm slipping in and out of the hayseed lingo, I wanted to smack the shine off his oily face, try out a little amateur dentistry on his ragged teeth; but I let Bobby keep working him.

Bobby said, "We're told you tipped a few drinks with him last Saturday over to the Forest Club."

"Who said that? That's a lie."

I picked up a salt shaker in the shape of a country boy with a straw hat. With one quick motion I turned and threw the shaker through the plaster and through the lath wood of the wall just over Thrumm's head. It was closer than I had intended, the missing eye playing hell with my depth perception. Thrumm didn't have time to flinch. I glowered at him long enough to see the eyes get big under his pomaded, plaster-flecked hair. Then I turned back to the cabinet to thumb through a stack of photographs: smiling Toby Thrumm, half toked, some women, a few other colored men standing around an alley. Back home, backwoods, Deep South. I thought of Thrumm with some disdain. But the photos brought up a twinge of regret in me. Whatever his faults, Thrumm was a man who could feel easy, who could make and keep friends and enjoy himself.

"There's no sense lying to us," Bobby told him. "I've got the time to stay right here breathing on you until you tell me exactly where to find Donny Pease. We're on the public payroll." Bobby pulled out a pack of smokes from his jacket and offered one to Thrumm. "No sense making Detective Caudill break out a sweat this early in the day. If he starts to sweat, you start wishing you were a cool breeze." Bobby leaned close to offer Thrumm a light and spoke in a whisper. "He's wound up tighter than a dress on Rita Hayworth."

"Well," said Thrumm, licking his lips again, "last I hear, he's staying with a woman two doors up from the Forest Club, you know, on Hastings over there, on Forest and Hastings."

As I stepped next to the telephone table, I could see that Thrumm was almost ready to jump up from the sofa.

"Don't lie to me!" Bobby almost laughed.

"I don't lie! If it's one thing I ain't, it's a liar!"

"You already lied to me once, at least," Bobby said, running his hand back amiably over his forehead. "Why would I figure you'd beat that habit so fast?"

I stood before the telephone table and angled myself so I could make out Thrumm squirming at the edge of my sight. With my right hand I picked up the handpiece, listened, and put it back, then ran a finger over the edge of the table. I still hadn't taken my left hand out of my pocket.

"I ain't so stupid as you all try to put on me. Donny Pease been known to have a temper on him, that's all. You put me in a hard place. But I guess he ain't so much to me, now that I think on it a while."

"Because you understand," said Bobby, "if you send us over there and we find out you're yanking our dicks, we'll be back here pretty quick, and plenty hot."

"Well, I don't know he'll be there," Thrumm said hastily. "That's just what I hear."

I felt Thrumm's eyes nailed onto me; I was right on top of whatever he was worried about. So I pulled my left hand slowly from the pocket and gave Thrumm a good long look at it. Pink flesh, bright and shiny where the two littlest fingers should have been anchored to the mangled palm. A lobster claw. With the claw I fingered over Thrumm's war production ID badge from the Packard aircraft engine place, the money clip filled out with small bills, and his keys. I started to pull open the little drawer in the table. I figured it to be some kind of dope, but since we had no intention of taking Thrumm in, I wasn't about to go through the trouble of actually finding anything.

"Two doors up? What's the woman's name?" Bobby asked.

"Listen, I ain't, I ain't exactly sure about that." Thrumm squirmed, and strained his attention toward me. "You know how that goes. So thick with extra women around here now with the war and all, they lookin' all the same to me."

"Well, let's put it this way. Some advice. If we have to come back here, you'll want to be somewhere else." Bobby stood up and shook down his clothes to a proper hang. He looked down at Thrumm but let his eyes go out of focus, as if considering something carefully. Then he gestured to me. "Let's get out of here. If we hurry, we can finish all this before lunch."

I let my lips curl a bit. I left the drawer as it was, picked up the telephone, and ripped the cord from the base. Then I turned and followed Bobby right out the door. As I trudged to the car through the rising heat of the cloudless day, I thought about what Thrumm had said.

Bobby said, "We'll take it around the block and up the alley and see if Toby Thrumm's a rabbit like I think he is."

Nobody else ever drove if Bobby Swope was around. He fished the keys from his pocket and we roared off, pretending to be hot for Hastings Street. But Bobby drove around to the next street, parked, and cooled for a few minutes, time enough for Thrumm to throw a few things in a bag. The alley was quiet enough. I guessed that there were plenty of white folks off playing tennis somewhere, getting rich by renting out the broken-down houses to all the colored families. They were jammed in tight in the Bottom and in Paradise Valley, jammed in, as I had read somewhere, as tight as Calcutta. And more Negroes were coming all the time, hitching up from the Deep South or riding over from Chicago or Cleveland to grab a job at one of the big auto plants or making airplanes at Willow Run.

We walked up the alley and waited out of sight in front of the garage door. In a minute Thrumm hot-stepped it toward the garage and began to swing open the big door from the inside. I ducked in and grabbed Thrumm by his spotty shirt and lifted him onto the hood of the old Fargo truck. Thrumm's head and backbone bounced all the way up to the windshield as I dragged him up over the front of the vehicle, and then again on the way down to the dirt floor of the garage. Bobby quietly pulled the garage door closed, cutting down the light to what could squeeze through the murky windows.

Thrumm's eyes got bigger when I pulled out my revolver. I held the barrel of the pistol hard to the base of Thrumm's neck and watched a snaky vein grow fat with stoppered blood. Bobby pulled a little knife from his pocket and absently cleaned his nails for a moment, watching Thrumm with lazy eyes. Then he stooped and eased the blade slowly into the sidewall of one of the truck's precious wartime tires, twisting to let the air hiss out more quickly. Thrumm gasped and jerked but made no attempt to escape. I watched his eyes jumping and judged that I was about to hear another lie, so I twice brought the butt of the revolver down onto the bridge of his nose.

Thrumm yelped and coughed, then held up a pale, dry palm in submission.

Bobby leaned close. "Lie to me again, lover boy."

"Shoo!" sputtered Thrumm through running blood. "I won't tell no more stories." Thrumm blinked to get the water from his eyes and moved to get up, but I pushed the nose of the gun into his neck again. "Okay, okay. He stay out on Wyoming, little apartment building next to Bidwell's on Fenkell there, you'll find 'im."

I stood up, wiped the muzzle of my gun on my trousers, and holstered the piece. I wanted to spit the coppery taste from my mouth. *You could have just told us that in the first place,* I thought.

Thrumm said nothing more. He drew his arms and legs in close and pulled up his shirttail to dab at his bloody nose. Bobby folded his knife and slipped it into his pocket with a wistful look on his face. He turned to push open the big door of the garage. Bright light washed in to show how small Toby Thrumm had become: all out of lies and bluff, smacked down to the dirt floor of his own garage, his blood let out. I turned away from him because the rich redness dazzled my eye.

I knew that the quick escalation of low-level violence had panicked Thrumm into telling the truth. But one thing troubled me as I followed Bobby out of the garage: Why was Thrumm so reluctant to spill Pease's whereabouts? Thrumm was not such a big man, but he was hard in the arms and back from his labor, and Pease had never been anything more than a loser on a slow downward slide, small and soft and used to talking his way through trouble. I was thinking hard as we walked back to the car.

Another thing tugged at my gut. Because I did not see how it

could be useful, I had not told Bobby of my acquaintance with young
Jane Hardiman. In the late fall of 1941, not long before the Japs came
to Pearl Harbor, I was walking my beat as usual. Two girls came out
of Bland's Liquor and turned up the street toward me like it was the
Easter Parade. To see them walking arm-in-arm like they were, in a
district where there wasn't anything but bump shops and beer gardens and grubby factory rats—well, it put a jolt in me. It was getting
toward dusk, and I knew the type of trouble that percolated on my
beat after sundown. As they came close, I pulled out my billy and
spread my arms to corral them to a halt.

The tallest one spoke with a twinkle in her eye. "Some trouble,
officer?"

"Not yet there isn't," I said. "That's the way it's going to stay.
What kind of business you girls have with Bland?"

The smaller girl kept her eyes down.

The other said, "He wouldn't sell us any liquor, if that's what
you're wondering. He did sell us a pack of smokes, though."

"Jane!"

"I don't mind the smoking, girly," I said. "But the two of you can't
be anything but trouble for me down here."

"I'm Jane Hardiman, and this is my friend Missy—"

"Jane! Don't tell him—"

"I don't care who you are," I said. "I want you off my beat before
the wolves come out."

"Rousted by the authorities! I suppose we're criminals now," Jane
Hardiman said. Her tone was flippant, but her eyes smiled warmly.
"Will you have to take us in? I don't think Missy's constitution can
accommodate any hard time."

"If you won't get into a cab, I'll have to call a scout car to take you
home."

"We'll take the cab!" piped Missy.

I brought them along to the cab stand around the corner and put them in the first car.

Jane rolled down the window and beckoned me near. "Officer, I don't suppose you could front us a dollar or two for the cab? We're a little short."

The cabbie said, "I don't take no charity case."

The girl was not more than fifteen years old, I judged, but she had managed to confound me. I put my hand on the door and stooped down to get a look at her face. I was ready to pull the money from my pocket.

"I'm just teasing, Officer," Jane said. "I have plenty of money." She put her hand over mine—the bad one—and then brought it up to touch my cheek softly just below my patch.

"You've been kinder than you had to be," she said.

The girl was trouble, all right. I could see that. Smart as a whip and used to having her way. But there was something close and familiar in her eyes. She looked warmly at me, as if she felt *sorry* for me. Sorry about the eye and the fingers, sorry that it was my job to roust the trouble from my little corner of the world.

I stood up and took a step back from the cab, then tapped the door a couple times with the billy. "I don't want to see either of you down here again," I said.

"Don't worry," said Jane. "We can take care of ourselves."

She sat back and squeezed her friend's knee. I could hear her clear voice giving the cabbie a Grosse Pointe address as the car pulled away from the curb.

That was the only time I had ever seen her, and I hadn't thought of it again until Bobby mentioned the name to me for the side deal he had cooked up. She was a smart girl, and I hoped that she had learned enough in the two years since then to keep her safe. As I settled into Bobby's car for the drive to Pease's place, an odd tug of emotion pulled at me: No matter how seamy the situation turned out to be, I hoped that the girl would recognize me when she saw me. I hoped she would appreciate what I was trying to do.

"What a city, eh, Pete?" Bobby asked, his pale face lit up with exhilaration. "I tell you, if this isn't the greatest city in the world, I'm as ugly as Churchill." He lit a smoke and sucked on it till he trembled, then laughed and coughed the smoke into the air. "Industry! Manufacture! It's all right here! Right here in the middle of the country, down along the beautiful Detroit River. What else could we need?" Bobby sat with his back off the seat, clutching and slapping at the steering wheel with both hands. "Brother, look at those trees. You think they have trees like that in any other city?"

I let my attention wander, knowing that Bobby's spiel would blow itself out after a time. *Nothing is ever as simple as people make it out to be,* I thought. Why would Pease be worth a busted nose to Thrumm? And why would he be willing to cut out like that, just throw his things in a bag and light out? I guessed that Thrumm had to be making at least a decent wage to be able to afford to stay at the flat without a dozen little niggers running about the place, too, and a garage and what looked like his own truck. It was a sweet deal for Thrumm, no doubt about it, and not likely found anywhere but here.

We were heading to the west side, a little pocket around Wyoming where they let the dark folks stay. *She's somewhere in the city,* I thought. *She could be anywhere.*

"Take it easy, Bobby," I said. "You're driving like a rumrunner."

"I tell you, Pete, what a town! It's taking the war to show the world what's really important. Detroit steel! We've got to think ahead to what's going to happen after this whole Hitler thing blows over. We should put our money where it'll make a little something for us. You think Chrysler or the Dodge brothers or Jasper Lloyd sat around waiting for things to happen? No! Got to stay ahead of the game!"

Bobby made himself at home as he drove. When he didn't need it for the clutch, he hiked his left foot up onto the seat and rested his knee against the open window. He put the old Chevy through a workout, drove six blocks the wrong way down John R, clipped the mirror off a new Lloyd City Cruiser parked on the corner at Harper. He eyed the crowds flashing by full of women shopping and running out for lunch dressed in office wear. "This is the place to be, all right. Anybody could get laid in this town. I'd bet my ass on it, even a three-letter man could get laid around here!" He glanced at me and rapped two bony knuckles onto my chest. "Hell, even a one-eyed gimp could get some action now and again if he put his mind to it. You should get out a little more, that's my take on the whole matter."

"You talk like a woman sometimes," I said. "Just talk and more talk."

"I'm always ready for action," said Bobby. "Trouble is I get nothing but dragging feet whenever I try to scare something up."

"Okay, I got you." I let my face go slack. The last thing I thought I needed was Bobby Swope's advice on how to improve my social life. "How should it go with Pease?"

"You're the man with the rough-stuff experience, Pete." Bobby ditched his butt out the window and fumbled for another smoke. "But see, think of it this way. Pease is a known felon from the auto beef in St. Louis, and he's been known to carry a weapon. He might also be found in possession of a small quantity of an illicit substance, namely a little packet of reefer"—he patted the inside pocket of his jacket—"if he gives us any trouble. That won't look bad if we end up having to make a report of all this. So you can use your discretion about the persuasive stuff."

"What about the girl?" I asked. "If she's that type, she'll be back over as soon as things cool down."

"I call that job security, Pete," said Bobby. He tapped a finger three times against his forehead, leaving three white marks on his skin that took their time coming back to pink. "I'm always thinking ahead."

I wondered if Captain Mitchell had expected that his new detective would receive such errant guidance when he paired me with Bobby to learn the ropes and get a handle on procedure. Mitchell was hard to figure, but he was not a fool. It had been such a surprise that I had done so well on the detective's exam that nobody in the brass knew what the hell to do with me. They all knew me as a pug, a big lug, and I guess people in general don't want to go to the trouble of thinking twice about anything if they don't have to. In fact, I wasn't sure myself why I took the exam in the first place. Bobby had told me that it seemed like somebody higher up was pulling some strings, maybe on account of my old man's popularity. So there I was with Bobby, so full of go-go-go, and I just fell into the rough stuff because it felt comfortable. I knew I could throw a scare. But it isn't easy to change into another man, and I wondered if I'd ever get to be much of a thinking detective.

Trying to feel Bobby out, I said, "You're saying it would be okay to bust his nose?"

"Okay with me," said Bobby.

"Break a couple fingers?"

"That'll hurt." Bobby grinned and flicked his butt out the window, half smoked.

"Break his arm?"

"Well, we don't want to make too much of a fuss, after all."

"I got you."

I guess I was happy enough just to do what I was told. Maybe that was the one thing about me that always rattled my old man. He was looking for a little initiative out of me, and he never found it. I guess I took the detective exam as a nod to him. Sure, he would have wanted it. What you go through with your family works on you, underground, no matter how much you try to tell yourself that you've put all of it behind you. My old man used to talk about freedom and independence—and he seemed to want to hold on to an idea about this country like he was an immigrant. But freedom, as I had it figured, was just a way of saying that you were responsible for what you did every minute of the day. You had to decide all along what you should do. It could tire you out from thinking. So when it came down to it, I had always been willing to be told what to do, as long as it wasn't too far out of line.

But nobody would ever tell you exactly what they wanted. Bobby was an example: I could bite my way closer to a picture of the situation by asking questions, and sooner or later I'd get an idea where the lines were drawn. But Bobby liked to hint around, to wink and lay a finger to the side of his nose. For Bobby, the lines were always part of a negotiation; they could always be shifted or ignored if a better deal showed up, especially if they weren't drawn in anything firmer than sand in the first place.

It was a bit of a drive to get to the little colored section on the west side. As we rolled toward Pease's apartment building, we pulled a lot of eyeballs from their business in the overcrowded district. The rows of small apartment buildings, though generally made of brick, dropped bits of spalled masonry and crumbling mortar to the walk. Everything sat too close to the road. Along the edge where the concrete met the buildings and in all the cracks in the sidewalks, weeds poked up and spilled out in fronds to catch sun and water. In between the small businesses, a few rickety wood houses stood, all with big porches on the upper and lower flats. These were filled generally with older folks and very young children, and I could feel them staring. I guessed the colored folks were probably tired of the shit that seemed always to roll their way.

Bobby crept along the curb, casing Pease's building. It was like all the rest; the windows were open to let the feeble breeze through, and yet the blinds were drawn shut to keep out the sun. I thought, *Why would she want to come to such a filthy place? What in her private-school life of leisure could make her want to dirty herself this way?* Roger Hardiman should have had enough money, I imagined, to keep his family from falling apart. I checked my mind from wondering too much about what Jane and Pease might be doing inside, or what kind of fussy talk it must bring up in the district to see a white girl going up to a colored man's apartment. It was only a job for us. We had not been hired to involve ourselves any more than we had to, and yet I found myself gritting my teeth and squeezing my hands into fists. Maybe the girl would turn out to be a foul-mouthed shrew, and we'd have to drag her kicking and screaming back to the car. But I was stirred up with feeling, with jealousy or anger or an odd protective instinct, and I did not want to put a reason to it. I was glad when Bobby parked next to a hydrant and killed the motor.

"Some joint, ah?" he said. From the outside, from the street, it wasn't easy to see anything wrong. Colored kids were just out of school for the summer, running and screaming, ripping up the tiny patches of grass, and scrawny old gents sat on benches and chairs and tried to soak up warmth into their dry bones. But when we stepped into the cramped vestibule and scanned the mailboxes for Pease's name, I knew something was up. I could smell every onion that had ever been cooked in the building. The odor hung in the air, seeping from the soggy, piss-grade lumber of the trim and doors and from the plaster flaking from the ceiling. *The air just isn't moving,* I thought. It was like the hush that falls over a room after somebody sends glass crashing to the floor. Blood came up in my face, and my scalp bristled.

Bobby tapped one of the boxes: Pearson, scrawled in uppercase letters in smudged pencil, a name Pease had used in St. Louis. Second floor, straight shot toward the back. Bobby took the stairs at the front of the building, and I walked through the dim hallway to the back stairs, feeling my shoulders brush against the walls. As I thumped up the steps, colored boys began to pass me on the way down, creeping along the rail with their eyes put aside, the only sound the swish of their too-big trousers. One by one they went. Then, as I got to the top, the last of them tried to push past me. I grabbed the boy's bony arm and jerked him back hard enough to make him yelp.

I judged him to be no more than thirteen, tall for his age. His bones seemed recently grown and now waited for the flesh to catch up. He couldn't stop his big wet eyes from staring at my eye patch. I almost let him go.

"What's going on here, boy?" I said, growling and pulling the boy close to me.

"I don't know nothin'," he said, too scared to wriggle or pull away.

"What's your name, boy?" I could see the boy's eyes begin to skitter. "Don't lie to me!"

"Joshua."

"You know Donny Pease?"

The name lit up the boy's eyes, but before I could say any more, Bobby's voice boomed in the still air. "Caudill! God damn it, Caudill!"

I pushed the boy aside and hoofed it double time to Pease's door, pulling out my revolver as I went.

I couldn't see anything at first because Bobby stood just inside the doorway. The heavy revolver at his side seemed to stretch his arm, so that his white wrist stuck out from his sleeve. He had pulled off his hat, showing the few black hairs he had left on his prematurely balding head. I shouldered him aside with my pistol up, thinking—if I was thinking of anything—that I could protect him from whatever was inside.

But it was too late for protecting, and more trouble than a gun could blast away: Young Jane Hardiman sat sprawled on the couch, her legs spread, her pleated skirt pulled up to her chin, and dried blood covering all but a few glimpses of the pale skin on her thighs. It seemed like a big wind had blasted her there. Seeing her arranged that way, facing the door, with her hair flying up and stiff from dried blood, I felt like I ought to run berserk. My teeth gnashed together, my lips pulled back, and the blood ran into my arms and hands; I would have squeezed off a shot into the ceiling if the pistol had not been so close to my face.

I had not been used to making words about something like that, even though I'd seen worse, and plenty of it. The girl was dead, and any thought of making a happier life for her would have to be put to rest, too. Part of me heard Bobby quietly closing the door behind us, and another part thought, *Nothing will be simple again for a long, long time.*

CHAPTER

2

The day had been too long and too hot, so I smoothed my hair back with my palms and pressed my white handkerchief over my forehead and nose to wipe off the oily sheen that had collected. As I sat in the car with Bobby on the long circular drive of Roger Hardiman's mansion, I could see stiff-postured shadows moving across the great windows.

"Listen, Pete, try to be polite in there," said Bobby. "You have to know how to talk to people. Just let me take it. Let me do the talking."

I felt lousy enough that I wanted to stab someone with my bitterness. "I guess this means I won't ever see my thirty-five bucks," I said.

"Jesus, Pete, don't say anything about that. We'll be lucky if we keep our jobs after this."

"That girl was out of luck before we came anywhere near that place," I told him.

"You're not getting the point here, Pete. It doesn't matter what we *could* have done. That girl is dead and we're mixed up in it. If Hardiman decides pull the rug out from under us, all he has to do is give the word to Old Man Lloyd and we're finished. Finished."

"All right, Bobby," I said. "Don't think I don't feel bad about the girl. I feel like hell about it. But Hardiman can shove his money up his ass if he thinks I'm going to take the heat for it. He should have been looking after his own. Some big shooter if he can't keep track of his own little girl."

"All right, all right, I hear you," said Bobby. "Let's just go in and see if I can smooth things out a little bit."

By sticking with Bobby, I was walking into a mess. I just shrugged and put my hat back onto my head. *She's gone,* I thought. *All the way gone.*

Since the heat of the day hadn't yet settled in like it would later in the summer, the evening had brought a cool breeze off Lake St. Clair. I thought that maybe the moneyed folks here in Grosse Pointe had managed somehow to bring the cooler weather with them when they moved out of Detroit. Downtown, the high buildings and parking lots and wide paved streets seemed to trap the heat in a way that the lush lawns of the Pointes did not. I was not envious, exactly, of the big homes and the fancy automobiles. It was too much work and trouble to maintain all of it. But I'd take the money without the mess; money would let me live like I wanted to.

We walked over the cobbles of Hardiman's drive and up the steps to the vestibule. Bobby lifted a shaky hand toward the knocker. The doors opened inward suddenly, and a well-dressed man with a medical bag brushed past us. He didn't even have to look at us to decide that we weren't worth looking at. Inside, a colored servant woman looked at us with bright eyes.

"May I help you?" she said.

Bobby said, "We're—"

"Let them in, Louise," boomed a deep voice from within.

She stepped back from the door and dropped her head a bit, but stole an oddly curious glance at my face as I passed. When I turned to look at her, she met my eye and smiled a little with her mouth— but kept the same look of bright interest in her eyes, like she was looking to remember. In truth, since I'd never had a servant, I didn't know how to take it. Was a servant supposed to look you in the eye like that? So I gave her the dead-eye and turned away.

I took in the place all at once. *This is what she had to think of as a home,* I thought. The glittering chandelier, the wide, sweeping staircase, the dark wood paneling, and the rich leather furniture made me think it was a put-on, a mockup like a set from *Gone With the Wind.* But I knew that this house was the real thing, and much older than the motion picture. *She couldn't even put her feet up in a place like this without worrying about wrecking something.*

"Step this way, detectives," said Roger Hardiman, who stood at a set of double doors leading to his library.

As Bobby and I stepped through the doors, I looked Hardiman over. He was like an aging Ivy Leaguer, his blond hair gone to dull straw and traces of gray, pushed back in pretty waves from his forehead. His skin was red from too much drink and, I guessed, too much worry about getting somewhere. He was not quite as tall as Bobby but cut a better figure. His suit was cut precisely to his flat shoulders, and the trousers broke neatly over his shiny wing tips.

We all walked to a circle of leather armchairs and sat down. Hardiman sat down, too but got up immediately and walked to a cabinet to fix himself a drink.

"So," he said, "Swope, maybe you can tell me how I'm going to explain all this to my wife."

"Well, sir, first let me say that you have my most heartfelt sympathy, and I—"

"Swope, you ass, you're not a friend of mine! I don't look to you for sympathy! What I want to hear is how, in a city like this, with all the law enforcement we have, and with all the legal apparatus in place, all the industry and all the commerce, how could such a thing have happened to that little girl?"

"Well, I—"

"You understand that Jane was our only daughter and the youngest of our children. My wife and I still have our two sons, whom we love dearly, but a girl—try as you might not to have favorites—Jane was the apple of our eye." Hardiman raised his tumbler and sipped, keeping a steely glare on Bobby.

I set my jaw and sank back in my chair, watching intently. That was how they got you. From the moment you walked in the door, the money on one side of the table made it so that any blame to be passed around was going to fall your way. It never mattered that you hadn't before that moment played any part in it. Even if you were in on the same side with the money, as long as they had it and you didn't, you could never make it an even game.

And money was worth more than that. Hardiman had to be a good bit older than me, but his skin looked young, aside from the alcohol damage. There was a soundness to his teeth and his bones and a clarity to his eyes that brought home to me what might be bought with money. It was easy to imagine that the rich were not different, but I noted Hardiman's way of talking, how he controlled what was coming out of his mouth, how it sounded so full but gave away nothing. Maybe it was the real advantage of a good education.

Bobby drew in a deep breath. I could see that he was rattled, and yet there was always a certain shrewdness to him. He began to speak slowly. "It's a messy business, sir. A tragedy, I would say. But I can say, at least, that the people I've called in to take care of it will act with the greatest discretion. And Detective Caudill and I will get to the bottom of it, you can be sure."

Hardiman sucked the rest of his whiskey through the ice and set the tumbler down. "Think of what you've done so far as the last botched job you'll be allowed." He stopped for a moment to judge how his speech was hitting us. "Now, I've lost a little girl, and this grieves me deeply. I've invested so much in Jane's upbringing. But there is also a war to be won, and I'm sure you know how crucial Lloyd Motors is to the effort. So it should go without saying that you and your—your pirate friend here must find a way to perfection of effort from this point forward. And I'll hold you responsible if some sort of justice—"

A muffled commotion from the foyer cut off the rest of his blather. Raised voices struck the doors like dampened blows, and then the doors opened suddenly. A woman I guessed to be Mrs. Hardiman came in, followed by Louise, the servant, who was flustered now, her lips pressed thin. Bobby and I stood up.

"Dear, you must introduce me to our guests."

"You should rest," said Hardiman. "You shouldn't be walking." He stepped toward her, his jaw set, his blue eyes glittering. "Louise will help you to your room."

She waved him off and flounced into a chair, her eyes bleary. I could see that the doctor had underestimated her constitution.

"Fix me something, will you, dear?" she said. She sat like a shaky ballerina at the edge of her chair and regarded Bobby and me. She passed right over Bobby, but when she looked at me, something like a tight school of fish or a flock of pigeons angled in her eyes. She was angry, she was amused, she might have cried—all at once. She said, "The police, are you? I'm Estelle Hardiman."

"Well, ma'am, I'm Detective Robert Swope, and this is, may I introduce my partner, Detective Caudill."

"I see. Sit down, please. Please. Good. Louise, just go." She fluttered her thin fingers at Louise. "Close the door behind you."

Hardiman brought her a drink, Scotch on the rocks, watered down a bit.

She said, "So you're the gentlemen who found my daughter?"

Bobby looked at Hardiman.

"My husband tries to keep things from me," she said. "One of the many things he does not do well."

"You'll understand that my wife is not herself tonight," said Hardiman. "She is usually more reserved."

Mrs. Hardiman stood up and said, "I carried Jane for nine months. And delivered her breech. You see, she was a difficult child from the moment she was conceived." She choked down a bitter laugh, kept it locked inside. "You detectives don't know much about childbirth, I suppose. It isn't often brought up in polite conversation, at least in mixed company. But you see, I am a woman who insists on being treated with respect. I believe in marriage as a partnership. Roger doesn't keep things from me, because he knows I'd make his life a living hell if he did." She teetered and looked over our faces, then pulled a slim silver cigarette case from somewhere in her dress. She put her hand on my arm, leaned close, put a cigarette to her lips, and murmured, "You look like a man who could give a woman a light."

I raised my eyebrows and slowly shook my head. I pulled my left hand from my pocket and tipped the palm upward, empty, making sure she took a good look.

Bobby stood up and fumbled with his lighter until the lady managed to catch the flame. He sat down gingerly and rubbed his thumb over the silver case, looking for a place to cut into the conversation.

"Well," said Mrs. Hardiman, "my little girl is gone. Taken from me by a madman, I suppose."

"Estelle," said Hardiman, "perhaps liquor isn't the thing just now." He made a halfhearted motion to take the glass from her.

"It's just the thing," she said. "Nothing else will do." Her rings clacked on the tumbler as she tipped it back and sucked out a mouthful of whiskey.

I watched her delicate throat bobbing, watched the movement of her blue veins beneath the pale whispery skin. She might still have passed as beautiful but seemed to have lost her vitality unevenly—bits of flabby flesh contrasted with the odd dazzle in her eyes, and she had quick way of moving, even with the influence of whatever the doctor had given her. I moved my eye slowly back and forth between Hardiman and the woman.

Mrs. Hardiman glanced at me, her eyes just shy of control. "Oh, dear, I'm afraid Mr.—Cudgel, is it? Mr. Cudgel doesn't approve. Do you think I'm entirely without feeling for my daughter, Mr. Cudgel? Do I seem cold to you?"

"Ah," said Bobby, "I'm sure Detective Caudill doesn't have anything to say about that."

"I venture to say, Mr. Cudgel, that you can't begin to appreciate what's been lost here. Am I right? Do you know yourself?" She was a slender woman, and small, and half broken down, but still she turned something my way that made me think she knew how to wreck things.

I met Estelle Hardiman's eyes for a moment without letting her pull anything out of me. Then I turned my head slowly and stared blankly at her husband. You could see that she had more than a little something on him, and you can bet I was taking careful note of how he was handling her.

"It's a delicate situation," said Bobby. "It's going to take—"

"Shut up, you idiot!" Hardiman walked to his desk and shook the ink down into his fountain pen. He scrawled a note on a half-sheet of letterhead, folded it, and handed it to Bobby. "Detectives," he said, gesturing toward the doors, "I suppose you can find your way out. It's been a long day, and I should see to it that my wife gets her rest."

We stood up and walked toward the library doors. Bobby placed his hat on his head, then turned to the woman and lifted it slightly. "I'm sorry, ma'am," he said. I kept walking.

Darkness had fallen, and a chorus of crickets sang out from all over the green, leafy estates of Grosse Pointe. I was thinking about Hardiman's liquor cabinet as I slid into the car. It was obvious that he got a lot of use out of it. Since I couldn't make much out of the situation in the house, I kept from thinking about it. It was like stepping into a whole other world, where the usual rules for dealing with people had been warped, where gin might not be gin and whiskey not whiskey, where names on bottles might not say anything about what was inside. It had only been from lack of imagination that I could not see before how things might have been hard for Jane, why she might have wanted to get out of the Hardiman house.

Bobby sat down next to me and opened the paper. "Grosse Pointe Shooting Club, noon," he read.

"Well," I said bitterly, "it's a cinch they won't be feeding us any lunch over there."

CHAPTER

3

Friday, June 11

Morning? No sun yet peeping around the shades, I thought. *What kind of jackass would telephone in the middle of the night like this?*

I stumbled from bed, working my jaw, stretching my neck. Rubbing the eye in a bad attempt to see my way to the telephone in the living room. I picked it up. "Yah?"

"Jesus, Pete, how much sleep do you need?"

"Bobby." I stretched my mouth open painfully as wide as I could.

"Time to wake up, pretty boy. Things got deeper after you cut out for your beauty sleep."

"Is it five o'clock like I think it is? Anything new happen that you couldn't wait till seven to tell me about?" My jaws slowly loosened from the night's grinding.

Bobby said, "Listen, Pete, this is serious. *The Old Man himself* called Captain Mitchell last night, wants to know what the hell's going on."

"Who called? Jeffries?"

"You think I'd've been up all night if it was just the mayor? *The Old Man.* Jasper Lloyd himself called, cussed Mitchell out till his ears were bleeding."

"So?"

"So that means you'd better get your ass moving. I'll pick you up in half an hour."

"Yeah, okay," I said. I hung up the phone and made a quick breakfast: coffee and four fat slices of toast with butter. Then I ran a rag over my face and combed my black hair straight back. I worked up a little lather and brushed it onto my cheeks for a quick shave. Then I considered myself in the mirror: pale, a good build but getting thicker around the middle, jowls getting heavy, teeth okay, a soft pink empty space where my eye had been. With the maimed hand I squeezed the water from the rag and carefully wiped and dabbed away the goop that gathered each night in the cavity.

As I waited on the front steps for Bobby, I considered it lucky that school had just let out for the summer. I wouldn't have to suffer the Catholic schoolgirls as they passed me on their way to class, wouldn't have to endure their discomfort at my presence. They were good girls, for the most part, living in their own little world. Something like me, I guess, they didn't usually have to think about. Something older, and hard, and cut up some. Young Jane Hardiman had only laid eyes on me the one brief time, but she wasn't put off, and had even reached up to touch my face. It was an odd thing to do. Thoughts of the girl drew me on to a crashing remembrance of the trouble we had stumbled into.

I drew a deep breath and then let it pass through clenched teeth. *Maybe it's better to live alone,* I thought. For me at least—better not to have to haggle about small things every day. Imagine Hardiman having to deal with that woman every day of his life. You could go through a fortune just figuring ways to keep yourself away from her.

I found myself at thirty-five with regret and a bit of relief. Never married and starting to get to the age where it wouldn't be expected anymore. I could think of it as one less responsibility to shoulder, one less obstacle between me and a simpler life.

Simplicity.

I tried to think of the exact time I'd crossed over the line to where I could no longer keep everything straight in my head. Maybe as a young man I'd just been better at ignoring all the things outside my immediate circle of concern. I'd done all right for myself, even during the lean years before the war. Now it seemed that for every problem I worked on with my full attention, two more popped up, so that I was always behind in what I needed to do. It was a terrible feeling, waking up in the morning already in the hole.

And now, burned into my mind's eye: a young rich girl I never really knew, violated, jagged end of a cracked broomstick jutting out of her. Skin torn from her neck by a garrote. But what clenched at my gut was the way she had been set up like a picture show on the sofa, with her legs spread open toward the door, so that whoever walked in would get it right in the eye. You could do a bad thing because you were stupid or weak or afraid, sure—in every city, every day, it was bound to happen. When I saw that girl, though, something cold got into me, like I had come down with the plague.

What did it matter to me? After all, I knew nothing about her, and I realized I was a dope for hoping she'd recognize me. I tried hard not to take it personally, like a family thing. But I could not. It wasn't just the doing of it, it was the rawness of the show, like spit in the face.

We'll ask Captain Mitchell for a bit of free rein on this one, I thought. *We'll go over and squeeze all the punks in the neighborhood till something leaks out about Donny Pease, and then we'll find the cocksucking bastard and make sure we don't need a trial.* Simple enough, even for me.

But it wasn't Pease. So many other times I had been able to forget what I couldn't quite grasp, but this was a truth I couldn't push far enough away. Though I had bumped up against enough scum to rub away any illusion about the human character, I knew that a small-timer like Pease—a car thief, a purse-snatcher, a creep-and-run coward—could never have the marbles to pull a thing like this. It wasn't Pease. I knew it with a certainty that felt as solid as a good shot to the heavy bag—*thunk!*—when the bag goes weightless on the chains for just a second. But when I tried to scare up some idea of who might have done it, my mind felt the old fog setting in. *It's just like they say,* I thought. *I'm not cut out for this kind of head work.*

As Bobby squealed around the corner, leaning on the horn and leaving precious rubber on the pavement, I let the decision fall quickly: I'd have to think about asking Mitchell to drop me back down to sergeant. But first, there was this one thing to set right: Though I could not yet explain it to myself, I knew that I could not allow the killing of the girl to stand. I stood up and walked toward Bobby's car with my hands and my feet tingling and my mind worrying over a young girl and a broken family.

"Shut the door, Caudill. Close it. All the way."

"Listen, Captain, I see it this way, if—"

"Shut up, Swope. It's too early in the morning to have to listen to your claptrap."

If Captain John Mitchell had not slept, I couldn't see it. His wiry gray hair bristled neatly over his head, and his cheeks had been shaved so closely that his skin looked as if it had been scrubbed with steel wool. His small eyes were dark, his uniform pressed and formed as if it were a part of his body.

Mitchell pushed a neatly folded copy of the *Detroit Times* across the desk to Bobby.

Bobby picked it up and began to read. " 'The body of Jane Hardiman, daughter of Lloyd Motor Company vice president Roger

Hardiman, was found yesterday on family property in Dearborn, the apparent victim of a riding accident.'" Bobby grinned and said, "Things move fast in this town."

Mitchell let out a long breath. "How long do you think a story like that can hold water?" He trained his eyes on Bobby. "How many people saw that girl in there? And how long do you think it will take people to put two and two together and figure out what happened? It seems far from your mind, but how are we to carry on an investigation when no murder is supposed to have happened?"

"Well, Captain," Bobby began, "something like this... It's a messy business, and the Hardiman family—"

"What you figured," said Mitchell, "is that Roger Hardiman would want the whole thing hushed up. So you decided to set aside your duties to pony up to him. I'm guessing also that the two of you had to put aside your assigned caseload to chase after Hardiman's daughter in the first place."

I clenched my teeth. I glanced at Bobby and wished he could have the sense to keep his mouth shut.

"I just thought that with all the trouble with the colored—"

"It does not matter what you think ought to be done. You are a civil servant. You are paid to do your job, and part of that is doing what you're told. If you don't feel like you can follow the chain of command, remove your badge and sidearm and place them on my desk."

Bobby's face went blank for just a moment. "I don't want that at all," he said.

"Then keep your mouth closed and listen to what I'm telling you. I'm well aware of the trouble we've got smoking in the Valley and down in Black Bottom. From the looks of things, it's going to be a long, hot summer. It's my job to stay right on top of things, and that gives me a perspective you don't seem to be able to muster. I'm not just concerned about putting a few extra dollars in my pocket. I've a better idea than you do, apparently, of the shortage of manpower we're facing here on the force, as well. Think, now, think. Think about how it looks when you and Caudill—given his history—pay a visit to Toby Thrumm and beat the hell out of him—"

"Hey, I just busted his nose, that's all." I felt heat rise over my chest.

Mitchell turned to me without expression and spoke evenly. "That's another thing you'll have to explain to me. I received a telephone call late last night from the Reverend Horace Jenkins. Seems he and his people had to take Thrumm to Receiving Hospital with a broken arm and a concussion. If what he's telling me checks out, it also looks like Thrumm was *bullwhipped.* They say he had almost bled to death when they found him. Blood coming out his ears."

"You'd take Jenkins's word over mine?" I let my look get as dark as it wanted to. "I busted enough noses to know he wasn't hurt that bad."

"I'm not saying it was you just yet. But Jenkins says he's got several witnesses who saw a certain one-eyed man and a dandy jackass on Thrumm's front porch early yesterday. And given your history, Caudill, you can see why Jenkins might want to get involved in this."

"Ah," I said, "that's a bum rap."

"I'm thinking about how this will affect the mood in the colored neighborhoods. You, of all people, should know that our old city isn't so rosy as it once was. We're not children. I know that sometimes heads will get busted. That's part of the nature of our business. You're not so stupid as you'd like to be, Caudill. Don't insult me by pretending you don't know how it is." He looked at me with his black eyes till I shrugged.

"Now, Swope, if you're so concerned about keeping things quiet, you'll understand that Jenkins is exactly the man I ought to talk to. I'm guessing you and Caudill don't have too many friends among the

Negroes." Mitchell drew a breath. "Jenkins is marching his people down here this morning. I want you two out of this building and out of sight."

Bobby spoke up. "Captain, we'll just see what we can do about finding Pease—"

"No you won't. You'll stay clear of anything on the west side until I see what Jenkins has to say. When I get all the information I can, then I'll decide what you should do."

I shifted in my chair. "What are we supposed to do, sit around holding our peckers?"

"Look here, Caudill. Don't talk to me like you're equal to me. I've given a lifetime to get where I am, a lifetime of service to the people of this city. I don't have any concern for you beyond the job you're supposed to be doing. Now, I worked with your father for many years. We went through perilous times, and I appreciate all he did as an officer for this city. But if I say the word, you'll be out of here and lugging engine blocks for Chrysler's. If they'll take you." Mitchell drew a deep breath and let it out slowly. His tone softened. "You can see that when Jasper Lloyd himself calls me on the telephone and tells me that this particular case is highly important to him, I feel like I need to get a handle on things. The situation is messy enough. And this news story of yours, Swope, just makes it worse for us. Right now you two are what I have to work with. Frankly, I'm not sure how much I trust either of you."

"But Captain, how are we supposed to get at the bottom of it if we can't poke around?" Bobby's tone was unnaturally sincere.

Mitchell looked hard at us. "It looks like there are more players here than we know about. If Jenkins is playing straight, it looks like somebody is deliberately stirring things up in the Negro districts. And any kind of trouble we have in Detroit can only mean lost production, and lost production means that more of our boys will lose their lives overseas."

"For God's sake," said Bobby, working his knobby fingers over his jaw. "They'll start a riot if things get any tighter."

"Just keep your eyes open."

"Is that all?" I clenched and loosened my fists. "Is that all you want us to do? Keep our eyes open? How are we supposed to find out what's going on if you want us to lay low?"

"Take it easy, Caudill. I've got two recruits coming in, and I'm pretty sure they're straight. One of them's my nephew—Will Johnson, my sister's boy. His father's sheriff up in Kalkaska. The other's a colored boy just on the force, name of Walker, one of Jeffries's little concessions to Jenkins."

"What the hell are we supposed to do with two green frogs?" I asked. "At a time like this?"

"Send them over to the west side to canvass the area. Find out if anybody will talk about Pease. They might be more likely to talk to the colored boy. And Caudill, you see to it that my sister's boy doesn't get in any trouble."

My agitation spilled over. "You want me to hold his dick for him when he takes a piss, too?"

"I expect you to start acting like a detective if you're going to be walking around with the badge. Now get the hell out. And you'd better get some results pronto or you'll find out how the wind around here can blow a man right out the door." Mitchell pushed an old brass key across the table. "I've set up the old interrogation room in the basement for everything you do with this case. Walker and Johnson are waiting down there for you. I shouldn't have to tell you, Swope, to keep your mouth shut about it. Now get out before Jenkins shows up."

We got up slowly. In the pit of my stomach, my undigested breakfast had turned sour, and I felt acid gnawing at me. "We'll set things right," I said, though I didn't believe it.

The four of us squeezed into the unused interrogation room. It had been made small with the idea that the cramped feel would make a man more likely to talk. But none of the bulls could stand to be in it, either, so the room had been abandoned.

"That's a nice notebook, Johnson," I said, eyeing the leather pad holder. "Your mother buy you that?"

"No, it was…Captain Mitchell. Gave me this pen, too, my first day on the force. It's a Waterman."

"You're not fooling with me, are you, boy? There's no need for any of that." I meant for it to seem like a joke, but it just went out in the air with a nasty feel. My social graces had fallen out of use. I sipped my black coffee. "You can put that pen down for now. We'll keep the paperwork out of this."

Johnson said, "You don't want us to take field notes?" He lifted his eyebrows and folded his notebook.

I shook my head. I could see that Johnson was a bright boy. He was a good-looking kid, tall and blond and carrying a bit of color from spending time outdoors. I thought he looked a little soft, but the jaw was big enough to carry it for a time.

"Detective Caudill likes to keep things simple," said Bobby. "Like his clothes, see? The other day, a lady tried to put a nickel in his coffee cup." He waited for a laugh and didn't seem to mind that he didn't get one. "See, he likes to keep things to himself."

"I put my clothes on to keep my ass from hanging out, that's all. Listen, Johnson," I said, "You can scribble all you want with your Waterman pen when we finish up this particular case. But for now"—I tapped my forehead—"keep it up here."

Bobby threw a leg up over the edge of the old table, sat, and said, "What do you think of all this, Walker?"

"Well," said the Negro patrolman, "since I'm stuck here in these blues for a while, I don't see any point in getting het up about my clothes." His face showed nothing.

"But if you were off duty and you were trucking down in the Valley, wouldn't you want to wear something to get yourself noticed?" Bobby asked.

"Well, sir, I am a family man."

"Swope's a family man, too," I said, "but that don't prevent him from dressing like a rooster." It didn't seem funny even to me. I tried to read Walker's tone, his expression, but found no trace of bitterness in his reserved manner. Maybe that was what they were looking for when they hired colored men for the force. He had just finished the officer's training course, like Johnson, but Walker was evidently some years older. The nicks and scars on his hands and face showed that he had done some real work in his time.

"You might have some luck with the ladies if you picked up something a little more modern, Caudill," Bobby said.

"I got enough problems already." I had given up on the small talk. Bobby enjoyed it so much that he seemed willing to forget our present troubles, just to try to impress these two bland rookies. It was hard enough, I thought, to figure out what things meant without having to entertain these punks. I let it pass on the chance that Bobby's patience, his instinctive feel for wheedling, might pay off somehow with the pair. Still, I couldn't get over the idea that things could work so much more briskly without the social bric-a-brac.

"Okay, fellas, let's get down to brass tacks," said Bobby. "Did Captain Mitchell tell you what it's all about?"

Johnson said, "He told us to listen to you."

"Are you with us so far, Walker?"

"Yes."

Bobby said, "What we have here is a situation where you need to keep everything quiet. And quiet means quiet. We don't want you whispering with your buddies or anybody else. We don't want to hear any of this getting around." Bobby pulled out a cigarette and tamped it on the table. "Because it's my ass, and Caudill's ass, on the line. So, can I count on you two to keep it under your hats?"

"Sure," said Johnson.

Walker nodded somberly.

"You heard about Jane Hardiman? Riding accident?" Bobby looked the pair over.

"It's too bad. I met her once," Johnson said. "Funny girl."

"She's not funny any more," I said. "Murdered." I saw Johnson's predictable look of surprise, sincere concern. Walker's expression did not change. He only nodded.

"How do you mean she was funny?" asked Bobby.

"I met her when she was sixteen, I think. She just seemed funny. She was always making jokes but didn't seem happy. A real looker, too."

"It wasn't just that she was killed," I said.

"That's right," said Bobby. "We'll spare you the details. Maybe you didn't read in the social column, Johnson, about how young Jane Hardiman liked to hobnob on the poorer side of town. On the colored side. We found her in an apartment toward the west end. You know this area, Walker?"

"I've been there, yes."

"We had a tip she was with a colored boy named Donny Pease. Now this is just a small-time thief, lately out of St. Louis, with a big smile and flashy clothes—a zoot-suiter, you know the type. So we ran down the tip, and he was gone before we could get there."

"So," said Johnson, "you think this Donny Pease—"

"Don't start in with the thinking just yet, Johnson," I said. "You're here to keep your mouth shut and do the grunt work for us."

"That's right," said Bobby. "We just want you two to go over to his apartment building, knock on all the doors, sniff out what you can find about where Pease might have gone. After that, just keep on knocking down the street and see what turns up. And for God's sake, keep it close to the chest. All we're looking for is anything about

Donny Pease we can find. Nobody said anything about the girl. As far as anyone should know, there's no girl involved in any of this. You can understand how all this could be hurtful to the Hardiman family."

"What should we tell people if they ask why we want Pease?" asked Johnson.

"Tell them he's wanted for buggery," I said.

"No, no! Jesus, Pete. Tell them it's traffic tickets or some such. Drunk and disorderly." Bobby slugged down the last of his coffee. "One thing, though. You fellas remember when you're talking to these people, you can expect that every last one of them is going to try to lie to you. That's the way it works when you're in the uniform. If they start talking, let them keep talking until they say something funny, and then you'll have something on them."

I continued to search Walker's passive face for any trace of emotion. I would have been relieved to find anger flashing in his eyes or a smirk or a look of disgust. It would not have angered me to see Walker looking bored. The lack of reaction told me only that Walker was smart but not which way he leaned. I looked carefully at his tired eyes and wondered what he thought of me. If it was on his mind, he kept it buried.

"Walker," I said, "you have any acquaintance with Donny Pease?"

"Not to my recollection, no."

"Colored folks tend to stick together, isn't that right?" I asked him.

"That's fair to say," he said, measuring his words. "But just the same—"

"It's only natural," said Bobby. "You can't expect Walker to know every Negro in the city."

I choked down the words that wanted to pour like hot gas from my mouth. "Maybe," I mumbled, "maybe Walker could ask around, that's all."

"You can do that, can't you, Walker?" said Bobby.

"I'm willing," he said. "But from how you talk about Pease, I don't think anyone from our church would have any familiarity with him."

I kept quiet for the next few minutes while Bobby laid out our plan for the day. Then we all stepped from the little room and walked up the narrow stairs to street level. Bobby kept close to Walker and made an effort to chat amiably on the way. After a few steps, I took Johnson's elbow, drew him aside, and let Bobby and Walker walk on ahead.

"Listen, Johnson," I muttered quietly. "I got something for you. If you see a tall, skinny colored boy, about thirteen, big eyes like a cow, maybe name of Joshua, you let me know, all right? He'll be shaking like a leaf, probably. Maybe wearing his pants too big, hoisted up with a belt. You find out what you can, you don't do anything, you just let me know. And keep it under your hat. Don't say anything to Walker or Swope about it either. You follow?"

"Sure," he answered. "But what—"

"And don't ask me any questions until I see whether you can handle that much."

CHAPTER

4

As Bobby drove through the gates of the Grosse Pointe Shooting Club, I hung my arm out the window and dangled my hat. "Some joint," I said. I took in the heavy, ivy-covered facade of the old building and listened to the popping of pistols and shotguns from the range out back. "Looks like a funeral home."

"This is where the big money comes to socialize." Bobby rubbed his palm over the panel of his car door. "There's more money changing hands here than in any of the big offices downtown. Mark my words, Pete," he said. "Pretty soon I'll be kicking up my heels in a place like this."

"When you get rich."

"When I get rich, that's right. It's in the works, Pete. Someday remind me to tell you about the little thing I'm running on the side." Bobby tightened the knot in his tie and smoothed his sparse hair close to his pate. "A little foresight, that's what it takes. You think

Lloyd or Chrysler got rich, excuse my French, standing around with his thumb up his ass, working for somebody else? This police thing is just a temporary stop for me, mister, on the way to something better."

I mulled it over. I knew that Bobby had been with the department since he was twenty or twenty-one, and so the temporary stop had stretched to something approaching twenty years. And though I had been paired with Bobby for only a short while, I had heard derisive references to his moneymaking schemes and failed side jobs for years.

I said, "Money's just sitting around waiting for you to find it, eh?"

"That's exactly right. You have to train yourself to see it. It's everywhere. Every little thing you see is just floating on a river of it. It's like a fish floating along in the water. If he never says to himself, 'Hey, what's this stuff I'm floating in?' then he's never going to be able to take advantage of it, you see? And another thing," he said, fluttering his hands for emphasis, "it's always about money, no matter what anybody tells you. Not just in business but in every other thing. Every bit of crime that gets done in Detroit or anywhere, it all comes down to money. You follow the money, and you'll always get to the bottom of things."

"So somebody's getting rich off this dead girl, is that it?" I felt disgust well up. "Big market for dead little girls around here?"

"Jesus, Pete, don't get hot. I just said that, at the bottom, it's all money. I don't say I can attend to every detail. I'm letting you in on some of my stuff, that's all. I thought you might appreciate it. Listen, I know they all like to get a laugh out of me in the locker room. But let me ask you, do they laugh when they consider the number of good collars I've brought in? Is there anybody else with a nose for the dirty stuff like I've got?"

"Take it easy," I said.

"I'm just telling you, it's like a shell game. Keep your eye on the money. God knows there's a lot of it floating around here. It seems like you just don't care about it enough to really think about what it can buy for you. You don't let yourself care."

"If I had money, I'd go down to Rocco's every night and buy me a big porterhouse and a sweet potato, put some brown sugar and cinnamon on it and some butter and dig in. Wash it down with a bucket of Stroh's. I'd do it every night till I got sick of it."

Bobby shook his head slowly and slipped a finger under his collar to ease the pinched skin of his neck. I thought I caught a glimpse of real fear in Bobby's eyes but laid it off on the brightness of the midday sun and the play of light and dark in the car.

"Money makes you slippery, Pete. It gives you a little insurance, a little room to angle when they come after you, see? If you've got money, you can use it to get more for yourself than you would have if you started out with nothing and put in the same amount of work and sweat. I'm not just being greedy, Pete. You know I've got Anna and the girl to think about. But it's no sense being a sap about it. If you can at least get a handle on what's going on around you, if you can figure out what makes everybody scramble, then you're halfway there."

I gave him the eye for a moment and then said, "Halfway to where?"

"Don't get hot about it, Pete," said Bobby. "I'm just trying to help you out."

We left the car on the big circular drive. As we stepped into the cooled air of the building, I whispered, "I told you it's like a funeral home."

The place had been carefully modeled after an English gentleman's club, with heavy dark paneling over the walls, dark leather furniture, subdued light, and submissive waiters carrying drinks on silver trays to lounging old men reading financial papers. Shelves of leather-bound books lined one entire wall, broken only by the stone hearth and fireplace, idle now. A bank of windows, tiny panes of beveled glass, looked outdoors onto the rear of the club, over the target range and back to the hill beyond the trap and skeet areas. I took a moment to orient myself and realized with a smile that any stray bullets or shot making it over the hill would probably land over the city boundary in Detroit proper.

We found Roger Hardiman on a fieldstone patio out back, barking orders to a colored boy, who tried frantically to load clay pigeons into a trap quickly enough to suit him.

"Pull, damn you!"

The boy let loose two low-flying pigeons. Hardiman followed the first sharply with his shotgun, blasted the thing to dust before it had gone thirty yards, and blew apart the second just as it reached the crest of its flight. I studied the executive's sweating forehead, his leather-shouldered shooting jacket, his fancy colored shooting glasses. Another man might have been attending to family matters, to funeral arrangements, or to his own grief after losing his only daughter, the apple of his eye—but Hardiman, I could see, approached things from his own angle.

"Mr. Hardiman, sir," said Bobby.

"Swope, you've finally made it, I see." Hardiman broke the gun over his elbow. He pulled the two hot shells expertly with his glossy fingernails and dropped them to the patio. To the colored attendant he said, "Lose yourself, boy, we've got some things to talk about." He drew a bright white handkerchief from his pocket and mopped his brow.

"Caudill, is it?" he said, extending his hand. "I have come to understand you have quite a reputation."

I returned Hardiman's powerful grip, met his look. "I didn't know I had a reputation."

"I knew your father as well. Did you know that?"

"No."

"It seems you don't know much," said Hardiman.

"He doesn't let on," said Bobby. "Mr. Hardiman, sir, we won't take up too much of your time—"

"No, you won't. I called *you* here, remember? I've some things to say that couldn't be spoken last night with my wife present. What progress have you made?"

"We've got two men canvassing the neighborhood. They'll turn up something, I'm sure. We're about to see what we can do to track down Toby Thrumm, a known associate of Pease." Bobby held his hands clasped together like the director of a funeral home.

"In other words, you've nothing at all. A whole day has gone by and you've nothing at all."

"That's right," I said. I sized up Hardiman. Natural-born salesman, confident, pushy, the worst kind: believes what he's selling, entirely oblivious to anything but what's on his own plate. "Pease probably skipped out by now."

Hardiman turned his attention from Bobby to me. "You think it's possible that Pease went back to his people in the South?"

"Likely. If you get hooked up with something like this, no matter how much of a dope you are, you know how hot it's going to get."

"What sort of authority do you fellows have to go down there and get him?"

"None," I said. I wasn't about to lower my head or put my eye aside for him.

"Well, listen. I've got a thousand dollars—that's five hundred apiece—if you'll get that jigaboo and bring him back here for me."

"And then what happens to him?" I tipped the brim of my hat back and stared down my nose at him.

"You leave that to me."

"You got some other flunkies you can pay to do your dirty work so your pansy hands don't get bloody?"

"Pete!" said Bobby. "Take it easy!"

"Listen here, Mr. Caudill. My hands have seen their share of blood. Unlike you, I know how to wash up afterward, and I've the social grace to think of it as an imperative. My concern is directed by a head for business. If it makes sense for me to a job myself, I do it. If a job doesn't require the use of the skill I might bring to bear, I shop the job out to someone whose time isn't as valuable as mine. Now, I could buy ten of you with what I keep in my petty cash account. With one telephone call I could have you sweeping streets and cleaning sewers in Hamtramck. So no matter how tough you think you are, you're only getting half the picture. Without money, without a wide circle of influential friends and a deep involvement in the community and its running, you're nothing. Nothing. Rootless like a dry leaf blowing." Hardiman pulled in his breath deeply and let it out as he put his handkerchief away. "Now, I want that nigger found and brought to me. If the two of you can't use the money, I'll find someone who can."

"How is it," I said, "that a bright boy like you can't keep a teenaged girl in line?" I pulled my hands from my pockets, felt heat throb in them, felt the heat radiating from the barrel of Hardiman's shotgun.

"That mouth of yours will dig your grave one of these days, Mr. Caudill." He paused and tried to drive that home with a level stare. "Now, you bring me that nigger's balls or don't show your face near me again. Our business here is finished." Hardiman turned, red and sweating.

As he drove, Bobby tapped his nails on the roof of the car. "Jesus, Pete, what was that all about?"

"Just seeing what Hardiman's made of."

"Couldn't you find a nicer way to do it? You need to learn how to grease people a little bit."

"I'm giving him more credit than you are," I said. "Why's he want Pease's balls?"

"Jesus, Pete, if you had a daughter killed like that—"

"Leave off with that. You know as well as I do it wasn't Pease," I told him. "Probably Hardiman's guessed it, too."

Bobby spent a few moments looking from me to the road and back. "You're probably right."

"Sure I'm right. First off, Pease is an idiot. You read the book on him? How he got caught in St. Louis? Stole a car and drove it over a fire hydrant right in front of a scout car." I worked my hands around the brim of my hat in my lap, thinking of Hardiman's long neck and of the lack of concern he seemed to feel for Jane.

Bobby said weakly, "I don't hear much on Pease except that he's been running numbers in the west side neighborhoods."

"Listen, it takes some kind of stomach to do that to a girl, such a young girl. For these guys, slapping them around is one thing. But a small-time lifter like Pease couldn't come up with the marbles for this type of treatment, not especially with a rich white man's daughter, and not especially with the way things are right now in this town."

"So you don't figure him at all," said Bobby.

"Hell, no."

"Who, then?" Bobby gestured with both hands on top of the steering wheel, showing blue veins below the pale skin of his palms.

"You're the senior man here," I said. "I worked up a good sweat just thinking that much." I could see that Bobby had hoped Pease's guilt would not be called into question. Pinning it all on Pease, finding him, and dragging him to Hardiman would settle things easily and maybe lead to a big payoff. It was just lazy, slippery thinking, and I was getting to feel that lazy thinking could be dangerous. But it fit Bobby like a second skin.

"You'd almost have to be crazy to pull something like this," said Bobby. "The way things are down in Black Bottom—it's just too many people crowded too close together, see? Come the real summertime, when it all boils over, know where I'll be?"

"Standing on the corner of Chase Alley and Riopelle," I said, "selling baseball bats for ten bucks a pop." I adjusted the eye patch a bit and moved the strap higher on the back of my head.

Bobby pulled back his face into a smile. "And you'd head for the hills, if there was any hills around here."

"I'll be cooling my heels on a boat in the middle of Lake St. Clair, pretending to have some bait on the line," I said.

"Well, Pete, if things ran good all the time, there wouldn't be any need for us on the police force. We'd be sweating like pigs at Chrysler's."

"I'm sweating like a pig now."

"So you don't think it was Pease went back to beat up Thrumm, either?"

I closed my eye and leaned back. "Pease is too little to have done something like that all alone."

"Some other niggers got something for Thrumm?"

"It's too much to believe all at once."

"So you think," said Bobby, "that whoever killed the girl came back for Thrumm after we left?"

"That sounds right."

"But that would mean—"

"That they've been watching us." I breathed deeply and worked a point into my hat's brim with the three digits of my left hand. "We've been putting on a monkey show for them."

"Jesus."

I stared out the window as the bustling city rolled by. The Arsenal of Democracy, they called it. Detroit was a great steaming engine, pouring out a steady supply of steel and power to the front lines of the war. An idea flickered through my head, and it felt right: Someone was deliberately trying to mess things up in the city. Looking at it Bobby's way, what profit could there be in that? In terms of business, I never figured out how everything could work like it did. I could not bring my mind to understand what all those men in the white shirts could possibly be doing at Chrysler's or Lloyd Motors to bring in a profit—adding up to millions for the men in charge. It seemed to me that they were just talking all the time or shuffling numbers on papers. And if I couldn't understand how a regular company might work, how could I understand how it might profit anybody to wreck things?

But then it was in all the papers; you heard it every day on the radio and every time a gaggle of old broads stood gossiping at the back fence: Loose lips sink ships; there were enemy agents among us. I could see that the Japs or the Germans might like nothing better than to foul up production in Detroit. Even if it would cost them millions, they wanted to wreck us, and I could understand that. But I couldn't quite make myself believe that there were spies about. The war seemed so far away. If I hadn't already lost a brother to it, I would have wondered if it was real at all.

If I could trust my gut, I knew that our problems slept closer to home. No spy would come halfway around the world just to meddle with a rich man's daughter when he could put dynamite to almost any plant in the area. Our trouble, I knew somehow, had sprouted up from our own soil, our own foul history. As I began to realize how deep the water had swelled up around us, I mashed my teeth together and clutched at my hat. Detroit, like any big city, was built atop the flimsiest house of cards imaginable, the basic civil cooperation between its citizens. I had been a police officer long enough to know that civil behavior, when it broke down, did so in a flash. A husband breaks a bottle over his wife's head; a rummy knifes another drunk over a half-empty bottle. If we could not find a way to handle things quickly, I sensed, the pending summer in Detroit would be one to remember. My throat clenched as I considered it. Detroit was the only place I had ever lived. Where could I go if it all broke down?

CHAPTER

5

I wondered what Bobby thought of the early brush-off. To me, the day had been a waste: talk and more talk. We had not made any progress toward finding Pease or whoever was responsible for the girl's early exit. In fact, everything seemed less sure, and the situation had become spongy, too soggy to get a firm grip on. Nobody knew anything, nobody had anything to say. Walker and Johnson had turned up nothing. They had run into either a stone wall or genuine ignorance in their door-knocking. Nothing on the boy, Joshua, and no indication that the people near the apartment had heard or seen anything amiss. It was all coming together to remind me that too much thinking always took something away from you. Even if you got somewhere by thinking, it always left a rawness in your throat that you couldn't wash down.

So when the regular end to our shift came, I told Bobby to drop me off at home. To Bobby's objections I only raised my bad hand like a traffic cop. I knew that Bobby was probably still out driving somewhere, scrounging for some hint of information, driven by the vague tickling at the back of the head that dicks get when they know there's a piece somewhere that'll fall into place and wipe away the fog. In Bobby's case, it was not so easy to say what kept him going day and night. Though he had a beautiful wife and a little girl at home, Bobby did his best to avoid the place. He seemed most at home swimming through the tangle of petty motivations he found in the dark corners of the city. There was also the dangling carrot of Hardiman's money, which seemed like something that got talked about but never showed up in anyone's hand.

After cutting out on Bobby, I stood in my shorts before the mirror in my bathroom. I pulled the patch off my eye and rubbed the red outline on my nose and cheekbone, tried to smooth away the groove pressed into my brow by the thin leather strap. When I bought the patch, it seemed hard and funny to me that I'd spent a small fortune on the finest one I could find, beautifully tooled and stitched and lined with thick red satin cloth, but none of that saved me from the discomfort I could have bought more cheaply. I hung the patch on a hook alongside the mirror, and then I drew up cool water from the tap and splashed it on my face. *Fair enough,* I thought. *Bobby can go hang himself. I've got things to do.*

I placed a shallow bowl in the sink, poured a small portion of table salt into it, filled it with warm water, and mixed it with my hands until I could no longer feel the scraping of the salt over my knuckles and my nails. With a turkey baster I kept in the linen closet, I sucked up some of the salty water, leaned over the sink, and washed out the cavity of my eye. Then I carefully removed my glass eye from its box, rinsed it in the salty water, and placed it in the socket.

I winced a little as it went in. Holding a towel over my face, I squeezed my eyelids shut as my tears started spilling over from both sides. After a time, the stinging subsided, and I was able to open my lids again. It was good for a chuckle to see how the glass eye stared out, blank and bright. The doctor was right; I wore the eye so rarely that it was beginning to fit poorly in the changing flesh of the socket.

I ran a hand over the thick stubble on my chin and considered shaving again but decided against it. I found a clean shirt and put the rest of my clothes back on. As I stepped out the door and felt the evening's heat still hanging on, I stopped, thought for a moment, and grabbed my hat from its hook.

I hoped my old Packard would hold up for a few more years. I didn't look after it like I should have. Though I drove with the windows down, and though I couldn't hear any extra snorting from the exhaust, I was sure that fumes were coming up into the interior. My nose always recoiled and my eye and eye socket always watered whenever I drove for more than a few minutes. I wondered if I could get funny in the head from sucking up exhaust. I wondered if I already had. I had seen more than a few suicides in their garages after the stock market crash, soft-handed businessmen too cowardly to use a gun. But I let it roll off me like the hundred other things I might have found to worry about.

As I rolled up to my sister-in-law's house at the northern edge of Hamtramck, I tried to avoid running down any of the kids heading for the movie theater on Campau. I had seen the marquee: an Alan Ladd movie, something about the war. I generally avoided the movies because I felt that it would be best not to strain the eye. Now they were starting to make them with too many colors, too many bright colors. I had never seen such colors in the real world. Even though Detroit was a city of trees in many areas, their green could never match what I had seen on the movie screen. And there was something about Alan Ladd as a hero. You could see that he was just a little guy, but he always acted so tough. I guess that's where the acting comes in—but he wasn't such an actor after all. You could see that he wasn't tough in real life, just pissy.

My brother Tommy's widow, Eileen, lived in a house with a big basement on Carpenter Street, just half a block off Campau. It was a nice place with a big attic, too, probably too big for her and her son, Alex. I had arranged things so she could keep it after Tommy was killed, done some things I shouldn't have to come up with the money to pay the mortgage down. Eileen got by all right with the widow's pension and by taking a few odd typing and filing jobs. In fact, the house was better than the place I had been renting for the last four years.

I stomped up the wooden steps to the wide porch and pounded my fist on the doorframe before coming in.

Alex was sitting on the sofa, working the pocket of his ball glove. "What's with the skiff, Uncle Pete? It's a hundred-ten degrees out."

"It might cool off later, you never know," I said. I pulled off my hat and looked at the boy, tried to see his father in him. But Alex was softer at the edges than Tommy had ever been; he favored his mother, maybe.

"Your uncle is a formal guy with his hat and all," Eileen called from the kitchen. "At least he dresses for dinner."

"At least I'm not wearing my spikes!" Alex's voice wavered, a bit too loud, a bit too blustery.

"He's crazy about baseball," said Eileen.

"Well, don't get fresh with your mother, kid, or I'll wallop ya." I felt the lead weight of my joking with the boy. I wanted to make up for what he was missing since his father had been killed, but I could not think of a way. Though I had known him since he was shitting yellow in his diapers, I couldn't just grab up the know-how to deal with a kid of any age overnight. It was clear that he felt some resentment about the way things were, but he covered it well. Fourteen years old. A bad age to be without a father.

"Dinner's almost ready," Eileen said, draining potatoes in the sink.

"Maybe we'll go see the Tigers sometime, ah?" I said. "Yanks coming to town next week." I watched the boy closely.

"Maybe," said Alex. He shrugged.

Alex had grown up in Pittsburgh, where Tommy had graduated from college. After I lost my eye and our father died, Tommy thought it best to pull up his family and come back to Detroit. When the boy finally saw me with the patch over my socket and the missing fingers—he was only seven or eight years old at the time—he was the only one who didn't offer any sympathy or try to get me to look on the bright side of things.

"Man oh man, Uncle Pete," he said. "Man oh man."

I let him rub his thumb over the long, ragged scar on my hand, and on the sly I even gave him a look at the empty socket. He marveled like it was monkeys riding bicycles at the zoo, which didn't bother me. Kids don't give a damn what you look like. Alex had been goofy as a kid anyway, prone to laughing out loud when he was playing alone. He was clumsy, forever falling out of trees or getting hung up by his trousers from the top of a fence.

Alex hadn't changed so much even two years ago, when Tommy and I pulled him out of school to play hooky at the ball game. We had box seats just a little beyond third base, right along the rail. Even though I was loopy from lack of sleep, having worked the graveyard shift the night before, and even though I had only the one eye, I managed to snag a hot foul tip with my bare hand. Pinky Higgins, who was playing third base, cranked his head and tipped his cap to me as I was sitting back down. It went so quickly that I don't think Alex even knew what had happened until I handed him the ball.

"Man oh man, Uncle Pete," he said. "That's some pepper."

"That's the lightning right that laid down the Bomber," said Tommy. "Laid him out like a bindle stiff on the Bowery. Crossed his eyes and—"

"Don't start telling stories," I said.

"Did you or did you not lay down the Bomber with that right hand?"

"He wasn't the Bomber then," I said. "He was just a kid."

"Don't try to bog me down with technicalities, Pete. You should have seen him, Alex. What a mauler your uncle was!"

"You weren't even there," I said.

"Technicalities," said Tommy. He had been saving up to try to go back to school for a law degree.

"Can you teach me how to fight, Uncle Pete?"

"Well," I said, "you better ask your mother about that."

"All right!" Alex turned his attention back to the game, working the ball in his glove and squirming with excitement.

It was a crisp fall day in 1941, and even though parts of the world were already fighting, it seemed nothing could touch us. But things fell like dominoes for the boy shortly after that: Within a year he'd stand stricken at his father's graveside, his body erupting with change and the world turned blacker in his eyes.

I couldn't blame him for changing. Standing there looking down at the bristling young man working out his frustration on his old ball glove, I could see that he was a world away from me now. He was not five feet from me, sitting on the same sofa we'd roughed up listening to games on the radio while Tommy was alive, but I could not in my fumbling manner find a way to touch him.

I had made the mistake of telling Eileen that my favorite meal was meat loaf with mashed potatoes and lima beans. So now she made the same meal whenever I stopped by. Still, it was good, solid, heavy food, and tasty, and I was glad to sit down at the table to eat, especially after the grim and unsatisfying day I had suffered. I mumbled a terse but serviceable grace before the meal, adding a silent prayer afterward, more like an undirected birthday wish, that I could somehow bring back the easy feeling of family that I had known as a child. When Tommy and I were kids, we scrapped and tussled bloodily, as boys will do, and our father tarred the both of us regularly, but at the end of the day we were a family, tight and loyal. But here it was like a minefield of emotions that I did not feel I could navigate. Alex seemed ready to burst, as if he were holding his breath all the time. I knew that it was a problem of his age. The world was opening up for him; he was finding out about any number of things that he couldn't well share with his mother any more. It's a normal thing for a boy to go through, and in a regular family, the house holds together. But with Tommy gone—especially Tommy— I could see that pressures were building up and that something would have to give.

It was hardest for me to judge how I should act toward Eileen. Tommy had been our connection, and with him gone, I had a slippery feeling that somehow things were improper. I continued on the same way I always had, or so it seemed to me, but I had more and more come to feel that I was missing something that everyone else could see. Early on in life, I had skipped out on the lessons in social grace and etiquette, and now I was a rube, a laughing-stock. It could be that I was just generally uncomfortable in my own skin. Had I always been?

I could see that Alex was in a big rush to get away, though he clamped down on his squirming well. He ate quickly, smart enough to head off any objections by wolfing down a hearty portion of food. He had lately taken on an odd smell, with all the chemicals in his body churning and roiling, and this, too, was hard for me to handle. It would have been better for the boy to have a father or some other older man that he could trust to help him through this part of his life, someone to show him the ropes of shaving and showering and talking to the girls. But how was I to be of any help, when my own life and history had become such a botched affair? I ate slowly and chewed thoroughly, rolling the salty gravy over my tongue to get all the flavor I could out of every bite. We ate for a time as if famished, and an uncomfortable silence grew.

"Well, it's a year this week," said Eileen finally, "since Tommy died over there."

"Mother," said Alex, "we shouldn't talk about it during dinner."

I swallowed my words. *If she wants to talk about it,* I thought, *she can talk about it.*

"I think that's just silly, Alex. If we don't talk about him, who will?" Eileen's voice seemed too young for her thirty-three years, almost girlish, and I noted that it wasn't the kind of voice that could keep a boy of that age in line.

"What I meant was, it's not a good thing to talk about while we're eating. It's not good to talk about dead people for dinner conversation." Alex's hairless cheeks blushed livid red.

"Listen, son," I said. "It's your mother's house, and I guess she can talk about what she wants. When you get to be in charge, then you can talk about whatever suits you."

"I'm not your son," muttered Alex. He didn't meet my eye.

"That's right," I said. "Because if you were my son, you wouldn't be talking to me that way. And if I know your father, if I know Tommy, if he was here he'd slap you out of that chair."

Alex said nothing but let his eyes focus somewhere beyond the remainder of his food. He gripped his bread and worked his jaws. He seemed about to burst or run.

"You're not the only one who's lost a father, boy. At least you can be proud of the way Tommy went out. Not like your grampa, hung himself like a coward. Too young to remember how that was? Or is that another thing we can't talk about at the table?"

Silence.

Since I had opened my mouth, I felt like I had to go on, and I tried to angle my approach. "As long as you're still eating food at your mother's table," I told him, "you'll show her some respect. Do you think you really want to act like the punks I see every day down on the corner? You better think long and hard about it. You haven't got much family left to be careless with."

Alex swallowed his anger and slowly composed himself. He pulled another bite from the dry bread and worked it down his throat. Without looking at Eileen, he said, "May I be excused? I've got to get down to the field while it's still light out."

"Drink your milk and you can go," said Eileen.

Alex sucked down the last of his milk and turned away from the table with his eyes averted. He stopped at the foot of the stairs to grab his ball and glove and hurried out the front door.

I wiped the gravy from my plate slowly and said nothing. I chewed the thick bread and tried to think what to do. It was plain to me that the boy needed a man around the house, someone hard enough to keep him straight. I wondered if my weekly visits were keeping Eileen from meeting another man. Tommy, I knew, would not have waited a year before stepping out. And Eileen was shaped pretty well, she laughed easily, kept a clean house. There was no reason for her to grow old alone, though of course most of the eligible men were caught up by the war. I thought also of how much simpler my life would be if I didn't have to worry so much about Eileen and the boy. As I kept working at the food and my plate came clean, I knew I'd have to say something.

"Maybe it's bothering him that I'm over here so much," I said.

"Oh, no! You're practically the only family we've got," said Eileen. "It's good for him to spend time with you instead of going around with those hoodlum friends of his."

"Every time I come over here he runs out the door."

"He's crazy about baseball."

"Maybe." Alex was not on the short list of those who seemed to enjoy my company. Offhand I could think of only two for the list: Eileen and Bobby—and Bobby, I thought, was in the same boat as me, at least around the precinct houses. I tried to think of a way to ease out of the house without hurting Eileen's feelings, but nothing came to me. *Maybe,* I thought, *I should think of how Bobby would weasel away.*

"Pete, let's do something," she said abruptly. "It's been a year. Let's go out and do something to celebrate that it's been a year and we're doing okay."

"What do you mean, go out? You mean like boozing it up?"

"No! I mean let's go dancing. How long has it been since you've cut a rug? It's been ages. Honestly, I haven't been in ages."

"You know I'm no good as a dancer." I felt heat rise quickly over my chest.

"Nonsense. The last time you danced with me was at that wedding, that Polish girl, do you remember? Your neighbor? I think she would rather have married you than that little clerk. She must have been in love with you and Tommy, growing up across the street."

"I don't remember," I said.

"And don't worry about anybody seeing us. My friend Sally told me about a place up in Mount Clemens where her husband takes her. I'll go change, and we'll run out just for a little bit." She pushed her chair away from the table. "We'll just leave the dishes for tomorrow." She turned from the table and hurried to her room to change.

I felt the dropping feeling again. It was easy to see that men ran most things in the world—we kept most of the money for ourselves, and we owned most everything—but in the little things, the day-to-day things, women had the advantage because they were better at *talking* than men. It was like boxing. If you were good at it, if you'd spent years in the gym, sparring and scrapping, you got so you could

put your fist on a man's chin. You got so you could weave and duck
without a thought. In a household, the little things got settled with
talk. The women had all been raised up talking, just sitting and talking, and it gave them the instincts to duck and bob in a conversation,
so that they could slip in a punch and be gone before you could do
anything about it. Long talk always made my skull crawl, and if there
were too many characters or if the story was too complicated, like in
a book, I couldn't keep everything straight. I pushed myself quietly
from the table and walked toward the door. In the usual place, inside
a cookie tin atop the old china cabinet, I placed two folded twenty-
dollar bills. I picked up my hat and held it, scratching my head. Then
I pushed the screen door open and winced as the spring squealed.

I slipped out onto the wood porch and tried to keep my big shoes
from clumping. Could I just sneak away? My heart pumped thick
sludge in my chest. I scratched at the back of my head and around
my neck and tried frantically to think of something. After working
through all the legitimate excuses and all the far-fetched ones, I realized that I could not bear to crush Eileen any more than she had
already been crushed. And not especially after driving her son from
her house. It was only a little something to pay, an hour or two or
three of discomfort and embarrassment, to ease her mind a little. She
deserved it, if anyone did.

So I sat on the gliding rocker and tried not to think about how
awkward it would be. I tried not to think about anything. The sun
was getting low and hung just over the rows of houses and businesses
to the west across Campau, glowing through the haze kicked up by
the auto factories out that way. A breeze came through now and
again, cooled my cheek, and drew a bit of the heat out of my unbut-
toned jacket. I turned toward the door and strained to hear Eileen,
but my eye fell on something out of place. On the far side of the wide
porch, tucked under a wicker footstool, lay Alex's tattered ball glove.

I lifted myself and felt my knees flutter as I crossed the porch to the glove. I scanned the area quickly but saw no sign of Alex. From the placement of the glove, I could trace the steps he had taken across the porch, but it was impossible to tell where he might have gone. He might have run off in any direction. He might have turned down the alley next to the house and holed up in the garage. He might have been watching from a bush or from the window of a house across the street, or, for all I knew, he might have arranged to meet a girl somewhere. This last was too hopeful, I knew. The anger I felt stewing in the boy wasn't the kind of emotion you'd have if you were thinking of meeting up with a girl, if I could remember well enough.

Voices carried from nearby houses, laughter and table talk, squeals of babies. I heard the thump of a big woman beating a rug across the street and saw the puff of pale dust rise up with each stroke. On Campau the cars rolled up from downtown, full of tired laborers heading home from their day of backbreaking work. An old, old woman tended the roses that grew in front of her porch down the street, and it seemed that I could hear the gentle clipping of her scissors. Though I had not traveled much, I could imagine that it was pretty much the same the world over. In the evening like this, folks would be eating and tending to things, settling in for the coming night. It worked me over somehow, and I felt like I could get choked up just knowing how the world had to go on, knowing that you couldn't ever escape. With all that I had seen and lost myself, I wasn't sure that I could ever bear to have a child of my own in the world. I looked up to the sky and tried to picture how it would feel to worry about bombers dropping death down onto my own city, down onto my family.

I picked up Alex's well-used glove and the ball inside it—the same ball I had snagged at the ball game?—and carried it to the other end of the porch. To show the boy that I had found it, I placed it in plain view on top of the upended crate that served as a table on the porch. It took something from me. My legs trembled as I sat down on the glider to wait for Eileen.

By the time we finished the long drive up Gratiot to Mount Clemens, darkness had fallen. I didn't worry about the gasoline, since I had been filling my tank at the department pumps since rationing began. The place was off a dirt road that followed the Clinton River toward the lake from Gratiot. The grass parking lot was just beginning to fill up. Out of each car poured a gang of excited young men and women, unpacked like clowns from their jalopy at the circus. I backed the old Packard into the closest spot I could find and parked it.

No amount of trim or decoration could conceal the fact that the Royal Ballroom had started out as a warehouse. The exposed beams and timbers had been painted and covered with baubles, and three big truck bays had been closed up and hung with shiny fabric, but still the place had the air of industry, which seemed suitable. The band had already started up, just a few skinny youngsters playing what might have been an original tune, though obviously copied from the sound of Jimmy Dorsey's band. It was too loud for me but the commotion of all the dancing and milling about made me feel like I could get lost in the crowd. I wouldn't complain about that.

The small tables near the floor had all been grabbed up by groups of kids dressed as well as the war would allow. A few zoot-suiters mixed in with the crowd, standing out like roosters, but generally the men wore suits that looked like hand-me-downs and the girls wore dresses that might have been homemade. A few of the girls, I noticed, had drawn a line up the backs of their bare legs as if they wore stockings. Since there were no tables available, I pulled Eileen toward a couple of stools at the bar. I put my hat on the bar as a marker.

"I feel out of breath just being here," said Eileen. She looked off through the smoky room toward the dance floor. "When I was a girl I used to want to be a flapper. I used to cut my hair in bangs like Louise Brooks. That was all the thing in those days."

I looked her over. I couldn't imagine her as a boyish, flat-figured flapper. The dress she wore had been bought some years before and seemed a little tight, but it seemed modern because the young girls all wore tight skirts and form-fitting dresses now. Some even wore trousers, as they had seen in Hollywood picture magazines, Eileen's dress was cut low over her chest, and her breasts swelled up with each quick breath she drew in.

"You look all right," I told her. "You look pretty good."

"Pete," she said, looking up at me, "you're a charmer, in your own way. Such a gentleman." She peered again toward the dance floor. "Do you know this number?"

"I can't say so," I said. "It all sounds the same to me, just jumping music, how the kids like it." For once I was glad for the small talk, since it kept me from thinking too much about how I could have ended up here with her. I knew it would only be a moment before she took my hand and pulled me to the dance floor, and I knew I'd go with her. Dancing would give me a break from having to say what I knew would come out of my mouth wrong. If she was eager to go out and dance, to have fun, then it was clear that I should step out of the picture. I knew that I was a fright to look at, even without the disfigurements, and few men would dare to show any interest in Eileen with me lurking around.

"Well, Pete, we're not getting any younger sitting here," she said. She hopped down from the stool and took my hand.

Her hand felt small and warm and damp. We threaded ourselves between groups of standing revelers and tables toward the dance floor, a square area of wooden planks laid over the concrete floor. We walked on in the middle of a number, and I tried to shake some feeling into my old legs as I stepped over the shaky planks. I felt Eileen squeezing my hand as we drew near to an open area of the floor. She turned toward me, and I began to lead her in a fair version of a fox-trot. At least I thought it was fair.

I watched the younger folks dancing and saw that the new dances were largely just variations on the few I had practiced as a spryer man. There were embellishments, sure, lifting moves and spins, and drops to the floor, and I watched the footloose roosters perform with a sense of resignation. It was enough work for me just to keep the beat. I moved Eileen in slow counterclockwise circles over the floor, keeping to the side of my good eye to avoid bumping into anyone. Between numbers, we stood and tried to catch our breath. Though I was sweating heavily, I kept my jacket on. I knew that the leather shoulder rig I wore during the day had left marks like dim smudges on all my white shirts.

Eileen looked happy to me. As she danced, her wavy hair pulled loose from the clips and pins and caught the light that poured down from above the dance floor. She gripped my mangled hand without any flinch or hesitation as we danced and in between numbers, and she smiled up at me, with sweat beading on her upper lip, her neck, between her breasts. I wished she could be ugly. You could talk to an ugly woman. Though she seemed at ease with me and seemed to accept me like family, I could not find my words when I talked to her. Even simple remarks about the progress of the war or the weather just tripped out of my mouth. Her face was sweet. She had some wrinkles starting around her eyes, and her teeth seemed a little big in the front.

It all preyed on me, and it made my throat close up whenever I tried to think of a way to tell her that I could not continue to visit her. I guess I knew that the problem was with me. Sure, I knew it. It wasn't anything in the way she acted. You could see from knowing her that she had come from a good family. She had been brought up right, and there was nothing shifty in the way she behaved. If she squeezed your hand, it was just because she wanted to squeeze your hand. It was all me. I couldn't say if it was the scrabbling way I had been brought up or the things I had to deal with every day or the parts I'd lost. It wasn't just the eye and the fingers gone; in some other way I wasn't a whole man anymore. Somewhere along the line I stopped being straight. There was no way to say if things could ever be straight or simple for me again. But I had seen her face twisted up, torn with grief, and I did not wish to see any of that more than once.

"Okay," I said finally, "time for a break." We had danced just a few numbers, short and peppy, but I felt the rubber in my legs and knew that I'd be aching in the morning.

We went to the bar but found only one open stool in front of my hat, so Eileen sat there and I stood close to her crossed legs. After a time I was able to get the bartender's attention, and I ordered drinks. Then I put my hand on the bar and watched the crowd. I watched the young girls and guessed many of them to be underage, high school girls probably, unless things were really different from the days of my youth. I turned my attention to the bartender, who kept a big mug for tips near the cash register. I could see that the youngest boys tipped best to avoid being refused service when they bought drinks for their dates, but I was too tired to be sure how I felt about it. On the one hand, I regretted that such a simple law could be side-stepped two bits at a time. On the other, I realized that if the war dragged on, many of these boys would be called to service, and soon.

"My God, Pete," said Eileen, "what is it? You look like a cloud just blew over you."

"A long day, I guess." I had to lean close to her to be heard over the noise, and I worried that my breath was sour. I picked up my drink and drained the little bit of watery liquid from the overiced glass.

"I'm sorry, Pete. I shouldn't have dragged you here. It was selfish of me, just selfish. You must be so tired."

"I don't sleep so well," I said, forcing a smile. "Maybe this'll wear me out enough to have a solid night's sleep."

"Is it something bad at work?"

"In my work it's all bad," I said with a shrug. "It suits me."

"No," she said. "You're a good man, Pete. You deserve to be happier." She squeezed my arm just below the elbow I had propped on the bar.

"You're seeing Tommy," I said. "Tommy was the good one." *The whole one,* I thought. *The one who could fit in anywhere.*

She winced and eased her grip on my arm, but before she pulled her hand away, she smoothed her palm up and down the sleeve of my jacket. We had been leaning close together to be heard over all the noise; now she let a little space open up between us.

"You could find a better way of looking at things, Pete," she said. "You should ease up on yourself. It's the same world for a gloomy person as it is for a hopeful one. It's still the same world, however you look at it."

"I can't hear you so well," I said. "It's so noisy."

"We'll go, then," she said. She gripped my arm again, and she put a breezy tone to her voice. "It's already been more fun than I've had in a year. I guess I'll have to teach you something besides the foxtrot, though."

"I think I danced myself out for this year," I told her. "I'm glad we came, but—the old bones ain't what they used to be." In spite of my reluctance, I had to admit that I had enjoyed myself. Anything would have done it, any kind of physical activity, like playing ball or digging a ditch. It was possible to glimpse another world where I might even get more comfortable going out and dancing once in a while. But now, sweating and conscious of the time, my mood dropped suddenly. I knew all of this could not help me to get to the base of things or to make my life any simpler. There was always the shadow of trouble and duty pushing everything else aside.

"We'd better beat it," I told her. "Early day tomorrow." I took Eileen's elbow and guided her toward the door, clearing a path with my bulk through the crowded dance hall.

I drove back down to Detroit without saying much. The car had no radio, so Eileen tapped her fingers on the seat beside her and hummed bits of the swing tunes she had heard at the club. I figured she wasn't talking because she had sensed my mood—I had a natural way of killing conversation—but I knew also that she was a woman who could keep quiet. Tommy would not have married a chatterbox. Her hair had been naturally blonde and sun-lightened in her younger days but had darkened now to plain brown. She was short but had a shapely figure, a small waist, and breasts heavy enough to sway when she danced the fast ones. *She could find someone,* I thought. *That's one place I can cut things down to the bone. She doesn't need me coming around so much. Maybe I can set her up with—what! Now I'm thinking like a woman.* I thought, *It'll be enough to tell her how it is.*

We pulled up to her house and looked up at the dark windows. I killed the engine.

"I won't walk you in," I said. "I don't want to set the boy off again."

"If he's home," she said.

"If he's home! What business does a fourteen-year-old boy have staying out till midnight?"

"He doesn't listen sometimes. What am I supposed to do? He's bigger than I am."

I turned a little darker. "Does he push you around?"

"Oh, no. He just doesn't listen. He's a young boy. From what I've heard, you were worse when you were his age."

"I had a father to whip me up when I didn't stay to the right side of things." I thought for a moment. "If he gets out of hand, you let me know. I'll stand him up and see if he's as tall as he thinks he is."

She laid a hand on my arm. "It's not as bad as all that, Pete. He's growing up, and he's a sensitive boy."

I wanted to pull my arm away but resisted the impulse. She was expecting or hoping that I'd say something reassuring about Alex, I knew, but instead I said, "I have to tell you, Eileen, I don't think it's a good idea for me to come around so much anymore."

Her eyes fell. "Don't feel like you have to."

"I don't mean to say it like that. I like coming here. It's the only good cooking I ever get. But it's about time for you to be moving on now that Tommy's been gone for so long."

"Pete, I'm not what you'd call a spring chicken anymore. I'm not a little girl. You don't have to worry about hurting my feelings or anything like that." She looked up at me and squeezed my arm. "Don't let anybody tell you different, Pete. You're a good man."

"I'm not so good." Though she was making it easy, I felt that cutting loose wasn't going as cleanly as I had planned. I felt like a heel for pulling such a thing right after we had enjoyed a night out. But what else could I have done? Somewhere in the past several years, I couldn't say when, the world had begun to move faster than I could keep track of it. I felt like the world under my feet might shift whenever I walked.

"It's not a pretty world," I said. "Sometimes things get wrecked. Some people get hit with bad luck. You can't explain it. You can't always see it coming."

"You don't have to say anything more, Pete."

"I don't feel like I can ever—" I stopped speaking and looked at her in the dim light. The night had begun to cool, and a warm, thick breeze passed through the open windows of the car. Her eyes were crinkled lightly in a little smile, I guess, or from worry. I drew in a great breath and let it out as I turned toward her, then took her shoulder with my bad hand. Her eyes were calm, even grave. I was thinking that she might rightly be afraid of me or put off by my deformity. But when I found her soft mouth with my own, she did not stiffen or cling too much, and accepted the kiss as if it were the most natural thing in the world.

CHAPTER

6

Saturday, June 12

Things were getting so snarled that I wasn't sleeping right. I didn't want to get out of bed, but the pressure in my bladder forced me up, and I shuffled into the bathroom to relieve it.

As I stood before the toilet, I thought, *It always comes at you sideways, blindsides you.* Then a laugh like gravel worked up from my belly. Blindsided, so to say. Letting down a heavy stream of piss, I brought to mind a time when I felt like I could do what I wanted. Or maybe I just didn't want so much in those days. The first couple of years on the force, I was big and swaggering, I looked good in the uniform, and I knew the punks wouldn't sass me when I walked by swinging the nightstick. It was still Prohibition, and everybody was drinking twice as much as they do now that it's legal. It's the only time in my life I ever really drank much.

I didn't need to know much about what was going on in those days, just had to worry about what was happening under my nose. Right before my eyes. The bigger picture was a problem for lawyers, politicians, or rich folks who could afford to make the effort. You had a beat to take care of, a clear area of responsibility, and you could go home to another life at the end of the shift. The rumrunners could bump each other off, and that was not a problem unless it spilled over to the civilians or unless it became incriminating to some judge or elected official. Later, during the lean years, when folks broke the law a little to bring home some bread for their families, you could look the other way.

Now it was different. I didn't remember the other war being this way. Though I had been just a kid, it seemed over before it began. I could not remember worrying during that war, even though my own father had gone over for a time. But this new one seemed to have sucked something vital out of the city. All the good men had gone off to fight Jerry and the Japs. All the men who could see what had to be done had gone off to do it, leaving a makeshift crew of decrepit grandfathers, 4-F rejects, head cases, and teenagers to hold things together till the storm blew over. All the buildings were the same. The streets, the stink, and the muddy river still rolled along as before, but the city tottered somehow. From my black view, it seemed at the brink of collapse. While all the whole men were off fighting the enemies overseas—the ones you could pick out easily—the rest of us were left to sort out the lurking demons living beneath the husk of the city and inside our own skins.

Well. I had kissed my brother's wife. My dead brother's wife. Widow. So what? A moment of hunger had flared up and I had quickly snuffed it out, or at least pushed it below the surface again to pop up another time.

I washed up and ran a dull razor over my cheeks. I let the nicks

bleed till they dried over and cleaned the blood off with a rag after I
finished dressing. It was too early, I knew, to expect Bobby to pull
around the corner, blaring the horn. So I sat in the kitchen and
waited for the coffee to percolate. There was nothing left to eat, no
eggs and no sausage, not even bread for toast. When the coffee
looked dark enough, I poured out a cup and sipped without tasting,
staring across the table with my head propped on my bad hand.

Well, I thought, *it's done. I've been kidding myself, I guess. Maybe that's
what's been eating the boy. He could see it coming. He can't help seeing me as a
duller and meaner version of his father. So how does this work?* I wondered.
And then I thought, *It doesn't. It doesn't go forward until this thing with the
Hardiman girl is straightened out.* Something deep and messy had been
stirred up, and Bobby and I were into it. I'd put whatever I could
into figuring it out and going along with Bobby—night and day if
necessary—until the whole thing was in the ground. And then we'd
see what was left. I thought I would call Eileen later in the day and
tell her to hold on for a time, to let her know the clumsy kiss hadn't
been a shove to get myself moving in the opposite direction. The
Hardiman mess might veer toward the sort of trouble that involved
blood and beatings and bullets, I knew; and in the unforgiving
morning light, I thought to myself that there was something more
frightening to me about dealing with Eileen and all the emotional
entanglement than about facing another man's gun.

I swore I could feel the hot trickle of the coffee all the way down
my gullet and into my stomach. *That's another thing,* I thought. When
I was a kid, my digestion was always good, no matter what I ate or
when I ate it. *Enough of that. Straighten things out, let the lesser things fall
away, and maybe the old stomach'll even out, too.* I downed the last of my
cup and filled it again, then grabbed my coat and hat and went out to
the porch to wait for Bobby.

"Chesterfields, Pete," said Bobby, considering the cigarette he held between bony fingers as he drove. "Know what they taste like to me? Just like *chocolate cake.* Can't live without 'em. Wouldn't want to."

"I don't see it," I said. "I don't like chocolate cake." I thumbed through the files from the coroner's inquest that Bobby had obtained late the night before. I forced myself to look at the photographs long enough to burn the images into my memory. Atop the pile of grisly pictures, there was a studio head shot of Jane Hardiman. I thought the photo might have been made for a debutante's ball. You could see the darkness in her, the anger, even with the lovely smile on her lips and the way the studio lighting fell down over her wavy pressed hair. Her eyes were calm and reminded me of the Rembrandt pictures I used to look at as a boy. Like one of those pictures the sad old painter had made of himself toward the end of his time, she seemed to look out onto the world with living eyes. The photograph, without color or breath, was more lively than my paltry memory of our brief meeting. *You should have known,* her eyes seemed to say—a trick of my sorry mind. She was dead; she was clearly gone, as I had seen too plainly for myself, and it was only ink and paper before me now.

"That's why I always give two bits to the kid collecting for the cigarette fund for the boys over there, see? 'Cause I'd be crawling the walls in two minutes if I ever ran out."

"Shut up, will you? I can't read and listen to your flapping gooms at the same time." I scanned the written report. Cause of death: suffocation, evidence of garrote around neck, though several dozen superficial knife wounds had been carved into the girl, most prior to death. Carpet fibers mashed into all the wet and bloody places. No trace of semen but severe damage to genitals and anus, presumably from the broken-off broom handle found protruding from vagina. It had not been quick. It had not been done in a fit of passion or stupidity or jealousy. I read the worst parts over and over until I could carry the girl's violation deep in the pit of my belly. I wanted to let it stain me enough so that I wouldn't have to think when the time came for action.

Finally I looked up from the papers—I could not afford to lose the use of my only eye. I looked over at my partner and noted the darkness under his eyes, deepening to black toward the base of his bony nose. I said, "Jesus, Bobby, you look like a toilet."

"Time enough for sleep in the grave."

"If you don't sleep, you won't be able to do anything right. You've got to give the old carcass a chance to catch up."

"Black coffee and Chesterfields, that's what I need," Bobby replied, smiling thinly. "Listen, Pete, maybe you don't understand how serious all this could be for us."

"I got it fine."

"I mean that somebody, almost anybody here, if he had a mind to, could make real trouble for us. Just takes one call to the Old Man and we'd be in it up to our chins."

"Like Hardiman? What's he got to gain by rolling on us?"

Bobby stretched his long fingers over the top of the steering wheel. "I don't worry about Hardiman so much. See, he's in it up to his neck already, and there are some things that just can't be smoothed over, no matter how much money you might have. I'm being funny now, when I shouldn't. But you know, I usually walk around with half a feeling that everybody is out to get me. That just helps to keep me alert to what's going on. In the usual case, though, I might joke about it, but it's not really so true—got me? In regular times, there's always somebody you can count on being in your corner. With what we're stepping into now, though, who can say?"

"You think Mitchell's on the funny side somehow?" I asked. "In a tough spot like this, he gives us what to work with? Johnson and Walker?"

"You can bet," said Bobby, "that Mitchell's got other pots going on the back burners. But I don't worry that much about him. I've made my place skating over the top of things—I'm a slippery guy and all of that. But this here... it seems like the heat is melting things. We don't have a place to stand."

My brain continued to plod along, as if I had ever been able to get to the bottom of any problem by a simple process of going through the elements one by one. "Well," I said, "Johnson seems like a good kid. But Walker's hard to read."

"You've got to figure that Walker—and every other colored officer on the force—knows what you did to that colored boy. That's still a raw spot. You've got to understand that it's always going to figure in the social situation." Bobby scratched at his stubbly chin. "But that's neither here nor there. What I'm thinking, and what's been bothering me, is that something's going on and nobody wants to say what it is. It's like we're being set up for something."

"Sure, you got it right. You and me, huh? Who'd be better for the job? We can do all the dirty work, and we've both been under the bridge enough to take the heat if it comes down to that. Who'll miss us if it doesn't fall to the good side? Just now the big fish are taking notice of us, that's all. Maybe we've been lucky it didn't catch up to us before now." I felt a dry pang of hunger work through my gut. "Or it could be that you're spooked because you need some sleep. What do you think, Mitchell isn't telling us something? Then why would he send his own nephew to get mixed up in it?"

Bobby said, "Maybe Johnson isn't on the level."

"Nah," I said, "that kid's a Boy Scout if I ever saw one. But I'll tell you what. You take Walker aside and see what he's found out. He's not likely to spill too much with me around anyway. I'll take Johnson and see what's what."

"Pete," he said, sliding to a stop at the curb, "I have to take the blame for dragging you into this. I honestly thought—"

"We're partners, aren't we?" I took a long look down Beaubien at the spectral figures already hustling to their offices. So early in the day, and the heat already made everything waver like a mirage over the concrete. "Just make sure you get me out of it."

"Jesus, Johnson, I told you to scratch that notebook," I said. I stood with my foot on the dressing bench while Johnson smoothed his tie. We were alone in the locker room except for the attendant, who puttered out of earshot, fixing a mop head to a handle.

"I know," he said. "But it makes me look official. When I'm talking to someone, if I'm writing, they get an idea that I might give them a ticket or something. When they know they haven't done anything I can arrest them for, sometimes they talk a little funny. You know how it is. But a ticket, well, they know that's going to cost them something, and they might not think I'm so funny after all."

"Don't get too smart too soon, Johnson. That notebook won't do you any good if some big nigger decides to knock a sap across your skull."

I studied Johnson's smooth face. The young patrolman was different from the boys I had hired in with so many years ago. Back then it was a good job for a big boy to try out for. Maybe times had changed. In the old days, it wasn't a full day if you hadn't cracked a wino or a racket boy with your nightstick. Simple fear let you do your job and let the decent folks know they'd better stay decent. But I could see that Johnson would never walk a beat in the way that it used to be done. He didn't look like he'd smack anybody's mouth just for being lippy. Still, he'd grown up with his father as the sheriff in Kalkaska, and the men from the lumber camps up that way weren't soft. He must have seen some of that.

I said, "What's the story with you and Walker?"

"As I think about it now, I should've let Walker go in by himself first, to see if he could shake something loose. But we both went in together, so we didn't get much. I don't think even Walker, by himself... you know how it is."

"How is it?" I asked.

"Even though he's one of theirs, so to speak, even though he's a colored man, when he steps up wearing that uniform, they clam up on him. I think it's even worse for him than me." Johnson stopped to think. "We didn't have much in the way of colored folks where I grew up. We had Indians."

"Listen, Johnson," I said, "this isn't a job where you can afford to be soft."

"I know that, Detective. I don't intend to let anyone get the best of me. But I just keep thinking about different ways to get around the problem."

"Things have been bad between the Negroes and the police since long before you were born. You've got a lot of ideas now, and maybe you're thinking you'll be able to do a little something about it. That's all right. From where I'm sitting, I know you'll get over that." I leaned closer to him. "But for now, what we're worried about is cleaning up this little mess without going down the toilet ourselves. I expect you'll do what you're told so I don't get shot in my ass while you're off talking or thinking somewhere."

"I can follow orders."

"I expect you can follow orders," I said. "I don't care about that. But I get the feeling lately that I'm stepping into a big heap of something smelly. I aim to come out on my feet. Can I count on you to help me out with that?"

"Well," said Johnson slowly, "Captain Mitchell gave us clear instructions to follow your lead."

"Is that all he told you to do?"

"I don't follow you."

"What I'm asking you, Johnson, is if there's anything fishy going on that I should know about."

"You mean between me and the captain."

"That's right."

"Well," said Johnson, "let me ask you something. Is it true you once knocked Joe Louis down in a scratch fight?"

"That's true enough," I said. "But he was just a kid then."

"Then there's nothing fishy going on."

I looked hard at Johnson, and he looked right back. We stared at each other till I was satisfied. I said, "So you didn't find anything to speak of."

"Hold on," said Johnson. "I didn't say that. We were getting the stiff-arm from everybody, sure enough. I was getting a little hot, I guess. It's hard not to take it personally. But Walker was all right, so I kept as cool as I could. Anyway, we got to a place a few doors down from Pease's building, just as dumpy—I guess I'd hate to live like that, just the smell of it—and we rapped on one door. You could hear the old man talking long before he dragged himself to the door. 'I'm coming, I'm coming,' he says. 'You got my boy?' He opens up the door finally. It's an old man hobbling around with two canes. I can't say what's wrong with him except he looks like he's jumped off a grain silo. His legs are all splayed out so bad that he's walking on the inside of his ankles."

"I don't give a shit what he looks like," I said.

"I know, I know. But I'm just remembering. You told me I couldn't write anything down. The old man figures we're there to help him find his grandson. Starts mouthing off a little. Walker tries to calm him down, you know, tries to talk to the old fellow, but he wasn't having any of that. He starts cussing us out. 'You think my grandson jus' *run off*? He a altar boy down to the Holy Sepulcher—'"

"Did you get the boy's name?"

"I didn't want to look too interested, and Walker was doing the talking. The boy didn't come home Thursday or Friday night. And I looked up Holy Sepulcher, it's only—"

"I know where it is," I said. I stroked my chin for a moment, sliding my thumb and forefinger slowly over the places I'd missed shaving. "Tell you what, Johnson. You go down to Sepulcher and have a word with the priest, have him keep an eye out for the boy."

"I think I can do that."

"And keep it under your hat, got me?"

Johnson nodded. "I can do that, I guess. I get the feeling I'm lying when I leave Walker out of it, though."

"Walker can take care of himself," I said. "He's a grown man."

"I don't worry—it would just be easier to be able to treat everybody the same. Wouldn't have to remember so much to keep the stories straight."

"Everybody's not the same." I stood up and worked out the kinks that had formed all down my spine. "If everybody was the same, we wouldn't have a job."

I turned away and walked slowly out of the room. Johnson closed his locker and followed. We made our way down the stairs to the old interrogation room. I wondered if Captain Mitchell was like Johnson when he started out on the force. I couldn't see Johnson ever getting that hard without going through a war, as Mitchell had. It seemed clear to me that Johnson would be moving up in the department, though, with or without his uncle's help. It was like he walked onto the job expecting advancement. What did he think of me? I guess I've always had one foot out the door. With everything I've done and everywhere I've been, I never quite felt like I belonged on the inside.

"You wouldn't believe it at first," Bobby was saying as we entered, "but it's true. Just like chocolate cake." He looked up and waved an arm as a theatrical introduction. "Caudill and the boy wonder have arrived."

"Morning, Detective," said Johnson. He nodded to Walker.

"Listen, Pete," said Bobby. "I was just telling Walker about my rules for living."

"He doesn't seem amused."

"It's not a laughing matter," said Bobby. "We've got just a short time here, just one life to live. Any shortcut you can get to figure things out is going to help you in the long run. Am I right, Walker?"

"If you say so, Detective."

"Can you tell Detective Caudill what you told me about Pease?"

"Well," said Walker, "if he wants to hear it." He paused for a signal from me and satisfied himself with my attention. "Johnson probably told you that we didn't find much of anything. The folks in the neighborhood weren't happy to see us. They didn't give us much. I gather they didn't think much of Mr. Pease. He didn't seem to have any friends among his neighbors."

"You think that might have something to do with the fact that he liked going around with white girls? How would something like that go over in the colored district?"

"Jesus, Pete, do we need to get into that?" Bobby asked.

"That's all right," said Walker. "Detective Caudill is trying to get the lay of the land. I can understand that. He's right. I don't expect Mr. Pease was well liked down there for a number of reasons. He was going about with white women, it's true. That's one thing. But he was also known to be a thief with a criminal record. Johnson and I heard some whispers about possible use of marijuana. We also managed to figure out that Pease was a pickup man for the numbers racket over there. Now, colored folks tend to look fairly well on the numbers. They have the idea that they can make a little money with it." Here Walker paused. He seemed to hope that Johnson might pick up the tale. Then he said, "But I guess in this respect, colored folks are something like white folks: We don't like men like that in our neighborhoods, where our children walk to school and play on the stoop."

I guess he might have been directing this last comment toward me. It struck me so, but I couldn't say why. I said, "So, boiling it down, we don't have a clue where Pease might be."

"Do we know who's heading up the numbers down there?" Bobby asked.

"He was getting to that," said Johnson. "I made a few calls and picked up the name. Rufus Beamon. Turns out that's an old friend of Walker's."

I was thinking about Johnson making a "few calls," but I said, "That so, Walker?"

"That's right," said Walker. "We grew up together over in the Valley. You might say we were partners in trouble in the old days. You know how boys go. But old Rufus kept a liking for troublesome ways." He paused and pulled a drink from his coffee, gone cold. "It took the better part of the rest of the day to track him down. I spoke to him, and he claims he hasn't seen Pease for a few days."

I felt like my skin was getting red all over, like I was flaming up somehow. I was dizzy. It was me and not Walker, I guess. Maybe it was my blood fizzling out from not eating. But all I could think was *I'd hate to have to sit in on a poker hand with him. Not only don't I know what he's holding, I'm getting so I don't know what's in my own hand.* It seemed that Walker was talking directly to me, trying to stir up something personal, but I couldn't really say that he wasn't just being polite. If he was playing, I couldn't beat him, and I couldn't even say if he *was* playing. I managed to say, "Could you tell if he was on the level?"

"I've always known Rufus to be an easy liar, but he knows me, and he knows I haven't been putting any extra money in my pocket. If Pease has gone missing, it wouldn't mean much to Rufus. He could get another pickup man anywhere. Rufus wouldn't go to any trouble for him. So I would say he hasn't seen Pease."

"Bobby," I said, "can we lean on this guy?"

Bobby shook his head slowly. "Not without drawing a lot of attention."

"If anybody had a beef, we could send them to Mitchell."

"I'm not worried about anybody beefing," said Bobby. "I'm just thinking that it wouldn't be worth the commotion."

"So you think"—I had exhausted myself somehow, though I hadn't really done a thing—"we can take Walker's judgment on this? This guy doesn't have anything to tell us?"

Bobby let the question hang in the air for a moment. Then he shrugged his shoulders and said, "Sure. I think we ought to send Walker around on his own to see what he can find out with his people."

I looked sharply at Bobby and blurted, "You think that's all right?"

"I think Walker's a man who knows when to talk," said Bobby. "Am I right, Walker?"

We all looked at Walker intently. He looked from man to man and then nodded slowly.

"I'm telling you, Pete, Walker's our man."

I thought for a moment. Though I had set up Johnson to dig for me without telling Bobby, I felt that I had lost some footing, like I was the odd man out instead of Walker—and I wasn't sure that didn't make sense. All of it rattled around in my head for a moment, and then I said, "You don't have a car, do you, Walker?"

"No, sir."

"Well, Bobby," I said, "are you going to send Walker out by himself in a scout car? How do you think that'll go over with the boys in the garage?" I knew that to the men on the force, the few colored officers trickling in represented the cowardice of Mayor Jeffries in the face of pressure from Jenkins and other civic leaders pressing for change. If we took Walker to check out a scout car, it would surely mark the first time a colored officer had been allowed to take a car alone, and probably the first time a colored officer had even been allowed to drive one. I couldn't help thinking that men had been lynched for less. And if something like that came along by the time we had finished all our business, wouldn't everyone suppose I had a hand in it?

Bobby stood up and wafted his hat back and forth, brushing it against his leg. Then he let a big grin burst over his face and said, "We'll find out, I guess!"

I had never touched a colored man in friendship. I had rousted dozens over the years, cracked a few heads, arrested my share, and shot more than one colored man dead. I guess a colored criminal didn't feel so much different to me from a white hoodlum. Certainly they were no filthier. But standing there, with my mind bugging out, and with everyone waiting on me to say yea or nay, I couldn't remember ever so much as shaking the hand of a colored man. Certainly, I had never been known to be the chummy sort. I hadn't ever laid my hands on a great number of white men, either, to put it that way. If my father hadn't been such a terrific backslapper, I could say it was something in the way I'd been raised. Finally, as I could see they were waiting for me to say something, I muttered, "You better go with him, Bobby. They'll dump a load on him if you don't."

"You should go instead," said Bobby. "I'd like to see the look on Farley's face if you and Walker came up together."

"Piss on that fat bastard." I just shrugged. "He's been a pain in the ass since before I was on the force. My old man used to take me in there and Farley would try to scare me with his stories, rolling his fat ass around on that chair of his. How can a man spend his whole life on the job sitting down?"

We all walked out and stood to the side of the building, where the early sun bounced off the marble and the sidewalk and wanted to cook us from every angle. Bobby and Walker crossed the street to the garage.

When they were out of earshot, Johnson said, "What should I do with the boy if I find him?"

"Take him out for ice cream," I said.

"I mean how should I handle it? What should I tell the people at the church if he's there and I take him away?"

"Johnson, you are a police officer. People will do what you tell them, if you can look 'em in the eye. You carry a weapon. You wear a uniform. If you can act like you're in charge, then you'll be in charge, and you won't have to take any guff from anybody."

That shut him up. Johnson said nothing more as we waited for Bobby and Walker to return. He followed as I sidled toward Bobby's car, which was parked, as usual, blocking the hydrant in front of headquarters. We watched as the scout car pulled out of the garage with Walker behind the wheel. I could see Bobby's white hands moving inside the cab, directing Walker to pull up right in front of the building. Bobby jumped out and slammed the door, but stuck his head immediately inside the open window and began talking excitedly to Walker.

I walked up and rapped my knuckles on Bobby's bony back.

Bobby pulled his head out of the car. "Priceless, Pete, I'm telling you straight. Farley's eyes popped right out of his head when I gave Walker the keys. He says, 'You can't let that darky drive! He's not certified!'"

"What did you tell him?"

"I told him Walker was my chauffeur," said Bobby.

"You're a laugh riot. It'll be even funnier if they find Walker with his toes pointing up." I leaned toward the window of the scout car so Walker could hear as well. "I'm thinking, now, with what's happening, maybe we should be looking for Toby Thrumm, too. You know anything about that name, Walker?"

Walker shook his head.

"It was Thrumm that set us up to find Pease. Seems after we got done talking to him, he got the tar kicked out of him and ended up in the hospital. At least that's the story we got from Jenkins."

"Jenkins!" Walker perked up. "You mean Reverend Jenkins?"

I said, "Is that funny to you, Walker?"

"Not funny exactly."

"Well, what is it, then?" I had intended just to send Walker on his way, and now found myself engaged in a conversation that seemed likely to drag on. My neck began to ache from craning my head into the car's window.

"Reverend Jenkins, there's a man who went from nothing to something in a hurry, that's all I'm saying."

"I hear he's a real big shooter down in the neighborhoods," said Bobby. "Has a line on everything."

"*Now* he does," said Walker. "You all probably don't remember how it was maybe ten years ago with Jenkins. That man knows how to talk is all. Back then he wasn't much more than a street-corner minister, if you catch my meaning. But when the unions started coming in, and all the organizers and such—Communists and all, they were—when all those boys started coming in, wanting to stir things up, they couldn't find anywhere to talk. No sir, none of the colored churches would touch 'em. Mr. Lloyd saw to that. Time was, a colored man could only get a job if he was going to church regular, and then the minister might put him on the list for Lloyd's."

"And Jenkins found a place for the union boys to have their meetings, that right, Walker?" Bobby let loose a wide grin.

"That's right. See, back then, he wasn't anything but a talker. He didn't have anything to lose."

"So our Mr. Jenkins is quite a gambler, then," said Bobby. "Now he's up there with the big boys because he jumped on the bandwagon when it was just starting out." He slapped his palm on the roof of the car. "See, Pete, it's what I keep telling you. You have to try to look forward a little, see what's in the wind."

"Never mind all that," I said. "Walker, I want you to sniff around, talk to your people about Pease, see if you can come up with a location for Toby Thrumm. Receiving says he's busted up pretty bad, somehow he slipped out, they don't know where he is. Don't talk to Jenkins. Try to get back with Johnson here after lunch. Got all that?"

"Sure, Detective. Should I bring Thrumm down if I find him?"

I looked at Bobby.

"Well," said Bobby, "see what you can get out of him, if he's around. Maybe...it would be better not to bring him down here."

"Try to get a description of the boys who messed him over," I said. "And tell him I said hello."

"All right, then. Okay."

Walker drove off carefully. I was aware that we had drawn a crowd. All the uniformed officers and detectives trickling from the building glared at the car until it passed from view.

"Okay, Pete, why the bum's rush for old Walker?" said Bobby.

"Johnson's got a lead on a colored boy that I saw in Pease's apartment building. Seems the boy's gone missing. Now, if I can find him, he may not know much, but at least I'm sure I can make him tell us what he did see. Since I know him by his face, he can't clam up about being there."

"Maybe it would have been better to let Walker talk to him."

"Maybe. Maybe not."

"Walker's all right, Pete. We got to talking. He says he's getting it bad from both sides. Colored folks down there calling him Uncle Tom and all of that. One old lady got so worked up cussing him out that her dentures came flying out of her mouth. Spit all over his uniform, you know." Bobby let loose a laugh and a deep cough. "Can you picture that?"

"Nobody twisted his arm to join the force."

"Jesus, Pete, you can lighten up a little. Not everybody's out to get you! I'm telling you, Walker's decent enough."

Johnson said, "If it's trouble, I—"

"Get to it, Johnson," I said. "You won't have the same trouble getting a scout car. Farley knows you're Mitchell's nephew, I'm guessing."

Johnson nodded.

"Then get to it," I told him.

Johnson wanted to say something but held it back. He turned from us and made his way across the busy street to the garage.

"Let's go," I said to Bobby. "I feel like we're putting on a show out here." I slipped into Bobby's unmarked car.

"Where to?"

"I say we head over to niggertown on the west end and see if we can spot any familiar faces leaning on lampposts, maybe roust a few, kick up something about Pease."

"Hey! What about Mitchell?"

"Hell with Mitchell," I said. "If he's looking to knock us down, he could get plenty on us without all of this. I figure he's telling us to stay away to cover his ass if it gets too ugly. Let's go. I want to wrap this thing up and put it away as soon as we can manage it."

"Okay," Bobby said. "I'm game. It's good to see a little initiative out of you. Could be I'm starting to grow on you a little bit?"

"When something like you starts to grow on me," I muttered, "I chop it off with a hatchet."

CHAPTER

7

Bobby let the car into gear and eased slowly into traffic. He took the car through a nonsense route of side streets and back alleys that left me wondering at times where we were. I gripped the top of the door with my good hand to hold myself steady.

I couldn't get a handle on the numbers, but it seemed like there were too many people in the city, especially with so many men off to the war. Detroit was a big magnet, sucking people up from all over. Though I had lived in the city my whole life, and though I had been thrilled to see the great skyscrapers come up in the twenties and all the other changes, I thought that the city had become too big to keep track of. As a child, I had roamed all over, thumbing rides or hitching on the streetcars, and I felt like I belonged anywhere Bobby went, except on the property of the old auto barons. You always knew where there was too much money and where they wouldn't let you just walk around free. I thought I knew every corner of the city. Maybe it was Bobby's careless driving, circling, speeding up and slowing down, but I looked out now at the streets that had become strange and wondered how I had lost even my feeling of home. I caught glimpses of street signs and began to realize that we were far south of where we should have been on the trip westward.

"You need to stop and ask directions?" I said. "This ain't exactly the best way out."

"Well," said Bobby, "it's just a little business I need to check up on. The way things are, it's been a few days." He turned and leaned to poke his elbow into my shoulder. "Listen, Pete," he said, "you strike me as a man who can keep his mouth shut."

I said nothing but looked at him and raised my eyebrows dully.

"You don't make me for a chump who's going to work all his life, do you? Don't answer that." Bobby sucked in a deep, shaking drag from his smoke. "See, I got a little thing going on the side. It's not much for now, but give me a couple years. I got a place rented out, it's just down here if you want to swing by and have a look."

"Sure," I said. I thought with wonder and worry about the endless vitality my partner seemed to have. It seemed bad to keep on hustling when your juice had to be run out. I wondered if it wasn't eating Bobby up from the inside, or storing up bile to turn into cancer or something. For myself, I had decided long ago that a slow and steady course was best and in fact the only one possible.

"Flavored syrups, that's the racket," said Bobby. "Watch where it gets me."

"I'm not following."

"See, I've got this little thing going. I get the flavorings and the bottled water and the sugar. I pay a couple Polack ladies to mix it all together. These babushka ladies can work hard, but you have to keep an eye on them or they just sit and gabble in Polish. I sell it to Pops Brunell over in Paradise Valley, he puts a little fizz in it, a little water, bottles it up, and sells it to all the colored kids on Hastings Street."

"You're selling syrup?" I loosened my tie and ran my palm over my forehead.

"Well, I know it sounds like a dope's racket. But the markup I'm able to take is—well, it ought to be illegal. I got these ladies doing the messy work, and all I've got to do is set things up on the business end. This way I get to keep my hands clean, know what I mean?" Bobby considered his pink fingernails over the steering wheel.

"Don't you need a license for that sort of thing?"

"Ordinarily," Bobby grinned.

"Well, where the hell are you getting all the sugar?" We both knew that dodging the ration system could bring federal dicks swarming around like ants at a picnic. And the federal dicks wouldn't have any reason to smile at Bobby's antics.

"That's the sweet part! I've got this guy up north, outside Mio— you know where that is? Twice a month I borrow one of the paddy wagons and make a pickup down there over the weekend. Sugar beet country, that's all them hicks got up there—"

"That's your big idea? Selling syrup? How much could you be making on all of that?"

"You'd be surprised, Pete, let me tell you. It adds up to a pretty penny. Pops sells a truckload of that stuff because it's cheaper than the Coca-Cola. Maybe you haven't been up to the Valley in a while— I know you're not exactly welcome—but the darkies up there are falling all over each other, it's packed in so tight. And they're plenty thirsty."

"I guess I'm having trouble seeing it," I said.

"Open that eye up a little wider. This is just the start of it, see? If I can put up three or four setups like this, I'll be making enough to quit the force and concentrate on the business. No more dirt under these fingernails. No more hustling punks for information. I'm telling you, Jasper Lloyd was forty years old before he ever—hold on, here it is."

It was an old warehouse from before the turn of the century, fitted out now for a number of small businesses. I knew that the area had once been Jewish, and I figured that the places were all rented out now by Jews up in big houses in Oak Park or farther out. The front of the structure filled half a block and ran along the alley all the way back to the next street, and it made me wonder how many bricks had gone into the face of the building. I fixed the place at no more than sixty years old, but already the bricks were cracked and the mortar had started to crumble in places. It would have suited me to think of bricks as something like stone, good for thousands of years. *Still,* I thought, *enough of it's still holding together to keep it up for a while.*

Bobby pulled into the alley and left the car there, midway between the sheer walls of two four-story buildings. He pulled out a key from the watch pocket of his trousers and opened the door. I felt the flush of hot, wet air on my face as I entered and smelled the sweetness of thick sugar bubbling. A few heavyset Polish ladies padded around in house dresses and flat shoes, toting heavy bags of sugar, dropping them into big kettles lined up along a sturdy bench with gas burners built in. There were six kettles, and one of the ladies moved slowly from one to the next, lifting a long wooden paddle at each and patiently stirring the brew. All the ladies seemed cut from the same cloth: bow-legged, thick about the shoulders, hips, and forearms, and each squinting through the drooping flesh above her eyes, peering out briefly at Bobby and me through dark pinholes. I couldn't decide if the faint trace of cabbage smell came from the ladies or from Bobby's makeshift setup.

A fan blew out through a high, narrow window to the alley but didn't do much to cut the thickness of the air inside the room. I sauntered along, eyeing the setup. It reminded me of some dank scene from the Old Country. I put it together. Except for the running water of the washbasin and the spigot set on the wall for washing out the kettles, a century might not have passed, to judge by what I could see before me.

Canvas sacks tight with sugar had been piled up neatly along one wall, enough, I judged, to be worth a pretty penny on their own. Everything, all the benches, tables, and stools, seemed to be made of heavy, oil-darkened wood, and the lights overhead seemed yellow enough and threw light dimly enough to be mistaken for candles or torches. The papers that Bobby searched through on the little desk seemed yellow and curled and were in general written out by hand—often in the crabbed hand of the Polish women, marking production.

It felt bad to me. I propped myself against a wall under a window, where I could feel the slight breeze from the tilted pane pass over me. Maybe Bobby's sugar supplier had given him the stuff on credit as a way of lessening the risk of selling it; maybe Bobby really had the sway to fix up such a sweet deal on his own. I wasn't much for figures, but I couldn't help wondering how a farmer could make more money selling on the black market than by selling on a fat government contract. It occurred to me that perhaps Bobby had some sort of hold on the farmer; it was easy enough to imagine how a big-city police officer might dig up dirt bad enough to nudge things along that way. But it seemed like too much trouble to go through, too much risk, and too much complicated hustling for the profit that might be involved—especially for a man like Bobby, who had a nose for the dirty stuff and could easily amass a small fortune in well-placed graft and hustling. I knew plenty of officers, even beat cops, who had done just that. Certainly a few muddy bills had crossed my own palm. What it boiled down to, I finally decided, was that I did not trust Bobby's judgment enough to allow that he could run something like this without something going bad in the end.

When Bobby at last found the papers he was looking for, I pushed off the wall and sauntered after him into the alley. I said nothing but spent some time trying to place all of it into what I already knew about Bobby. All the thinking and fussing just left me aching to do something rough with my hands.

On the road again and heading toward Pease's side of town, I set my face grimly and thought about Walker. There was just the one other thing, and Bobby seemed to want to forget about it. I knew that I could not afford to forget it myself and that Walker could hardly ignore it. The whole Negro community held on to it, I had to figure. It was not the kind of thing that would ever just fade out from the back of your memory. I had killed a young colored boy in cold blood, it was true, and I had done it without hesitation, dropped him in his tracks because he wouldn't put up his hands. However I felt about it after, however it was settled, that was somebody's boy. If the colored folks had a mind to remember, the whole business was still sitting with them, waiting for a time when they might be able to do something about it. How it sat with Walker, I couldn't say.

It was a bad time for everyone, when everything just seemed to dry up. Folks were poor enough and hungry enough to set aside some of the lessons they had learned in church. In the dark part of town, especially, it wasn't unusual to note a Blue Monday party on every block, where all the ladies gathered together and cooked a little something, hoping to scratch up enough dough to keep a neighbor from being thrown out onto the street. And it was a winter, a cold one, even for Detroit, and the boy was lifting some shoes for himself with a couple of his pals. Though the inquiry had cleared me of any wrongdoing—the department had closed ranks for me, as a matter of course—that one incident made it easy for people to think they knew me, knew what I was about.

I had fallen into it easily. Because of my size, my lack of easy words, and the set of my face, men and women had always been leery of me, but that one moment put me down forever as a heavy man, as someone best kept to the outside. Even before I lost the eye and the fingers, I was apart from things. I've got the kind of face that looks dark in photographs, like I've got a shadow following me around. After I killed the boy, my mother cut the pictures out of the newspaper like she was proud, like she couldn't understand how anyone could see her boy as anything but good. It was useful as a beat cop to have that weight behind me, though, and easier than trying to explain myself with words. After I shot the boy, I had seen it working: More than once I'd been grousing with a lippy punk when something made the punk realize who he was dealing with. The change would come like a bone stuck in the throat, and the bravado would fall away like a wave. In a town like Detroit, any number of two-bit hoodlums wouldn't get pale at the prospect of a beating from a particularly tough cop—a crack on the head, maybe a couple more teeth gone, in the worst case a broken arm or jaw. It also meant at least one warm night in the can, a full belly, and the added weight that such a thing might bring in the dark corners of the city. But it was another thing to come up against a man who had killed a boy for lifting a cheap pair of shoes in the dead of winter.

With the heat and the stupor brought on by the extended reminiscence, I might have dozed off if not for Bobby's chatter, which had started up again. I was glad that my left eye was missing because it made it easy not to look at him. The question of what to do about Walker stayed with me, and I worried at it like a piece of gristle stuck between my teeth. I wanted to smack him down to see if he'd come up swinging, as if that could settle things the way it had between me and my brother Tommy. I wanted to tell him that I was sorry I'd killed the boy, that I was older now and maybe I wouldn't do it again if the situation came up. I cared less about the law, less about keeping things in order that way. Nothing so clear-cut would happen, though; I knew it wouldn't be settled that easily.

"Whoa! Stop the car, Bobby."

"Why?"

I thumped two heavy knuckles on Bobby's chest. "When I say stop, you stop."

Bobby slammed on the brakes and squealed to a stop.

"Back it up to the alley there." Though the street was thick with pedestrians, I thought I had caught something hinky in the corner of my eye: three men banked up against another in a way that jolted my attention.

Bobby cranked his head around and zigzagged the car in reverse until we had a view down the alley. Two big white men were working over a smaller colored man while a third white man, short and very slender, dressed in a suit and smoking a cigarette, watched with both hands in his pockets. The colored man was up against the wall, on his feet but crouched down with his back arched, his fanny sticking out to pull in and protect his privates. His arms were in front of his face, his fists and elbows tight together, making a shield. With the two gymnasium boys looping in punches from either side, it wasn't much use.

I fumbled with the door while Bobby let the clutch kill the engine. The smoking man looked down the alley at me, turned slightly, and then smiled as if in recognition. The look on his face made heat rise up in me, a flash of fury, as if the whole purpose of the altercation had been to bait us. But I quickly realized that there was no way in the world, with Bobby's aimless driving, that anyone could have expected us to stumble onto this scene.

"Bobby," I said, "go for the runt!"

"I got you," said Bobby, already out of the car and hotfooting it toward the fight. The two white boys lobbed a few more punches with their brass knucks and tore off down the alley. The runt trotted after. I made it out of the car and ran as well as I could after them. I knew it was useless. I was pretty fast with my hands, but my legs were thick and sturdy, good for standing, not running. So I let the big boys go and stopped to check the condition of the colored man while Bobby shagged the runt.

The Negro sat on the pavement, shaking his head and working his tongue in his mouth. "Man, I didn't even *know* those hunkies," he said.

"How do you feel?" I stood over him, panting as if I had done some real running. "You busted up in the stomach? Broken bones you can say?" I glanced down the alley to see Bobby spreading the runt against the wall of a hat shop, almost down to the next street.

"This ain't right. I'm just tryin' get some lunch. Then these white boys..."

"Just keep quiet." I pulled a handkerchief from my inside pocket and opened it carefully over my hand. I felt under the man's jaw and found it unbroken. His lips were smashed and bleeding, and the black skin over one cheekbone had been split open, but his eyes looked okay. I knew he'd look like a pile of guts after he'd had a little time to swell up. But if his ribs had been broken up, he'd be wheezing and maybe frothing up blood already. He was lucky in that regard— I could see that he was hard like a working man, and that was what kept the blows from tearing up the insides. He'd be feeling it in the morning, probably reaching for the whiskey to tide him over, but unless he started pissing red, it didn't look like any more damage than a typical smack-around.

"You're all right," I said. I offered him the bloodied handkerchief. "Take it now. It's ruined anyway."

"This is just not right." The colored man took the handkerchief and pressed at the rip over his cheekbone, then dabbed softly at the blood that ran down his cheek and chin.

Still on one knee, I glanced up the alley to see the runt approaching with his hands cuffed in front of him. Bobby walked behind, slapping the runt occasionally on the back of the head. The face was not familiar. I watched carefully as they drew near, concentrating, trying to remember. The runt's face, though turned down and toward the wall, seemed lit up with something funny, as if I ought to know him and there was a joke in the making. But though my mind had lately been playing tricks, making every stranger's face seem somehow familiar, I could say that I had never seen the face of this oddly undersized man before. It was a face you'd remember if you had a reason to. He was sized like a boy, almost, with a thick and tousled mop of hair, and he moved with his head down and his shoulders loose and forward—a posture that might be taken for submission. The face, though, was clearly outside boyhood: The skin about the eyes and mouth had gone thin, the eyes were not clear, and he had a general blue cast to his puffy flesh. He was older than me, and showing it, on close examination.

They passed by me on the way to Bobby's car. I watched their backs as they went. Something about the way the runt shuffled down the alley, striking and stomach-turning like the sight of a big rat shambling along a wall in broad daylight, lit up my memory. Powerfully, the way that certain scents could do—the smell of coke dust worked into my hands, the smell of my sister's hair on her deathbed—that runt's walk opened a dusty back closet in my memory. Just a flash it was, like a scene from a movie I couldn't name. For a moment I wondered if I might be asleep in my bed, dreaming a pointless dream about alleys and flavored syrup and punks hammering a poor nigger for no reason. Or I might be dead, trapped in a never-ending bull's nightmare of dead-legged chase—a type of purgatory. But that runt's odd shuffle, the way he kept to the shadow along the brick wall instead of walking down the middle of the alley, struck me hard and went into me like the bits of gravel that now dug into my knee. Bobby looked back at me and grinned.

Then I remembered.

I remembered crying. It was eight years almost. I remembered that my first thought was that I was crying. But of course I was not crying. There was an image I could not shake, visiting me less often now in dreams than it had in those first days following the loss of my fingers and eye. Huffing down the side of the empty Clark Rubber factory in my beat-walking days, right down by the bridge to Belle Isle, chasing a little man who seemed to shamble like a rat down the alley.

I remembered the brightness of the day and the color of the sky. When the little man slipped through the jimmied steel door and into the rubber factory, I pulled out my revolver and hurried after him. But as I opened the door, time seemed to skip forward. I had been standing with my left hand on the door, peering into the darkened building—but then I was facedown in the street, thirty feet away. I remembered how quickly I jumped to my feet, as if embarrassed; the revolver had not stopped sliding over the pavement. And then I looked down at my hand: not quite right. I reached up with the good hand to feel the wetness dripping from my eye. Crying! But not tears. I did not know it then, but the explosion had driven a tiny sliver of metal through the cornea, the lens of my eye, and into the flesh inside the bony socket. And the humors dripped down like tears.

The little man, the little man, I thought then. What's become of him?

Bobby flipped me a thumbs-up, stepping proud, full of air and himself, as if the quick chase and capture had puffed a little life into him.

"Watch him, Bobby!" I felt my legs churning but could not make them quick. I fumbled to draw my piece from the shoulder rig as I stood up.

I could see a shadow move on Bobby's face. He turned back just as the runt wheeled around and plunged a short, broad blade into his stomach. A quick jerk dragged it a few inches upward. The runt's knife hand was free of the cuffs. Bobby grabbed for him and managed a grip on his lapel, but the runt shook free. Then he was gone, running with remarkable speed for the end of the alley. Bobby pulled the blade from his midsection and threw it after the man, fumbled with blood-slick fingers for the seldom-used revolver in his shoulder rig, failed.

By the time I made it over to him, Bobby was on his knees on the pavement and tearing at his shirt, which was already soaked with blood.

"Bobby, just stop moving for a minute."

I pressed down on his shoulders and forced him to sit back against the wall. I tore open the shirt and saw blood and bile pouring from the wound and could think of nothing to do but press my good hand over it. I glanced back down the alley and saw that the colored man had run off the other way and was about to turn the corner onto the next street.

"Listen, Pete, make sure about Anna and the girl. Make sure they get some money. It's in the wall. Everything's in the wall."

"What money?"

"Just promise me you'll watch out for them a little bit, okay? She needs somebody to watch out for her. She always has."

My heart was like a quail in my chest. I hadn't ever thought that I might care so much about Bobby. "You're all right, Bobby. A little blood ain't gonna kill you."

"You know," Bobby said, "I never heard you lie until now." He laughed, and the blood pushed through my fingers with the laughter. "You've always been a straight shooter. You can't help it. That's what I always liked about you."

Bobby's warm blood streamed over my hand and ran down wet enough over his clothes to pool onto the pavement. I felt the wetness soaking the knee of my trousers. I felt like I should cry out for help like a woman might. But I could do nothing. After a moment, I felt Bobby begin to relax and heard the clatter as a bullet rolled from his palm onto the pavement, a bullet at the end of a little silver chain. With my mangled left hand I stroked Bobby's hair, murmuring, "You're all right. You're all right."

CHAPTER
8

For once I was glad for the rain. It did not seem fitting to be buried on a sunny day. The soft rain pulled down the temperature and allowed me to survive the lengthy service in my heavy black wool dress uniform. The heat that rose from deep in my belly had washed down as well, so that, as a pallbearer, I stood at attention through the formal proceedings in a half-stupor. I hoped that the ceremony would lend Bobby more dignity in death than he ever cared about in life. *It's for the wife,* I thought, *and for the kid.*

I could do nothing about the mob of reporters and photographers or the gawking civilians who braved the rain to witness the spectacle of a police funeral. If I had had concern to spare about it, I would have viewed the circus with more disgust. The morning papers had blared headlines. HERO OFFICER'S FUNERAL TODAY: CAME TO AID OF NEGRO MAN. I knew Bobby Swope wasn't well known in the city, though he had been mentioned in the papers several times. Crooks were far more interesting than the cops who nabbed them, it was commonly known. The everyday grind of police work was no more interesting to the average newspaper reader than an account of life on the assembly line. But now that Bobby had been killed, he could be seen as something like a fallen soldier. You could hook him up to the whole mess overseas and get weepy about it if you had a mind to. If I had wanted to be fair, I might have admitted to myself that such a ruckus over one officer's death might be a good sign. It was still a rare and disgraceful thing in Detroit for an officer to be killed in the line of duty.

I was in no mood to think about fairness. My thoughts were black as I stood at attention before the casket. The pastor of St. John's Episcopal said a few more words, mumbled something biblical and apologetic, and then turned away. I watched him go: a sad man, wrapped up in a world of books and weak prayers. The boy holding his umbrella tripped after him, unable to keep himself or the pastor from getting soaked.

Dressed neatly in black, Anna Swope sat with her knees together under the canopy that sheltered the few family members from the rain. Most of the police officers who had accompanied the procession from the church to the old cemetery on Mt. Elliott had gone on to their duties. The remainder now passed by Anna, who nodded without expression and allowed her hand to be squeezed as each mourner expressed condolence. I lingered at the grave, wishing I could muster the gravity to make an oath of revenge, but I could not do more than scan Bobby's coffin and study the wet earth piled up beside the grave. My hands felt swollen.

The rage and guilt that had blown through me over the last two days had left me hollow. Clearly, I had thought, as a man lives, he's responsible for what happens on his watch. And Bobby had gone down on my watch. *On my watch.* Because I did not believe in coincidence any more than I believed in divine providence, I knew that there was some deeper guilt I had to shoulder. If this same rat-shambling runt had been responsible for the loss of my own eye and fingers, so many years ago, then there must be some reason, some careless ember left smoldering below the surface, for what had happened to Bobby. It all turned on me, as if I had done something wrong but couldn't remember what it was. I had some debt to pay. I could not see what I had purchased at such cost; my life was not all roses, clearly. But if I had collared the runt years ago, as I might have, then maybe the present mess might have been avoided, and Bobby's carcass might not have been boxed up until his natural time. It seemed right to believe that there was some connection between Bobby's death and the Hardiman case, too, though there was nothing but the white-colored mix in both incidents. On the basis of intuition, which I didn't want to believe in, either, everything seemed connected. Maybe I had become addled enough with feeling and shame that I was inclined to take on any stray guilt that drifted my way. I'd accept the blame for Jane Hardiman's death, too; I'd have to put all of it to rest before my life could ever be right. But that was as far as I could go. The awful guilt had left me unable to string together any line of thought or deduction worth following.

I had given the sketch artist a good description of the runt, and so at least I had the assurance that half the police in the city were on the lookout. The runt was oddly small and wore clothes that cost a little something. My optimism wavered; on the one hand, there were so many people and so many nooks and crannies in the city that it seemed unlikely that we'd find someone who didn't want to be found. But I also knew that the beat cops and the dicks would all make a little effort to find something out. They'd ask around, spread a net of conversation around the city, and maybe turn up something to go on. I had not mentioned to anyone that I felt—I was sure—the runt was the same man responsible for my maiming. In that case, so many years ago, I had never seen the man's face as I chased him. Why had I been after him anyway? It was his walk that struck me. I could tell a familiar walk a block away, long before I could see well enough to recognize a face. I can see it in my mind now, even standing grave-side in the pissing rain—how the little man's bandy-legs wavered in the heat bouncing off the paved parking lot as he scurried away from me—

"Pete," said Anna, hovering near my elbow, "you're getting soaked. Let's go."

I was startled out of my daydream. It took a moment for me to feel the rain again, to bring my mind back to the sodden grass, the dull light, and the hiss of the cars passing over the wet pavement of Mt. Elliott.

"Let's go." She held an umbrella out to me, and I took it, bending toward her as we walked to my car.

"I'm sorry, Anna. I guess it was my fault."

"Don't be foolish, Pete. It happened to him because—I know—he wasn't a careful man." Her English was clipped and careful, the German accent muted.

I flinched to hear her speak so plainly. She was a tall woman, slen-der, with a handsome, square-jawed face, and this suited her person-ality: grim, plainspoken, and businesslike. Yet I could not accustom myself to her practicality.

"He was careless, but he wasn't stupid," I said.

"He could be stupid." She stopped at the passenger door and let me open it for her. "Pete, you can teach me how to drive one of these things?"

I said nothing as she slid onto the worn seat. I thought dully that from anyone but Anna the request would seem a come-on. "Sure," I said. "But it'll have to wait a couple weeks till I get things straight-ened out." I took down the umbrella as I walked to the driver's side and shook out the water as well as I could. Then I slipped out of my soaked coat and put it in the rear seat with the umbrella. Behind the wheel, I sat for a moment watching the water running down the windshield.

"The ladies are putting out some sandwiches and coffee," said Anna, "in the basement of the church."

"No disrespect, but I think I'll pass on that." I started the car and began to drive toward the church.

"It's okay," she said. She crossed her ankles and folded her gloved hands on her lap and stared listlessly out the window. "I would skip it myself."

I hoped that the rain might suck the heat right out of the air and wash it away, but I knew that the heat would rise up like steam after the clouds blew away. It didn't seem fair. I glanced at Anna's angular profile and made out no trace of emotion. I had not seen her cry during any part of the proceedings.

"It'll be better in a while," I said.

"I've been through worse things," she said. "It's Lucy I worry about. Someone told her that Bobby had just gone to sleep, and now—and now she's terrified of the bed."

I could think of nothing to say. I felt numb and weak and wanted to smash through something.

"I can't imagine what we will do now," said Anna. She worked with long fingers to adjust the pins that held her little black hat to her hair.

Something about the way she was sitting or a murmur at the back of her voice seemed too open to me, too intimate. We had not spoken much before. I ground my teeth together and wondered how shook up I must be to let my body feel what it was feeling, with my partner's stiff, made-up fingers folded over his belly not half a mile away.

I drove slowly, peering through the bleary windshield. I could not quite suck in enough air.

"I am not fit for anything," she said. "And who would hire me?"

I knew that her accent and history would make it hard for her to find something. I knew that most of the Japs in the country had been rounded up, even the ones who had been born here. Though I had never asked Bobby anything about it, I had gathered that Anna had come over from Germany in the 1930s with her brother, an engineer. Even if she had become a naturalized citizen since that time, her accent would hang like a cloud over her, at least until the war was over.

"But this is America," said Anna. "Widows and orphans are not left out on the street."

I saw no trace of humor or bitterness in her words. I could not say what she was feeling, though I could see that she, too, was clenching her jaw.

"Listen," I said, "do you have any family over here?"

"No," she said. "Not here."

"Well, we'll think of something, I guess." I scrambled to think of a way to come up with a little money. I could run over to Bobby's business and grab up all the sugar, unload it on the black market. Bobby had mentioned something about some money. It seemed clear that money could buy some flexibility, at least, or a little time.

"I don't really worry," she said. "When I was a girl, it was much worse. You perhaps cannot imagine."

We arrived at St. John's, and I pulled around to the side, where I knew the old ladies of the church would lay out their sandwiches and cookies. Though the sky still looked heavy and close, the rain had stopped.

"It's not my business," I said, "but how did Bobby leave things?"

She coughed or choked back a laugh. "He was always at the end of his string, you know. At the end of his rope."

"He worked pretty hard. He was always looking to get ahead. Had he saved anything up?"

Now she laughed bitterly. "He had hoped he could be a good man. He was always running away!"

"Running away?" I held both hands on the wheel and met her eyes.

"Pete, you are a dear man," she said. She gripped my forearm hard enough to shift my muscles under her fingers. "But you seem to know nothing sometimes." She loosened her grip on my arm and stroked her hand over the damp fabric of my jacket. Then she turned and opened the passenger door.

I could not imagine what to say.

Anna stepped out of the car. She leaned her head back in and said quietly, "You should know it, Pete. You should know what it means. Don't think less of me for the telling. Bobby was a *queer.*"

"Ah," I stammered, "queer?"

Anna closed the car door, turned curtly, and walked into the church.

I put the car into gear and let the idling motor drift the vehicle away toward the street.

Probably at a dozen other beer gardens or back rooms in the city, the better part of the police force swallowed liquor that day, not out of remorse for the way Bobby ended up but because the situation allowed a certain show of self-pity. I found a place where I knew there would be no company and guzzled half a dozen highballs. But the alcohol could not produce much feeling for me or offer relief from the ideas slamming inside my head. I sat for an hour in my car, watching the rain come and go and wishing that I could fall asleep in the backseat. I pulled my revolver from the glove box and looked it over. I dropped the shells from the wheel into my palm and then held them up, one by one, turning them and eyeing them between my fingers. After reloading the shells, I put the gun into its holster and worked it into the squeaking leather the way a ballplayer might work a glove. Since I knew that the burning ache in my gut would not go away no matter where I went, I decided I might as well try to get back into the swing of work.

The police headquarters were empty for a Tuesday. In a room behind the main desk, I rummaged over the cluttered desk.

"I told you to take a few days off, Caudill." Captain Mitchell's voice sounded close to my ear.

"I enjoy my work so much," I told him, "this is a holiday for me."

"You're his partner, you should have stayed at the church. A lot of the men are there." Mitchell stood close and spoke softly. "I could smell the liquor on you before I came into the room."

"They won't miss me." I thumbed the pages of the order book. "Roscoe!" I called. "Where's the roster for the Fourth Precinct?"

Faintly, through the open doorway leading to the front desk, came Roscoe's thick voice. "It should be in there, I'm telling you."

I told Mitchell, "I'm trying to find out who was supposed to be on the beat where Bobby got it." I fumbled through the heavy book. "Hell with this," I said. "I'll just run over there."

Mitchell took me hard by the elbow. "Come up to my office for a minute, Caudill. And keep your mouth shut."

I fought the urge to jerk my elbow free and followed Mitchell through the building to the back staircase that led up to the offices on the third floor. It always bothered me to pass by the second floor, tiled and furnished cheaply with desks for the detectives, and then to step up to the third floor, where the big brass kept house. Oak paneling as dark as mud, separate offices with walnut desks and windows overlooking Beaubien, a bank of secretaries set up in the middle of the floor. We passed into Mitchell's office, and I stepped to the window and looked down at the street. Mitchell closed the door.

"I won't mince words," said Mitchell. "Frankly, Caudill, I wish I could see a little more spark behind that eye of yours. It's a disappointment for me to realize how limited your thinking is always going to be."

"Then why the hell did you make me a detective?"

"I've told you before about that swearing. It's good enough for the tough-guy act down on the street, but up here you're supposed to be acting like a detective. It's an honorable position. I expect you to take some pride in yourself."

"Why the hell did you make me a detective if I don't even look right?"

"I didn't," said Mitchell. He sat behind his desk. "You don't seem to notice that there are people working behind the scenes here that you don't see every day. You did all right on the test, but I always thought—I still do—that you haven't got the temperament for the job. You don't have the patience. You'd rather just slug right through everything. We're not children here, so I can admit that your talents can be useful in a certain arena. But I'll tell you right now, if there wasn't a war on, you'd still be in the blues as far as I'd have a say in it."

"Bust me back down," I said. I stared down at the street. "I won't kick up a fuss about it."

"No," said Mitchell. "I won't do that. The only thing that's saving you right now is that I know you're not smart enough to lie to me effectively. Swope might have been smart enough, but he didn't have the grit that you do. He couldn't quite throw himself into his lies with enough vigor or lack of concern to be convincing. That's what made the two of you together so valuable to what we're into here."

I wished I could think faster. I reminded myself that Mitchell knew more than I did. Had he known about Bobby? Was he trying to tell me something by speaking this way? Maybe it was the booze still muddling things up, but I could not make my mind race through everything fast enough.

I asked, "What are we into?"

"Barton Rix was on the beat where Swope got killed."

Barton Rix. I rolled my back toward the window and stared hard at Mitchell.

"So you can guess the situation," said Mitchell, "without thinking too much about it. I know that you've known Rix since the old days. I need to figure out if I can trust you to handle things with some tact from here on out."

"It won't take much tact for me to put a slug between his eyes," I muttered.

"One thing we know, it wasn't Rix that killed Swope."

"You don't think he knew what was happening there? Three guys socking up some poor nigger in an alley, that doesn't sound like Rix to you?"

"Sure it looks like something Rix might be involved in. But does that mean you should just run right over and commit felony murder? Can't you stop and think what it might mean?" Mitchell was half out of his chair, leaning toward me. "Do you think Rix is smart enough or sneaky enough to put anything like this together? Think for a minute. Think. He's got no more initiative than you do."

I lowered my eye and felt like sleeping. Maybe it was a dream coming on, a nightmare; I let my mind come up with the idea that Mitchell wanted. *The Black Legion.* My memory wandered back ten years or more to the leanest years: 1931, 1932. Even then we had been overrun in Detroit by poor southerners looking for work. They came up on the rails, hoping to land a nice job at one of the auto plants. For a lot of those crackers and hill people, the only thing they could hold on to to make themselves big was that they weren't niggers. Even before that time, during the years following the Great War, the beginnings of the Legion had taken root. They splintered off the Klan up here in Michigan, and for a time it seemed that the Legion might overrun everything. At least fifty murders, I knew, could be laid at the foot of the Legion, and probably more, since the stiffs were usually the wrong color. The bulls didn't spend much time investigating murders on the dark side of town, especially in those days. There were other things happening in Detroit, too many starving and living on the dole to worry about a few less nigger mouths to feed. I guess I knew about the Legion as much as any outsider. Certainly many men on the force were members, or would have been, if they could have stood for the hokey ceremonies and were willing to pay the dues. Though I never cared enough about it to find out, it was understood that a number of city councilmen, state lawmakers, and judges were members or sympathetic to the Legion.

But the Legion has gone to dust, I thought. Or so the story was told, after the murder of a white man, Charles Poole, in May of 1936. Dayton Dean, the triggerman, had embarrassed the Legion by singing his canary head off for a grand jury. They had taken Poole on a one-way ride because he had supposedly beaten his wife on occasion. That was how it was with the Legion. They weren't particular about who they smacked around. They hated Negroes first and foremost, but they also hated the Catholics, the Jews, and especially the Communists, all swarming around Detroit during the Depression. Poole's wife was in Kiefer Hospital giving birth to their baby when the Legion took him, and she later denied being beaten altogether. The papers went wild, of course, and the publicity forced a scramble to stamp out the Legion. It only went as far as the level of the goons, though, because it was clear that further investigation would implicate many powerful men, judges, state senators, and police officials. They put up twelve of those lamebrained crackers on trial, and convicted eleven of them on Dayton Dean's testimony.

And Barton Rix, a patrolman like me at the time, on a beat, was rumored to have been in the third car, I now remembered. *The car that didn't make it to the Poole murder because it was caught at the Rouge River drawbridge.* Without the rope they carried in the third car, the lynching party was unable to hang Poole. So Dean shot five holes into him with a pair of semiautomatic pistols.

I chewed on it for a while. I couldn't pull together what it might mean down the road because my mind was half taken thinking about

Bobby. What Anna had told me made me feel that I needed to go back over all the times I had spent with Bobby to figure out if they meant what I had thought they meant. And now, with the suggestion that the Legion—it had been a dirty time. It was all beyond what I could do to sort it out.

But a smile crept to my lips. I fished down into the inside pocket of my jacket and pulled up the chain and the bullet that had rolled from Bobby's hand while he was dying. I rolled it around my palm with the index finger on my bad hand. A bullet on a little chain, kept inside the lapel: the calling card of the Black Legion. I had forgotten. A whole world I had forgotten. But now the two, Rix and the bullet, came together to spark certainty in my mind, like two words matching up in a crossword puzzle. And another thing: The Legion boys, I remembered, were deeply involved in busting up the unions in the old days; though we never spent much time investigating such things, it was standard practice to blow up houses of organizers. Just around the time I lost my eye in an explosion. I tossed the bullet on the desk toward Mitchell.

Mitchell picked it up. "Who does this belong to?"

"I guess Bobby pulled it off the runt that killed him."

"So this is evidence, then."

"Well," I said, "I guess you'll have to decide about that in this case."

Mitchell dangled the bullet by the chain. "We won't find any prints on it now, that's for certain."

I sat quietly, rubbing the pink nubs of my bad hand, waiting. I figured, the way things were, it was just me. There wasn't a person on the earth to trust, at least until things shook down enough so that I could see who stood to lose what. I kept my head low and peered up through my eyebrow at Mitchell.

"You're wondering," said Mitchell, "if you can trust me."

"Don't worry about it, Captain. I don't trust any man that doesn't get his hands dirty when he works." I watched him with a slack expression.

"Make up your mind, Caudill. Do it quick. I won't sweet-talk you. If you don't think you can act like a detective on this one, go along with me as far as it goes, then you're out. I can put you anywhere you like, directing traffic, helping little old ladies across the street. If you're in, you'll do just what I tell you and be happy with what information I think you need to know."

"You figure the Legion is trying to come back up?"

"I can't imagine how it could be done these days. It looks like a few of the Legion punks trying to pull a few things over while we're busy thinking about other things. That's the best guess I have."

"You're just guessing?"

Mitchell let his shoulders roll. "Where I can't find good information, I make my best guess. This requires a modicum of faith, nothing more." His black eyes seemed to smolder at me. He said, "I'd like to see this case wrapped up before the first day of summer."

"But that's—"

"It's almost a week. What do you think you can pull together if you spend the week sober? Can I trust you to make an honest effort or not?"

I looked down at my hands and studied my nails while I thought it over. I couldn't feel anything hinky in Mitchell's manner, but I knew the captain was hard enough to lie without a flicker of feeling if necessary. It hardly mattered; whatever percolated below the surface, the situation stood as it was regardless of what I knew about it. Either I was being played for a sap or I wasn't. Either Mitchell was in on it or he wasn't. And now that blood had been drawn on my watch, I'd sink my teeth into it and shake until things fell loose. If I had only a week to make the whole thing good—I'd have to find a way to do it. Though I could not be sure that I would get to the real root of things,

I knew at least that I would drag more than my share down with me to hell. When it was done, they'd remember my name.

"I'm in," I said.

"One last thing," said Mitchell. "You leave Rix to me. I'll ask around, see what he's been doing on his own time. If you go anywhere near him, you're out. I'll send the men after you myself. There's no way I could gloss over something like that. That's all. Now go on, clean yourself up. You look like a wino."

"If Rix turns up dirty," I said, "not you or anybody can save him from what he's got coming." I stood up slowly and felt the coolness of my damp clothes. Without another word, I turned and left Mitchell's office.

I tramped slowly down the stairs and left the building. Then I fired up the car and turned out onto Beaubien, my blood thick.

CHAPTER

9

Wednesday, June 16

I could not say why I had obeyed Mitchell's orders. Instead of tracking down Barton Rix, I had spent the remainder of the rain-soaked day poring over all the photographs of the Legion I could find in Records. My eye regretted it. The strain of looking so closely at so many pictures made the eye feel dry and tired. I hadn't slept well. And I was afraid that somehow the sight of all those unlucky faces might erase the image I kept in my mind of Bobby's killer—the runt who had been able to change me into a partial man.

When that search came up dry, I further taxed my vision by reading the entire report of the coroner's inquest on Bobby. He had bled to death, and very quickly. The short incision had been only about three inches deep, enough to open up a major vein and to spill Bobby's stomach and bile duct. *He was weak in the belly,* I thought. *Too*

skinny. A solid layer of fat and he might have been all right. Then I thought,
That runt can handle a knife; he knew just where to put the blade.

And now, though the new day promised to be clear, there was no
feeling that the rain had refreshed anything. I worked at the conges-
tion that was always on my chest, now and again hacking up a glob
and spitting it out the car window. The rawness of my throat made it
fail to close off properly, so that every sip of water or coffee seemed
to dribble into my lungs. With my addled brain and everything else I
was choking down, this sense that I couldn't even breathe properly
made my teeth clench and my neck ache. My shoulders wanted to
pull up to my ears. No matter how often I emptied myself, I always
felt like I needed to piss, and my legs were weak.

I wanted to visit Eileen. It was the lure of a pretty woman, a
friendly face, a decent home. I thought that I could just step into it
like any other man, like a regular man. The idea played in my mind
like a nice storybook or a cinema show that could have a happy ending. Mornings, I could wake up to a hot breakfast, I could pull up my
tie and slip into my neatly pressed suit, and I could hop on a streetcar to my office downtown, like a regular man. Maybe there would
even be a little one, a bright-eyed girl with a curl in her hair to tod-
dle on my knee when I came home in the evening. On weekends,
we could drive up north to a little cottage on a lake, and the little one
could play in the sand while I taught Alex how to hook a fish. Eileen
would wave at us from the beach, her face hidden by the shadow of a
floppy hat, her legs and shoulders freckling in the sun.

But I could not allow such thinking. I knew it could never be true
for me. However it fell, I knew that my own life could never work as
a happy story. I was born without the confidence or the courage or
the faith to imagine myself a happy or fulfilled man. I carried my
own trouble with me; and if I went to visit Eileen, if I set myself toward making some kind of life with her, I knew that, as things stood,

I'd just bring trouble to her as well. Still, I had the choice: I could steer the car toward Eileen's house, or I could try to negotiate my way forward in the case, try to settle the scores it seemed I had accumulated, by finding out what I could from Anna. There was a third choice: I could just drive away from Detroit and try to make a new life somewhere else. And finally the fourth choice, as always the last desperate choice available to anyone: I could take my own life as my father had. I didn't want to, really, as roiled up as things were, and it made me wonder what my father's state of mind had been to make that monstrous decision.

As I pulled up to the curb in front of Bobby's house, I was thinking about how Bobby always seemed so frail beneath the bluster, how long and thin his fingers were, how his hands looked like they had never done a day's labor.

I walked up and knocked on the door.

Anna opened it and gestured for me to enter. In her face and her way of walking there was nothing like the stiffness that had stood between us while Bobby lived. It was like she felt that her admission of the previous day had cracked apart the need for any show between us now. I lingered in the doorway because my feet didn't seem to want to go in.

"Lucy, honey," Anna called, turning from me, "why don't you run next door to sit with Mrs. Koppel for a little while. Mr. Caudill wants to talk about adult things now."

I stepped aside to let the little girl skip past me out the door. She was pretty but had a small mouth and thin lips. Her blonde pageboy was fluffy and frizzy, and the natural curl lifted into the air. As in the past, she didn't greet me or even look at me as she passed. I didn't watch her go.

"Step inside, Pete. I have coffee made."

Though I had been inside the little bungalow any number of

times, still I stumbled as my eye adjusted to the dimness of the interior. I turned my head back and forth to make a picture of the place—but nothing had changed. The house was the same, but I couldn't get my feet to move like I wanted them to. I moved to the little table in the kitchen, where Anna Swope tippled a bit of Canadian Club into two cups of hot black coffee. I sat down across from her.

"You are glad you didn't come to the church after all. Old ladies clucking about what the world has become," Anna said. "And talking behind their breath."

"The world is not a place for old ladies anymore."

"Well, I suppose that will be me one day, soon enough." She tipped up her cup and held it thoughtfully to her lips, as if she could make the coffee cool down enough to sip just by thinking. She pursed her lips and blew, staring vacantly over my shoulder.

"Could be," I said. "You get older before you know it." I took a quick sip of the coffee and swallowed, clenching and reclenching my throat and coughing a little. "It's good you sent the girl away."

She cradled the cup delicately in all her long fingers and brought her eyes to bear on me. "You're going to say something about Bobby. It's all right. I know what kind of things he was after."

I drank more coffee and swallowed hard, glad for the whiskey.

"He was into some things he should not have been, I know." Anna did not look at me directly. It seemed like she was looking at my neck or my jowls—whiskers I'd missed with the razor. "But he was a good man, a good husband in his way. Do you know what I mean? When we are children, we think we know so much. We can tell what is right and what is wrong. But when we are older, we cannot be right all the time. There is more to regret, always more as time goes by."

"Don't make too much out of it," I said. I looked down at the backs of my hands: hairy, nicked and scarred, callused, beefy and rounded but for the two biggest knuckles on each hand, which bulged out like goiters. "Anyway," I said, "you don't have to say any more about it. All of that, I guess that's your business. You say too much."

A flash of quickly subdued anger passed over her angular face. Maybe it was the German in her, something cold that made me think that her little speech had been some kind of act. My mind was too slow to reconsider everything like I should have, all the things that had to change their meaning because of what I now knew. I could see why Bobby and Anna might have hitched themselves together; but I couldn't see what the balances were or how it could work day after day, year after year.

"Well, what is it you want to know, Pete? What brings you here?" With two fingers crooked in the handle of her cup, she tossed back the rest of the coffee.

"Did Bobby ever say anything to you about a hiding place or a safe he had around the house?"

"Why?" She tipped the bottle and poured a finger of whiskey into her cup.

"I guess I figured a guy like Bobby might have a little something put away. It could be ... some money or papers that might be worth a little something."

"Well," said Anna, narrowing her small dark eyes, "there is nothing like that, nothing that I know of. You know he left no will. He never told me about the police work or any other ... business he had going."

"The garage?"

"It's just ... wood. There is no plaster or anything. But he might have hidden anything out there. I never cleaned it. But he didn't spend much time there." She slowly sipped from the cup. I could see her pressing her tongue tight in her mouth, but she didn't wince from the straight whiskey. "He wasn't handy."

Anger welled up in me. There was too much to consider, and the added element of sex skewed things. Her attitude seemed wrong but not in any way I could figure out. The thought flashed through my head that she might be some sort of enemy agent. I had heard from Bobby that she and her brother had fled Germany when the Nazis took over. Of course, it must have been a story already when Bobby first heard it, and Bobby had heard it, as I now let myself realize, doubtless from her. In fact, there was nothing about her past that I had ever bothered to verify. Had Bobby seen any photographs? I understood that the brother had been killed in an accident at one of the plants, but now it seemed that anything I had learned through Bobby needed more consideration.

Briefly I considered that Anna might somehow be involved in all of what was happening. Maybe she wanted Bobby dead because she was sick of living with it. But I reminded myself again that Bobby and I had stumbled onto the beating by pure chance. To believe anything else would mean that the whole world was against us. And that, I thought dryly, would leave little to do but to head out of the world snarling and flaming, lashing out against the most obviously rotten. It would be easier than thinking through it all.

"Maybe I shouldn't ask," I said, "but I guess I need to know how he left you. There's nothing, no money put away anywhere?"

"No," she said, shaking her head grimly. "He didn't leave us much. For all his ideas, there was not much to show. A bit of life insurance. Maybe we'll be able to keep the house or to eat. Not both."

I poured a strong shot of whiskey into the dregs of my coffee and drank it all in a swallow. It seemed that I could swallow the whiskey well enough. I felt it fuming through my sinuses and burning down my gullet, and I liked the sharpness of it. I kept quiet for a moment, hoping my silence would make Anna nervous enough to spill something. She just stared absently out the window.

"So there's nothing that you know of, nothing stashed around here?" I stared hard at her.

"It isn't sensible to pretend about it, Pete. There's nothing. You think I haven't looked myself? We're alone here now. Of course I am willing to work," she said, "but perhaps if I looked, I would find wherever I went that there is nothing suitable for me. You see?"

I wondered if the little bit of liquor could be working on me so quickly. Sometimes you don't know what the booze can do—but I can't lay it off on that. The way the whole thing was playing out, I could see what a dope I had been and still was, how anybody could dance around my fat head or tiptoe right past me. It brought up something foul in me, and I pictured my right hand knocking her down to the carefully scrubbed floor of her kitchen. I had that feeling you get when a smart guy is trying to put one over on you, working up a laugh for his buddies. But she wasn't playing to her buddies, and I felt how sharp it was that we were all alone in the house. When she reached across the old table to grasp my mangled hand, I drew it back, then reached out and grabbed her above the elbow. I stood up and my thighs lifted the table, tottering the glasses and the bottle of whiskey.

Maybe it was wrong. I guess I've done wronger things. With the three fingers of my left hand squeezing down to the bone of her skinny arm, we stumbled to the bedroom. I pushed her ahead of me to the center of the room, just to the edge of the bed, and watched while she undressed. She took everything off carefully, her thin fingers crawling like spiders over buttons and clasps. There was nothing like anger or desire in her face, nothing at all, and she didn't seem afraid of me.

I became two men. One watched with a weary eye, and found the workings of the muscles under her pale skin to be more interesting than the dark nipples and the dark patch of hair she exposed to me. The other man seemed to grow up from my legs, and I felt my prick stiffening inside my trousers, like the whiskey was a kind of fuel in my blood.

When she finished undressing, she did not pull down the

bedclothes but climbed to the center of the small bed and lay on her back, looking calmly up at me but not at my face. She tipped one knee to the side, spreading her legs a little. I stepped to the edge of the bed, pulled my belt loose, and opened my fly just enough to let my baggy trousers and shorts fall. Then I shrugged out of my jacket and moved over her. I wasn't sure how it would go in. I squeezed my prick with one hand until it was stiff enough, and then, moving between her legs, I groped and guided the part of me into her.

We did not speak while I huffed away on top of her. The one Caudill watched her face carefully, watched her eyes rest on some spot on the ceiling, and he wondered what she was thinking about. He wondered if his trousers would be badly wrinkled, gathered as they were now above his shoes as his knees scrambled for traction over the silky lace of the bedcover. The other Caudill plunged into the warm wetness and felt glad of it, felt the give of her soft thighs and the rhythmic thump of her heels over the small of his back.

When I finished, she dropped her hand from my shoulder and let it fall lightly to the bed. Then finally she looked at me. I met her eyes, but there wasn't anything to communicate. I only rolled off her and dropped my legs over the edge of the bed. Quietly I sat for a few moments, thinking of nothing but the way my prick slowly drooped. Then I scanned the room and wondered if Bobby had ever shared it. Behind me, Anna slipped from the bed and began to gather her clothes. The rustling made me wonder what sort of transaction had taken place, if I could really understand the workings or be able to afford what it would cost. It wasn't much, after all, bodies pushing together. But things didn't always hold their meaning in the time or effort it took to make them happen. You could throw away your whole life with one stupid move.

I stood up and dragged my shorts and trousers up to my waist. As I fumbled to button myself up, I stared blankly at the wall just next to the bed.

"What's this?" I croaked, sliding my fingers over the uneven surface.

"That was a crèche," murmured Anna. "The Catholics and their graven images. Bobby didn't like it. He covered it over."

I rapped my knuckles up and down the plaster and heard nothing but hollow reverberations. Had I expected—what? Something to knock back in answer? But with an idle interest I pressed my thumb into the patch job near the bottom edge, pressed hard until my thumb cracked through. I kept pressing until I had made a hole wide enough for my fingers, then I pushed them through and felt along the bottom of the crèche. Nothing but bits of plaster, mouse droppings, and dust. Certainly nothing like a valise or satchel of money, nothing large enough to be of any value. I pushed my fingers in until I could feel the old wall at the back of the crèche. The tip of my middle finger pressed against something small and cool to the touch. With some fumbling, I managed to snare it between two blunt fingertips.

I pulled it out and rubbed it clean as I moved to the window. A key it was, a small one; in the bright light of the morning sun, I brought it to my eye. I could smell Anna's breath, coffee and the sharp bitterness of whiskey, as she struggled to get a view of what I had. Tiny numbers, burnished brass: the key to a safe-deposit box, I thought. And almost as quickly, I thought of another thing: This was the first time, as a detective, that I had actually found something I had set out to find.

There was a way to get into police headquarters through the garage, and I used it. I had heard the newspaper stories and the gossip about the runt since the news broke about Bobby. As with any case that made the papers, citizens had filed reports. The runt and his boys had been seen digging up an old lady's geraniums on the northern perimeter of the city; he was living on the top floor of an apartment building downriver, south and west of the city, playing that swing music too loud at all hours of the night. He was running a laundry down on Riopelle, stealing buttons off shirts. One lady was convinced that the police sketch printed in the paper was her husband, though he had been obese and bald when he ran off on her ten years earlier. People from the American Legion kept calling, insisting that the man was some sort of foreign agent sent to undermine the war effort. The two thugs were certain to be Nazi spies.

The slightly more reliable sources, other officers, had turned up nothing. I knew that some of the officers still on the force must have called themselves members of the Legion or the Klan at one time or another. The stories were as wild then as they were now, but it was said by many that the Legion had once claimed over a hundred thousand members in Michigan. Certainly few men on the force felt inclined to coddle niggers or anyone else. I began to wonder if I could count on anything from anybody on the blue side of the line.

Maybe somebody had caught wind of Bobby's leaning. Maybe I was too slow to see that some of my fellows had put it together this way: Some guys who hated niggers had sliced Bobby the queer. Bobby the queer, married to the *German*. Probably it wouldn't be worth any special effort to track down those boys, and it could be that some on the force would go out of their way to lose any information that turned up. As I walked into headquarters, I lifted my head to take a really good look over all the officers milling about. Aside from a few nods in greeting, they ignored me, as always. It made me think that maybe Mitchell was right to be so tight-lipped about everything.

I made my way down to the little room in the basement, where I found Johnson and Walker poring over books of old mug shots.

"Detective," said Johnson.

"Johnson," I said. "Walker."

"We weren't sure you'd be coming in," said Johnson. "Captain told us you had a few days coming."

"Hell with that," I said. "What do you have to tell me?"

"Roger Hardiman's secretary has been tying up the phone lines trying to call you. He was getting so hostile that I told Mary at the switchboard just to tell him that you're out of town for a few days. We thought you weren't coming in. Your sister-in-law Eileen called, too. She said for you to call, it's about the boy."

At the mention of Eileen, my brow muscled down over my eye, and I tried to bluff away the stab of emotion. "Hell with that. What kind of luck did you have tracking down the bastards?"

Johnson looked at Walker. "Walker had a little talk with Horace Jenkins. Jenkins says—you tell him, Walker."

I turned my head toward Walker.

"That's right. The Reverend Jenkins dropped a little information about Toby Thrumm. He says he doesn't know where Toby is right now. I can't say if he was lying or not, but I guess if Toby was anywhere in this town staying with colored folks, Reverend Jenkins would know about it. So we don't have any kind of way of finding Toby right now. But I also heard from Jenkins that old Toby was knocked about by two big fellas and a little guy—same as in Detective Swope's case. Toby thinks it was the little guy who whipped him up."

I felt no surprise. I only felt that this new bit of information locked together a few things I already knew, and so I could be free to admit the truth to myself. Of course the thugs who killed Bobby were the same thugs who had killed Jane Hardiman. Of course—of course they had put Thrumm in the hospital. I remembered the feeling I had talked about with Bobby: Someone had been following us around. But that wasn't so; I now guessed that the thugs were probably sitting in a car on Thrumm's block, watching, waiting. Probably laughing as Bobby and I tore off toward Pease's apartment, knowing that Jane Hardiman had already been killed and arranged for the unlucky bastards who found her. So—it was a good bit of thinking for me to do with the thought of Anna hanging over me now—I guessed Toby Thrumm did know a little more than he was letting on. He must have been mixed up in the whole thing somehow.

Johnson said, "It's the same three guys knocking colored folks around that killed—"

"Don't walk through your whole life being surprised by everything, Johnson," I said.

"Maybe it's some out-of-town beef or a syndicate play—"

"Hold off with the thinking, Johnson! If it's the same guys, maybe that'll make it a little easier for us, that's all. So far as anyone knows, Jane Hardiman died in a riding accident. That's how we aim to keep it."

Johnson was ready to bust, but he saw from the look on my face that he should keep his trap shut.

"We'll just keep on working like we've been doing," I said. "Is that all right with you two?"

Both men nodded grimly.

What Johnson and Walker did not know was that I had seen the runt before, long before all of it. I wondered how they would look at me if they knew.

"So I'm guessing from these mug books that we don't have any tips about these boys," I said.

"We ran down a few tips, but it was nothing," said Johnson.

"I guess these guys are getting some help from somewhere." I rubbed my stubbly chin. "Hell with these pictures. You two get out and talk to a few people. Wear out that shoe leather. Walker, go down and ask around if there's been any other times lately where a colored boy has taken a beating like this. Johnson, get on the phone and see if you can talk up the sheriff where Pease used to stay in St. Louis. Don't tell him anything specific but let him get a whiff of Pease hanging around the white girls."

"Yes, sir, Detective," said Johnson.

"I'll do that," said Walker. "I guess folks will be glad to talk about that."

"Listen, now," I said, "you make sure you remember what you're talking about to people. Nobody needs to know anything about Jane Hardiman and all of this."

After the two officers left, I made a few telephone calls. I finally located the bank where Robert Towne Swope held a safe-deposit box. I hung up the phone while the clerk on the line was still spewing legal mumbo-jumbo. I walked upstairs, grabbed a cup of muddy coffee from the pot in the swing room and headed out the door back to Bobby's house to pick up Anna.

There was no way around it: I needed her to get at the box. Since I suspected that the box might contain something really fishy—*hell,* I thought, *every cop's got a little stash somewhere*—I had located the box outside police channels and had neglected to obtain a warrant or a court order to open it. It shook me up a little to bring the woman, but I figured I could use the poor-widow leverage. I thought about bringing the girl, too, but it was only half a thought. I wanted to bluff my way in and out without any mess. Because Bobby had been murdered in such a public way, the department brass would want a look at the contents of the box—if they knew anything about it. Any cash would certainly be taken and tied up forever, and I had decided that the money, if any, would go to Anna and the girl. I didn't want questions or trouble from anybody I wasn't sure I could handle. The way it was, I wasn't sure I could handle Anna, either, but at least I knew for certain that she didn't ordinarily carry a gun under her clothes.

I pulled up to the bungalow and tapped on the horn. In a moment, the little girl ran out the door and off the porch and slipped through a bare spot in the hedge. She disappeared into the neighbor's house. Anna stepped out wearing a fancy little hat and a severe skirt and a jacket, what they called a utility suit. She turned and locked the door behind her and stepped smartly toward the car. When she neared the door, she bent down a bit to look at me and smiled brightly, showing all her teeth.

We spent a few fruitless minutes arguing with a teller at the bank.

"What's the trouble here?" The voice seemed fat over my shoulder.

I turned slowly and eyed the natty prig.

The teller drew a deep breath and said, "This lady here wants to get into a safe-deposit box held by her husband. But her name is not on the box. I've tried to tell her that it's against bank policy, but she just—"

"This woman's husband was a decorated police officer who was just killed in the line of duty," I said. "He couldn't come here himself to open the box."

"Now, just a moment. Please lower your voice. I'm Mr. Nicholas, a vice president here." He eyed my patch. "And you are?" He held out his hand.

I took it and squeezed the soft pink thing a little hard. "Detective Caudill," I said.

"And Miss Perkins has explained bank policy to you? That we can't give you access to that box without a court order signed by a judge or a search warrant signed by a judge?"

"My husband left no will," Anna said, "and it could be months before the courts get through with everything. And in this meantime I need to find some way to get by without a man and to put food on the table for my little daughter."

"I sympathize, madam, but bank policy—"

"We're not leaving without having a look in that box." I did not move my feet, but I insinuated my attention and my bulk toward Nicholas.

He flinched and glanced nervously toward a security guard who stood near the door, ready to rush over at the slightest signal.

"Why don't we go into my office," said Nicholas.

We followed him across the marble floor to his richly appointed office. At the door, I barred Anna from entering. I had to push her outside the door so I could close it. The last thing I saw of her was the sharpness of her eyes. I followed Nicholas right around his over-sized desk. *Clearly,* I thought, *that desk is supposed to be imposing.* And maybe that sort of thing worked when Nicholas was looking across his big desk at somebody coming cap in hand, begging for money. But when the little man sat down and turned to see me next to him, he jumped in surprise and tried to lean away.

I took his flabby elbow and leaned to whisper in his ear, making sure he could smell my breath and feel the heat thrown off my head.

After a few moments, I came out, followed by Nicholas. The three of us went to a private booth, and soon a clerk came in with the box. Nicholas shook himself out of the booth and left us alone.

Anna said, "What did you say to him?"

I said nothing and tried to ignore how hard she was. Despite the softer parts of her body, I considered that there wasn't really any-thing extra to her; she was as tight as a wire and always sharp in her purpose. It was not clear if she already knew what was in the box, but I could feel how she strained toward it. I noted with worry that the box was far too light to contain any bundles of money or anything of value except perhaps a few tiny jewels; I might have thought it was empty except for the scraping of paper inside. Maybe an envelope, I thought, but not heavy enough to add up to much if it was cash.

"What did you tell him?"

"It's always easier when they start out afraid of you," I said.

"Why should he be afraid?" She did not look at the box.

"I told him I was going to send a big nigger over to rape his wife and daughter."

I looked for a reaction on her face, but there was nothing, no sign of disgust or humor, nothing. In fact, she seemed to be thinking of nothing. She seemed to be dancing to steps she remembered from long ago but didn't really care for, like twiddling her thumbs to make time pass. I opened the box and pulled out the contents: an interoffice mail envelope from the police department with only one name on it. My own.

I broke the seal and pulled out a short stack of glossy eight-by-ten photographs. Anna leaned closer when she saw that the photographs showed flesh. As I looked through the pile, sliding each topmost picture in turn to the bottom, Anna grew more intensely interested, and I turned my shoulder a bit to control her angle. They were peep photos, taken from behind a mirror, showing Bobby and his naked white ass, Bobby going down on another man. Near the bottom of the pile, two photos showed clearly that the other man was Roger Hardiman. Anna drew in her breath sharply and sent out her slender hand to grasp the pile and draw it closer. I resisted, angled myself between her and the photos, and pulled them free. She was quick enough to see plenty of money there, I guess, but I was just thinking how ugly human flesh could be in photographs.

I reached the last photo, and it was my turn to draw in my breath. A coal black Negro, dead or thereabouts, was tied to a tree with a heavy rope around his waist, his belly smashed up against the rough bark. His face, lolling toward the camera, was just meat. Finger-wide gashes from a horsewhipping covered what was visible of his back. Both arms were behind him, shoulder-snapping, his wrists pulled hard by a rope held taut by something off the edge of the picture. Drooping in death and held up to the tree only by the thick ropes around his waist.

In the background, a lineup of men posed as if with a hunting trophy. Smiling, elbowing each other, boys at play. One young boy looked up at his father. From the clothes, I guessed that the photograph had been taken some years before. I couldn't see any face that might have turned into the runt's sunken look. Taking pride of place next to the Negro stood a small man with military posture and round glasses, leaning on a cane, unsmiling. Around his head, some-one had drawn a crude circle with a china marker, like a black halo. I leaned close to see if I could recognize the man. Nothing.

But there was one man I did recognize. At the far left of the pic-ture, arms crossed, staring blankly at the dead man, I saw my father.

CHAPTER

10

I couldn't depend on my gut anymore. Driving toward Eileen's house, I wasn't sure if I wanted to vomit or if I was hungry like a Jap for rice. I wasn't sure that I could bear to see her. I wasn't sure anymore if I ever knew my father. When I heard about the men on the Briggs stamping line going out on strike because they were being forced to work next to niggers, part of me understood it. But when I thought of the two big boys beating on the poor nigger in the alley, my blood flamed up till I was sure I'd kill the boys on sight if I managed to track them down. So much of what I knew had been built on creaky information, I could see now, and it made me wonder what I had left to get knocked out from under me.

So many people got hard in their ways as they got older. The oldest, most withered-up people got sharp and lost all their patience for disagreement because they thought they knew it all and didn't see why they should spare the effort to suffer any fools. But it seemed that I was heading in the opposite direction. I wasn't sure that I cared anymore what was right or wrong or if I could even put the proper names to them. The deeper I fell into all of it, the more I felt that I wouldn't ever be sure about anything. The thought of brushing up against Eileen and maybe putting that germ into her made my skin crawl. Though I wasn't clean enough to put my face before her, I had to do it.

I made a pass by Eileen's place and saw that the door was open, so I drove down the block, turned around, and parked in front. I sat for a while, but the engine kept ticking like a clock, so I pushed myself out of the car and onto her porch. My knock rattled the screen door, and I could see that the hinges were loose. Screws always work themselves out of wood over time.

"Pete, thank goodness," said Eileen as she hurried from the kitchen. "Thank goodness." She pushed the door open and held it.

I stepped inside, and the door clapped shut. As I pulled my hat from my head, she stepped close and embraced me lightly. In that short moment, when I sensed her straining upward, I bent my head low and let her lips find my cheek.

"I'm sorry," I said.

"Sorry?"

"Things have been—"

"There isn't a thing to be sorry about," said Eileen. "Don't be silly, Pete."

She seemed so small. I reached around her, not as an embrace but to pat her on the back; my hat sounded hollow as I did it. We were so close that I could feel the heat trapped between us. I couldn't bear it.

"I feel like I need to be sorry for something," I said. I took a step away from her. "I haven't been keeping up with things like I ought to." I guess, thinking back, that I should have been able to find better words. More and more, the talk was failing me.

She took my elbow and tugged me along to the kitchen. It hit me that her kitchen was laid out something like Anna's. We sat down at the little table in the kitchen just as I had at Bobby's house.

"I wasn't sure if I should go to Bobby's funeral," she said.

"It wasn't any fun."

"Funerals aren't supposed to be fun," she said. "But I couldn't get a ride, and it was such a miserable day. I wasn't sure if you wanted to see me."

I looked down at her. "I like seeing you," I said.

She looked across the table at me. It might have been the light in the kitchen, which was situated in the darkest corner of the house, but it seemed to me that Eileen's eyes had lost some of their brightness since the last time I had seen her. She kept her head tilted a bit, considering me, and then slowly reached across the table to touch my hand. With the table between us, I didn't mind, but I knew that if we somehow wound up with our bodies pressed close together, I'd flame up again. It was more than I could bear or think through clearly.

I let her caress my bad hand for a few moments. Her own hand was white and a bit plump, and her fingers grew more slender toward the tip. Her nails were fine, buffed but not painted. The two remaining fingers of my hand had begun to veer oddly away from the thumb at the first knuckle, either from a general tightening of the disrupted tendons and skin or from adjustments due to hard usage. Compared to Eileen's clean white skin, my hand seemed foul and dirty and hard. My nails were thick and blunt and needed a trim. When I turned my palm up to grasp her hand, the whole effect was like a white hare or a dove clutched in the foot of an awkward and shy bird of prey.

"I'm bound now to clearing a few things up," I said finally.

"I understand, Pete. I don't mean to make any more trouble for you," she said. "If you'd like to stop coming around—"

"It's not that," I said. "Of course I don't want—there are so many things I'd like to—"

"Stop, stop, Pete. Just stop. There is no reason for any of this to hurt."

"But I just can't see how to do it." I was squeezing her hand a little too hard. "I'm no good. I'm no good for this."

"Oh, Pete." She brought her other hand over and took up my bad hand as well as she could. For a few moments we sat there quietly. She began to draw in her breath more sharply, and I feared that she would begin to weep. I regretted that I had not removed my jacket. She looked at our hands and then looked up at me with a trace of a wry smile. She pulled in a deep breath, and when she let it out, I could feel it fall warmly on my hands and on my face.

"Can we at least carry on like we used to?" she asked.

"Sure," I said. "I think so."

"Don't blame me, Pete. Do you blame me?"

"Huh," I said. "I blame myself for everything. That's my policy."

"But that's not fair," she said.

I shrugged. "That's how it is."

She gave my hand a final squeeze and then pressed her index fingers to the inside corners of her eyes. "I've been missing sleep."

"That's probably my fault, too."

"No," she said. "It's Alex. He's just been so *bitter* lately. He's never home. He goes out in the morning and sometimes he doesn't come back till after dark."

"You don't know where he goes?"

"He doesn't bother to tell me anymore. I can't stop him, can I? He doesn't even pretend he's going to play ball like he used to."

I mulled it over. I tried to picture myself as a boy—had my mother ever felt like this on my account? She would have had good reason, certainly. But things were different then. Despite the current war, which of course weighed over everything, I think it was a harder time, a harder world, in those days. Alex was softer in some way than

Tommy and I had ever been, and we had always had each other to fall in with when a scrape came up.

"I'll stash the car up the street and wait for him to come home to-night," I said. "There's at least one thing the old man was good for. If Tommy or me ever pulled anything like this, we'd get the strap. And it wasn't anything to argue with."

"I don't know if that would do any good, Pete. You know how he is," she said. Her eyes softened. "He misses his father."

I knew she was right. I could tan the boy once, but I couldn't be at the house all the time. He'd already had a taste of sneaking around and hiding things, and I knew that he'd get better at it quickly. He was smart enough to put on another face if he had to. Like everything else, my ability to figure out this new situation seemed limited.

"And there's something else," Eileen said. She stood up and walked over toward the sink. She drew down a cookbook from a shelf, pulled out a folded piece of paper, and brought it back to the table. "I found this in the back pocket of his trousers yesterday."

I took the paper and opened it. Across the top in big letters it read A NIGGER'S BRAIN. The rest of the sheet was filled with a cartoon of a colored man shown from the side, with huge lips, drooping eyelids, and nappy, bug-infested hair. His brain was shown in cutaway, divided into sections labeled "Love of Watermelon," "Laziness," and a bigger part, "Lust for White Women." But three-quarters of the brain had been darkened by crosshatched lines and labeled "Unused." It was an old drawing, and I had seen a copy of the picture before, tacked up for a time on the board in the swing room at the old precinct. So soon after I'd seen the photograph of my father at the lynching of the colored boy, the smudged paper I now held in my hand struck at me. Everything at the edges of my vision started to go white.

"You don't have any idea where he's going at night? He's not seeing a girl?"

She took it in for a moment. "I think if it was a girl he wouldn't be so angry. He just won't talk to me."

"Know any of his friends?" I asked.

"I think he had a hard time at school this past year. He told me there were some colored children in his classes. I didn't think anything of it. You know how Tommy was. He wasn't like that."

"No," I said. "Tommy wasn't like that." *But our father was,* I thought. *Maybe I am, too.* I stammered, "Let me ask—Alex found some different friends lately, is that right?"

"I guess that's right. He used to just play with the boys on the street here, but now he won't have anything to do with them."

We were still sitting at the little kitchen table. I kept my hands flat to the top because they seemed so heavy. The legs of the table were a little uneven, and I caught myself rocking the whole thing back and forth as I listened to her.

"He brought a boy named George here for dinner one day about a month ago. Redheaded boy about Alex's age. But he didn't seem like a hoodlum."

"A month ago?"

"Oh," she said, "I guess it was more like two weeks ago, I guess. George Dix is his name, I think. He lives just the other side of Campau, behind the Catholic school."

I felt my blood stop. "Dix? Or Rix?"

"Rix, I think. Sort of a funny name."

At once the room seemed too small. I wanted open space, room to swing my fists. At least in hell you've got some room to kick around. She must have seen it come up in my face.

"What is it, Pete?"

"I'll have a look for him," I said. I stood up and made a step toward the front of the house.

She caught my sleeve and stopped me. "Pete, please," she said.

I couldn't bear to tear my arm away from her.

"I won't hurt him," I said. "If I find him, I'll just bring him back here, that's all."

Her upturned face and the plain smell of her flamed through me and wrenched my gut. I wanted to crush her in my arms and carry her to bed, but I bent and jerked down to touch my lips to her cheek. To get her loose from my sleeve, I put both hands on her shoulders and held her down in her seat. Then I turned and walked out—and felt a fool for ever having thought of a happy life.

What should a man be? I thought of my father and how he treated my mother toward the end of their time together—not such a pretty story, as it turns out. I can remember him as a happy fellow, taking my mother dancing in the long-ago days. He knew how to tell a story. He'd have everyone hanging on his next word, sure, and ready to throw their beer mugs at him when they heard the bad joke that topped it all off. Tommy and I would lay awake in our bunks with our ears to the wall, taking it all in. They talked and laughed halfway through the night about the drunks they'd rousted and the fingers they'd broken, letting out the spiel of a life of pickpockets and grifters and mashers, three-letter men they'd tossed into the Detroit River in winter, graft and petty thievery and dope fiends and wrong turns. They talked loud to keep from falling to the wrong side them-selves, to keep from putting their own guns to each other or to their families. Or to themselves. Maybe the talking had finally failed my father; maybe that was what finally led him to his sorry end. I should have learned something from all of it. Tommy picked it up, the gift of gab, but I never did.

He must have loved my mother once, he must have. Things went sour, but I could imagine that once upon a time, life must have seemed like a happy proposition for them. I tried to see how I could make that kind of life with Eileen—but I just couldn't. With Anna, I could kid myself that I could handle things. At least sex was sex. It was like fighting or sparring, two bodies coming together, no more;

there wasn't any sense in getting sentimental about it. With Eileen, it was more. And I had not picked up the trick. I had not ever learned how to manage it.

After I left Eileen's house, I felt sour with all the tangled mess of my life. I knew that I should have ignored Captain Mitchell's warning about going after Rix. Up from the dusty locker of my memory floated the nasty image of Barton Rix, always sneering, with his tuft of bright red hair pushed back on his head. Time had darkened everything, and yet the hair and the name and the timing stuck me like a needle. My mind raced through the possibilities. I could no longer ignore my own involvement in all of it. Maybe some of it could have been coincidence, after all—but it was too much. I knew Rix, all right. The blood between us wasn't good. If my father had been messed up in the Legion, and if Rix had been wrapped up in it, too, then Rix might have a reason to target Alex. But with the old man dead, and Tommy dead, there was only me to rake over. Messing with Alex might be a way of coming at me from a blind side. At his young age, and shaky from all he'd been through, the boy wouldn't be able to fend off anything they threw at him.

Whatever it was, I decided that I would find out tonight, Mitchell or no Mitchell. There wasn't anything to keep me from it, and I knew it would be best to wade in while I was still hot. I wasn't sure I would match up against Rix anymore with the bum eye and the bad hand, but I figured I might be able to make him see things my way if I could get a drop on him.

I drove across Campau and parked at the farthest edge of the St. Ladislaus parking lot. From the trunk I pulled out a box of shells for my revolver and dumped enough for two reloads into my coat pocket. I pulled an oversized sap from under a blanket and slipped it up the left sleeve of my coat, through the loop of cloth I had sewn in, resting the handle end in a little pocket inside the cuff. It was very heavy, filled with grapeshot, but I liked to carry it in my sleeve rather than in my pants because it was easier to handle and harder to spot. When I was all set, I closed the trunk and got behind the wheel. Just then it occurred to me to look around to see if anyone was following me, if anyone was watching all of it—perhaps a nun peering from one of the hundred windows of the school or the rectory. It made me realize that I was not much of a detective. It did not occur to me to check a telephone book, and I couldn't very well call anyone at headquarters for Rix's address. Even if Mitchell didn't get wind of it, there was no way to be sure that anybody else I might talk to would be clear of the whole thing. But hope sprouted like a germ in me, despite my worst inclination; I had the idea that if things ended as badly as I thought they would, I might somehow be able to crawl away clean if nobody knew I was going in after Rix.

I drove slowly through the neighborhood behind the school, peering through the failing light at everyone passing by on foot, hoping to recognize Alex from his walk. After half an hour of driving, I began to work my way westward. The terrain began to open up a little to empty lots and older houses, left over from long-gone farms and country life. I saw that several cars and trucks were passing me, heading for a long driveway through a break in a small stand of trees. I turned around and followed until I came upon a little house swarming with hayseeds and shift workers in overalls and shirtsleeves. Out back of the house stood a large barn, spilling light from the door and from all the cracks in the siding boards.

I turned the car around to face the road, parked along the grass next to the driveway, and walked up to the barn. It seemed like a religious tent show except for the ring of hard faces near the big doors. Though it was still warm, I buttoned my coat to hide the revolver. I lingered in the yard, slowly taking in the scene. None of the faces looked familiar to me, though in the dim light I could not tell if my eye was faithful. I looked for a shock of red hair bobbing about but saw nothing of the sort. There were several young boys and smooth-faced men, but I didn't see Alex. A general movement toward the doors and into the barn drew me along, and though it didn't sit well on my face, I tried to look friendly.

At the door, one of the hard faces stepped up to block my path.

"Do we know you, brother?"

I squinted down at the little hayseed in dungarees. He kept his lips pressed tight to hide his bad teeth. I lifted my hand slowly and moved the man gently to one side. There was little movement but a good deal of bright attention from all the men in the doorway. I worked myself into the barn and glanced about to gain my bearings. The place was lit up well from a couple of big electric lamps hanging high up in the rafters. Perhaps forty men sat on plain benches arranged in rows like church pews. Another thirty stood along the walls of the barn, and I wedged myself alongside them, settling into a dark hollow between two framing studs with my arms over my chest. Two of the hard cases from the doorway, older men of about fifty, ambled up and took position on either side of me.

A table had been set up on platform at the far end of the barn, and I heard a kind of barking language from that direction before the standing men found their seats. When it cleared out, I could see the pale eyes and the bright red face of Barton Rix. He began to bang on an upturned milk pail with a metal ladle.

"Quiet! Quiet down, damn you! This isn't a social club!" After the crowd settled, he continued, "Now, I know you all aren't here for a quilting bee. We've got some pressing news about the mud people and the Communists that I know you all need to hear. So let's get ourselves organized.

"First of all, I've got some grave news about our own police force, which as you know I have been proud to serve on these many years. But it might not surprise you to know that even on our own force and higher up in the government, there are a few Commie- and nigger-loving bastards."

Laughter rippled throughout the room.

"Some of you might read the paper or listen to the radio. You might have heard about Jane Hardiman dying, thrown from a horse, they say. That's a lie! I know for a fact that little white girl was killed up in niggerville on the west side of town! That girl's father is Roger Hardiman, and you know who he works for. If you don't, I'll tell you. Jasper Lloyd. You heard me right. Backstabbing, union-kissing, nigger-loving Jasper Lloyd. There's a man—you all know this— made himself rich off the sweat and blood of decent white folks, and now he's sipping whiskey on his yacht off Belle Island while the darky hordes are killing little white girls! And telling his flunkies to lie about it! What could be the reason for all that? I'll tell you! He's a goddamned coward, that's right! He made his money, and now he can afford to run scared while the Communists and their unions let in any old coon and his mother to take jobs away from the very people that made this country great! And that little girl laying dead! Raped by a nigger! How many y'all prepared to let that sort of thing go on?"

A roar went up from the crowd. Bottles were going around, and they were all getting plenty juiced up. I kept looking through the crowd for Alex and George Rix, and also for the runt and the two big blond boys I had seen in the alley. I realized that I might never recognize the two thugs if I saw them. They might have dyed their hair black and stepped right out of the feeble description I had been able to give. I kept looking, and since I figured it was just a matter of time before Rix or somebody else noticed I was there, I started to figure out how I might best draw the revolver with my right and drop the sap from my sleeve into my left hand.

"But I won't jaw at you all night," said Rix. "There's someone here I know you've all been waiting to meet. And I hope you'll listen up. Because there ain't many times you'll ever get to hear someone of this stature up close. You want to meet a man that's not scared to stand up for what's right, here he is. You want to meet a man that won't run off with his tail between his legs when a big nigger says 'Boo,' well, here he is. You want to meet a man remembers how the automobile industry made Detroit into one of the greatest cities in the world, before the Jews and the niggers and the unions started taking over everything, here he is. Ladies and gentlemen, only there ain't no ladies here, I give you the Colonel."

There was a smattering of applause, but it died quickly as a hush fell over the room. Rix took a seat behind the table. I finally caught sight of a head of bushy red hair, what I took to be George Rix, sitting about midway to the back in the row of benches. Next to him sat Alex, watching with his mouth open.

A very old man with a grim-set mouth limped into the barn from the small door at the back. As he came into the light near the table, I saw his face bloom into view. Though it was wrecked by time and whatever else, I knew it was the same face I had seen in Bobby's photograph. The cane, the bearing, and the round glasses, thicker now, came together in a sharp point for me and made me sure of the identification. From the way my head was swimming, though, I could have sworn I'd seen him in a bad dream somewhere. My gut churned and churned, and I was sure, though I couldn't remember it, that I must have taken some lye. They say the appendix can burst and it'll eat your guts out like that. I guess they call it adrenaline, what pushes your heart faster. I raced through my options. With the two hard boys right next to me, I might, at best, squeeze off one or two shaky shots at the old man before they took me out. And that would be the end of me. They'd have me six feet under or ground up for hog meal before anybody realized I'd gone missing.

Alex would see all of it. He'd know me at a glance, he'd watch them take me down, and he'd feel nothing so much as *embarrassment* that he was related to me. I would never have any opportunity to explain or to try to talk sense into him. But Rix would be there to tell it to him, to fill the boy up with that easy food that says it's best for a man to be tough and not take any guff.

I thought I might just walk up and arrest the old man. Arrest him for what? For having his picture taken with a dead nigger who probably couldn't be identified as a murder victim anyway? What would it help? How much could the old man really mean to a barn full of men, half of them probably armed and ready to slit the throat of any unlucky nigger they could corner in a dark alley? It would be like kicking a hornet's nest. I held myself still.

Bam! The man slammed his cane flat on the table, and the whole room jerked. He drew himself up to his full height and looked around the room, studying the faces of the boys and men. Then he poured himself some ice water from a sweating glass pitcher and sipped at his leisure.

He began to speak. "Now is the time," he said in a reedy voice, "to choose up sides."

The sound of his voice brought every man in the place to stillness. Only the moths whirled silently about the lamps in the rafters.

"The summer of purgation is almost upon us. We shall be privileged to bear witness to the joy and awe of a holy endeavor here in Detroit and across this great nation of ours."

My head felt light. I wasn't sure if I had decided to move or if my weak knees made me topple forward, but I stepped away from the wall and began to jostle my way across the back of the barn. Foulness seeped from the speaker like noxious gas, and I only knew that I had to pull Alex away from it if I could.

"I do not doubt," said the old man, "that you have heard it said many times, from your city fathers, from *politicians*, that we ought to welcome the Negro race with open arms. Welcome them into our factories and even into our *homes*."

My feet were never clever, and now they scraped along the plank floor like carcasses being dragged. Many in the room turned to stare at me, as if the one thing they couldn't bear was rudeness. Rix rose from his chair and broke into an ugly smile as he recognized me.

"Never!" shouted the old man. "Not while I live and breathe!"

I stumbled forward to Alex's bench and reached to gather the boy's shirt over his chest. I pulled hard and dragged Alex from his seat, dragged him struggling toward the side wall and back toward the big doors.

"What's this? What's this, brother?" The old man whacked his cane down on the table twice. "Do I not speak the truth?"

At the old man's words, the men at the back closed up the opening before the doors and surged forward to surround us. I could feel hands on me.

"Leave him go! Leave him go!" The old man whacked his cane again. "He can turn his back on us now, but he knows in his deepest heart that there is no place safe for him to call home. When he looks in the mirror, he'll see a coward staring back at him every day of his life."

They could have pulled me to pieces, but the old man's voice held them from it. The crowd at the doors didn't loosen up, so I bulled right through, still with an iron grip on Alex's shirt. The boy held tight to my forearm to keep the shirt collar from digging into his neck and armpits, and his sneakers pattered over the floor as we went.

I broke through the gang and sucked in a chestful of cooler air, shaking. I stood Alex up and took a grip on his upper arm, which was growing harder but was still scrawny enough for my hand to wrap all the way around. We left a trail of yokels as we made for the car, and I kept my ears open for the heavy foot of Rix. Alex would not meet my glare, so I yanked the boy along with me to my car and hoped I had done the right thing.

CHAPTER
11

Thursday, June 17

I had managed to grab three hours of jaw-grinding sleep, but I felt worse than bone-tired. If I had not slept at all, I would have been dry and tired, bitter and narrow-eyed. The little bit of sleep had left my body sluggish, still clutching at slumber. There was a delay in my reaction to what I saw. My breathing was slow and deep and regular, and I felt my prick getting stiff from rubbing inside my trousers, like it might do in the middle of the night. I shouldn't be driving, I knew, but there was no longer any choice.

I had not been ready for the scene with Alex and Eileen. Going in, I thought I was sure of myself and my position, but I could not find the words to convince Alex of any of it. Tommy could have found words, I was sure. Even if Tommy couldn't have moved the boy on moral grounds, he would have shown somehow that the cagey move, the smart move, was to stay clear of Rix and that gang. Tommy could have made the boy see the profit in it for himself. I wondered if it was a natural gift or if it had to do with Tommy's years in college. Was a college education a way to find the language to sway people over to your point of view? Our father seemed to think so. Fred Caudill was sure that Tommy would wind up as a mayor or senator or some kind of big shooter. I guessed that he might even have approved of Tommy's enlistment as a way of gaining the stature necessary for that kind of public sway.

I had the bulk to move people to my way of thinking—as long as I was in the room. After an hour of shouting and silence and a mother's crying, I had seen the softening of Alex's face and his posture. The boy kissed his mother before he went to wash up for bed. But I knew that things had not changed. Alex was smart enough to lay back and deflect the heat till it died down. And that was the sense of it for me. More hurt would have to come before the whole issue could be laid to rest. Without the gift of real persuasion, I could not hope to make a lasting change in his view of things. So, after my night of grinding and not sleeping, I decided that my best move would be to try to fight the problem at the root instead of messing with the boy.

Since everything seemed to revolve around "the Colonel," as Rix had introduced him, it looked like I had tipped too much of my own hand by pulling Alex out of the meeting. Rix would be looking out for me now, or maybe coming after me, and all the strange faces at the barn would be able to spot my one-eyed face anywhere. It was like I had stepped into the light. Because of the eye patch, people wanted to keep from looking right at me, and that's usually how I played it. Now, at least as far as the dirty business went—and it seemed to go everywhere—I was front and center. I had an idea that I might be able to muscle Hardiman with the pictures, but to tell the truth, I didn't feel smart enough or like I had a strong enough handle on it yet. What I wanted was time and peace to think things over. I wanted to be left alone. It was because I couldn't let things alone that I was in all the mess.

Since I couldn't think of anything else, and since, playing like a detective, I figured that all the aspects of the case might be important, I decided to check out Bobby's little syrup racket as a way of wrapping up any leads. It was a part of the mess I could maybe clean up and put away. Though I couldn't see how the ridiculous little syrup business might tie into it all, a hunch told me that there might be some odd connection to the Black Legion there, too. Bobby had told me that the beet sugar had come from up near Mio, and I knew well that there were any number of country places north of Detroit where groups of hateful rednecks liked to gather and stew their grievances together. My mouth had a bad taste like metal from all the talking I had done the night before, and I had a thought that a little sugar might sweeten things.

Bobby's crazy driving had confused me about where the building was exactly. I rifled Bobby's desk at headquarters until I found the address in some of his papers. Then I picked up Walker and Johnson and we drove westward, past the alley where Bobby was killed, south along a dirt road following the railroad tracks, and up to the address. The corner of the building that Bobby rented looked like it was unused. The windows were papered over from the inside. The door was padlocked, so I sent Johnson for the crowbar in the trunk. I was about to twist off the lock when Walker hollered from the side that the alley door had been broken in.

I went through and turned on the lights. It didn't seem as if any of the Polack ladies had been in for some time.

"This is quite an operation," said Johnson.

"Well," I said, "this ain't the high-rent district."

The place had been tossed, but gently. Papers were scattered over a table making duty as a desk, and Johnson began to shuffle through them. Walker, his hands clasped behind him, stepped gently throughout the room. On the wall nearest the alley, several gallon tins of syrup stood stacked near the door. Along the opposite wall lay the heavy sacks of sugar, untouched except for the rat-nibbled holes along the bottom row. I moved closer to inspect them. There was no inscription or indication of their origin. It was the same with the tins of syrup, though they had handwritten labels showing their flavors. Sensibly enough, I thought. It wouldn't do for black market sugar to holler out a howdy-do. The folks in Washington seemed to be taking the war pretty seriously. Anyway, I thought, it was clear enough where the sugar and syrup were going, to Pops Brunell and into his soda drinks. And Pops would be easy enough to find.

Johnson gathered all the papers and boxed them up, but I knew it was useless to search through them. What interested me was the source of the sugar, the supplier. I guessed that the search of the place had been made to ensure that Bobby had left no way to trace the source, and this piqued my interest. It was not surprising that black marketeers should lurk in the shadows, and it was common knowledge that Bobby had been killed. So anybody with a muddy hand in it might have come over to throw the joint. It didn't need to be anyone mixed up in all the rest of the mess; maybe there was no connection at all. The truth of it, though, was that the whole deal smelled odd to me. Bobby was a hustler and a hard worker, I knew, but still I wondered how Bobby could ever set up an ongoing deal to obtain rationed sugar in such quantities, and at a price—sure to be at a premium on the black market—that would allow a decent markup. Pops Brunell couldn't very well charge an arm and a leg for his juice in the part of town he did business in. I wanted to sniff the air for some confirmation that the sugar was indeed connected to the Legion and to all the rest of it, but my senses were dull.

After Johnson filled a crate with everything that could be connected with Bobby, he and Walker carried it to the car and tossed it in the trunk. I stepped into the alley and gathered my bearings. Had I come to the time in my life when my brain was so full up that I had started emptying out what I had known? Of course I knew the area, of course I remembered now; there was a pretty good butcher on the next street over, so I walked down the alley and called him out.

"Listen," I said, flipping up my lapel to show my shield, "there's a pretty pile of sugar down in there, never mind where it came from. If you think you can use it, go down and take a couple sacks. Just a couple, hear me? But don't keep them out in the open for now. I'm about to call the rationing board, have them come over for a look-see."

The butcher was a little DP, and he looked me over with his head tilted to one side.

"I use little sugar in my trade," he said. His English was good but he spoke with a thudding accent.

"You don't want it?"

"It would be wrong for me to accept such a thing," he said.

"You can't take a sack home for your wife?" With all the problems I had, and all the worries I was trying to sort out, the little man's attitude struck me funny. To top it, he was looking at me like he knew me, like he expected me to recognize him as well.

"You mean to tell me that you won't take a sack home for your wife?" I said. "You don't think that would be fine?"

"I am simply unable to accept such a thing," he said. "I am unable."

He was half my size. He stood with his hands clasped politely behind his back, and he had me rooted to the spot. I couldn't very well smack him down, though the idea worked through my mind.

"Well," I said finally. "If that's your position."

"Yes," he said. He seemed gravely disappointed that I could not muster a more proper attitude.

"Go on, then," I said. "I guess it's all wasted."

"I'm sorry," he said. "Good day. Good luck to you, after all."

He walked with a quick step back to his toil, and I watched him go with some regret. I wouldn't have cared overmuch about the illegal sugar, even without the present mess taking up all my attention. I had offered him the sugar because I knew how it was: A leg up in tough times could make all the difference, and I knew that he worked hard for his money. It wasn't costing me anything. But he wouldn't play along with it. By the time the rationing boys were through, the rest of the sugar would be parceled out to a hundred cronies as presents for their wives or as bribes to other wartime agencies. Though I wasn't altogether fussy about following rules, it made me sick to think that a solid, weighty piece of *something* could just disappear like smoke into the petty rot of bureaucracy. The rationing boys would come in and kick up dust to show that they were earning their pay, and nothing much would come of it. When I talked to Brunell, I would make it clear that I had no concern for the laws involved, and perhaps that would be enough to loosen his tongue.

By the time I made it back down the alley, Johnson and Walker had slipped into the car, Walker in the backseat. As I approached, I noticed Johnson's wild look and curt gesturing. I turned my head and looked up the street. I saw a big Lloyd Cruiser full of hard guys standing half a block down. The windows were smoked. I stared at the auto, and it began to creep along the curb toward me.

"What'll we do?" said Johnson. "Call it in?"

"Sit tight for now. You'll know real trouble when it hits you in the back of the head." I stepped to the front of the car and waited for the Cruiser to approach. I could see only the driver clearly in the bright light of late morning. I heard Walker sliding across the backseat, heard the door latch open quietly.

"Hey, mister, did you get your eye shot out in the war?"

I turned to the young boy at the curb, who stood pointing his stubby finger at the black patch.

"Don't get fresh, kid." I saw that the black car was almost upon me. "Beat it."

"Was it Jerry or the Japs?"

I slowly pulled up the bad hand and drew back my jacket enough to give the kid a glimpse of the shoulder rig and the butt of my revolver. The kid's eyes sharpened, and I wondered if it was the sight of the gun or the mangled hand. "I said beat it, kid."

The boy stared blankly for a moment and then skipped away down the street. He ran a few steps, stopped to pick up a bottle cap, and turned off across an empty lot.

I turned my attention now to the Cruiser, which had stopped opposite my unmarked car. I sensed that Walker had slipped out of the car and now stood just behind the rear bumper. Because the driver of the Cruiser had let his window down, I could see the young thick-neck's disinterested face drooping forward. The darkened rear window lowered slowly, and a haggard face came into view.

"Pete Caudill?"

I said nothing.

"I guess it couldn't be anyone else with that kind of mug," said the haggard man. "Frank Carter. I work for Jasper Lloyd."

I had recognized him the instant his deep-set eyes came into view. Frank Carter, Lloyd's head beef-handler, once chief of security for all of Lloyd Motors, and now reduced to running errands and providing personal security for the Old Man.

"Mr. Lloyd has asked me to bring you to him, if you'll come."

Still I said nothing, and there was a stiff silence all around.

"Will you—" Carter broke off in a fit of coughing.

I turned away and leaned in to speak in a low voice to Johnson. "You take the stuff, you stash it somewhere funny, right? And keep an eye out for anybody following you. I'll leave word at the station for you later." I tossed the keys to Johnson. "And call the rationing boys over here, will you, before the whole neighborhood cleans the place out."

Johnson nodded and slid across the seat. "Is it all right?" he asked.

"Don't get weepy, Johnson. Just do what I told you."

I walked toward the black car, then stopped. I turned and gave Walker a little nod, then climbed into the luxurious sedan, my stomach gurgling, wondering how long it would be before I could eat a little something.

I had an idea how it was. Jasper Lloyd's yacht was the biggest on the Detroit River—but that wouldn't last. There had been a sort of gentlemen's agreement about the pecking order among the auto barons, and none of the pirates had built a yacht larger than Lloyd's. But as the Old Man was in decline, and as the company was floundering under the management of Lloyd's young nephew, it was inevitable that soon the mantle would pass. Another monstrosity would roll down the dirty river and settle into a berth at the Belle Isle Yacht Club or the Grosse Pointe Yacht Club, and Lloyd would settle into oblivion. The Old Man, who had begun his life over eighty years ago, when much of the area was still farmland and undeveloped acreage, would go to dust like any other man.

The gateman at the Belle Isle Yacht Club began waving us through as soon as he saw the big Cruiser turn into the drive. Carter led me out onto the long pier, which had been specially built to accommodate Lloyd's yacht. We climbed onto the yacht, and I followed Carter up the stairs to the big deck up front. A colored boy in a neatly pressed white jacket brought iced tea. Carter's men stood and loosened their ties in the sun while I looked for a place to set my glass. I took in the skyline of Detroit across the bow and let my eye come down to the Belle Isle Bridge, far enough from the Yacht Club to separate the riffraff from the upper crust. The bridge was clogged with people heading onto the island, trying to escape the heat. Nothing much was doing at the rubber factory or at the naval yard at the land end of the bridge. I thought idly that it might be nice to have a place like this, a place where you could step back and take a look at the city from a little distance, separated by water like a moat.

I pulled a long draught from the tea and found that it went a long way to easing the discomfort in my belly. Carter and his men had not tried to take my revolver. If I was another kind of man, I might have been insulted that they weren't worried about me getting rough. Not a word had been spoken since they picked me up in the street. I sat next to Carter during the trip, hoping that whatever it was the old man kept coughing up into his handkerchief wasn't contagious.

"When I was a boy, Mr. Caudill, cows used to graze over much of what you see here."

I turned and was surprised to find Lloyd standing next to me. The tiny man had crept up without sound.

"It seems I can remember what happened long ago more clearly than what happened yesterday. Age does that to you, I'm told." Lloyd brushed a thumb to smooth the lower edges of his long mustaches. "As I remember it, the colors and the odors were sharper than they are now. Horse and buggy days, they were. Things were slower. For a man with a little initiative, it was easier to get ahead. And now..." He drifted off.

"Old age makes you soft," I said.

"Soft! I should be able to afford to go soft now, after all of it." He stared out over the rail and worked a little spit over his thin lips. "I suppose the old days are gone forever, and it wouldn't quite be manly to mourn their passing. The good Lord knows I've seen my share of barbarous custom pass into disfavor. But I do regret the passing of the mannerly way. It was a mark of civility in my day to share a drink and a cigar with a business associate, to start out as men before talking about money. You couldn't say that we were innocent. We knew well that every man in the business world tries to gain his advantage however he can. He tries to gather something for himself and his family, and a simple application of arithmetic made it clear that profit and gain for one must mean loss for another; but we always took care to nurture our measure of social grace like a kind of gift. These days, though, the rush of commerce sweeps us along. Right down to business without so much as a kind greeting to ease into things. I like to get to know a man before I really talk to him, Caudill."

"I'm not friendly, that's all." I met the old man's watery gaze. "I don't put out the glad hand. I'm all business."

"You're no businessman," Lloyd said. "But your time here will be well spent. I would not go to the trouble and the risk to invite you here only to socialize." He eased back a bit like he was satisfied that he had put in his piece. "Frank," he said, "take the boys down and get them something to eat, will you?"

Carter herded the men down the short ladder below the deck and then followed, suppressing the racking cough that shook him constantly.

"Did you know that Mr. Carter was a police officer when I hired him? He's been with me over forty years," said Lloyd. "That kind of loyalty seems to have lost its currency these days."

I looked down at the old man's hands gripping the rail: a mummy's hands, dried and knotty, the fingers askew from arthritis. It seemed a wonder that such a tiny bit of flesh and purpose could hold control over such a massive fortune. Kings and presidents had asked his advice and sought favor with him, I knew.

"Were you aware, Mr. Caudill, that I knew your father?"

I couldn't help it; I tensed up a little and turned my unhappy eye toward Lloyd's face.

"He was doing a little work for me," Lloyd went on.

"What kind of work was that?" I wanted to throttle the tiny man beside me, squeeze out whatever information I could and then toss the desiccated carcass over the rail. But the old man had a kernel of strength in him that I had to appreciate. He knew I could snap him in two, he knew I wanted to, but he wasn't afraid.

"We'll get to that in time, perhaps. I'll be blunt with you, Mr. Caudill, since that seems to be the tack that suits you. I'm not sure I can trust you. In fact, the only thing that works to your favor is that I know you've been floundering around like an oaf for the past week. You couldn't survive long as a crooked man."

"You dragged me over here to insult me? It's a hell of a lot of trouble to go to, old man." I realized that I still held the glass of iced tea in my hand. I tossed it over the rail.

"The truth is, Mr. Caudill, as you can see, I am not the man I was. It's true; I have made my share of mistakes in my time. You can take it as a sign of weakness, if you like, of softness, but when a man gets close to the end of his time, he starts to think about how he'll be remembered." He stroked his snowy goatee. "Mr. Caudill, answer me bluntly, if you like. What's your feeling about the situation of the Negro in Detroit?"

"I don't give a good goddamn about the Negro, any more than I care about anyone else but myself, my family, and the few friends I have. And in case you hadn't noticed, there's a war going on."

Lloyd waved his hand dismissively. "Don't worry about the war. It's all but taken care of already. The pressing thing for us now is to shore up the foundation of our city. You are not a naive man, I take it, Mr. Caudill. You understand something of the working of business and economy. To accomplish any lofty goal, to beat back the forces of chaos and anarchy, it is often necessary to do business with men . . . not worthy of the greatest respect."

"Don't make excuses to me about it. I'm just a dick, and not a good one, either. Nobody cares what I think."

Lloyd sniffed. "You understand that none of what I tell you can be verified. Some years ago, during the first years of our troubles with the unions, Mr. Carter and I purchased the help of a diverse group of men—thugs, in the main, you might call them. Young men out of work. This was after the crash, of course, and it seemed for a time that somehow the Reds and the Communists might swarm over the country. America is the greatest, most blessed nation the world has ever known, and yet it seemed to us that these union organizers might strike in such a way as to pull apart the structure of what we had worked so hard and so long to build. So we fought back however we could. I still believe we were right to do so. But there came a time when we might have let our judgment slip a little, and we became too closely associated with a certain element that became a clear liability over time."

"Why do I need to hear all this?" My feet had begun to ache from standing.

"I believe you have gathered already that some of the men we hired were members of the Black Legion. Many of them, in fact. They were such a slipshod group that we failed to take them seriously. I admit that I was not as involved in the process as I should have been. Perhaps in those days Mr. Carter's efforts were scattered over too broad a field. What we knew was that these men hated the Communists and the unions with great passion and they were willing to address the problem in ways that the Lloyd Motor Company could not do officially."

"So I guess your popularity with those guys has gone to hell, then, now that you've let the union in."

"Exactly. You surprise me, Mr. Caudill. I didn't think you were following me so closely."

"You could say I know a lot of men who got the shit end of the stick when you caved in to the union. A lot of boys got their heads busted for nothing."

"In every endeavor, Mr. Caudill, there are winners and losers. That would not be a problem, for the most part. When the tide changes, it's foolish to try to swim against it. I suppose even the dimmest of the Legion boys could recognize that. It's business, after all, and I have always believed that the workings of business could serve a moral purpose. Some must lose. For our great country to continue as it has, for our great city to blossom into the greatest industrial center in the world, some must suffer. But there are always a few who will take things too personally."

Lloyd sighed. "When the Legion broke up after that foolish incident with Mr. Poole, we were gratified, as we expected that our problems had dissipated." Lloyd blinked and let his eyes wander over the Detroit skyline. He pulled in a deep breath and let it out. "I'm not what I used to be. And Mr. Carter... You can see that he hasn't long to live. It's the cancer." There was a long pause. "One man in particular was a problem for us. The workings of the Black Legion were so murky, so secretive. We never knew his name, really. I suppose the union contract was a bitter pill for him to swallow. We had rid ourselves of him and his cronies—it's another story, and I'm sure you haven't the patience to hear it. But now, as my sources have noted, he appears to have returned. When he's after, I can't quite say."

"You can't say, or you won't say?"

"For your purposes there is no difference."

"And you want me to make this fellow disappear again," I said. "Without any fuss."

"Mr. Carter has suggested to me that this man is responsible for the deaths of your partner and the Hardiman girl. But I can't imagine he'll stop with that."

"You understand that I'm investigating these things as well as I can."

"I'd like your investigation officially to remain as fruitless as it has been so far. This seems to come naturally to you. I'm willing to pay you twenty thousand dollars to get rid of this man before he's able to make his point, whatever it is. I want him to disappear without a trace before his actions can be connected to me or to the Lloyd Motor Company."

"That's a fair amount of money these days," I said. "I could use it."

"Of course you could."

"But that would make me sort of a whore, wouldn't it?"

"Mr. Caudill, I should think you're hardly in a position to moralize with me. I'm offering you the money. And certainly, if you're successful, you'll be helping the city, the war effort, yourself, and me. Nobody loses but this man and his accomplices." Lloyd closed his eyes. "I'm tired. Make your decision, Mr. Caudill. There is some sense of urgency here."

"Now there's a rush on? You feel time ticking away for you, old man?"

Lloyd looked at me bitterly for some time. He seemed for a moment to have forgotten our business as he let his eyes wander along the skyline. Then he murmured, "Mr. Carter believes that some catastrophe has been planned for the coming week."

I tried to follow his gaze to a specific point in the city but his eyes were looking beyond what I could see. "You mentioned something about my father," I said.

"Your father," said Lloyd, "was a smarter man than you are. He wasn't too proud to accept my money."

"I didn't say I wasn't going to accept it."

"Have you wondered, Detective, how a plodding man like yourself should have advanced to such a position of responsibility on the police force? Had you imagined it was entirely due to some innate talent?" Lloyd's bleary eyes sharpened. "I said your father worked for me—arduous work, and I should think it placed him in quite a difficult position."

"Difficult enough that he'd want to hang himself?"

Lloyd's face went slack, and he looked away. "It's impossible to say what shame might drive a man to do, Detective."

I know something about shame, old man, I thought. Then I looked away, too, across the expanse of muddy water to the glut of tall buildings crowding the waterfront. After a moment, I worked up a mouthful of spit and lobbed it over the rail of the yacht. Fatigue lent me an odd feeling of stillness, stiffness. I felt like the hollow shell of a cicada clinging to the rail.

"I'll need five thousand now," I said.

"It's impossible," said Lloyd. "You'll be paid when the job is done. I am a man of my word."

"Your word isn't worth as much as you think it is."

Lloyd turned and took a few steps toward the lower deck. "Frank! Give this man what he wants and drive him where he needs to go."

I stood for a moment at the rail and felt all the fingers in the world pointing at me.

CHAPTER
12

I drove up Gratiot to the shoddy house my mother kept in East Detroit. Six Mile, Seven Mile, Eight Mile Road—out of Detroit proper and into the suburbs at the frank dividing line. I knew there had been a ruckus a few nights earlier at Eastwood Park, near my mother's place. Colored jitterbugs, zoot-suiters begging for trouble in their pegged trousers and big coats, had come up from the city looking for a place to relax in the heat. Came looking for trouble, and found it. The young white boys in the area swarmed into the park, and the local police soon arrived to drive the colored punks out.

My chest and throat felt raw, and I worried that I might be coming down with a cold. *Hell of a time for it,* I thought, *with this heat.* It seemed funny when the idea flashed through my mind that, like Frank Carter's, my lungs might be rotting out from the inside. I wondered if Carter had thought it was a cold when it first came upon him. The money I had bluffed out of Lloyd sat in neat bills in an envelope against my leg on the seat. I had riffled through it, not bothering to count. It was a pile of bills thick enough to be heavy, and that seemed enough. My mind was so bogged down and off track that I could not say why I might want such a sum. I knew that if I stopped at a beer garden for a drink I'd either fall asleep with my head on the bar, start a fight, or pull someone into a boozy hug. So I drove to my mother's house, following the only lead I could lay my hands on, the photograph of my father I'd found in Bobby's box.

My mother stood inside the doorway in her housedress, half in darkness, arms folded over her loose, fleshy bosom. It seemed that she expected me, though I knew this was not so. I stepped over the curb and onto the patchy grass and made a mental note to talk to the neighbor kid who took two bits a week to look after the lawn.

"Hey, Ma," I said, my feet sounding out the water-damaged parts of the wooden steps and porch.

She tipped her head up and then turned her slumping back toward me and stepped into the dark house. I followed her to her usual spot at the little table in the kitchen and watched her settle into her battered old chair. The curtain behind her was smudged at the edge where she held it when she peeked out at the neighbors.

"You need a shave, Peter," she said. "You look like you just came off a boat."

I thought I knew how she had become such a wreck. Even from my earliest recollection, she had seemed unhealthy, but now her mottled flesh sagged unbearably, her eyelids drooped, and all the knotty veins showed beneath her grayish, almost transparent skin. She had borne five children, all boys except one; two died as infants, and the girl as a child of eight. And Tommy died in the war. Her husband, a man friendly to everyone but her, had hanged himself on Fighting Island, Canadian side of the river. *And now,* I thought, *all that's left to her is a one-eyed, unshaven cripple of a son who can't bear to look at her.*

"You won't get a girl with a look like that." She waved her hand in a vague gesture. "Your father, when we were courting—"

"Hell with all that," I said.

"You've got the anger, too," she said. "Just like him."

I pushed the envelope toward her.

She pulled out the photograph and studied it, turned it toward the light filtering in through the thin curtain. "Poor little nigger boy," she said. She began to make a clucking sound, and I realized that she was moving her dentures in her mouth with her tongue. "That's old Joe Wolociewicz. He's got the cancer now."

I stood up and leaned over her. I pushed my forefinger onto the chest of the central figure in the photo, the man with the cane.

"Why, that's—I guess that's Mr. Sherrill. Colonel Sherrill, they used to call him. But I don't know what war he was in. I guess he's too young to have been in the Civil War. My mother—your old grand-mother, she used to tell me—"

"What do you know about him?"

"Your father knew him from the time they were working on the railroads together, I guess. Used to call him Harlan, seems like to me. Oh, you couldn't have been born yet. Or you were just a baby. Such a hairy baby."

"Do you know where he might be living now?" I stepped back. She smelled like salami and Ivory soap.

"Oh, he's gone now. Died some time in, I guess it was a few years back. Sure, before the war. That's how I heard it, anyway. He and your father, they had a fight of some kind, they fell out some years before. I guess it was a couple of years before, anyway. So I didn't see him when he died. And after that, your father..."

I looked at her carefully. "When did Sherrill die?"

"Oh," she said, waving both hands in irritation, "it must have been when that fool Dayton shot that Red Poole, back when the Legion fell apart. Bunch of hoodlums anyway. But your father wouldn't have any talk of it in the house. He thought I didn't know anything about it, I guess. Thought I was stupid."

"So Sherrill died right after Poole got killed."

"Right after, right. But it wasn't in the papers, though. I heard it from somebody—who was it? Somebody from the old neighborhood." She shook her head. "Your father wouldn't hear any talk about it in the house. He thought I didn't know. Going out all the time at night—police business! He used to try to tell me. I know he didn't have another woman. He never had another woman. He had the anger, just like you."

"And Pop died right after that?" Even as I said it, I knew the truth. What Lloyd had said to me—I had been so struck with the idea that Lloyd might have pulled strings for me with the brass in the force—I had not been able to gather my thoughts enough to realize what he was really saying. *My father had not taken his own life. It had been taken from him.*

"Hung himself!" said my mother. "Can you believe it? With times so bad and all. People begging in the streets."

I took the photograph from her and slipped it back into the envelope. Without a word, I turned and bumped through the tiny hallway toward the light from the front door.

"Peter, honey, do you want some coffee? I can make you a sandwich if you want!" She called after me but did not rise from her chair.

I tripped through the door into the fading sunlight. Shame made me want to run—not brought on by some grave responsibility but because I had been too weak to let myself know the truth about my father. I could see how all the pieces had been there the whole time, just waiting for me to put them together. But I could not run; my legs worked like pistons thrashing through water. Over the porch, down the crumbling steps, and no way to keep buried anymore what I had known all along: My father had not taken his own life, and I was a coward for not facing it.

————

I left my mother's house wondering if I could take a room some-where for the night, someplace nearby but clear of the city, where no one knew me. I thought I might sleep better between two clean sheets in a rented bed. There was money enough to swing it, money to burn. I could call up a steak sandwich from room service and duke the delivery boy with a ten-dollar bill for a tip. But there wasn't any-where I could go to forget that it was my old man who kept trying to tell me what a chump I was. Punch drunk, he'd call me, though I hadn't ever been hit that much. He tried to take me under his wing, but I wouldn't have anything to do with it. I'd just look at his worn-out shoes and the early gray in his hair and figure he wasn't in any shape to tell me anything. *Use your head,* he'd tell me; *keep your head up and your eyes open.* Now it was like he had reached out from his grave to smack me up again: *See, jackass, you couldn't even let yourself know that I'd never take my own life, such a simple thing. So many other things you might have seen, and now you're in this hole because you wouldn't see, you wouldn't listen, you never wanted to go to the trouble of pulling things together. Now you'll have to pay for it. Everybody has to pay.*

There wasn't any reason at the front of my mind to keep me from hopping on a train to someplace cool, to the far north or up to some high mountains out west where the breeze was dry. But I steered the car toward Eileen's house and let my head loll toward the open win-dow as I drove, hoping for a breeze to cool my rattled head.

The house was dark as I pulled up, the front door closed. I had seen the dim glow from the kitchen light, though, so I trudged up the steps and thumped on the door. Hearing no footsteps inside the house, I thumped again just as Eileen pulled the door inward. We looked at each other for a moment, long enough for me to gather that she had been crying. She stepped back and motioned for me to follow. We sat together on a sofa in a little parlor just off the front room. Only a bit of light came in from the doorway and from the open windows, where lacy white curtains waved weakly and silently.

The close walls of the parlor bounced my own heat back at me, or so it seemed, and left me sweating and short of breath. I pulled off my jacket and draped it over the arm of the sofa.

"He's gone," she said. "He packed up some things and left this morning after breakfast." She sat primly at one end of the sofa with her ankles crossed and her hands limp in her lap and a folded white handkerchief smoothed over one knee. Though the heat seemed unbearable to me, she wore a white sweater over her dress, buttoned at the top.

"I'm sorry," I said. I hoped she would not begin to cry again.

"I shouldn't have started in on him again," she said. "I should have just let him be."

"You have to do something. You can't just let things happen when you know it's a bad way to go."

"I could have let him cool down about it for a few days. I don't know, Pete. I just wanted to know why. It seemed like all of a sudden he just turned so sullen. Just in the past few weeks. So I asked him about the picture again, 'Honey, why did you want a picture like this?'

" 'It's funny,' he said. 'It's like a joke.'

"I guess I should have just kept my mouth shut. Pete, you can't know how a mother feels. He's my only child, and you know I almost died when he was born. I couldn't bear it. I couldn't bear to feel so apart from him. It felt like he was going to become a stranger to me. How could I just let him go?"

"It's all right," I said, though I didn't know how such a thing could come out of my mouth.

"So I said, 'But it's just such a hateful thing.'

" 'No,' he said, 'it's the truth. Everybody knows that niggers are stupid and lazy. It's a scientific fact. If they weren't, how could white people make them into slaves so easy?'

"I hardly knew what to say. You've always been so strong, Pete.

I had always thought I was strong, too. I thought I held up so well when Tommy died. I never let the housework go. I tried to be cheerful. And I thought things would be all right."

I moved closer to her until our knees touched, and I took her hand. As my eye had adjusted to the dim light, I could see from the way her eyes were moving that she was working herself up for a good cry. Her pupils were open wide, her lips were pressed together, and her chin was beginning to pull up. She squeezed my hand and smoothed the handkerchief over her knee.

"So I said to him, 'What would your father think?'

"'Just shut up,' he told me, 'and don't you talk about my father. You don't have any right to talk about him.'"

I stood there like a dummy. Even with the family I had lost—my sister Eliza, Tommy, and my father—I couldn't kid myself that I could really understand the depth of feeling and attachment she had for the boy. "You shouldn't," I said, "you shouldn't have let him—"

"Pete," said Eileen, "he's bigger than me now. I told him, 'I have every right to talk about Tommy. He was my husband.'

"He said, 'What do you think he would say about you being such a roundheels now? You think nobody knows about you and Uncle Pete!'

"Well," said Eileen, "you can imagine how that felt to me. I couldn't believe he would say such a thing. I guess that made me angry."

I said weakly, "You should stop apologizing."

"He's my child, Pete! I told him, 'When you get to have a house of your own, and pay your own bills, and raise your own children, then maybe you can give me a lecture about what's right and what's wrong. Until then, you remember, *I'm* the mother and *you're* the child.'

"He said, 'I don't need you to pay my way anymore. I can make it on my own.' And then he pulled out a little wad of dollar bills and waved it in my face. 'See?' he said, 'that's real money. As much as you get in your little cookie jar from Uncle Pete. Or does he give you more now that he's getting a little something?'"

I said, "You should have smacked him."

"Oh, Pete," said Eileen, "I tried to. I shouldn't have—I never have before—but it just made me so angry. I wasn't thinking. I just raised my hand to slap him across the cheek, and he put his arm up to stop me. Then I tried with the other hand, but he grabbed my wrist and pushed me away."

I said nothing. It was like watching a wreck on the highway as it happened, or like a train wreck, and I was a part of it. I could see up ahead a little ways, and I knew that the whole weight of my life was crashing, or about to crash, and I could do nothing to step out of it. I was grateful, at least, that she seemed to have gone past the need for tears.

"You should have seen the look he gave me, Pete. It was like he was *disappointed* in me. He just turned away. He was just packing up his clothes in his father's duffel, and all I could think was *He needs a haircut.*"

I felt something like a knife turning in my belly. All my mistakes, all the things I'd neglected to take care of in my life, came together inside me like a capsule of cyanide. "Okay," I said. "Okay."

"He's gone," she said. "He's gone."

I let go of her hand and put my arm behind her. I could see too well in the darkness that she was wrecked with emotion. With my hand at the back of her neck, I pulled her to me, I held her tight. She was shivering and small. I could feel how tightly she had closed herself up and how tight she kept her fists. But when I slipped my fingers through her hair and cupped the back of her skull gently, she softened and brought one hand up, still clutching the handkerchief, and laid it on my cheek. She let her head fall back on the support of my hand, and we slowly went over until she was reclining against the

arm of the sofa and I was half on top of her. Our faces were close together, and the feeble breeze from the nearby window did little to
brush away our shared breath. The auto shop across the alley was
closed and dark, but some light from the streetlamps on Campau fell
warmly over her.

The hammering of my heart in my chest seemed to sap my
strength. I was shaking and barely able to keep myself from crushing
her with my full weight. When I brought my mouth down to hers,
she seemed willing, and so I kissed her. I continued to kiss her as
gently as I knew how until my heart began to settle and I no longer
feared that I might faint or simply pass away. It might have gone on;
we might have pulled off our clothes and made love on the couch or
on the floor or in the bedroom, but it didn't seem right or necessary.
In truth I had been afraid to touch her. I had been afraid or disin-
clined to touch anybody, and in the course of my normal life, this often continued until it seemed impossible for me to think of touching
anyone ever again. But here with Eileen, after the first few panicky
moments, it seemed—at least while it lasted—like it might be possible for me to accept a little comfort.

After the kissing petered out and the wild emotion settled somewhat, we lay for a time without speaking. I found a way to set my elbows so that I wasn't crushing her, and I began to remember what a
pleasure it could be to touch a woman's soft skin with my fingertips.
With the two long fingers left on my bad hand, I smoothed her hair
along the top of her forehead, each individual hair, and the two faint
wrinkles that had creased the skin between her eyebrows. It seemed
to soothe the both of us. Her breathing grew deep and steady, her
eyes softened, and it seemed that she might at least be able to sleep. I
sat up on the couch and drew her legs to a comfortable position.
There was a dusty blanket along the back of the couch crocheted
from scraps of yarn. I pulled it down as I stood up, and opened it over
her.

"He's still just a boy, Pete," she whispered. She reached out to take my hand as I stood over her.

"I know," I said.

"You'll bring him back to me, won't you?"

It seemed so late in the evening. I imagined that my eye looked as dark and droopy as hers did. "Okay," I said. "Okay." I bent down to lay one more kiss on her forehead, and with that I turned and stumbled out of the house.

The moon hung up in the sky like a nickel. Vaguely, I could make out a few bats fluttering silently across the tree line, pulling bugs from the air. Though the evening had brought cooling to the air, I felt that I could not escape the halo of heat surrounding my head. I walked slowly down to the car, fired it up, and drove off.

CHAPTER

13

Friday, June 18

Funny thing was, I slept pretty well that night.

When my eye found focus and began to send groggy pictures of the real world to my brain, I felt the weight of unfinished business come crashing, the desperate sense that crucial details were being lost and forgotten in my mind. It made me want to sleep, to shut off the worry for a few more hours. But I knew that the day would be full of something. It had to be.

Acid hunger burned in my stomach; I had not eaten since early the previous day. I had not thought to ask for anything to fill my stomach at Eileen's house, where there would surely have been something. No food in my house—no clean clothes to wear, either. I ruffled through my set of five white shirts, stiff with dried sweat, all hung over the ladder-backed chair next to my bed. Then I walked to the closet and looked over the few older shirts I owned—all too small. Deciding I'd rather smell bad than be uncomfortable all day, I chose the cleanest of the dirty shirts and began to dress. I owned three pairs of decent trousers. From my trip to Lloyd's yacht, the pair I had worn the previous day smelled of the briny water of the Detroit River, so I picked up the cleanest of the other two, whacked it against my leg a few times to shake the dust out, and tried to rejuvenate the crease with my thumb and forefinger.

The hunger was playing tricks with me. Though my mind seemed in a fog, my body felt thinner, leaner, sharper. Ready to do what I needed to do. *Best not to eat too much,* I thought. *I can get a cup of coffee, maybe a little omelet.* With my eye on the envelope of Lloyd's bills atop my low dresser, I thought, *Hell, I can have a kid bring me some breakfast over every day if I want. I can buy some new shirts, a dozen.*

That's right. Money buys things. Money can buy freedom, time. Maybe, with enough of it, money can buy more money. But the trick of it was, I thought, to know what you really needed and what was just a cushion against the same grating things that happened every day of your life. Dragging your ass into work every day. Dragging your ass over to look at every dead wino, every dead hophead plugged through the heart for a few nickels or just for a flash of anger, a fight over the last biscuit at dinner. No matter what kind of personality they might have had in life, the dead always looked the same. The earth pulled them down all the same. Whether they were on the floor of a ratty flat, dumped in a vacant lot, or in an alley somewhere, their baggy clothes always seemed to pour like liquid onto the ground.

And usually it wasn't anyone who'd be missed, really. It was always the same—an old bag would come out in her housecoat and slippers, hair smelling of cigarette smoke and beer, screaming to Jesus that her man, poor Henry, who didn't have an enemy in the world, had been taken from her. God! How could it be true? When the evening before she had probably locked him out for staying late at the beer garden, thrown his things out the window into the street. Or took her clothes off for the tamale peddler who pushed his cart up the street every night. And really, there wasn't any shortage of people in the world, so what did it matter? In my experience, it was usually the ones that didn't matter that bought it unexpectedly.

Except for Bobby, I thought. I was not young enough to believe anymore that the law was the best way or the only way to help keep things together. Sure, Bobby had a lot of wrongness in him, and he might have lifted a few things that weren't his, but on the whole, I figured, he was always there, trying not to tear things apart but to get something going. He had gone so suddenly, and in such a drab place. That was just plain bad luck for him. Even if we had been followed, such a setup could not have been made so quickly. We had stumbled onto the men we were looking for all along but could not recognize it. Clearly it would stick bristling in my craw until this was over.

And now I knew that my own father had been murdered. For so many years I could not admit to myself the most obvious of answers: Of course my father had not been alone on the island. It came to me as if I had always known. Maybe in my hunger for a simple way of doing things I had never allowed the thought to form itself fully. It was another thing that would not rest, another tapeworm of regret gnawing at my gut. And Lloyd knew all along; of course he knew. There was the possibility, I thought, that I'd have to squeeze the head off that old mummy before this was over. How many others knew? I wondered if I was the only one who hadn't figured it out for myself before now.

At least I could muster some good feeling now that I could hold Hardiman over a barrel. I guessed that Hardiman knew about the pictures, and I wondered again what Bobby needed them for. It was a dicey business at best. Hardiman clearly couldn't afford to have such a thing out in the open—but neither could Bobby. It might be a good day to drop in on Hardiman and watch him squirm.

Images of Jane Hardiman crowded my mind. I had looked over the bodies of whores, half-decayed and rat-bitten, and found it easy to forget, but something about this society girl pulled at me, even while I slept. I dreamed about her being alive. I couldn't keep from dreaming about what it would be like to put the sex to her, and even in the dream I knew how wrong it was, how it meant that there was indeed the shadow of a monster lurking inside my own brain. Bobby and I had been hired—though we had never seen a nickel—to find her, to bring her back over to the right side of things. Even though I had met the girl just the once, I had always known that the exercise was futile. Whatever made her act like she did, it wouldn't go away just because Bobby and I threw a scare on her or her colored fellow. Something in her family life wasn't right; she wasn't getting what she needed. Maybe, like me, she had a bad mind. I wondered how a kid could manage at all with the Hardimans for parents. Still, I could not really say why I cared so much about her now. Maybe I was mixing her up with my dead sister Eliza somehow in the sleeping part of my mind.

I had dreamed again about my sister. She had simply been too weak to hang on to life, I thought. She had come out of our mother a step behind. It wasn't until after she died that I began to feel the guilt, though. I had always been strong, even as a kid. The other kids called me Bull. I never knew the two older brothers I might have had, of course. Somehow, even though I had been only two years old, I thought I remembered when Tommy came along. And then, another two years later, little Eliza. Weak, pale, and thin from birth to death. It was not a surprise that she should die in 1920, after so many others fell from the flu. It was not a surprise, but I could never erase from my mind the one image that summed it all up for me: on her deathbed, Eliza clinging with her limp fingers to my big paw, already rough and strong and scarred up, though I was only twelve years old. I kept reliving that image in dreams. To me it meant that I had somehow robbed her of something, health or physical strength or grim determination, that she needed to survive. I had been given more than my share.

So. I lived in a world where my father could be strung up by a group of hateful rednecks. It was a world where a detective like Bobby could take a blade in the gut and spill out his life on a sunny day in an alley as if it were just the luck of the draw. It was a world where a girl like Jane Hardiman could get ripped up and killed and the boys who did it could still walk around. There was malice enough in the world to make Alex a target—a boy without a father, a boy who shared the tie of blood with me. I had promised his widowed mother that I'd bring him back to her.

Enough, I thought. *Enough thinking. While I've still got juice in me, while I can still squeeze a trigger, somebody's going to pay for all of it. I won't change the world any, but somebody's going to pay.*

I walked darkly into police headquarters, my head down, eye straight forward. I saw Johnson jump up from one of the steel chairs in the lobby.

"Detective!" said Johnson. "I guess you're all right, then."

"Keep your voice down, Johnson. This ain't a swing joint."

"Well, I have something for you, finally. It's an actual break."

"Johnson, goddamn it, spit it out," I muttered. "You're acting like a woman."

"I'm sorry, I know I'm talking too much. The coffee does it to me. I've been here all night, haven't slept." He rubbed the sparse bit of stubble on his chin. "Yesterday after you left, I got back here and took a call for you—priest at the church said he'd been watching out for the boy, just like you said—and spotted him laying up in a tool shed on the grounds."

"So?"

"So I went and picked him up. He's in one of the cells downstairs."

I looked around the lobby to see who might be listening. "Anybody else know about it yet?"

"Just Kibbie, watching the desk last night. Kibbie's all right, I guess. And Walker's down there with him now."

"You talk to the boy?" I asked.

"No. He's scared to death. Been moaning for his granddad all night."

"Did you feed him anything?"

"No."

"Good, good. See if you can find me some food around here. Bring it down." I pulled at my lower lip. "How long has Walker been down there with him?"

"Ten minutes, maybe."

I turned and made my way down the narrow stairs to the first basement. I was surprised to see the old colored janitor shuffling along with his mop and pail of water, and I grunted a low greeting and watched him keenly as he passed by me, heading into his maze of storage and records rooms. Toward the back, in front of the few seldom-used cells, I saw Walker drooping in a chair. I motioned, and Walker stood up and walked toward me.

"He say anything to you?"

"No," said Walker, "he's just laying on the bed. Lets out a little moan once in a while." He gave me a careful look. "Poor kid."

"Poor kid my eye. Girl gets killed and he knows something and runs off like a sissy."

"I don't know what he could tell us that would help. You say it's the same guys that killed Detective Swope."

I said, "Whatever he's got to say, he's going to say it now."

"You're not going to rough up that boy, are you?" Walker's voice was quiet.

I stopped in my tracks and stood square to Walker. I rubbed my thumbnail across the stubble on my chin. "I might," I said. "Does that bother your stomach?"

"Not my stomach, no," replied Walker.

"If you've got something on your mind, Walker, I'd just as soon you did your thinking out loud. It ain't good to keep yourself cooped up like that."

"I'm just thinking," said Walker, "that I could get that boy to tell everything he knows without making a fuss."

"I guess you could," I said. "I don't doubt that you could. But some days, you get up and what you want is a little fuss. You want to let out a little anger. You keep it all stoppered up inside, like I figure it, you wind up with the cancer, see?"

Walker stood stock-still for a moment. He wasn't challenging me with his eyes, but he wasn't exactly turning away, either.

"Can you see it my way?" I asked him.

"I follow you," he said. "You're the senior man here." The tone of Walker's voice betrayed nothing of what I figured he must be feeling.

"I want you to stay right here by the stairs," I said, "and give a little whistle if you see anyone coming. Can you do that?"

Walker nodded. He seemed eased a bit that I had not sent him away entirely.

"When Johnson gets back," I said, "send him on down to me and sit tight here by the stairs."

Walker nodded and leaned against the wall, one foot resting on the bottom step. There was a stillness about him, a way of standing without fidgeting, that worried me. It meant he was thinking so much that he forgot about being restless.

I pulled the key to the cells from a metal case on the wall and slipped it into my pocket. I let my shoes slap the floor as I made my way down the short row of cells. When I caught sight of the boy's sharp shoulders poking through the fabric of his old shirt, I stopped and watched for a moment. On a ratty tick mattress, Joshua rocked himself slowly and mumbled, hummed a few words. I guess he must have heard me and seen me in some part of his mind, but he seemed intent on blocking things out.

I barked, "Get up, boy!"

Joshua jerked and turned and immediately pulled back when he caught proper sight of me. He sat up and pressed his back against the wall and drew his knees up to his chest.

"I said get up!" I threw as much grit and gravel into my voice as I could, but it was hardly necessary; if the boy hadn't wet his pants already, he would soon. "Get up and come over here!"

"No!"

"Did you just tell me no, boy?"

Joshua slowly let his legs drop and stood up from the cot. He stood shaking, his clothes falling off of him.

I stood a step back from the bars and glared. I said nothing but clenched my jaw and breathed deeply through my nose as I watched the spindly boy fidget. He brought an embarrassing smell to the place—unwashed, in between boy and man.

"I didn't see anything!" Joshua blurted. "I won't ever say anything about it! I haven't told anybody about it!"

I lurched forward and shook the bars with both hands. I yelled, *"Why'd you kill that girl?"*

"No! No!"

"Don't you lie to me!" I shook the bars again but eased off when I realized that the concrete they were sunk into was flaking loose. "Answer me!"

"I never killed her!"

I stepped back and shook my head slowly. "That's not what I want to hear, boy." I drew the key from my pocket and pushed it into the lock, turned it, and felt the bolt sliding in, metal over metal. "I want you to think real hard, see if you remember how you did it." I entered and swung the door closed behind me, locked it, pulled the key out, and tossed it across the floor outside the cell. "Now it's just you and me, all alone."

Joshua skittered away, searching the cell blindly for the farthest place from me, panicked, now a mouse before a gnarled alley cat.

"Sit down!" I said. "If you make me chase after you, it'll be worse!"

Joshua sat on the edge of his cot, as far from me as he could get, and began to stammer and sob, snot and tears running down his face. "I-I-I never killed her! I-I-I never touched her!"

"Shut up, kid! I know you didn't kill her. How could a sissy kid like you do that? Do you think I'm stupid?"

"What? N-n-n-no."

I stepped toward him and leaned close. I whispered, "Now you tell me everything you saw that day and don't leave anything out or I'll rip you limb from limb. And it won't do you any good to cry for your mother down here."

"M-m-my m-mother's dead."

"Shut up about your goddamn mother and tell me what you saw!"

"Well, I didn't see anything until the guys made me go up—"

I placed a hand on either side of the boy's head and lifted him from the cot. I kept lifting until Joshua's feet dangled and the tips of his bare feet scraped the floor. I drew the boy close until we were nose to nose and said softly, "Bullshit."

Joshua's wet brown eyes danced and twitched. "Okay," he said. As I lowered him to the bed, he sighed and croaked, "I wet myself." He looked down dully at the spreading stain on his trousers.

"Just tell me everything you saw. Everything."

"Well, it was three guys."

"Was one of 'em a big fat guy with a mustache, bald on top?" I watched the boy closely.

"What? N-no. It was two big guys and a little guy. Smaller guy dressed in a suit."

"Well, what were the other two guys wearing? What did they look like?"

Joshua looked up at me.

"What did they look like, boy? I'm not playing footsie with you anymore!"

"They looked like the police. They was wearing uniforms and all."

"The police." I thought for a moment, rubbed my jaw. "Were they driving a police car?"

"No, it was just a regular old car. A big car, almost like a truck."

"So you saw three guys. And then what?"

"Well, they was carrying a... looked like a old rug. Big old rug. And the little guy was watching out, you know, peeking around. Just smoking a cigarette, you know, walking up and down. Then they all went up to Donny's place." Joshua stole glances at me as he talked, beginning to relax.

"A carpet." My eye went out of focus as I took it in. *Carpet.*

"That's right, a carpet, like. They was in there for a while, and then they come out. And this little fella, he's looking around, looking out for something, and we's all right there across the street, and he's acting like he don't even know we's there." Joshua was looking down at his pants.

Johnson came down the stairs and ambled toward the cell with a sack of pastries and a cup of coffee for me.

"Johnson!" I said. "Let me out of here. This boy's pissed himself." I felt the acid rise from my stomach, bubbling up so that now the tail end of my throat felt raw. "The key's on the floor there."

I turned to the boy. "Now, kid, you tell me what you saw when you went into Pease's place."

The boy turned away and hung his head between his bony shoulders. "They made me look."

"What did you see there?"

"I saw the girl."

"Did you touch her?" I spoke almost gently.

"I wouldn't! We didn't none of us touch her! We was afraid!"

"All right. All right. Stop that sniveling."

I stepped out of the cell and noted that Walker had quietly moved himself close to the cell. I spoke to Johnson softly. "Take the boy out the side door. Give him back his shoes and his belt. Clean him up a little. You and Walker can take him back home in a scout car. Maybe we can make some points in the neighborhood." I took the sack and the coffee from him. The heavy, buttery pastries had made a greasy stain on the waxed paper, and the sight of it turned my stomach; I tossed the sack to the boy.

"Listen, Johnson. After you drop the boy off, let Walker take the car. You go home and get an hour or two of sleep. Then you get back here and dig up anything you can about a Harlan Sherrill. Check the property records here and in Macomb and Oakland counties, marriage records. Possibly military records if you've got the time. You go up and talk to Mitchell and see if he'll let you have that secretary you've got your eye on—that Betty or Sally or whatever her name is—to help you out. I'll be back here. I don't know when. And keep it all under your—"

I turned away abruptly. I saw that Joshua was hunched over and sobbing gently over the bag of pastries. "What the hell is wrong with you now, boy?"

"I don't want you to kill me," he said.

"Boy, why would I kill you?"

"Because I know it was the police killed that girl."

"If I was going to kill you, I'd've killed you already. You listen here. Them boys wasn't the police, and if they were, they won't be for long. You understand? That was just some guys playing dress-up, see?"

"Okay."

"Stop that goddamn crying. You're acting like a girl."

He turned away and tried to pull himself together.

"Walker," I said, "I want you to go down to the Valley and talk to Pops Brunell. See what he knows about the syrup he's been getting from Bobby. You tell him I sent you, and if he gives you even a little bit of lip, bring him down here and throw him in one of these cells, all right? And you don't need to be nice about it. Can I trust you to do that?"

"I'm generally trustworthy," he said.

I had a good long look at Walker's face. His eyes were almost black and seemed very watery to me, but from what I could see there, he was a solid man. It galled me to think that he might be smarter and know more than me, and so I turned away and stalked down the hall, gulping coffee. The liquid swarmed down my gullet and over my bare stomach, hot but still soothing.

Carpet. The word screwed into my brain. This was not new information. I knew well that the body of Jane Hardiman was covered with fibers, looked on all the bloody parts to be fairly sprouting fur, and it was easy enough to guess that she had been transported in a carpet to Pease's place. Tossing a body in broad daylight, there wasn't much else that would do the trick. A carpet was the thing.

I took the steps slowly, submerged in thought. A dead girl, a dead father, a dead partner; missing eye, missing fingers, missing nephew—and the face of another man, one of many victims of the so-called Black Legion, floating up from the back of my mind like a bloated stiff at the bottom of the Detroit River, waving in the current. Floating up: the face of a man found murdered in a gully downriver, found wrapped in a carpet, too. Found to have been tortured to death, his face battered with a ball peen hammer till most of the teeth were gone, parts of the shattered jawbone raking out through the skin.

I stood at the top of the narrow staircase and gripped the rail. Ten years ago, maybe. Bad days for everybody, 1933. A young Communist, involved in the struggle to organize the autoworkers, had been taken for a ride by the Legion. So what? In those days, no one cared about any Reds. I remembered it as well as I could remember the first time I had smacked a baseball over the playground fence. All the boys in the squad room had laughed about the poor Red. Laughed and showed around the picture in the *Free Press* that showed the Red's movie-star-pretty fiancée and said that they'd have to pay her a visit. I could still picture her little mouth, her pressed hair. The picture looked like a movie still. That girl was the only reason I remembered the dead Commie at all.

But now I remembered another thing, something many had found laughable, too. The carpet they had used to roll the body was brand spanking new, still had a tag on it. Stupid or full of balls or both; that was how it was with the Legion in those days. They traced the carpet right back to a little mill here in town. Things being what they were, nothing came of it. As a matter of routine, I could remember, the police rousted the owners of the mill, made a bluster over it till the papers settled off.

The carpet mill, I remembered now, could not have been more than two or three blocks from the alley where Bobby Swope found his early end—within running distance. The memory kept surging up through me, through my blood till my fingers throbbed. *The carpet mill had been owned by Clyde Rix, brother of Barton Rix. Barton Rix, Barton Rix.*

I was so busy thinking that I wasn't looking out when I burst through the door from police headquarters, and so I was not prepared to meet the line of dark faces in fancy-cut suits heading toward me. The Reverend Horace Jenkins led a pack of three assistants or bodyguards like a shark pulling pilot fish in its wake. The hired meat looked as big as Jenkins but didn't have the confidence. Jenkins looked like a man on his way up.

"Detective Caudill! Just the man I'd like to have a word with." Jenkins stopped, and his flunkies fanned out behind him.

I fought the urge to duck away and let Jenkins talk to my backside. "Take it up with Mitchell. You've got nothing I ain't heard before."

"Oh, I think I do."

I fought the urge to sink my fingers around the colored man's Adam's apple. That look of smiling good health begged to be notched down.

"A man's nothing if he doesn't look out for his family, isn't that right, Detective?"

"Hell with you, nigger," I said.

One of the men behind Jenkins lurched forward, apoplectic. The veins in his neck bulged over his tight bow tie.

Jenkins put out his arm to block the smaller man. "All right, Mr. Noggle. Plainly Mr. Caudill is not an educated man." Jenkins let his eyebrows rise, but his smile did not diminish. "I may be a 'nigger,' as you say, Detective, but I am at least able to carry on a civilized conversation with another man. And where I come from, that makes me a better man than you. How does that make you feel, Mr. Caudill, to think that a colored man is better than you?"

"Noggle? I know you, Noggle," I said. "Still beating up on your wife?"

"Mr. Caudill," said Jenkins, "we're all entitled to our mistakes. Clearly Mr. Noggle has made his share, perhaps more than his share. He's had some trouble with the bottle, it's true. But is your view so petty, Detective, that you can't believe a man can change for the better?"

I looked from Noggle to Jenkins. "Are you going to jerk my kielbasa all morning, or are you going to spill what you got to spill?"

"Can we walk?" Jenkins laid out his hand, smooth palm up, toward the sidewalk.

I grunted, and we began to walk slowly. The rest of the men followed behind, just out of earshot. Since Jenkins fell naturally to my left, I could not see him as we walked abreast; but in the game of jousting confidence, it would have been bad form to object.

"I'll be brief, Detective, since I know you have things to accomplish—criminal investigations and such, service to the good citizens of our city. Early this morning—very early, at a time when most decent folks are in bed—some of the brethren at our church along State Fair interrupted a pair of white youngsters painting a crude little sign on the front door of the building. An image quite unflattering to our Negro brethren. Now, one of the cowards ran off like a yellow cur, but the other we managed to pull into the church for a little scare."

"Call in a complaint."

"We're not foolish enough to think that such a complaint would be worth the effort. But what's of interest to you, I think, Mr. Caudill, is that though the young man wouldn't tell us his name, we're quite certain it was your nephew Alex."

I stopped walking.

"I see I've told you something you didn't know. That gorilla mask of yours could use some practice."

"Did you hurt the boy?"

"Nothing broken, I trust. Certainly nothing as serious as what Toby Thrumm had to endure." Jenkins let his smile go and now looked at me with a blank, almost serene expression. "We let him go, and he ran off."

"Thrumm got a busted nose from me, that's it. Less than he had coming."

"I'm well aware that Toby Thrumm is no angel. And I'm certainly aware that you didn't use the whip on him. But what I don't know, and what I must know, is what you're planning to do about all of it."

"Last I heard," I said, "you've got no more say about what I do than pigeon shit on a statue of Lincoln."

"Things are changing, Detective. We may not live to see it, but things will change."

"Things are always changing. So what? What's that got to do with you parading around here like a rooster, telling me what to do?" I realized that my tone was almost without anger. He had me interested.

"I haven't tried to tell you what to do. What I'm trying to ascertain, Mr. Caudill, is what side of the fence you fall on. Are you doing what you can to settle the situation here, or are you a part of it? May we assume that you're trying sincerely to get at the bottom of things, or are you prepared to stand back and let it go on?"

"What I do is my business. But since you let me in on something, I'll try out being civil, see if it fits me. That boy Thrumm, I don't give a damn about. You, I don't give a damn about. Big-shot Hardiman can go piss off a bridge for all I care. But that little girl didn't deserve what she got, and neither did my partner. See? Now all that means is I got a few things to settle. And you leave the boy to me. That's all I'm ever going to have to say to you."

"Can we walk a bit more?"

The anger had blown out of me, but I was still thinking about Clyde Rix's carpet mill. I looked Jenkins over. He held his hands clasped behind his back, and this made the buttons of his boxed shirt pull over his beefy chest.

"I'm on a schedule," I said. "Just spill what you got to spill."

"Something's in the air," said Jenkins. "Can you smell it?"

"I'm not a coon dog," I said.

"Talk and more talk. It's always there in the background. In fact," he said, "you might say that talk is my business. Lately in Detroit the whispers in the shadows have turned to words of hate and race war."

I shrugged and turned my palms up. "But I don't care about any of that," I said.

"You do care. Of course you do. You've lost your partner. You've shown an odd concern for young Jane Hardiman. Clearly you have deep feeling for your nephew Alex. Can you fool yourself into thinking that all of these things aren't related?"

"Where's your profit in all of this?" I blurted. "Where do you fit in?"

Jenkins looked disappointed. "We all have so much to lose—and I know that the burden will fall most sorely on the Negro population if we can't stem this violence. It always does. Now I ask, do you have so much left in the world that you can afford to turn away as it goes up in flames?"

My teeth clamped down. I turned abruptly and stalked off toward my car, cutting crosswise over Beaubien to make it hard for them to follow me.

Jenkins called after me, "Perhaps we can be of assistance to you, Detective!"

I kept walking, my eye now nailed forward into a tunnel of vision, thinking only of Alex, a carpet factory, and a little girl who died before her time.

CHAPTER

14

On the way out to the carpet mill, a cop directing traffic stopped me with a white-gloved hand, then whirled and let the cross traffic go. After a moment, the cop turned toward me again and peered into the glass. His white teeth flashed in a sneer of recognition; he formed a mock gun with one white-gloved hand and popped it off in my direction, and then he turned away. It might have been a good-natured gesture or a veiled threat. But I thought, *That's it. I might as well go home and sit out on the porch with a beer. They'll come for me if I don't come to them.*

I let out a long, slow breath through pursed lips and let the resignation wash over me, teasing out the kinks from my aching neck. Why not? It was simpler to let all the worry about the future go slack. I considered a quick visit to Eileen to see about the boy. But I reminded myself that the best way to care for Alex was to find the festering sore at the bottom of the trouble.

I leaned over and pulled half a box of slugs from the glove box. I dumped the bullets into the inside pocket of my jacket because I couldn't stand to have the weight bouncing against my thigh. Twice I stopped and turned around to make sure that no one was following me, but I felt that the effort was wasted. It seemed that every eye behind every curtain in town and in every darkened doorway knew me and would relay news of my whereabouts to all concerned—a great spider's web of alliances I had not the ability or the desire to understand. *Fair enough,* I thought. *The bigger the better.* Let them all gather round. If I could not hope to grasp the entire thing and make it right, I would burn like a poker of white-hot iron into the belly of it.

I trolled by the alley where the runt had cut Bobby and followed the street for two blocks more, turned west—there it was, another block away, closed up and falling to pieces. The old building looked to me like it had been built before the end of the last century. It could not have been closed more than a year or two, but already nature had begun to reclaim it. Greenery sprouted in patches all over the packed dirt drive and the gravel lot, and the surrounding area had not been mowed or tended for some time.

I drove twice around the block, looking the place over from all angles, and then parked the car. After dragging an old flashlight from under the seat and testing the batteries, I left the car and stepped toward the building. I took a slow walk around the perimeter and found no obvious trace of recent entry. Cigarette butts lay strewn about a small sunken truck bay, shielded from direct view from the street. Kids, probably, sneaking smokes. All the windows were closed and whitewashed on the inside, the doors padlocked, no fresh scratches on any of them. I had never possessed the patience for detail work and could not see a reason to start.

Without checking to see if anyone was watching, I leaned into one of the doors to gauge the strength of the locks. The padlock and the hasp were flimsy, meant only to present an obvious discouragement to idle hoods. The deadbolt felt solid, though, sunk into the old wooden beam like an anchor. It was too high up for me to kick through it; but one, two, three heavy shots with the shoulder on the opposite side of the door sent the upper hinge splintering away. Two heavy forearms hitting at that side ripped loose the bottom hinge, too, and the door scraped away over the floor till it hung only by the twisted hasp of the padlock. I went in.

There was no smell. No human smell. The clouds of dust I had stirred up now swirled in the light thrown in from the highest windows. I found no obvious trace of recent habitation or activity, no sour smell of men drinking, smoking, scheming. The place felt so peaceful that I didn't feel the need to pull out my gun. After waiting a moment for things to settle, I made a circuit of the building, looking down into the dust as I went. Bits of rat shit here and there, thin trails and tiny footprints wavering across the floor, but no footprints, no empty bottles, no cigarette butts. The dried carcass of a bird, gone so long it no longer smelled, lay below a window dotted with tiny holes in the whitewash, where the bird had slammed against it trying to escape.

In a big, open area, where they might have cut the carpets and bound up the edges, I stepped over the wide grate that covered a trough cut in the floor. I wondered what kinds of chemicals were dumped in the process of making carpets, and what place downriver they had fouled during the mill's years of operation. No matter. I walked across and felt that it might be nice to live in such an open, airy place. You could just take a piss right in your living room, right down into the sewer. Scanning the edges of the grate, I wondered if the rats were coming up from it, if the holes were big enough. I'd once been told that a rat could squeeze through an opening the size of a quarter. With the forefinger and thumb of my bad hand, I made a circle about the size of a quarter and peered through it at the grate. Plainly now, at my feet, I saw that someone had recently removed the grate and gone into the well below the floor.

I had been ready to turn back but felt no real pleasure at having guessed things correctly. Somehow I felt that my steps were not my own, that I was being drawn forward into a game set up just for me. What I needed was a shot of whiskey to settle my thoughts. I considered going to fetch the bottle from the car but decided against it, for fear that the booze would rip into my empty stomach. When I turned to check the window nearest the grate, one of a bank of little panes reaching up ten feet above the sill, I found it unlocked, of course, and just about big enough for a child or a small man to slip through on the run. I pictured it in my mind: The runt hoofed it for a couple blocks, trotted up to the window, pushed it in, rolled over the sill, closed it up, and picked up the grate and made it underground.

I leaned over and tested the weight of the grate. Not so heavy for me, but I would have figured a little guy would have a hard time picking it up—unless someone was there to help him. A quick scan of the surrounding floor told me that wasn't likely. *So he must be strong—stronger than you'd expect,* I thought. *Make a note of it.*

I stooped and laced the fingers of my good hand into the middle of the square of grating and lifted it away from the sunken bay in the floor. Quietly, I leaned it against the wall and then lowered myself into the deep trough until my shoes crunched on the dried chemicals that glittered like jewels at the bottom of a well. I could see that the trough fell away from the building through a flat opening barely large enough to squeeze through. Thinking that the wad of money hidden at home could buy me a new suit of clothes, I got down flat on my belly and peered into the darkness. The flashlight was weak, but I could see that there was a drop-off just the other side of the opening, maybe another six feet down. It seemed that a wider corridor led away from the well. It looked tight, but I thought I could squeeze through the opening and down to the lower corridor. Feet first, and covered now in dust, rat shit, and crystallized chemical residue, I lowered myself down till my feet landed on a round metal grate. Faintly, I could hear water moving far below.

I regretted the noise I made getting down into the narrow passage. I imagined a nest of vipers or rats springing to life, surrounding and overwhelming me, but when I stopped for a moment to gain my bearings, I heard nothing but my own raspy breath and the blood pounding in my ears. It seemed fitting to imagine a whole network of nigger-killing bastards skulking under the city; but what I saw in the feeble glow of the flashlight looked cramped and plain, like a maintenance passage between sewer lines or an old tunnel left over from Prohibition days, a way to get out during a raid. They were all over the city, I knew, and I expected that the narrow passage would lead only to a manhole in the street or to a shack at the edge of the property.

Before I started out down the passage, I closed my eye and tried to picture which direction I would be heading above the ground. I had twisted myself around so much inside the building that I could not decide. I wondered if I would be able to climb back up into the trough inside the building if the tunnel didn't lead anywhere. Without anything to step up on or a place to get a good grip, I knew I was in some trouble if there wasn't any other way out. I thought I might die down underground, and it flashed through my mind that I'd be reduced to screaming for help before that happened. From what I could see from the flashlight, there weren't any piles of bones stacked up anywhere. *If the rats can survive down here,* I thought, *so can I.*

As I stooped forward, I realized that I had forgotten my hat in the car. *Bad luck for me today,* I thought.

I kept the light at my feet as I crept forward. The passage went on for a dozen yards, a dozen more, and seemed to be sinking slowly, graded down away from the mill. In the dim glow I could make out a turn a few more yards ahead. It seemed like I was moving yards at a time, but I might have been moving only inches. The walls were smooth and damp, slimy with condensation, and I braced myself with my free hand because the floor was slick under my hard soles. As I neared the corner, the flashlight began to go. I turned it to my face and shook it: a brief flare, then darkness. I stood there like a dope for a minute, choking down the panic; I had always been afraid of enclosed spaces. But as my vision adjusted, I realized that the darkness was not complete. A meager light seemed to bounce along the corridor, reflected from beyond another corner some distance ahead.

I stooped to place the flashlight gently on the ground, then drew my gun and inched forward as quietly as I knew how. When I drew near to the light that seemed to swirl like fog at the next corner, I heard it: a low rumbling, not clear enough to sound in the ears but felt in the belly. I stood for a moment before I realized what it was. *Snoring,* I thought. *Bastard's sleeping like a baby.*

I stepped softly toward the light, trying to judge how far I had come from the carpet mill's perimeter. Maybe it was because of the missing eye, or maybe I had always been bad at such things. I could not even guess where I was. But as I moved forward, I decided what I'd do. Listen good, bust in, shoot 'em up, fall back down the corridor and up into the old building if I couldn't get them all. I almost laughed. Not much of a plan, but simple.

As I drew near, the snoring abruptly stopped. I heard someone drop his feet to the floor—no shoes—and the deep, heavy breathing of a man still half asleep. There was no other sound, no sign of any other man. From someplace behind me, I heard the faint scratching of a rat scurrying along, maybe checking to see if the flashlight would be good to eat. I crept forward at an achingly slow pace, trying to time my footfalls to the man's breathing. The corridor opened up into a room, and the dim light that filtered into it came from narrow windows high up on the walls. The man was holed up in someone's cellar.

When I was as sure as I was going to get that no one else was around, I curled myself around the corner till I could see the cot where the man sat scratching himself. The funk of the place burned sharply in my nostrils: piss and grease, sweat and beer. I took two steps toward the man and realized that the darkness of his skin was not merely shadow but pigment. I raised my gun and drew a bead.

"Pease," I said, my voice a gargle.

Donny Pease turned toward me with a world of weariness in his expression. "One-eyed fool," he said.

I extended the gun to arm's length and began to shuffle angrily toward him. "Go ahead and move, Pease. One good eye means I got real good aim now."

"I ain't goin' nowhere." There was a dull glimmer in his eyes. "You got me, I see."

I hurried around the cot to get a clearer view of Pease's hands. As I stepped forward to put the barrel of my gun to Pease's neck, the light seemed to spark like lightning for a moment and my head snapped forward. My knees buckled; I wanted to piss. Before the light faded entirely, I crumpled toward the cot and my eye caught a close view of the flaking skin of Pease's knees. *The floor is cool,* I thought, *dry packed dirt.* I remember that the familiar smell of that dirt floor gave me a sweet feeling before I blacked out.

In the dark, I felt a sharp pain at my knee. Maybe a cramp but— growing sharper and clearer.

I came to with a jerk and tried to lash my leg away from the sharp thing, but I could not move it at all. I snapped my head from side to side, trying to clear the cobwebs. There was a snicker and a lower chuckle, and I sensed a small figure skipping away from me. Still I could not see; my left arm was immobilized, and my right was cuffed to something heavy. Both legs were bound tight. I felt I had to fight to catch my breath. After a moment, I realized that a burlap sack covered my head.

There were figures around me: two, maybe a third, quiet behind me. Skittering before me, nervous and excited, was a man I guessed to be the runt. He came close and stuck me in the leg again—something like the tip of an ice pick welded onto some brass knucks. I strained and lifted myself in the chair I was bound to. But my right wrist was handcuffed to something heavy and metal and my legs could not move, so I sat back down rather than fall on my face.

Snickering laughter from the runt, giggling. *A retard, maybe, a head case.* My stomach, already churning and empty, heaved up a bit more from the general air of him.

"Fairy," I croaked.

The heel of the runt's little shoe cracked into my chest and sent the wind out of my lungs. The force of it tipped the chair back onto two legs for a moment.

"All right, Mr. Frye. We don't want to make Mr. Caudill uncomfortable."

I bobbed my head from side to side, trying to form a picture of the room from the spangled light I could see through the holes in the rough fabric. I felt warmth oozing from both legs just above my knees, blood trickling down the inside of my baggy trousers and along my calf and into my shoe. *Nothing serious,* I thought. *The fairy likes to poke his little pin into things.*

"You trouble me, Mr. Caudill. You disrupt my timetable. I suppose it's *Detective* Caudill, now, is it not?"

A snicker from the runt, and a raspy gut-laugh from a seated man to my right; dark, probably Pease. I heard a low grunt and heavy breathing directly behind me. That made three, plus the man who had spoken. Though the conversational tone was quite different from the speech I had heard in the old barn, I knew it was Sherrill. I could not guess where I was. If I had been unconscious, they might have taken me anywhere; I might have only been taken upstairs from the cellar. If it was some sort of hiding place, there might have been any number of rednecks lounging about in other rooms. I tried to let all the tension out of my arms, tried to save my strength.

"I apologize for my associate's behavior. You see, it's a grim business we're in, and he takes his amusement where he can." Sherrill took a step into the room. "You really should take better care of your weapon, Detective. This revolver is filthy. That makes it, perhaps, untrustworthy, as liable to kill the owner as anyone else. And yet I've heard you're quite a marksman."

Maybe my mind was filling in what my eye couldn't see, but I could make out his stooped figure in outline, leaning against a cabinet, waving the gun like it weighed too much for him.

I said, "Sherrill, is it? I heard you were dead."

"Clearly you are in receipt of bad information."

I worked my left arm and my legs. I was in a wooden chair. It could be broken, I knew, but my right wrist was handcuffed to something heavy and immovable; so if I broke free, I'd still be stuck.

"I believe the barrel of this thing has been bent! How can you shoot, Mr. Caudill, with a pistol so untrue? Is this the gun you used when you shot that little Negro boy in the neck?"

I said nothing, but I hoped he could feel the heat coming off me.

"Have I heard the story right, Mr. Caudill? You did shoot him in the neck, didn't you? For my money, that's the way to do it. I've seen a darky or two dispatched to hell with a shot to the neck. A true shot will sever the spinal cord, and the whole animal just flops over like a pile of soiled laundry. With only a fair shot, he'll at the least be discouraged from sassing you. Isn't that right, Mr. Pease?"

"I guess," said Pease.

"Mr. Pease is just waiting for the money he's been promised. When he gets it, I suppose he'll be on his way down to Dixie and his kin and all the little pickaninnies he's fathered. What's your feeling about the Negro situation, Detective?"

I thought for a moment, then murmured, "Pease, you know he's going to shoot you with that gun."

There was a moment of deep quiet, then the hiss of Pease's pent-up breath being expelled through his clenched teeth. I heard a rustle and guessed Pease was going for a gun; but of course he wasn't fast enough. Two quick shots sounded in the little room, followed by another, more studied one, and Pease let out a gurgling breath and slipped from his chair to the floor.

"We've been keeping an eye on you, Detective. We took note of your stroll in the park with Reverend Jenkins this morning. Touching. And we note that you've taken up with your brother's widow. That shows a surprising Old Testament flair, something I hadn't expected from you, Mr. Caudill."

I tried to remember if I had heard a gun hit the floor when Pease dropped, tried to judge how far away it would be or if it was still inside Pease's coat.

"What is your feeling about all those good white men fighting each other over there while the Negroes are moving right into their houses and bedding down their women at home? Not talking? Your father found his tongue when we strung him up. Couldn't stop talking, point of fact. He begged for his life like a woman. Shat in his pants, sorry to say, lost every shred of dignity he might have fancied toward the end."

I thought, *At least it means they're afraid of me, trussing me up like this.*

"It would be easy to think of me as a sort of monster, wouldn't it, Mr. Caudill? It's easy to fool yourself about things. That's how we can tell the weaklings, the cowards, from the brave men we all hoped to be as boys. Weaklings and cowards always shy away from making difficult decisions. When something true stares you in the face, you want to run away, don't you? You can think of me what you wish, but deep in that charcoal soul of yours, you are certain that I am right. You loathe the mud people just as I do. You'd like to do something about it, but you won't. You're a coward, simply. When was the last time you let yourself touch one? Have you ever touched a colored man, except in anger? That Hardiman girl was a Negro-loving whore. Your father was a Negro-loving whore for that pimp Lloyd. And I think you know why I'll shed no tears for your partner's misfortunate demise. Some things just aren't done or even spoken of, no matter how crude the company."

I forced myself to take deep, slow breaths.

"I have seen the way you feel about the Negroes, Caudill. Fool yourself if you will. Cowardice runs in the family, I suppose. I can't imagine what that fool Mitchell was thinking when he sent Walker to work with you. Don't you know he hates you as much as you hate him? And even now he's planning something for you. He sees the way you shut him out, take Johnson into your confidence like a puppy dog. What do you think that does to a man? Even a black man?

"I know you, Mr. Caudill. You can't sleep at night because you know that in twenty years the whole city will be overrun with little darkies, the whole country. Simple arithmetic should tell you that if they continue to breed indiscriminately, like the godless animals they are, they'll soon outnumber us. And you know as well as I do that it's something deeper than just the color of the skin."

I gently tried to stretch the knot at the back of my neck. "When I'm as old as you, and my dick doesn't work anymore, will I just want to talk all the time like you?"

Frye's quick heel struck my chest again, hard enough this time to knock me over backward in the chair. As I struck the floor, I rolled my eye up to try to see who was behind me. The man bent close and lifted me upright again without difficulty. Against the light from the window, I saw the flash of reddish hair: Rix.

"Really, Willard, it's hardly likely that Mr. Caudill could say anything intelligent enough to cut me to the quick." Sherrill moved a few steps closer. "Many times we have heard such words from desperate men."

"If you're going to shoot me, do it already."

"Surely, Mr. Caudill, you must be afraid of something, am I right?"

The runt came close and grabbed my throat with a surprisingly strong hand. He put his face so near to mine that I could smell his grassy breath. It seemed my whole body wanted to heave with revulsion. Was it only fear? I thought that this Mr. Frye was a freak, a sideshow freak, and he lived only to make others as freakish as he was. Then I saw a glint of metal near my face and felt the needle-like point break the skin at the corner of my eye.

I squeezed the eye shut but didn't flinch. I said, "Piss off."

"Ha! You're more spirited than your father, Mr. Caudill. But you needn't worry. We'll be on our way soon. Mr. Frye, step away from Mr. Caudill, please."

I tensed myself and lowered my head a bit to hide my neck from the shot I thought was coming.

Sherrill stepped behind me, reached forward until the gun was just next to my cuffed hand, and fired another slug into Pease. Spark from the shot stung my palm, and I had a taste in my mouth like burning hair.

"We're not going to shoot you, Mr. Caudill. You see? You've just killed Mr. Pease for us. You've disrupted our timetable, but not irreparably so. And now, if his usual schedule holds, Mr. Noggle, who squats in this charming little shack—I believe you know Mr. Noggle from your little rendezvous with the Reverend this morning—should be home momentarily. I suppose if he were of a different mind he might be amused to find a white man, a known hater of the colored races, in his house, having killed another Negro it's widely known he was searching for. Tied himself up afterward to make up some outlandish story about the Black Legion. Imagine it! Powder burns on his hand and the key to the cuffs just across the floor there. I'm afraid even Mr. Noggle, though addled by drink, isn't so simple as that."

The whole thing is ridiculous, I thought. But I knew it didn't matter to Sherrill. As the men left the house, I had only one thing in my mind: the image of the young colored boy I had killed so many years ago. I carried that picture with me like all the rest, in the back of my mind, covered up and festering. The boy, caught like a deer in the light of the big, head-thumping flashlight I carried in those days, would not remain still when my partner and I shouted out. The young boy made a move to his pocket, tried to pull something out, but he did not make it before my gun flared. We found a little identification card underneath him when we turned him over. He was trying to show me who he was. Now all my guilt had tied me to Sherrill's scheme.

Funny thing though, it's not something that you can tell anyone about, the way it goes with things like that. You can't try to explain. You just can't. You can only go along with the boys who hurry in to cover things over. *No one would have ever believed it, but I was aiming for his leg.*

CHAPTER
15

The chair snapped to pieces like kindling. Before Sherrill and the rest were out the door, I had pulled the arm and the two front legs loose from the rest of the chair. I thrashed and tore at the pieces, which hung by tight cords to my wrist and ankles. The ladder-back and bottom of the chair were still attached by a thick cord around my waist. I stood and straightened myself until the back snapped loose from the bottom and the greater part of the chair dropped to the floor. With the arm of the chair like a splint on my lower arm, I reached up and tore the sack from my head, then whirled to see about freeing my other hand. I saw that they had cuffed me to an old gas jet, just a narrow pipe coming up from the floor and ending with a sharp bend about head high. I could have slipped free of it at any time, if I had known what it was. I slipped the cuff off of it and rid myself of the remaining pieces of the chair.

First thing, I grabbed my gun and popped open the wheel—six shells, two shots left, the extras in my pocket gone. I slipped it into my shoulder rig. I kicked Pease over with the bottom of my shoe. One bullet had gone in below the eye, another smack in the middle of the chest, and a third had opened up Pease's throat. The last shot probably went in the back, I thought, but there wasn't any blood. There wasn't any other gun to be found.

I racked my head around wildly, trying to figure out where I was and what I might use to get myself out. It was an old shack with weathered plank flooring and no curtains, furnished on the cheap with junk from flea markets and junk shops. Maybe a lot of the stuff had been bought during the time when folks were selling what they owned to put food on the table. Out the windows I could see nothing but trees. Good. Some distance from anybody else, maybe.

Noggle would be coming, tipped off, maybe, by one of Sherrill's men. Or maybe—my mind seemed too clear, like I was thinking with a sharper mind than I'd a right to—maybe Noggle and Jenkins would be tipped off by Mitchell, and I could expect a storm of officers coming to jump me. It wouldn't do to trust anyone now. *However it goes,* I thought, *so it goes. I won't make it easy for them.* I scanned the floor for the key to the cuffs and found it under the toe kick of the old cabinet under the sink.

I took a strong grip on Pease's collar and dragged the body through the house to the back door and tossed it in a heap outside. Then I wheeled and began ripping through the place. In a tin cabinet beside the sink, I found a bottle of bleach. I opened it and splashed away at the blood that had leaked out of Pease. The sudden rush of fumes burned at my eye and shocked my throat and lungs, so I heaved the bottle right through the kitchen window. To get some air in, I smashed out a few other windows until I began to think of the fingerprints I might be leaving and the bits of glass that might show up on me if there was an investigation. I'd got to the point where I wasn't sure if I could ever wash myself clean.

Matches. The house was a firetrap. With the backs of my hands,

I brushed through Noggle's collection of junk, worthless broken tools and radio parts, ashtrays lifted from various colored restaurants, stubby bits of pencils. Matches. I turned up the table and bulled my way to the cast-iron stove. There I found a box of Ohio Blue Tips, pulled one out, and pulled it along the ragged edge of the stove until it flared and sputtered to life.

I blew it out and tossed it into the sink.

Thinking, thinking. *What will they expect me to do? What should I do?*

I hurried out the door to check Pease again for a gun. Nothing. Pease had spent more than a few nickels on the suit, more than I had ever been willing to spend. Ruined now, ventilated and bloody. Pease's pomaded hair had flipped forward and reminded me of a cockatoo I had seen on a post at a farmer's roadside stand once. I looked around. The setting sun told me that I was probably west or north of the city, and far enough out so that the grime blown up from the auto plants didn't show up in the bright sunset. I decided I'd need a way to get back to town, a way to carry Pease until I could make him really disappear. Lighting the house up now would surely bring some official attention, even out here, and I was still on foot. I tossed Pease over a little hummock and into some tall weeds.

With my ears pricked up, I trotted toward Noggle's old garden shed, which was leaning badly and half gone back to nature. Shovels, rakes, a watering can. Noggle grew some food for himself. There, in the corner, sat a big can of kerosene. I took the can, carried it to the rear of the house, and left it there. Then I dragged Pease around the house and over the rutted drive and wondered if the spotty grass growing there meant that Noggle did not own a car. If not for the body, I figured I could make it away on foot. Burying it would take too much time. I could incinerate Pease in the house, but the slugs would still be there if they raked through the ashes. I could try to dig the slugs out of him, but even if I could do it, there was a chance that the shot in the neck had passed through and the dumdum had splattered somewhere in the kitchen. They could match up the slugs with my gun, maybe, if there was anything left of them. And I couldn't really toss the gun.

I made my way up the shadowed side of the drive to the road that I guessed to be beyond a short stand of trees to the south. As I waited to see what would come for me, the thumping of my heart finally slowed. Darkness fell, and the mosquitoes and deerflies swarmed around me.

Some time later, headlights approached slowly, wavering and bobbing along the rutted road, from time to time swerving to one side, as if the driver could not find his own driveway in the darkness. I realized that the headlights would light me up where I squatted against a tree, so I quickly crossed to the other side of the drive. When the truck finally followed its bouncing beams of light through the scrub trees toward the house, I latched on and rode it out, crouching on the half-timber that had been bolted on as a rear bumper. As far as I could tell, Noggle was alone in the truck.

We bounced to a halt, and the old motor blurted and died. I dropped from the bumper and crouched at the corner with my gun drawn, waiting for the glow of Noggle's white shirt.

He's sizing things up, I thought. *He knows something's hinky.*

I set my course of action. *Just turn and look at me,* I thought. *If you see me, even in this bad light, you've had it.* To my knowledge, Noggle had done nothing to deserve a bullet. I knew that he had been arrested for pimping his wife and had done some time for breaking her arm. It would be wrong, then, by law and in a general sense, to kill Noggle. But not wrong enough to keep me from doing it. I needed the truck, and I already had one stiff to explain if I couldn't make it away clean.

A fumbling started inside the cab of the truck, then a frantic scratching; the door creaked open, and I tensed as a long leg slipped slowly toward the ground. I drew my bead where I figured Noggle's heart would be if he came out shooting. *Come on, you stupid bastard,* I thought, *save me a bullet.*

Noggle cleared the truck and stumbled in the dark, took a few tiny steps, and tripped over his own feet. He landed in a heap and grunted as the wind was knocked out of him. I was over him in a few quick steps and heard a hoarse, drunken, sniggering laugh. "Got-damn," Noggle wheezed, just before the butt of my revolver crashed with the weight of a cinder block at the back of his head.

I felt my chest aching, felt that I had been breathing too heavy for too long. I was dangerously tired. *At least they won't find anything of Pease,* I thought, feeling the unfamiliar pull of a smile on my cheeks. I glanced again at Noggle on the floor of the passenger side of the truck. I hoped he wasn't dead. They say the brain can swell up. Noggle had not twitched or moved an inch during the whole trip. *Bad day for you, I guess. You shouldn't drink so much.*

I had driven the old truck around the area of the carpet mill until I thought I might have located the house at the end of the under-ground tunnel. Though I couldn't be certain that it was the right house, I didn't care much about it, so I just parked the truck where the shade of a big tree blocked the streetlamp. I looked around for a moment, then tossed Noggle's big ring of keys on the seat beside me, leaned over, and pulled the burlap sack off Noggle's head. Briskly, then, I stepped from the truck and walked to my own car. I hoped there would be no late strollers; my trousers were dark with splotches of dried blood, my own mingled with Pease's. But I felt calm.

My neck was a single swollen lump, almost impossible to turn. The pain seemed to push my head forward so that I felt hunched over the wheel as I drove. As I stared out the windshield, I wondered if maybe I was delirious or dreaming. I felt no anger, none at all.

Things seemed too clear to be real. I knew that Sherrill had not warned Noggle or Jenkins to expect something, though it would have been easy to do so—and I knew that there was a reason for it. There was a reason for everything, but nobody ever bothered to tell me what it was. I wondered if I had not died somewhere earlier in the day, if this was only my last ride uptown to hell.

Sherrill was not merely toying with me, he was using me. How should I react to it all? What was Sherrill trying to get me to do? I should be furious, murderous, a flare of rage. But I felt nothing. *That old bastard wants me to come after him,* I thought. *And he wants me to be mad as hell.*

As I approached my house, air raid sirens began to moan. My headlamps carved a tunnel through darkness as the lights in every house blinked out for the drill. I was too tired to bear it. I trudged toward my door and did not care to check if anyone might be waiting in the dark for me. I flipped on the lights and let my hunger pull me through the kitchen and into the small pantry. Stooping down to the lower shelves, I saw a few cans of beans and a jar of preserved apricots from the old woman across the street. Something seemed unfamiliar far in the back corner, and an odd bit of hope came up that I might have forgotten something tasty back there, something worth heating up and eating. The jar was dark, and I thought that probably the seal had broken. But there was no smell. I leaned in until I felt the shelf cutting into my chest. With the tips of my fingers, I was able to drag the jar close. I held it up to the light, swirled it. Even with the exhausted dullness of my mind and the itch of my dry eye, there was no mistaking it: *Hell if that ain't a nigger's dick,* I thought. *Balls, too. I know I didn't get that down at Baker's Market.* With a sigh, I carried the jar of particulars and the jar of apricots to my table and sat down. I stared dreamily for a time at the hacked-off flesh turning slowly in the jar and had to guess that it had been stewing in the formaldehyde for many years. It was like a relic or an antique, something a proud hillbilly might pass down to his young'uns as a badge of family honor. Now somebody had put it into my cupboard, trying to make me look—I found I could not imagine anymore where all the stupid pranks might lead me.

A sharp, cutting rap at the front door jerked me to attention and raised my anger. I bulled to the door and whipped it open.

"What?"

"It's an air raid. Lights out."

I sized up the air patrol officer: short, fat, bloated and red in the face, his soft neck drooping over his tight collar. He wore a white helmet and slapped a white nightstick into the palm of his left hand.

"Beat it, you pig, or I'll shove that stick up your fat ass."

The man's jaw dropped and snapped back up with a shake of his wattles. He stepped backward from the porch, muttering, "It's a big fine, Mr. Smarty."

I closed the door and stepped slowly toward my apricots. Before I could reach the kitchen, I heard another knock at the door, softer. I wheeled and pulled my revolver from the rig, opened the door, and thrust out the muzzle.

"Ho! Ho! Take it easy, Mr. Caudill!"

I saw a tall colored man skip a step backward. His pink palms flew up. The gray wool of his hair peeked from under a chauffeur's cap.

"Mrs. Hardiman, she wants a word with you." He gestured toward the long black Lloyd Town Car that stood two houses down.

We walked to the car, and the chauffeur opened the door for me. I peeked in before entering to see that it was indeed a woman inside. The chauffeur closed the door after me and then stepped a few feet away from the car, politely, not quite out of earshot.

"Oh, God," she said. "What's that smell? Kerosene?"

"Some kind of lotion," I said. "Like your pretty husband might use."

"Mr. Caudill, oh, dear, you're a fright to look at."

I rubbed my bad hand over the thick black stubble that covered my jaw. "I am." I saw her blue eyes glittering, and I pulled in the thick smoke from her filtered cigarette—it filled me like food somehow.

"Well," she said, "I won't keep you. I've just come to tell you who killed my poor Jane." She turned away and exhaled rich smoke through the open window. "It was my husband."

I held myself still for a moment, wondering what new game was being played at my expense. I peered at her and struggled to see what her eyes were doing in the darkness.

"Lady," I said, "I don't know why you brought yourself all the way down to the slums to tell me that kind of a story."

"Oh," she said, "I know he would never dirty his hands personally. But it was him, you shouldn't doubt it."

"I do doubt it. But what I'm wondering is—and lady, you can see I'm dead on my feet here, right?" I tilted my head and wondered what sort of monster I looked like to her. "What I'm wondering is, why would you want to tell me about it even if it was true?"

"I should have thought you could use the help, since you haven't made any progress to speak of."

"Don't worry yourself," I said. "We'll get to the bottom of it. But go ahead and try your story out on me anyway. Why would your husband kill his own daughter?"

"Perhaps, Mr. Caudill, as a police officer, you've seen many things I haven't. You are accustomed to wallowing in the seedier side of things. But can't you imagine that there might be some things, some people who might be hurt, deeply hurt, by things that ladies in my society mustn't speak of? You've met my husband, haven't you? What was your impression?"

"He's a good shot with a long barrel."

"Is that as far as your powers of observation can take you?"

"He doesn't like niggers," I said, loud enough for the chauffeur to hear. "He's got a picture of himself as a big man."

"Yes." She slid the tip of her cigarette out the window and gently rolled it along the edge of the glass until the ash fell. She looked toward the porch of the bungalow next to mine and fell silent.

I felt the cogs in my head grinding dully. Hardiman hated niggers, he could handle a shotgun, he felt himself going places. The lady had lost a daughter the hard way. And at once it hit me, a deadened flush of what, at a better time, might have passed for pity.

"So you're trying to say," I said softly, "that your husband had his own daughter killed because she was running with a dark crowd."

"You can put it that way if you want to," she said.

"How would you put it?"

"Well, Mr. Caudill. You're unattached, unmarried—for the best, I'd say. You've a stunted sense of paternity. But try to imagine how you'd feel if you lost someone dear to you, perhaps a younger sister. You don't strike me as a delicate man. To put it delicately, though, I might suggest that my husband felt *unnaturally* possessive toward my daughter Jane."

My anger flared up, and I tried to clamp down on it. Here—was this woman talking to me about my sister Eliza? Could she really know anything about that? Or was she sensibly talking down to me, trying to help me to feel what I ought to feel if I wasn't a monster? I worked my jaws and swallowed hard. The day had been so long and tiring that I could not remember just what day it was. I let the pieces fall together in my mind. Of course Hardiman felt like he owned Jane; he acted like he owned or could own everything in the world. I could imagine that Hardiman had some acquaintance with the runt and his thugs from the earlier days when Lloyd was struggling with the unions. It wouldn't be a stretch to guess that he could hire them to take care of a wayward daughter, one who had kicked him hard in the only place he had any feeling.

"I never allowed myself to believe that Roger Hardiman married me for love, you see. Forgive me—you are poor. You're enough of a man to hear me tell you that, or have I mistaken you for someone else? Furthermore, I should say that you'll always be poor—or at least that you could never mount up enough money in your lifetime to make yourself into something else. There are circles here in Detroit, and across the country, in which you may never travel, do you understand?"

"Lady," I said, "all this just rolls off of me."

"Mr. Caudill, I can trace my family back to the *Mayflower*. We arrived here in Detroit in 1813."

Things seemed fizzy and soft at the edges. I said, "You're practically royalty."

She was too cool to be amused. "My husband has aspirations, you see. For the greater family's sake, I support him in those aspirations."

"And it wouldn't be good to have a daughter running around the dark side of town. It would be some sticky mess if she decided to spill her guts about the whole thing. It would be hard to cover up something like that. It could stop up a man's arse-perations entirely."

I felt like I was getting to something, but I couldn't see it all together. If Hardiman had some kind of involvement in the killing of the girl, then he had hired Bobby and me just to find Pease and kill him—or just to set us up as likely fools to hang it all on. Jasper Lloyd had plainly engaged me for the nasty task of chasing down Sherrill. I had become a piece of hired meat. Now the lady was trying to work me up for something, too.

"I have no intention of leaving my husband."

"That's your business," I said.

"Some things, Mr. Caudill, can't be changed. Some things can't be forgiven. I have faith that one day, when all is said and done, my husband will face some justice for what he's done in this life."

"Just what do you want from me, lady? You want me to see to that justice, is that it?"

"I forbid it!"

"You wha—you *forbid* it?" I felt the clutching of a chuckle in my belly. "Lady, you've got some nerve coming over here after the day I've had."

"Never mind my husband. In fact, I'm charging you with his welfare. If you or anyone else should harm even a hair on his head, I'll see to it that you live the rest of your life in misery. As I say, my family has been in Detroit for generations. Almost every sitting judge in the county is related to me or is a friend of the family. You must know also that we count as close friends the publishers of all the papers in this city. We can make you out to be any kind of monster we want you to be. A shame, a disgrace to your family, a coward. So you'll regret it, Mr. Caudill, if you think of trying anything with my husband."

"Why the hell did you come over here to tell me he killed your daughter if you didn't want me to do anything about it?"

"There are other things." She paused. "Roger doesn't think I know about the other things. Or perhaps he knows but trusts that I'll do what's necessary for the family name. There is a house up along the lake, where he keeps his harlots from time to time. My driver can show you where it is."

"Is he up there?" I thought of my jar of apricots and the pickled nuts and felt myself struggling to breathe.

"No. He won't be anywhere near there. He's in Washington for a few days."

"Who's up there?"

"It's rather secluded. Rustic, you might say. Just the place for hiding out—for someone unnatural—or for a sort of societal outcast. You get my meaning. But that's not really something I care to discuss. You can call it a favor." She pulled the butt of her cigarette from the holder with two slender fingers and slipped it out the window. "I've also come to tell you something you seem too thick to have guessed on your own."

"Spill it, lady. This is getting tired now."

"Your partner's wife, pretty thing, and her daughter—Lucy, is it? You're a crude man, Mr. Caudill, rough at the edges, really, but surely the arithmetic of your schoolboy days hasn't left you entirely?"

"Spell it out for me anyway," I said.

"Did you know Mr. Swope when he was first married? It's a simple subtraction: You know the age of the girl, and you know how many years they were married. You might have put it together yourself, if you'd take more of an interest in people."

I worked the numbers dully, and after a moment began to understand.

"So the child isn't Bobby's," I said. "Why does that concern you?"

"I don't suppose your limited education has exposed you to the study of genetics. What's the likelihood of a dark-haired woman giving birth to a girl with curly blonde hair?"

I said, "I think I'm starting to follow you now." An image floated up in my mind of Hardiman's wavy blond hair fluffing up like a cockatoo, snapping forward from the thrust of my fist on his face. Spelling it out for myself like a bad movie script, I could see how it might have worked out: After Anna's brother died, she was alone, and she needed someone to watch out for her. She started out with Hardiman, and her little girl Lucy was *his*—an heir and an embarrassment to the Hardiman name. Bobby had managed to get her clear of that mess. It was just what Bobby needed to throw the scent of perfume off of himself. The photographs gave him the leverage he needed with Hardiman.

"Mr. Caudill, something about your childlike nature is rather charming. If your hygiene should tidy up a bit, you'd be quite attractive, in an animal sort of way. The missing parts rather lend something to the mystique, don't you think? Or perhaps I've been reading too many potboilers."

"Lady—"

"Don't think of it! I only suggest it because—what would Roger think!" She opened her cigarette case and found it empty. "I've no rancor for the woman. It was a desperate time for her, I suppose. One trades on what one holds of value. My concern is for the girl and for any unusual or untoward interest my husband might take in her. I've given them a little money to make a new start somewhere. I ask you not to try to locate her, wherever she goes."

I was finally at a loss for words. I left the car and trudged back to my house, instinctively trying to ignore the literal sense of everything Mrs. Hardiman had told me. The lady wanted Anna gone, sure. Maybe because she hated Anna, maybe because a bastard child running around might snarl Hardiman's chances at the number one spot at Lloyd Motors, or maybe because the woman had some genuine concern for Lucy and could not have choked down her husband's behavior a second time. Then, too, as Bobby would have noted, it was a question of money. Little Lucy was worth money in the same way that the queer pictures of Hardiman could have been.

I heard the big Lloyd's engine fire up and drive away. The only light in my house came from the bare bulb over the kitchen table, casting a warm and yellow glow into the living room, where I stood with my hand on the back of the old overstuffed chair. My fatigue seemed to swell up my sinuses and press in my ears. I felt everything buzzing faintly.

I made my way into the kitchen and sat at the table, contemplating the jar of apricots and the prick and balls in the other jar. I stared for a time at the rudely cut flesh, whitening now at the edges, the stirred-up sediment collecting softly at the bottom. Estelle Hardiman had described Hardiman's relationship to Jane as *unnatural.* If I had been well rested, if I had not gone without food for so long, my mind would have been clearer—and I would probably never have let the thought form: Roger Hardiman had been putting the sex to Jane.

She had kicked him hard the best way she knew, by running around with the darkies, and it had gotten her killed.

Lucy was Hardiman's child... Estelle Hardiman knew about Anna, perhaps had always known... she had given Anna some money... Could she have known about Anna and me? Had Anna been talking?

I saw stars as I tried to jerk my head around. I stood up, dragged a kitchen chair over to the sink, climbed onto it, and carefully removed a piece of crown molding from the top of the cabinet over the sink. I squeezed my hand between the cabinet and the soffit and pulled out the envelope. Though there was no sense in looking—I could tell from the weight of the envelope that the pictures of Hardiman were gone—I opened it. The only thing inside was a little map showing the location of Hardiman's place by the lake. Even the picture of my father and the lynched boy had been taken. I turned again and peered into the hole over the cabinet. I saw the money I had taken from Lloyd, untouched.

My legs buckled as I hopped down from the chair, and I fell to my knees. I crawled to the living room. *It's cooler down here,* I thought. *The heat isn't so bad next to the floor.* I let my head drop, felt the back of my neck twinge in sharp pain, then subside, stretch out, relax. I dropped to my elbows, rolled onto my shoulder, and then lay flat on my stomach with my face pressed into the design of the worn rug. I slept.

CHAPTER

16

Saturday, June 19

They say that your mind works while you sleep, and your dreams can tell you something about your life, but when I woke up that morning after a few hours of dead sleep, I could remember only blackness. What brought me to waking was the searing ache at the back of my head, which seemed like the scream of a forgotten teapot on the stove. Though I had no memory of it, I had made my way to the sofa during the night, and when I opened my eye, I saw sunlight streaming through my open front door. Whatever effect the long, tiring events of the previous day had had on me, whatever I had learned or accomplished, it all meant nothing. I lay on the couch, wiping at the drool that escaped my mouth, and felt simply disgusted by the whole thing.

Gradually I warmed up. Clearly I had moved forward in clearing up the mess of my life—if not forward, at least *somewhere*. At least I could say that I had *done something*. Though I still could not find the optimism to put on a happy face or the presence of mind to pull all the elements of the situation together sensibly, I felt at least that I might be able to find a place to stand and think about things for a time. I could assemble a fair tally of what I had gained and lost, and of what I might stand to gain if I could hold myself together for a concerted effort. Thoughts of Pease need no longer trouble me, and it seemed that Anna and her little girl were now beyond my reach and hopefully beyond my concern. I had lost the photographs of Hardiman, it was true, but at least I had gained some information from the woman about Hardiman's cottage. I might doubt her motives, but I was reasonably certain that the information would be useful. Though I despaired of ever fully understanding what was happening to me, the feeble theory I had cobbled together about the connection between Rix, Frye, Sherrill, and the rest seemed at least now to be self-evidently true. It cut down some on the foul mood that had settled on me.

But then there was the thought of Eileen. I wanted her. I wanted to make a happy life with her. And just at this time, when everything else seemed to be falling apart as it never had during the simpler time in my life, I felt the bitter joke: I had never really wanted anything more than steady work and food enough to quiet my belly. Now that I had been surprised by a glimpse of that happy life, it was clear that I was farther than I had ever been from a chance at such a thing. The Legion mess, Bobby's death, the propositions from Jenkins and Lloyd and Estelle Hardiman, worries about Johnson and Mitchell and especially Walker, and my own galling guilt combined to leave me in a far greater pool of blood than I had ever known before. It seemed that my newly roused desire for a portion of real living had somehow brought all these troubles upon me. I could remember carefree days, but I doubted I'd see them again. I could not see any way to clear up all the troubles that plagued me, and—damn me to hell—I could not see a way to stop myself from caring.

Since it was a Saturday, the scene at police headquarters was more hectic than usual in the lobby. There were fewer officers and secretaries to handle the greater number of complaints walking in from the street, citizens too lazy to find the time during the week to air their petty beefs and gripes, now more surly than usual as they watched their weekend time slipping away in waiting. I walked through the unruly crowd, feeling light and awake but with a foulness of mood that made everything seem a shade closer to black. I found the stairs and went straight down to the little room, where Walker and Johnson sat in close conversation. I leaned in close.

"We're no longer looking for Pease," I said.

The two patrolmen looked up at me.

"Walker, what did you get out of Brunell?" I asked.

Walker said nothing. He glanced toward Johnson and then back at me. I swear I wanted to shoot the both of them.

"What?" I said. "Damn idiots, what is it?"

"Jesus, Pete, you look like a toilet," said Johnson. "When's the last time you ate?"

"What the hell," I said. "I got a couple girlyfriends now? Just tell me what you got out of Brunell."

"Well," Walker said, starting slowly. "He doesn't seem to know much. He's in the business of making money, and he doesn't get too particular about where his merchandise comes from."

"Did you get the feeling he was putting anything over on you? Was he nervous?"

"Well, he was plenty nervous," said Walker. "But it wasn't from talking to me. I think that we can say it was from the mob of folks gathered out on the walk, all set to string him up."

"What's that?"

"When I got there, Brunell was holed up inside, had all the shades drawn, you know. There was a mob of colored folk there, I guess they had got to talkin' among themselves. A regular character from the Valley named Willie Tompkins was firing them up—bug-eyed fella, been brought in drunk and disorderly many a time, but generally harmless. Excitable. He'd been pushing them all to smash in Pops's windows, not wanting to do any of it himself. Now, Willie Tompkins isn't much, on his own. But some of those men, if they get lathered up, they've been known to listen to some pretty paltry ideas. I guess all the men down there had some real complaint. They figured out it was something in the soda pop Brunell was selling that was making them all—" Walker glanced at Johnson, who pressed back a smile. "They were all having problems in the bedroom, if I'm getting it right, and they were steamed enough about it to want to burn Pops out of his place."

"Something in the soda?" I turned it over in my head, and then I turned it over some more. Something in the soda was giving the men problems in the bedroom. "That strikes me funny," I said.

"Well, Detective," said Walker, "you don't let a laugh get away from you, do you?"

I guess I just stared at him. "No," I said.

"I'll tell you, though," said Walker, "from the way those boys were swarming around Brunell's store, you could see they weren't tickled any. Some men take a lot of stock in that sort of thing, and just the sort that would be hanging around on the corner and drinking soda pop all day. They had been drinking that soda pop for months, and now just lately it seemed to hit them all in the same way, down in the pants."

Johnson said, "It seems like more than a coincidence with all this other trouble we've been having."

I could see that Walker was trying to get something from me. "Johnson," I said, "did the rationing boys come and pick up all that sugar from Bobby's place?"

"I phoned," said Johnson, "and we hightailed it out of there. I never said who I was. But I guess they ran down to pick it up pretty quick."

"Well, don't say anything to them about it." I liked the thought of the rationing boys going limp from skimming tainted sugar. The way it might spread out, that big pile of sugar, it made me wish I'd thought of it.

"They were after Pops because he's what they call high yellow, you know," said Walker. "They figure that since he could pass for white if he wanted to, he's in with the white folks somehow, trying to kill off the colored folks by hitting them at home, you see? I can tell you, they weren't any too happy with me helping out old Pops. If they weren't all a bunch of cowards, I'da been in it pretty thick."

I was nodding at Walker's words, just nodding.

"So you can see that Pops doesn't have much to say about all of it?" Walker said.

I fixed my eye on him. "You didn't bring him in?"

"I brought him in for a time," Walker said. "Just to keep his head attached to his shoulders. Then I let him go. I expect he's halfway gone by now."

"Jesus Christ, Walker! How are we supposed to find out what's going on if you keep letting go all of our witnesses?"

Walker said calmly, "It was clear to me that Pops didn't know anything, and it wasn't in our best interest to hold him here. He's a prominent businessman in the Valley, after all."

I glared at Walker's presumption for a time, but it just made my head throb even more. It occurred to me for the first time that Walker might already know about Pease and Noggle and the fire at the shack. Was he closing up ranks now, setting himself in opposition to me?

"Pete," Johnson said, trying to cool things down. "The captain wants to see you upstairs. He says if you try to duck out, it'll be your head." He looked at Walker and then said to me, "Maybe I shouldn't ask, but why aren't we looking for Pease anymore?"

I eyed them both. "Because I said we aren't. Is that all right with the both of you? Do you think we ought to take a vote on it?"

The patrolmen averted their eyes. "That's all right," said Johnson.

"Because we can vote if you want to," I said. "All those in favor of replacing Pete Caudill in charge of the investigation, raise your hands."

"Take it easy, Detective," said Walker. "We're just looking after our own selves a little bit."

I stared at Walker, not angrily, but with relief that the colored man should talk to me frankly.

"Fair enough, I guess," I said. "Let me say it this way: Pease is somewhere where he won't be found any time soon. And I know for a fact that he couldn't tell us anything we need to know about the men we're really after."

Both men looked up at me briefly, then set their jaws and adopted a slack expression. Their eyelids lowered, and they began working bits of their breakfast from between their teeth.

"Okay, Pete," said Johnson, "but maybe you can tell us a little more about what's going on here. Just for our own sakes, like Walker says."

"Been talking, eh? Good. I don't want you talking to anyone else about any of it. Not anybody, see? And Johnson, I don't want you running up to Mitchell with anything unless you pass it by me, see?"

He shrugged his shoulders as if dumbfounded.

I drew up a chair and leaned close. "Maybe I'm too dumb to put it all together. It looks like somebody's trying to rustle things up with the colored boys down in the Valley and in Black Bottom. Somebody's killing people, white folks, colored folks. Lloyd's mixed up in it somehow. So you can see it's something heavier than just a few crackers with a grudge. That ain't all of it, but it's enough to tell you that you better watch your backsides. I expect that some real heat is in the works."

"What would anybody stand to gain in all of it?" asked Johnson.

"Even when things get burned to the ground, somebody makes a profit," said Walker.

"I don't give a damn about any of that," I said. "My aim is to put a stop to it however I can. It won't be pretty. Now, you all can figure out for yourselves how wrapped up in it you want to get."

There was a long silence. The men looked each other over and finally nodded.

"Now, Johnson, I've scribbled a few things down here for you to look into."

"Not the library again?"

"Library, city hall, whatever. It's important. Did you come up with anything about Sherrill?"

Johnson shook his head. "Nothing in the papers, no property records, nothing. I think it must be an assumed name."

"All right," I said, "that's going to have to do. I've got something else, a little more personal. If either one of you catch wind of my nephew Alex, if you see him, you bring him in here to me. Just hold him in a cell till I can have a word with him, even if it means he has to spend a night or two here. I'll probably be back here again later today."

"Pete," said Johnson, "the captain did tell us to send you up to see him. Important, I guess. He said to mention the word 'noggle,' but I'm not sure that is a word."

My mouth notched toward grimness. I wondered when Johnson had decided it was all right to call me Pete. "Listen, Johnson," I said. "No matter how far down in the gutter it looks like I'm getting, no matter how stupid you think I am or how unprofessional my police work might get, you don't call me by my given name. You can keep calling me Detective. How does that sit with you?"

"I apologize," he said. "I was just—"

"You were just thinking that the captain's nephew can do what he wants, is that it?"

"You should give me more credit, Detective," he said. "It's not easy duty."

"All right," I said. I knew that the pain from all the lumps and cuts was making me meaner than I needed to be, but I decided to keep at it anyway. "Now, Walker," I said, "maybe we didn't settle this before. You are a Negro."

"That's right."

"And that means you can get into some places I can't, some places young Johnson here would blush to go into, right?"

"I'll go along with that." Walker's face was a mask. He was waiting to see how things would go before committing himself to any set emotion.

"Correct me if I'm wrong, Walker, but I'm guessing that when colored folks get together and there ain't no white folks around, the talk swings around sometimes to the general mood in the neighborhood, and how the white folks maybe don't treat people like they ought to, am I right?"

Walker nodded.

"I want you to go down to the Valley, down to Black Bottom for the next couple days, keep your ear to the ground. Just go around in your street clothes. Probably they'll know you're an officer. If you want to, you can tell them stories about how bad we treat you down here. Get what you can." I paused and clenched my stomach muscles to clamp down on a sharp pain of hunger. "Take your gun."

Walker nodded glumly.

"I got nothing more to say to either of you," I said. All along, I had been thinking about putting Johnson and Walker out of harm's way for the trouble I knew to be coming, and now I wondered if it wasn't stupid of me to send away the extra hands on idle errands.

Johnson stood up, his face still red. He picked up his hat from the table and the scrap of paper I had given him and walked out of the room. Walker sat slumped in his chair, his eyes out of focus on the floor, thinking.

I considered walking out. The days were numbered now. Captain Mitchell was waiting upstairs, I knew, and I was afraid that I might say or do something that couldn't be danced around or ignored. I thought I might drop the whole thing and hop a bus out of town, take the five thousand dollars and cut it all loose. I could make it last a year, easy. *Maybe,* I thought, *the game being played depends entirely on me playing the sap. Without me, it might all collapse.* I picked up my own hat and turned toward the door; but before I could take a step, I felt Walker take hold of my elbow from the blind side. The twist and jerk it took to pull myself loose and face him sent pain raking down my spine.

"You oughtn't to lay a hand on me," I said, hardening up like a flash.

"I don't intend any disrespect," he said. "But it seems to me we've got some business to settle." He didn't betray any anger, but he seemed set on some kind of action.

"The only business we have is for you to do what I tell you. Now, I've given you a job to do. Will you do it or won't you?"

Walker spoke slowly. "There was a boy got killed in the Valley some years ago."

Though I had long hoped for Walker to speak so plainly, I could not find a way to respond. My anger petered away as I said, "He some kin to you?"

"No kin," Walker said. "But that boy is still in the grave. He might have been a doctor by now, a scientist, a leader in the community. Who knows what you cut off that night?"

"Some day, Walker," I said, "you'll come up on a time when you have to draw your gun on somebody—"

"I'm not talking about any of that now."

I wished that I still carried a nightstick, something to hold on to: a way to settle the jangling nerves that always seem to end up in your fists. "Don't try to talk me down, Walker. I ain't much for talking."

"You know I have a wife and children who depend on me to be there day in and day out," he said. "All I'm trying to get out of you is some feeling that you're not ignorant to the human feeling there."

"You can't tell me what to do, Walker." I wondered if a blush might be coming to my cheeks as it had to Johnson's.

"You've got to choose for yourself," he said. "What I'm saying is, for my own self and for my family, I need to know how you're going. I don't care if you don't like me touching you. It doesn't hurt my feelings. But if you're the type of man that wouldn't mind putting a colored man in harm's way, I need to know that right now."

I wondered if he could see how he'd shamed me. Could he see right into me, even through my one squinty eye? We were standing eye to eye, man to man, and it was like Walker was holding up a mirror to me. There it was in front of me, the picture of a decent man, and I could see—with this and all the rest of it—how I had failed to be decent for so many years.

Walker said, "I don't want you to think that I'm afraid to go on. I can handle myself as long as I know that what's coming is out front of me, not behind me. My family can get by if I happen to lose this job but not if I'm gone. Not if I'm dead. Now, Detective, I ask you: How would you feel about tearing apart a family?"

"You know my family is already torn apart," I said weakly. "I don't feel too good about it." My stomach and my whole belly clenched and seized, and I thought I might start to well up with angry tears.

Walker stood for a few moments, watching. His look softened, and I felt smaller when he seemed to have something like pity for me. He said, "I guess that's as close as I'll get to a good word from you."

"Just stay out of it, Walker, if you're worried," I said. "I'm willing to handle it on my own."

"I can handle myself all right," he said. "It's you that's got me guessing." He turned slowly and walked out of the little room like he was tired in his bones.

After he left, I sat back down at the table. The scratched-up wood of the tabletop held my interest for a time, and it amused me to think of the heat pipes and the water pipes and the electrical lines in the little room, wondering where they went and how they worked. I fancied I could hear the gurgling and the ticking of water and steam and the hum of electricity waiting to flow; I guess I knew there was a cloud of doom coming my way. After what I had learned from the Hardiman woman, I knew I'd have to go out to the hideaway by the lake, and I knew I'd have to do it alone. It seemed funny. A man gone punchy like that can step as he likes, any way but the right way, but I had gone outside worrying.

I got up and left the little room and trudged up the stairs. I went up the final flight to the fancy offices, thinking, *I'll be damned if I'll go on like this without at least the support of Mitchell.* Passing the bank of secretaries, I set my jaw and rolled my shoulders. I opened the door to Mitchell's office without knocking and stepped slowly inside.

Mitchell looked up. He was haggard and red-eyed.

"Yeah?" I said.

Mitchell leaned back into his leather chair. He brought his thumb and forefinger to the bridge of his nose and pressed hard, eyes shut tight. Then he opened his eyes and peered brightly at me. "Detective," he said, "I want you to give me your badge."

I felt blood spike up into my neck, throb at my temples, and push up into my scalp. "What the hell?" I said. I stepped forward till my thighs pushed against the desk.

"You heard me. I want you to give me your badge." Captain Mitchell sat back in his chair, left hand pressed flat onto the desk.

I sputtered, "You—you—" I jerked forward in a spasm and placed both palms onto the desk.

Mitchell held up his hand. "Watch what you say, Caudill. Stop and think. All I've asked you to do is give me your badge."

I stood up and stepped back, dizzy from the receding blood. "My badge," I said.

"You're a detective, you have a badge, haven't you? You were issued one."

"Sure." I patted myself down but came up dry. "I don't—"

Mitchell flipped the badge in its charred leather case onto the desk. We both stared silently at it for a moment, and then I picked it up, slid it into my pocket, and sat down.

"I've been making do with less sleep lately than I'm used to," said Mitchell. "It doesn't agree with me."

"I been sleeping pretty good."

"Reverend Jenkins tells me there was a fire during the night." Mitchell placed his fingertips together gently and looked over them at me. "It seems Mr. Jenkins knows more about what you've been doing than I do."

"I've been doing a few things." I tried to parse the situation. I still could not tell what Mitchell had in mind. Jenkins knew I had burned down Noggle's shack; and yet the badge was still in my pocket.

"One thing—was it necessary to burn down the man's home?"

"I think so." I looked dully at the gray hairs crossing the bridge of Mitchell's nose.

"I'll give you three more days to reel this whole thing in, Caudill. After that, I'm going to ask you to spill everything you know and we'll let the rest of the department in on things."

"Three days ought to do it," I said, thinking of all the vague hints I'd heard about the beginning of summer—just two days away. "That should be plenty."

Mitchell said, "That's not the sort of attitude I was looking for.

Have you given up? Do you honestly have such a lack of feeling for what's at stake here?"

I squinted at him. "Pease is dead," I said. "I killed him. Had to cut off his nuts and I still didn't get much out of him."

Mitchell's fingers laced together tightly but his eyes did not flicker. He weighed what I had said for a moment. "We'll tally all of it up at the end."

"You and Jenkins?"

"Jenkins is a part of this because of our own shortcomings as a police force," he said. "If you could pull yourself together as a man and as a detective, we'd be on better footing. As it is—"

"You're only talking," I said. "I don't sit behind a desk."

Mitchell looked to be fighting a wave of nausea. "Sit yourself down sometime and see if you can live with yourself, Caudill. My nails are clean, but—if I were willing just to cut out and let things fall to pieces, I would have done it by now. I'm here for the long haul, however it turns out. You're just skating along like every other yellow pedestrian. You're a coward, a moral coward."

I could hardly answer. The badge in my pocket was like a gallstone.

"You just don't like the look of me, I think," I said. "I'm ugly. That's how the real world goes."

"If you ever read a newspaper, Caudill, maybe you would understand what's simmering here. Maybe you'd care. When a nationally distributed magazine says, 'Detroit is dynamite,' what do you suppose that means? Do you suppose the important men in the city are going to let things go? Do you suppose they'll let the hate strikes go on at the war plants, just now when we're knocking on Hitler's door? Don't fool yourself. You and I are nothing here." Mitchell wiped a fleck of spittle from his lip. "We're just treading water."

"I got you," I said. I stood up and turned to go.

"Three days," said Mitchell. "Then the tide turns."

"Is that including tomorrow? I always like to have a little pic-a-nic on Sunday."

Mitchell turned his chair toward the window and said nothing more. I went out softly and made my way out of the building without haste. I was thinking about Detroit, about cars and hard paved streets and regret.

There was time to kill. I knew it would be best to wait till night fell before I tried anything at Hardiman's cottage, and I thought that maybe I'd made a mistake in sending Johnson and Walker away. There was no way of saying how many crackers they might have up there, or if they were planning a party for me, or if the place would be empty. From what I could say, it might have been the whole army of night riders making a ceremony. After I left Mitchell stewing in his juices, I knew I'd have to find some way to keep myself occupied for the rest of the day—or else my nerves would get so bad that I wouldn't be able to shoot straight when I had to.

The time to go after Rix had passed, I thought. Alex, if he was anywhere close by, would not be with Rix or his boy. They were at least smart enough to see to that. According to Estelle Hardiman, her husband was out of town, and I couldn't have done much to roust him without the photographs anyway. I knew I'd find Anna and Lucy gone if I went to Bobby's house. The junk from Bobby's business might as well have been dumped into the trash for all the good it could do for me now; it was all pointless. I wondered about the possibility of shaking down old Lloyd for more of what he knew about it all, but it didn't seem likely that I'd be able to get near to him. *Carter, Frank Carter.* It occurred to me that it would be Carter who could tell me the most about the dirty details, since he had been on the inside of Lloyd's organization for so many years and had put his paw into all sorts of trouble—and it might be possible to get to him. I decided to wait to see what fell out of the business at Hardiman's cottage. If it had enough of a stink to it, I might be able to put the screws to Carter with that in my pocket.

All this went through my mind as I sat in my old car up the street from the headquarters on Beaubien. It must have been hell for anybody who wanted to tail me, watching me just sit in the car without going anywhere for such a time. All the fuss and the empty stomach and the constant throbbing pain in my head and neck had put me into a wicked mood. I wanted trouble. I thought I might go over to the deepest part of Black Bottom or Paradise Valley and get my hair cut in one of the colored shops. They'd have to find a way to trim around the lumps and the scabs on the back of my head. My presence would cut down on the happy conversation, I was sure, but I knew it would start up again after I left. I could just drive up and down the colored streets—or leave the car and go strolling, chatting up the shoppers on Adams or Hastings. Those colored folks had a reason to hate me, and for some reason I wanted to soak up some of that feeling for the work I had to do. A few restaurants down there served southern food, grease and greens and gravy all over everything. I thought I might be willing to ignore stares and the bad feeling I'd bring up if I dawdled my way through an early supper—*maybe my last bit of supper,* I thought to myself, *if my visit to Hardiman's hideaway goes as poorly as it ought to.*

You can be drawn to trouble like to a flame, and I didn't have any explanation for myself. Maybe I was just more likely to fall that way than most men. Or maybe troublesome ways suited me best—maybe it was all I was good for. Just sitting and thinking, fuming in my hot car, I knew it was making me meaner. For some things, you *need* to be mean, but up to this point in my life, I hadn't ever considered the cost of making myself and keeping myself so hard and mean. I wondered if I was even human any longer, if I could really ever fit in with regular folks. In some way, I had to admit that I was *choosing* to aim for trouble; I had to accept the guilt for that, too. It was my decision to go after Sherrill and the rest, though I knew it might mean the end of me. I owed something to all those who had been put down by the working of whatever hateful scheme was afoot. But just like any other man, I didn't want to die while I still had even a faint hope for a better life.

Finally I fired up the car and headed out.

CHAPTER

17

Although I remember not a single thing about the drive over, I was not surprised to find myself on Eileen's porch. It was another hot day, and the inner door was open. I could see that Eileen was in the middle of a day of cleaning. All the rugs had been rolled up and taken outside, and all the windows had been opened and the drapes and curtains taken down. I peered through the screen into the house and saw how much brighter it seemed inside than usual. Like a dope, I stood there admiring how nice the place seemed when it was all opened up. I knocked and knocked again, but Eileen did not come to the door. Gradually I realized that the sound of someone whacking the dust from a rug had been falling on my deaf ears for some time, and I stepped down from the porch and followed the little walk to the backyard.

She wore a white scarf and an apron and stood insensibly downwind from the rug she was beating hell out of. She didn't see me at first or hear me trip the latch on the gate, and so I stood there admiring her for a time. The neighbor's friendly dog pushed his snout through the fence and snuffed at me, then stood up with his front paws on the top rail. I patted him absently and scratched at the scruff of his neck.

When she finally turned to look at me, she gave a little start and then settled quickly when she realized I wasn't Alex. It rattled me to see the emotion move so quickly over her face. Then she smiled and put up her hands, embarrassed. I stopped scratching the dog long enough to put up a little wave. She hung the wire beater next to the rug on the clothesline that ran from the house to the garage and clapped her hands together to knock off some of the dust. Then she walked brightly over to me, brushing dust from herself all the way.

"Cleaning day," she said. "I must look a fright."

"You look okay," I said. "Better than me."

I bent down to lay a kiss on her, and I could see in her eyes that she wanted to ask if I'd found anything about her boy.

"He'll turn up," I told her. "He can't stay gone forever."

"Pete." She seemed to want to laugh. "It's good to hear you talk that way. If I could believe it—just look at you," she said. "You're falling to pieces."

Somebody in the neighborhood was frying chicken. "Listen," I said. "Have you got any food in there?"

It was as if I'd struck her. Her face fell; her eyes showed something of the emotion that boiled in her. "You should have called, Pete. I can always make you something, you know that. I'm glad to do it."

"I don't want you to feel bad. I'm just so hungry."

"Come on, then," she said. She motioned toward the door and crowded me to get me moving.

I pulled my hand from the dog and stepped inside. While she

washed her hands and put out bread and cold cuts for me, I sat down at the kitchen table and wondered if my stomach would be able to handle solid food anymore. It seemed that I could go without eating; it would be like giving up, which should have been easy.

"I'll have to talk to the milkman," she said. She stood considering the buildup of milk bottles in her icebox. "Alex drinks two or three quarts a day. I can't use all this."

"I'll drink it," I croaked.

She brought a fresh bottle to me. I pulled off the lid and began to suck it down. Though I never used milk except when there was no cream for the coffee, I had no trouble choking down most of the bottle. Eileen watched me with some concern as I ate at the bread and meat and mustard without taking the trouble to make a sandwich. My hand smelled strongly of the neighbor's dog, but that didn't concern me overly much. It would have been better to eat slowly and more lightly, but I just put it all away without thinking. When I was done, I fell back in my chair. My stomach was so full that it pained my chest; I feared that my ticker might give way. *If anyone ever really dropped dead from a bad heart at so young an age, it would be me,* I thought with a trace of panic. I was dizzy, I knew that my face must have gone red, and the veins on my head throbbed and seemed ready to burst. There was no way to escape, no way to avoid the trouble that was inside my own skin.

"Pete, what's happening? Can you tell me?"

"No," I said. "It's a holy mess." I wanted to belch but couldn't. "And talking won't fix anything."

"You have to talk to somebody," she said.

"I don't mind talking," I said, "but it won't do any good now."

She considered this for a time, leaning against the counter by the sink. Then she pulled the scarf from her head and dropped it to the table. I could not have said what day of the week it was, or what

time of day or night, or whether I would still be living tomorrow. I
thought that a bit of water might ease everything through my in-
nards, but I couldn't bring myself to ask for it.

"I'll make you a bath," she said.

The suggestion seemed as good as any other, so I did not resist.
While Eileen set the water going into the big tub in the next room, I
kicked off my shoes. I thought that standing might ease the pressure
on my chest, so I lifted myself from the chair and paced about the
kitchen.

"I can wash those clothes for you."

I looked down at my hobo's rags. "I smell bad, ah?"

She had moved very close to me. "You need to take better care of
yourself," she said. "Will I lose you, too?"

I couldn't find an answer. She took my hand in both of hers and
squeezed and worried over it.

"Eileen, I appreciate all of this. But I can't stay too long," I said.
"I'm supposed to be working."

"Maybe something of Tommy's would fit you," she said.

"I doubt it. Maybe."

With her next to me, so close to me, I felt almost regular. She
looked up at me like she might look up at any other man—just for a
moment—and then she let go of my hand and went to check on the
bathwater. I took off my jacket and settled it over my chair in the
kitchen. Modesty or plain common sense might have suggested that
I should wait until she could clear out before I began to remove the
rest of my clothes. But it wasn't that kind of day. I emptied the
change and the scraps of paper from my pockets, kicked off my
shoes, stripped down to my shorts, and placed all the clothes in a
pile. Though I couldn't see her from where I stood, I could hear her
soft hand splashing through the water, the squeak of the old handles
on the faucet as she adjusted the temperature, and her sighs. She

didn't fall back with embarrassment when she saw me. It was more like pity; and I reckoned that the sight of my battered body, dressed only in a black eye patch and threadbare white shorts, had only added to the burden of her womanly care.

The water was too hot, certainly too hot. My skin tensed with alarm even after I had sunk my whole self into the deep tub, but I kept lowering myself down, thinking that a good soak might loosen up the crusted blood at the back of my neck and clean out the holes in my legs. I heard music playing, but I could not be sure where it came from. Maybe it was only the rhythm of Eileen's washing machine in the basement. It seemed to me that I should be feeling something more, considering what I knew and what I had seen in the last few days. I should have been afraid of losing what I had, even my life. As the water slowly cooled and my skin began to pucker, I contemplated the tufts of hair that sprouted on my two biggest toes. I wafted my bad hand through the water to feel how oddly the scarred skin picked up feeling from everything, tingling and cool, like the fingers were not gone but only gone to sleep.

Eileen had crept into the bathroom. She carried a bundle of folded clothes in her arms. I could see a couple of white shirts and some trousers and at least one pair of stockings. Her expression was gentle, but I sat up as quickly as I might have if I had fallen asleep in church. I guess she saw the swelling at the back of my neck. She put down the clothes and knelt at the side of the tub. Then she found a cloth and worked a lather into it with a bar of Ivory soap. She seemed shocked at the damage that had been done; the blows I had suffered had opened up the skin, and I had not been able to get a look at it or clean it myself. Well, I sat through the pain and discomfort she brought to it, thinking that it might do some good. She kept hissing, as if to bring some voice to my silent suffering.

"This needs stitches," she said.

I shrugged. "Just some gauze."

She shook her head and eased me backward to rinse the soap away. I let myself fall back until I was comfortable again in the tepid water. It seemed to pain her to look at me, but she did. She rested her forearms along the edge of the tub and put her cheek down and stared deeply at me for a time. Then she sat up a bit and leaned over to pull the patch off my eye. My hands came up but I didn't stop her. She let out another sigh and found the rag again, lathered it up, and swabbed around my whole face and under my jaw. Her hair was spilling down and her big breasts were hanging over the edge of the tub. When she had finished, she used her cupped hand to let water fall and rinse the soap away. She left the sudsy rag on my chest.

"Look at that," I said. My prick, which had been sort of bobbing in the deep water, had stiffened up.

"Pete," she said. She flipped the cloth to try to cover the rude portion, but it was not effective. When she turned back to look at me, I could see at least that the shock had made her smile. I put my hands under her arms and hoisted her into the tub.

She shrieked and muffled herself immediately, writhed a bit, and then settled herself on top of me, hiding her face. Before too long I began to work at the buttons of her dress, and eventually we were able to slop the whole of her attire onto the bathroom floor. By the time we had finished washing up properly, the water had grown too cold to bear, even though the surrounding air was warm and muggy. Anyone looking through the bare windows of the house from the sidewalk would have seen two naked people walking through the dining room to the bedroom, two white and shivering bodies.

It didn't take long to warm up in the bed. We fooled around for a time under the sheet. I can't honestly say that I was so caught up that I forgot about the ugly hole on my face or what she might think of it. Her eyes were closed mostly. Maybe a dark thought about what I had done with Anna crept into the room with us, or maybe the ghost of the black boy I had killed or the specter of what I would have to do later on in the night—it wasn't something magical that could erase everything bad that had happened in the world. I thought, too, of all the soldiers who were fighting in the mud or in the jungle, and I supposed that many of them had found a way to accept such simple comfort, however far from home they strayed. But all of these thoughts didn't sway me much; Eileen was plush and soft and warm, and I mostly threw myself into the regular bout of lovemaking.

Before long we were both warm all over—except for her feet, which somehow didn't share the pumping blood—and I got up on top and moved into her. It was a pleasure, and I wasn't in any hurry. We didn't talk. Eileen was made for loving, for comfort, and in some way this gave me a bit of sentimental pride that my brother had done so well for himself. Gradually things worked themselves up to a more heated pace. Eileen lay with her eyes tightly shut. She huffed and tipped her hips upward, kept them still for me, and lifted her legs so that I could feel her cold heels on my backside. I must have closed my eye as well, because I was surprised to see her staring calmly at me during the time when my stones began to clench up and my movement was most ferocious.

In a soft, breathy voice she said, "I love you."

The effect of it was like a crash, like that train wreck I had been expecting all along. I was in the middle car and I was being crushed from in front and behind. The thing of it was, it wasn't entirely bad. It was like I had found the trouble I had been spoiling for, and at least it *seemed* that I had made a right move.

"Jesus Christ" was all I could manage to croak.

I collapsed in a great spasm atop her. She wrapped her arms and legs around me and squeezed hard for a long time, and we lay like that until things began to cool off and settle down. With my face in the pillow, I could not see if she was crying or if she had been disappointed. She kept her hand to the back of my head for a time, then lifted it and looked at it.

"You're still bleeding," she said.

I rolled off her and felt at the back of my head and neck. Blood mixed with sweat covered my fingers, a fair amount. "We'll have to cover it up with something."

"You should see a doctor," she said. Her face was calm and sleepy.

"I can't," I said. "There's no time for all of that. And those doctors, once they get their hooks on you—"

"I do love you, Pete," she said. "I care about what happens to you."

"You know me well enough," I said. "How do I know if I can get the hang of all this?"

"You have to be brave," she said. "You just have to be brave."

"But I'm not afraid," I said.

"You're not afraid of getting knocked around or killed," she said. "You're afraid to stay in one place and make things work."

Blood oozed from the back of my neck, gently pulsing with the beat of my heart. I had the odd feeling that the wound was allowing poison to drain from my body.

Eileen said, "You don't have to say anything."

"I want to be a good man. At least a better man. But I might need to do some bad things to get there."

She let her eyes go out of focus while she thought about it. "Sometimes trouble can swallow people up," she said. Her soft eyes drooped a little with weariness. "Like Alex."

"I know it," I said. "You can see how it has to go. Can't you?"

"It sounds like you're telling me good-bye."

"No," I said. Just then my tongue and my throat stopped up, and I could not have spoken, even if I could have found words to tell what I was feeling. I put my hand to her shoulder and then to her cheek, cupping her finely shaped jaw. With her head now sinking into the pillow, I could see that she was mulling things over with some resignation. With the cooling sweat and perhaps also from loss of blood, I shivered. My arm trembled so much that I withdrew my hand from her and balled up a fist close to my chest. I got up and sat at the edge of the bed. It would not be long before evening fell, I knew, and I wanted to scout Hardiman's place by the lake before I lost the light.

She said, "You'll have to choose for yourself what you need to do."

"I'm not sorry," I said. "I'm not sorry at all for what we've done here." I pulled the sheet over her bare shoulder.

Though it was only late afternoon, her eyes seemed dark and sleepy. She curled up a bit under the sheet and gazed at me steadily. It wasn't plain what she was thinking, if she was happy or regretful or worried; she was fully a woman, and not so easy for me to figure out.

"If I can, I'll see you tomorrow," I said.

"Pete, your neck."

I touched it gingerly. "It'll stop eventually." I stood up and felt how ridiculous a naked man can be. "It's just blood."

"Bring him back to me, Pete. He's all that's left of Tommy."

She fell completely under the spell of sleep while I dressed myself in my dead brother's clothes. I closed and locked her doors before I stepped out into the failing daylight and walked dumbly to my car.

Even the bugs were in league against me. I couldn't guess how many hundreds of crickets sang in the scrub surrounding Hardiman's hideaway. As I crunched over the gravel at the edge of the two-track driveway, I became aware that they stopped chirping as I approached and took up again after I had passed, as if I threw off a halo of heat and anger that could be read in the black night. *Still,* I thought, *at least I know there's nobody else around. I can't see a damn thing.*

After I left Eileen's house, as darkness began to fall, I made my

way slowly northward, then east to Lake St. Clair. Though the chauffeur had left me a nicely drawn map and detailed instructions, I had
to drive by a few times before I caught sight of the weedy drive heading down to the lake. After the glow in the west faded completely, I
ditched the car and walked through the trees until I found the drive.

I crept along until the drive opened up to a grassy lawn, then
stood for a long time in the deep shadows of the trees. Tommy's
trousers fit me a bit snugly and smelled of mothballs, but the shirt
was clean and white and fit well. Though the crickets told me there
was no one else around, I turned self-consciously from the cleared
area and toward the trees as I drained off one last feeble piss. Away
from the lights of the city, I could make out clearly the splash of stars
over my head. I wished for a moon. The house was very quiet,
though I could see swarms of bugs gathered at the lighted windows.
I stood still until I could make out the lay of the place: a long wooden
porch and the front door, probably another door in the back, and
maybe another in a Florida room, which I guessed might be facing
the lake. There was a big Suburban truck in the drive, and I made my
way toward it.

The hood was just slightly warm. What did it mean? I tried to
think, but it didn't seem important. That kind of truck was built for
hauling men and could probably carry ten in a pinch. My revolver
had six shots. I could reload, but it wasn't something I could do
quickly with the missing fingers.

There was no wind to push the gauzy curtains in the open windows. I thought I heard a radio playing somewhere inside. Why hes-
itate? I thought they must be waiting for me, expecting me. If
everyone else knew what I was about, surely these men, who had
made it their business to know my every move, would not be surprised to see me walk through their door.

I opened the door to the Suburban and slammed it hard, like

I had arrived in another car, but then I shuddered in spite of myself at the sudden sound. Though the night was warm, sweat soaked my armpits. I walked quickly onto the porch, stomping my feet like a man shaking dew from his boots, and tried the door. It was unlocked. I went through it like falling into a well. Inside, I twice forced a dry cough, hoping whoever was inside would take my lack of stealth as familiarity. After closing the door behind me carelessly, I pulled my revolver from the rig and stepped heavily down the hall, toward the lighted room where a hush had fallen but no movement could be heard, no scrambling, no scrape of metal on metal.

The three of them looked up at me in genuine surprise as I stepped out of the darkness. On another day I might have laughed. I pressed off a shot at Frye, the runt, thunderous in the little foyer, but the hollow bullet only puffed into the upholstery of the leather chair as Frye scrambled away. I put a bullet through the sternum of one of the big blond boys, who flailed his legs as if in a dream, running in a quagmire. The other blond boy could think of nothing to do but lift the little table that held his drink and a little hairbrush. He tried to shield himself with it, but I fired once under the table, hitting him just under the rib cage. My next shot splintered through the table and into his face.

I fired again at Frye, who had scrambled to his feet. The shot lagged several feet behind his small figure. My legs felt like cracking logs when I finally found the coordination to rush after him. Keeping my revolver ahead of me, I staggered into the dining room and turned, following, figuring to keep moving forward for a last good shot even though I knew I'd feel bullets slapping into me.

No bullets came. I bulled into the kitchen and found Frye there, scrambling at the lock on the door to the Florida room. *He's locked it by mistake,* I thought. *Or somebody else locked it.*

I moved in just close enough for a good shot and planted my feet. Frye stopped scrambling at the door and turned slowly. His face was a wild grimace or a smile, and his dull blue teeth seemed overlarge, hanging crookedly from puffy red gums. I had almost pulled the trigger when I was startled to realize that Frye had winked at me. The runt's pale yellowy eyes were lit up with merriment, twinkling in the dim light that made it past my blocky frame. He seemed to be looking at something behind me. Around the edges of my vision I saw stars, points of light swirling like lightning bugs. I couldn't get enough air.

Someone is behind me, I thought. *I'm caught like a dummy again.*

I whirled and squeezed the trigger, firing my last shot at the fourth man in the house, firing dead into the middle of where his chest should be—but there was no one there. Before I could turn to face him again, Frye was on my back like a tick. I felt a bony arm snake under my chin and clamp down on my neck. I tried to shake myself loose, brought my bad hand up to rip the arm from my neck, but could not find a grip. I tried to tuck my chin low, but he had taken hold solidly.

I could muscle up my neck enough to keep an airway open, but I knew that the arteries on my neck were outside the muscles. I lurched about the kitchen, hoping to dislodge Frye or scrape him off, but the little man was nothing but bone and gristle. We staggered through the dining room and into the foyer, where I stopped reeling and tried to think. I put the muzzle of the revolver back over my ear, pressed it into Frye's forehead, and pulled the trigger. The dull click did nothing to loosen his grip.

I turned the gun over in my hand and tried to beat Frye with the butt of it, but the thrashing only gave him an opportunity to tighten his grip. Then I dropped the gun and frantically grabbed at Frye's arms with both hands. I reached far back and pulled out a handful of his hair, then another and another, but soon felt my strength dribbling away. My heart was pounding. *Run,* I thought. *I can still run.* If I could crash through the Florida room and hoof it down to the lake and hold Frye under the water, he might loosen his grip a little, just a little, enough to let a bit of blood back in my head . . .

I dropped to my knees, then down on all fours. The strength in my neck went, and so I could not take breath any longer. I felt my stomach twisting up to vomit, but I held it down. In my ears there was a sound like rushing water, like heavy water falling a long way down onto jagged rocks. Someone was calling to me like in a dream— Eileen? But there was no hope of waking this time.

There was a louder noise, a cracking, like a splash that hurt my ears.

Frye gave a start but held his grip. Then he began to wriggle and jerk. When the wriggling became a spasm, his grip loosened; I reached back and pulled Frye off of me like a soggy shirt. Blood sprayed over my cheek and arm as the little man's squirming body fell.

I leaned back on my knees and sucked in a deep breath. My arms and legs were numb and buzzing, and I tried to shake some feeling into them, but then I fell forward again with dizziness. I jerked my head stiffly to the side as I fell to keep my nose from hitting the floor. Stars flashed in my eye as my head bounced, but I thought I saw a *colored* man in the room with a gun. It flashed through my mind: *The ghost of Pease has come to call.* I couldn't see clearly enough to know anything about it. Pushing myself back up to my knees, I felt some strength coming back.

Frye was still squirming and arching his back on the floor before me, blood pouring from both sides of his rib cage. I crawled over to him and took his bony head between my hands, one on the jaw and the other at the back of the skull, and I twisted with everything I had left. Frye turned over on his belly and scrambled for purchase with his hands and knees, but I got on top and pinned him down hard with a knee on his back, leaned into the job. With my hands wrapped around him, I could feel his ugly teeth gnash and crack as his jaw turned. The spastic writhing of his throat gagging and twisting onto itself shot like electricity into me through the skin and gristle of my good hand—and especially through the bad one. I felt a few small pops and one great grinding crunch as Frye's neck snapped. Then all the wriggling stopped.

I rolled off and heaved for my breath on all fours, expecting the slap of another shot and not caring. My mind blared in a white buzz, and I felt the quick flush of the familiar feeling that came whenever I had to kill someone: *embarrassment.* There was a sinking feeling in my stomach like fish were in there swimming, and I felt red, like everybody in the world could see what I had done.

Frye was watching me. His eyes were wide open and moving in his backward head. His teeth—his dentures—hung halfway out of his wrecked mouth. There didn't seem to be any life in him, but still he watched.

No, I thought. *You can't shame me.*

But he *had* shamed me. I felt like I had killed a retard or a gimp, something that had been dealt a bad hand by nature, something to be pitied. He was born wrong, and I was sorry that I lived in a world where there could be somebody like Frye, best off dead. But of course he would have killed me—he *was* killing me. I swung my head around, trying to clear things up. I wasn't thinking clearly enough then to realize that I'd killed the man who had made me in some way into a monster. After a few moments, his eyes stopped rolling, and—like a rat's eyes—I couldn't tell if there was anything behind them.

The colored man stood at the far end of the room, watching. I pushed back onto my haunches and put a foot flat on the floor.

"Ah-ah," said the man. "Maybe you next, bug-eye."

I leaned on my knee and focused on the colored man. Presently I recognized Toby Thrumm's battered face. His nose was still busted up and swollen where I had smashed it, and the swelling made it look like he was squinting. He stood in the entryway to the room, at the end of the front hall, shifting his weight from foot to foot. His right arm was in a cast and held in a sling across his body, so he held the pistol awkwardly in his left hand, half-trained on me:

"Thrumm, you stupid bastard," I croaked.

"If you ain't the sorriest, stupidest white man I ever seen," said Thrumm. His speech was sloppy from the swelling and the missing teeth, but he seemed full of purpose. "You ain't got the sense of a dog." He drew a shaky bead on me. "I ought to plug you," he said. "I might as well, lookin' at things."

I leaned forward painfully and stood up. I glanced around the room and saw nothing moving except Thrumm's aim.

"Shoot me if you want to," I said.

"I ought to," said Thrumm.

No shot popped as I turned my back and rooted around for my revolver.

"I followed your dumb ass all the way up the drive. When you stopped at the grass to scratch your ass, I could've reached out and touched you. You was pissin' on my foot," said Thrumm, following after me. "When you born a nigger in this world, you learn to sneak around."

I found my gun and popped the wheel. I pulled the empty shells out one by one with my fingernails, then drew out six bullets from my pocket and reloaded. I looked over at Thrumm, took a good, careful look.

"Thrumm," I said, "why ain't you gone from here?"

"Why ain't I gone? Where am I gonna go? I'm beat up all to hell, I got no money, I lost my work. I'm just as likely to be here as any-where in this world." Thrumm wriggled his gun around, trying to figure out what to do with it, then finally slipped it into the pocket of his baggy trousers. He started to shake his head. "You got no idea what it's all about, do you?"

"I don't claim to," I said.

"He got you jumpin', don't he?"

"Who?"

"You know who!" said Thrumm. "Who you think? Santy Claus?"

"However it is," I said, sliding my revolver back into the rig, "you better hustle your bony ass out of here."

"I ain't leavin' jus' yet."

"The way it looks to me, you're a nigger with a gun in a house with three dead white men. See how that goes?"

"I ain't leavin'. I got some lookin' to do here for just a bit."

"Hey," I said, cracking a stiff smile that made my face feel suddenly old, "you haven't lost your balls, have you? I think I might know where they are."

Thrumm furrowed his brows and muttered, "I never had any balls."

"That's a little joke," I said.

"It don't strike me funny."

"You looking for something the police ought to be interested in?" I hooked my thumbs in my pockets. "Or you just figuring to roll these stiffs?"

"Brother, you oughta be thankin' me somehow, ain't that so? If not for me, it would be *you* laying there with your tongue hangin' out by now, ain't that so? You can't just let me be alone in here for a little bit?"

I rubbed my thumb over my chin. I said, "I guess you got something there." I glanced at the clock on the wall over Thrumm's head. "It's getting late." I walked past Thrumm and into the darkened hall, my feet thumping, my hands in my pockets. When I reached the door, I turned and said, "Take the truck out there, if you can find the keys."

"I aim to," said Thrumm, following. "Listen, you know he wanted you to come up here and kill these dumb-ass crackers for him, don't you?"

I thought for a moment and saw it for myself. "I guess," I said.

"Man," said Thrumm, "you just the Devil's own rag baby doll, ain't you?"

I stepped through the door and into the night.

CHAPTER

18

Sunday, June 20

KILLERS IN SHOOTOUT WITH DEPUTIES, the header might read. THREE DEAD IN BATTLE AT REMOTE SHACK. Bobby would have loved it, anyway. I wished I had something left in me to enjoy it, too. But there was only the ache of every part of my body and the rawness in my throat, less from Frye's grip than from the splash of acid from my churning stomach. I had called the county sheriff's men too late in the night for the story to make the early Sunday editions, but no matter. Later in the day, or early Monday, the hacks would print it up. The county men would figure a way to keep Hardiman's name out of it. Things were a little different up in Macomb.

I figured I was through. The previous night's work should have gone a long way toward making me feel better, but I felt even farther away from a good life. I had left a foul, reeking mess at Hardiman's cabin, and even if the county boys and the newspapers left me out of it, I knew that one day it would come back to haunt me. Frye and the blond boys would never put their rotten touch to another girl like Jane, it was true; except as ghosts, they had lost all power to harm. But I understood that what had happened could not have been the culmination of anything.

Toby Thrumm seemed to know that I had been set up to take Frye and the two big boys out of the picture. Maybe Sherrill had come to think of them as a liability. Maybe the horrible violation of Jane Hardiman brought up the same bile in Sherrill that it brought up in me. I rolled it over in my mind to judge if Sherrill might hold to such an old-fashioned notion, and thought it might be so.

Revenge is supposed to be sweet, I had heard. *Sweet Revenge.* Though I had indeed found revenge for so many of the wrongs that had been done, I could not taste any sweetness—because I knew I had done nothing to stop the "catastrophe" that Old Man Lloyd was sure would occur. In fact, I had stupidly helped Sherrill along by ridding him of Frye. If Hardiman's cottage had been a base for Sherrill's operation, any trace or clue would now be lost to me. I had reached the end of my initiative. I only felt filthy and worthless.

What had Toby Thrumm been sniffing after at Hardiman's cottage? It must have been *something,* if Thrumm was willing to come for it after what he'd been through, up there in Macomb County where big stretches of scrub and farmland hid an awful lot of well-armed backwoods types. Bobby was right; it couldn't have been anything but money. I pictured a satchel of bills, taken by extortion or blackmail, or maybe from stickups or bank jobs. It was commonly known that the Klan and various other syndicates often pulled bank jobs to fund their operations. If a gang of men thought nothing of lynching niggers, they wouldn't mind taking dough from a bank the rude way; they thought Jews ran all the banks anyway. So it seemed sensible to me that there might be a big chunk of money floating around somewhere, maybe the same sack of dough that Pease had hoped to stick his mitts into. Gathered together in a bag, concentrated, it was enough to make men snivel after it, to make them forget their business and their better judgment. I thought of Jasper Lloyd and his promise of money for me, and I wondered how his offer might compare to the bundle that Sherrill seemed to control. I wondered, if I could find Sherrill and get a drop on him, if he'd stoop to offering me money to do his dirty work as well.

But how could I find Sherrill? How could I do anything? All I knew was that they were all smarter than me. I had bungled and botched everything I had put my hand to so far. I had killed the two blond boys, but that was only a sign of how meatheaded they were. Frye would surely have killed me if not for Toby Thrumm—poor Toby Thrumm, who figured I was worth saving even after I'd busted his nose. It all made me very tired. What had I ever done right? My father was gone, Tommy was gone, Bobby was gone, my sister Eliza was gone, Jane Hardiman was gone. Maybe Alex was gone for good, too.

I'm the one who drove him away, I thought. *Eileen knows it, too.*

Whatever catastrophe had been planned for the impending summer, whatever specific trouble Sherrill had in the works, I knew it was beyond my feeble power to help. He had been working with sense and purpose all along, and I had been fumbling stupidly after him. Briefly I thought of chasing down Rix or Hardiman, even Frank Carter or Jasper Lloyd, but it wasn't hard to give up on each idea. I was through. Though I had not earned it, I was ready to take a day of rest and wait for my end to find me.

It would have been a beautiful Sunday, really, except for the pressing heat. There was not a cloud in the clear blue sky, and there was a little breeze to keep the air from fouling. But the last day of spring seemed like a day in August. It was as if the earth had moved a bit closer to the sun. Would the government be afraid to tell us if such a thing had happened? From my school days I dimly remembered something about the way the earth went around the sun. Would tomorrow be the longest day of the year?

It will be for me, I thought.

I had been sitting in my car for almost an hour, mulling things over and sipping bottles of beer pulled from a tin bucket of ice on the far end of the seat. I thought it might actually be pleasant along the river, maybe on Belle Isle, but I knew that on a Sunday all the decent places to relax on the water would be packed with people, hot and snappish from bumping elbows. And I wasn't feeling sociable. So I just sat there with all the windows down, sat and stared out the windshield and over the rounded hood. Some of the neighborhood kids were blowing off firecrackers, too eager to hold their stash till the Fourth of July. I watched them idly and remembered all the things I had wanted to rip up as a boy.

How will it go? I wondered. Would the whole city go up in flames, or had Sherrill just paid off a bunch of crackers to storm the colored sections of Detroit? I had never given much attention to all the Bible-thumping preachers who'd tried to save me over the years, and so I could not form a picture of the fire and brimstone that seemed impossible to stop. The only smart move left for me was to take the money and sail my old car as far away from the city as I could. But I never went.

I've been playing the sap all along, I thought. *If they need me for the final hand, they can come and find me.*

I fired up the car and slipped it into gear. I pulled away from the curb and held the icy bucket to keep it from falling as I turned the corners and made my way to Eileen's house, two blocks away. I guess I had been intending to drive there all along. She was sitting on the top step of the porch as I came up, her hair tied up with a scarf, wearing a white dress that showed her shoulders. She squinted and tipped her head a bit as I approached.

I sat down near to her, a step lower. For what seemed like a long time, we said nothing. Though it was inching along toward evening already, I thought the sun might burn her pale skin if she continued to sit there. But it seemed unimportant. We did not touch.

Two big sedans rumbled onto the lazy street, one from Campau and one from up the block. They stopped on either side of the street in front of the house. I stood up and stepped down to the walk in alarm as well-dressed colored men poured out of the autos. They walked toward us in a semicircle. I kept my elbows tight to my sides and my hands in my pockets, so it wouldn't be obvious that I'd left the shoulder harness in the car with my revolver.

Horace Jenkins stepped to the front of the men with a businesslike smile. "Beautiful day, wouldn't you say, Mr. Caudill?"

"I'd say it's too hot for this kind of trouble."

"There's no trouble here, Detective. There's no need to look on the dark side of everything that comes your way. You might even say we've arrived with a mind to stave off trouble."

"What's with the mob, then?" I counted eight men altogether, but just a couple of them hard enough to matter.

"We are a group of men who love the Lord, that's all." Jenkins caught Eileen's eye and touched the brim of his pale gray hat. "We've just finished a little business at the church. There is strength in numbers, as they say."

"Where's your little monkey Noggle?"

"We take care of our own," said Jenkins. "Mr. Noggle has had a run of bad luck, as I'm sure you're aware."

"Bad luck, my ass."

"Mr. Caudill, it's the Lord's day. And there is a lady present."

"What do you want here, Jenkins? Does it look like I want to get friendly with you? Do you have a reason for dragging all this riffraff up to the nicer side of town?"

"Mr. Caudill, a little polite conversation wouldn't hurt you. It's the cornerstone of civility. I might ask after your health, as it seems obvious you've had a run of bad luck of your own. But I can see that you are busy, so I'll be brief." Jenkins stepped close to me and spoke softly. "You should have accepted our help earlier," he said.

"I'm listening."

"A few moments ago, I received news that Roger Hardiman was taking his supper alone, just a few blocks from here, at the Pigeon Club, a place I believe the police know well."

"You heard from who?"

"Detective, there are colored folks all throughout this city of ours, cooking, sweeping floors, mending clothes, parking cars. You shouldn't believe that we're any less intelligent or capable than white folks. A skin of color can make a person almost invisible in a way. We hear things, we see things," he said, sweeping his arm broadly. "Just as all the neighbors here peeping through their curtains can see a group of Negro men before you."

"Well," I murmured, "I don't care anything about it."

"I think you do. I think you must care," said Jenkins. "You have family to think of, just like the rest of us."

"Your people—have you heard anything about my nephew?"

"I'm sorry," said Jenkins. "Nothing."

"Well," I said, scrambling for footing in the conversation, "what's your interest in all of this? What's your profit?"

"The future of this city and the condition of race relations are of great concern to me," said Jenkins. "I'd like to leave something for my children to be proud of."

"That's fancy talking," I said. "If you know so much, why don't you go roust Hardiman yourself?"

"We all have a place in this world, Detective. The Lord provides it for us. All we have to do is listen."

I lowered my eye for a moment and considered. Jenkins was right;

I'd have to go after Hardiman, shake him up a little. It was my place to go. It looked like I had the choice: I could lay off chasing Sherrill, quit the force, find some kind of regular work, and see where things went with Eileen. We could make a good start with the money outside the city, where they were putting up cheap little houses on nice plots of land. We could at least make a go at being happy.

But then maybe the unsettled business would continue to eat away at me from the inside, and I'd go early to my grave anyway, hacking up my lungs like Frank Carter. Maybe Sherrill and his cronies would gain enough footing to spread throughout Michigan and Ohio and Indiana and even up into Canada, like a cancer in the heart of the nation that should have been cut out early. Even if I couldn't ever understand the whole tangled story about my father and Lloyd and Sherrill and Frye and Rix, Tommy and Bobby and Thrumm and Jane Hardiman, it seemed clear that I was mixed up in all of it, and reasonably there was no one else who could try to pull the plug on the whole sordid operation. I saw the choice before me: I could pick up now with Eileen and try to leave the troubles behind, or I could get down to the dirty business with Sherrill and Hardiman and probably die in the trying.

In truth there was no such choice. I could not simply choose between settling down with Eileen and chasing after Sherrill. What I had been after all along was a sense of myself as a good man, a whole man. Like any man, I guess, I had always understood at the back of my mind that there was such a thing as right and wrong. I had put off the decision to fall to the good side for too long. Now that time and misfortune had taken my youth, the task for me had become perhaps too great. But there was no choice for me; I could not rest anywhere unless I found a way to feel comfortable in my own skin.

"I don't know what's going to happen," I said quietly.

"Nobody does," Jenkins said. "There's still time. The trick of living is never to give up."

I turned my back to Jenkins and looked toward Eileen. She stood atop the porch with her feet close together and her arms crossed over her chest. She looked down coldly on the lot of us. I managed to get my feet up a few of the steps and leaned close to her.

"You should lock your doors," I said weakly.

"Why should it matter now?"

"It's a new moon tonight," I said. "Bad luck."

She did not seem angry exactly, but it was clear that she wanted to close herself off from me. I turned slowly from her, and my feet began to trudge back down the steps.

"Pete," she said, catching the shoulder of my jacket—Tommy's jacket. She pressed her lips quickly to my scratchy cheek. She whispered into my ear, "He's all I have in this world, Pete."

"I know it," I said. I thought—for an instant—that maybe I could make up for the loss of her only son with the remainder of the money Lloyd had given me. The idea shamed me so much that I felt my face go red. I was dirty, I was crooked, I was ugly, sometimes I felt sick in the head. I tried to take another step away from her, but she held fast to the jacket.

She hissed into my ear, *You're already a good man.*

I stepped down to the walk until I was close to Jenkins and his gang.

"You won't see it," Eileen called after me.

"You'll have to go on out of here," I said to Jenkins. "I can't leave her here with all of you."

Jenkins measured his response. "We're not animals, Mr. Caudill."

It was true; as I looked over the colored gang standing before me, I could see that they each carried their own share of worry and trouble.

"Fair enough," I said. "But you're still strangers to me."

"We'll take our leave, then," said Jenkins.

They turned and slipped into the cars. After they had gone, I walked slowly to my own car and drove off without looking back at Eileen.

As Johnson and I sat sweating in my car outside the Pigeon Club, the baking sun brought up a stench of stale beer from all the bottles rolling on the floor.

"Think we should just walk in?"

"Don't think about eating now, Johnson," I said. I had with some regret pulled the young man from the safety of his grandmother's house just as he sat down to an enormous supper.

Johnson grinned. "I bet they have some good eats in there. Good booze, too." He shot a sidewise glance at me. "If you go for that sort of thing."

"There's a ham sandwich in the glove box," I said.

Johnson opened the box, rummaged around, and pulled out the mason jar that I had placed there. He held it up to the light, his face blank and uncomprehending. The dark genitals swirled slowly, inches from his face. When he finally understood what he was holding, Johnson's hand shook a little and he placed the jar gently on the dash.

"Jesus, Detective, is that what you did to Pease?"

"It ain't Pease. I got an early Christmas present. Just put it back in the box." I felt like I had worked out enough banter for the day. We had been waiting almost an hour for Hardiman to appear. I squinted first at the red brick of the Pigeon Club, warm and orange in the low sun, and then at Hardiman's gleaming Lloyd Cruiser, parked by the valet just a few steps from the door. The place had been a speakeasy in the old days, one of the untouchable speaks reserved for the mayor and his cronies, the auto barons and their robber friends, steel

and rail magnates visiting from New York, Chicago, or Pittsburgh. I
had been inside it just once, when a patron had stabbed a cigarette
girl with a fork after she had slapped him, stabbed her twice in her
fat thigh. There was a tremendous ruckus before I managed to settle
it by squeezing five dollars from the patron for the girl. By the time I
left, the girl was back on the man's lap, pressing a napkin daintily
onto her punctures.

Finally Hardiman sauntered out. He pulled out sunglasses against
the brightness and snapped his fingers for an attendant. Though I
didn't figure Hardiman for a big tipper, the boy jumped up and ran
back to the big Cruiser, really just a few steps away. I heard the engine roar to life and then saw the gleaming black auto pull to the
stoop before the club. Hardiman got in and pulled the boat out into
the street.

I followed for a block or two. I was not sure that Hardiman would
pull over if I set out the flasher and used the siren. If he ran, it would
attract too much attention to a questionable stop; besides, my old
jalopy might not be able to keep up with the powerful roadster. But
after Hardiman's car washed around the corner and turned east, I
decided to risk it. I pulled up close to the rear bumper, set the flasher
on the dashboard, and cranked the siren briefly. Hardiman pulled
over.

I saw the door open a crack and Hardiman's glossy wing tip drop
to the pavement. "Go get him, Johnson. I don't want him to see me
just yet."

"Wh-what should I say?"

"Dammit, Johnson, just go!"

Johnson was in his street clothes but had remembered to bring
along his badge. He hurried out of the car and stopped Hardiman's ar-
rogant rush. I knew Hardiman wouldn't be able to see me, because the
sun was shining right on the back of my head. Since it was Sunday, all
the shops lining the street were closed and the street was empty

except for a few stray cars. I popped the leather strap that held my revolver in the shoulder rig.

Johnson wasn't doing well. I saw from the postures of the two
men that he was getting the short end of it. Hardiman tipped back
his head and let out a big laugh; his white teeth flashed. In an instant,
Johnson tipped his shoulder, swiveled his hips, and slammed a neat
uppercut just under Hardiman's ribs.

I scrambled from the car. "Jesus Christ, Johnson, what are you doing?" Hardiman heaved and gasped, doubled over, trying to get back
the breath Johnson's punch had stolen.

"He was getting funny with me." Johnson stood like a skinny
rooster, defiant and angry, unsure of his footing.

"I can handle the rough end," I said. *Still,* I thought, *that punch was
a little something, right on the money.*

Hardiman managed a hoarse whisper. "You're through in this
town, both of you. Do you know what they do to cops in the slam-
mer?"

"Any idea what they do with fellows who like little girls?" I asked.
"And don't think I don't know the rest of it."

"You've got nothing on me," said Hardiman, leveling his gaze at
me behind his glasses. "Because I haven't done anything."

I backhanded the sunglasses from Hardiman's pale, leering face,
putting some knuckle into it. "You're through talking, Hardiman. I'm
through and I know it. That means I can do whatever I want now. I
can piss on whoever I want and get away with it, just like you."

"You can't do anything to—"

I pulled the mason jar from my coat pocket and brought it
sharply to the side of Hardiman's head, shattering it and dousing
him with formaldehyde. The rubbery genitals bounced down from
his shoulders and off his hands as he brought them up. When they hit
the pavement, they wiggled a bit and stopped against Hardiman's
shoe. He kicked them away.

"What the hell is this?" he sputtered.

"That's Pease's balls, just like you wanted," I said. "Now where's my money?"

"You can't—I'm not giving you any money, you—"

I backhanded him again, spraying formaldehyde in a glittering halo. "I told you not to talk any more, see?" I looked around and saw that cars were beginning to slow as they passed. "Johnson," I said, "do you know offhand if formaldehyde is flammable?"

Hardiman's face, already pale, went green, and his eyes seemed to shrink back into his face.

"Should I get some matches from the car?" Johnson made a step.

"That's all right for now, Johnson, I was just thinking. Now you," I said, pulling my revolver discreetly from the rig and stepping close to Hardiman, "you get in and sit behind the wheel. We're taking a little trip." I nudged Hardiman toward the black roadster, shouldered him toward the door. "Johnson, you sit up front with Mr. Nothing, here."

We all got into Hardiman's car, me in back, directly behind the driver's seat. Hardiman started the engine with trembling hands and pulled away from the curb.

"I don't mind shooting you," I said. "Later I probably will. But I was thinking that it might be nice to find Jasper Lloyd and try to hash out this mess, just the three of us. I don't suppose you'd know where he is?"

Hardiman was looking me over in the rearview mirror. I wasn't sure if he could see my gun, but I know he felt it pressed to the back of his neck.

"Mr. Lloyd takes his rest on Sundays," he said. "He often takes a cruise along the river in the evening."

"Get moving, then," I said. "It's worth something to me to hear how you'll try to smooth it all over with Lloyd."

Hardiman said nothing. He drove slowly through the downtown

area along Jefferson with both hands on the wheel, glancing now and again in the side mirror. Each time he stopped at an intersection, I leaned forward and pressed the nose of my revolver to the side of his neck. To our right, past the tall buildings of the downtown area and then the cool streets of the swanky side of town, we caught glimpses of the Detroit River rolling along. It felt like we were heading against the current, heading upstream to spawn.

"If Lloyd isn't on the boat, Hardiman, this'll be your last stop. Like you say, I'm through. If you're yanking my dick here, I'll just figure the game is up and I'll put a slug in you. Nobody knows anything about Johnson. He can just slip out and get clean of it. The thing is, I'm tired. Dog-tired. If the Old Man's there, we'll hash things out real nice. Otherwise, you'll get it good, wherever we happen to be."

"He'll be there," said Hardiman. "Sunday is his day of rest and leisure, so to say."

"I wouldn't figure the Old Man to be up this late," said Johnson.

"Maybe he doesn't sleep well," I said.

"He doesn't sleep at all," said Hardiman.

As we approached the foot of the Belle Isle Bridge, all the foot traffic, cars, and buses snarled things up, so the going got slow. I noted that Hardiman scanned the crowd in the uneven light, hoping for a cop or a familiar face. As we made the turn onto the bridge, I leaned forward and kept close. I whispered to Hardiman, "I hope it doesn't cost too much to mop up your place out on the lake. Messy business it was."

Though the Belle Isle Yacht Club was not far from the bridge, it took Hardiman some time to navigate to the guardhouse at the end of the drive. Enormous crowds spilled onto both sides of the bridge, streaming homeward, hoping for a seat on the last of the streetcars and buses. Hardiman hugged the wheel as he drove through the largely colored crowd, his eyes wide. Nearby and in the distance, firecrackers popped loudly, pushing waves of pedestrians against the panels of the creeping car. I kept low in the backseat and watched the jostling crowds, noticing, too, the small clots of white picnickers huddling along.

Maybe, I thought, *I'm coming down with something. It can't be this hot, not even July yet. And the sun already down.*

The guard at the gate seemed to recognize Hardiman's car and lifted the flimsy wooden barrier to let us pass. Most of the boats were smaller pleasure craft and a few larger fishing boats. Towering above them, at the end of its specially built pier, Lloyd's yacht swayed slowly and pulled at the creaking pilings. Hardiman pulled the Cruiser into a spot marked RESERVED and cut the engine. He put his hands in his lap and hung his head.

"Give Johnson the keys," I said.

Hardiman did not move, so Johnson pulled the keys and slipped them in his pocket.

"If he isn't here," I said, "I'm going to have Johnson drop off a little package down to the newspaper office, so everybody can get a clear picture of you after you're gone."

"He's here," said Hardiman. "And you don't need to act like you have anything on me. I know how things are as far as the newspapers are concerned."

I held the revolver in the pocket of my jacket. I got out. I opened Hardiman's door and pulled him out by the collar of his jacket. Johnson moved to get out, too.

"Keep still, Johnson."

"I should come, too, Pete. You can see that's reasonable."

"Listen, Johnson, I don't need lip from you, too. I get the feeling our boy is lying to me, and I don't want you to be involved in what I do to him if he is. You sit here, and if there's a ruckus, you plug whoever comes down off of that boat, if it ain't me. You plug 'em or you get the hell out. I'll leave it up to you. You follow me?"

"I follow you." Johnson turned away and looked at the yacht, which was lit from within, like many of the other boats, and quiet.

"C'mon, Hardiman, let's get it over with." My mouth wanted something substantial, some good Scotch or rye whiskey, something to clean out the cotton. "It's been a long couple days."

I kept Hardiman in front as we walked onto the docks. We passed through a wrought-iron gate that led to Lloyd's private pier and stopped at an ornate stepstool leading onto the deck. As Hardiman's foot touched the stool, the inboard motors rumbled to life and sputtered in the water. I rushed up and tossed Hardiman onto the deck, then jumped up after him. I cranked my head toward the captain's chair up top but saw nothing. I pulled the pistol from my pocket, pressed against the cabin wall, and trained my eye to the fore end of the yacht.

"You should have searched me, you fool," Hardiman hissed, scrambling to his feet behind me. "You'd better believe I'm a good shot, even with this little thing. I never miss. So I guess you better hand that pistol over."

I slowly turned my good eye toward him and weighed the situation. Hardiman held a lady's gun, a little derringer with two barrels, and pointed it with remarkable steadiness at my neck.

"Hand it over, you pig."

I let the revolver dangle from my finger in the trigger guard, then moved it to my left hand and held it by the barrel. I reached to offer it to Hardiman, then gave a flip and tossed it onto the pier. It bounced and splashed into the water. There was a tremor in Hardiman's hand.

"It wouldn't be right to let you kill me with my own gun," I said.

"Just shut up and toss off the ropes," muttered Hardiman.

"Do it yourself." I turned to face him.

Hardiman adjusted his aim mechanically and fired without hesitation. He wasn't aiming to kill me; I was surprised to see the flash and let out a burst of air when the slug tore into the meat of my shoulder. I ducked down and hustled toward the front of the yacht. Though the report hadn't been particularly loud, Johnson had heard it and now scrambled from the car.

The engines roared and the yacht lurched forward, snapping the fore piling and dragging the aft piling and half the back end of the pier into the Detroit River. The pilings slipped through the looped ends of the lines and swirled off into the current. The yacht made a tight turn upriver, gaining speed quickly and washing up a tremendous wake over the seawall and onto the outdoor dining patio of the Yacht Club. My hard soles slipped over the deck as I scrambled to evade Hardiman. My brow smashed against the polished rail as my feet fell out from under me. Glancing back, I saw that Hardiman, too, had fallen. I held the rail with both hands and lurched forward. I had made it almost to the prow when I found myself staring into the double barrel of Barton Rix's shotgun.

CHAPTER 19

Barton Rix kept his legs spread wide to keep his footing on the slippery deck. He aimed the shotgun from his belly and leered at me.

"Should've come for me when you had the chance, nigger lover," he said. "A gimp has to take every advantage he can get."

I said nothing but steadied myself and slowly stood upright as the craft settled. We were heading upriver at a good clip, toward Lake St. Clair. I knew how much of a man's flesh a shotgun could remove, even with a bad shot, and so I made no move to escape.

"Climb on in," said Rix, tipping the gun toward the stairs to the interior.

I stepped down slowly into the boat's burnished brass and dark wood interior cabin. Though the electric lights were dim, I saw the two colored boatmen dead on the floor. In the alcove leading to a little galley, I saw a pair of feet indicating another body—Carter?—lying facedown. On a settee along the cabin wall, in white Sunday clothes and with his hands trussed before him, sat Jasper Lloyd. He was chewing on his lips so furiously that his goat-beard pointed wildly around the cabin. Rix used his foot to shove me to a seat beside the old man. Then he sat on a stool and leaned back on the chart table, holding the shotgun loosely with one arm. Hardiman scrambled in after us, huffing and beet red with anger.

"What's it all about, Rix?" I said. "This seems like more work than you're used to doing."

"I work better when I like what I'm doing," said Rix.

"The pay is good," rasped Lloyd. "That's what it all comes down to."

"You're the businessman here, old man. You'd sell your sister for a buck. You got niggers working for you makin' more than I ever made."

"What frightens you most, Mr. Rix, is the idea that a Negro man might be superior to you. It's natural to be afraid when you are in a position of weakness. Young David, here," said Lloyd, nodding toward one of the dead cabin boys, "was working for me to earn money for college."

"Old man," said Rix, "if you keep talking, you can die gut-shot." He stood up and pointed the barrel at Lloyd's gut. "Same for you, Caudill. You got born into the wrong family, I guess—born to lose, the whole lot of you."

I could not think of a reason why I had not yet been killed. Even if Hardiman's little pistol shot had not drawn any attention with all the fireworks going off on the island, the wrecked pier would surely draw some heat on the river, after the dimwits at the Yacht Club figured out what had happened. So there was some sense of urgency to the situation, and I, unbound, could only be seen as a threat.

"What's that stench, Hardiman? Some fancy French perfume?" asked Rix. "You're riling up my asthma."

"Formaldehyde, I believe. You'll have to ask our malformed

friend here, the one with the bullet through his shoulder." Anger and activity lit up Hardiman's pretty face with a glow.

I had forgotten about the wound, and at Hardiman's words I bent my head to examine my shoulder. It was to the bad side, so I had to crane my neck painfully to get a look. I did not see Rix raise the shotgun. In the enclosed cabin, the blast slapped painfully in my ears. I looked up and then quickly away as blood and disintegrated flesh splattered from Hardiman's face. The spray touched everything in a radius around him, wet and warm on my cheek and neck, brightly speckling Lloyd's white suit. Hardiman fell backward to the floor like a boxer already out for the count after a haymaker, his arms gently rising.

The violent scene gave new life to Rix's pale cornflower blue eyes. He let his breath out through clenched teeth.

"First and foremost," said Rix, turning the shotgun to me, "a man should look after his own. A man that don't take care of his family can't ever be trusted to go the right way. You can't turn your back to him."

Hardiman still writhed on the floor. I hoped Rix's aim would be better in my own case. Most of the lower part of Hardiman's face was gone, and he seemed to be struggling to understand what had happened to him. He sat up somehow, his one remaining eye turning wildly about. He was alert, but I knew that the blood coursing out of his open neck would shortly drain all the life from him.

Rix turned the shotgun back to Hardiman, but I knew he could not fire again because the gun held only two shells, and he would need the last one for me. He put his face closer to Hardiman and grinned. "How's that feel? Think you've got enough money to buy yourself out of this one?"

Hardiman rolled his eye up at Rix like a baby just learning to see. His chest heaved, his throat sputtered, and his fingers were doing a little dance.

I watched with great interest. I had seen dead men with similar wounds—but Hardiman was still alive and moving. The bright red blood and the exposed muscle and bone of his face and neck made his inner workings visible for that moment, and he seemed like a puppet.

"Just lay down, shit-packer," said Rix. "This time you lose. Did you think the Colonel would let you get away with doing something like that to your own daughter? What kind of a man would slip the pecker to his own little girl?" He lifted his foot to Hardiman's chest and tipped him over. "Not so pretty now, lover boy?"

"You're no better," I said. "Your men did worse to her."

Rix turned his attention back to me. His face had gone almost purple-red, and the whites of his eyes were as yellow as his teeth. "I'll give you that much. I never understood why the Colonel let Frye go on so long. Well, you cleaned up that little mess for us, didn't you? Between you and Lady Hardiman, you're about to put me out of work."

He walked back to his place near the map table and tried to mop up his sweaty face with his shirtsleeve. "Look here, Caudill. You got it in your head that what we're doing is wrong—but you don't think it through. I don't call it wrong to protect my way of living. You got no kids. You got no stake in how things turn out, see? You're walking through your days like an animal, and you're happy if you got a job and something to eat. You take the easy way through everything. Well, you've run out of people to do your thinking for you."

He turned away from me like I was making him sick and then looked down at Hardiman. "Listen, Hardiman, say hello to Caudill's old man when you get down there. See if he's still sore about you selling him out."

I felt the yacht make a slow turn back downstream. Then the throttle cut back and we stood almost silent, carried slowly by the current back toward Belle Isle. Through the hatch from above dropped a big canvas bag, flat-bottomed and gate-mouthed, like a mechanic might use to carry his tools. It landed heavily, though, without any crash of jangling metal. After a moment, with his cane crooked over his elbow, Sherrill struggled down the ladder.

"Get up there, Rix, and don't go until you hear the shots." He pulled out a big nickel-plated Colt and turned it toward me. "This is Frank Carter's gun," he said. "I'll tell you one thing: That man had a little pride in him before he died. He was a simpleton, but at least he knew something about loyalty. You should be proud to be shot with such a man's weapon."

Rix stood for a moment at the base of the ladder, trying to figure out how to carry the shotgun to the upper deck. Finally he broke the gun open and climbed up with the stock held between his cheek and shoulder.

"How much is in the bag?" I asked.

"Money," sputtered Lloyd. "That's what all this is worth. If you would have come to me, I could have sent you away with that much, or more, and we could have moved on like businessmen."

"If money were all I yearned after," said Sherrill, "I might have. But what I wanted was to make sure that everybody knew who wrecked this great city. What a stomach you must have to see them already naming libraries and schools after you. The Greeks called that *hubris*. You've allowed a plague of Negroes and Communists and moral degenerates to fester here, and it's my task to make you pay for it."

Lloyd said bitterly, "You picture yourself the hero in an epic tragedy."

"I expect no bard to sing of my long labor," Sherrill said. He seemed small and infirm, and his dim eyes were blinking and distorted behind his thick glasses. "And they'll not sing of you, as I have my way in the matter. I could unfold a tale to make you see how your name will turn to dust—but time draws short. You'll not see your beloved city as it burns tonight, Mr. Lloyd. But—do not doubt my word—after you're gone, your name will accept the proper burden of shame for what you've done."

"My only shame is that I could not rid the world of you before now," Lloyd said.

"True shame and humility seem to have expired from the earth," said Sherrill. "A pity. Yet I ask no pardon for the bit of money I reserve for myself. Perhaps it will be enough to secure a place where I can dwindle out my days—if there's still a place on this earth where a man can live without having to see a Negro scratching his backside every time he looks out his window."

I knew Sherrill would fire first at me, and I tried to judge whether the windy bastard had said his piece. I figured I could at least try to rush him, and maybe give Lloyd a chance to hop over the rail. But the settee was deep and soft, and it would take some doing to get off of it.

"I'll ask you once, Caudill. Would you care to sign up with us? Frankly, I'd rather have you about than Rix. You're more industrious. You lack only direction."

I stared dully at him; I had given up, I guess, and I felt so tired that I wasn't sure if my legs would move if I wanted them to. In a peculiar way, the sight of him hanging on to the satchel for his life made me feel sorry for him. But then I thought, *Alex is out there somewhere. Sherrill has his hooks in him.*

I asked, "What's your aim here?"

"My aim is to settle this Negro problem once and for all, to kindle the final flame here and now, so this nation can go on to the greatness God intended for her. Now, I don't expect that the Negro race will just lay down, but I'll swear by all that's mine, the last man standing will be a white man."

"Did you think I would sign up after all of this?"

"No, I suppose not. But you do seem to have a touching concern for your family. And I had hoped that you might have an eye for the future." He looked about the cabin with some melancholy. "I regret that the newspapers will make you out to be a villain in all of this mess. We had intended to blame the Negroes for Mr. Lloyd's death—but once again you disrupt our plan. Fortunately, you'll do nicely as a substitute scapegoat. Our men in the newspapers will write it up to seem—"

He was interrupted by the sound of a painfully raspy cough from the steps leading to the aft deck. There was a clink of metal and the sound of heavy rope sliding.

"God damn you, Carter, you yellow bastard! Can't you stay dead!" Rix bellowed from above. The shotgun kicked and blasted. "Colonel, he's at the hand-winch! He's letting the dinghy go! We'll be stuck here!" After a moment, the shotgun fired a second time.

Sherrill raked his head back and forth between the stairs to the aft deck, Lloyd, and me, and you could see that his old mind wasn't working so fast. He knew it would take time for Rix to get down from above, and I guess he also had to consider whether he had time to plug Lloyd and me properly before he had to step out to try to catch the dinghy rope. Maybe he even thought of dropping the satchel; but presently, with a crazy look in his eye and the wattles of his neck pulling at his collar, he lugged the satchel out the back to see what he could do.

I heard the little boat splash behind the yacht. I must have sat there for a moment with my eyebrows raised, but then I got up and pulled Lloyd after me up the fore stairs. Out on the deck, I looked up and saw Rix glaring down. The shotgun was open, and Rix was snapping the last of two shells into the breach. He closed the gun.

I lifted Lloyd up and tossed him over the rail. And then, as Rix leveled the gun at me, I dropped over the rail myself. The water of the Detroit River struck like a fastball low on the handle. Though the weather had been unbearably hot, it was still too early in the season for the water to be warm. The murky water frightened me more than the barrel of Rix's gun; at least with the gun, you could see it coming. I did not swim well.

I saw Lloyd's head bobbing and guessed the old man was doing a breaststroke or a modified dog paddle, heading for the city, making for the naval station at the foot of the bridge. *They mean for the navy boys to come out blasting niggers because of all this,* I thought. I turned and swam as well as I could for the lights I took to be Belle Isle, still some distance downstream. I thrashed across the current, hoping to catch the island before I was swept downriver. I knew Hardiman's little bullet had passed into my back and had settled at the edge of my shoulder blade because I could feel it tearing every time I stretched forward. I could not feel any pellets from Rix's shot.

From the yacht I heard shouting. I did not look back, but I guessed that Rix and Sherrill were arguing on the top deck. The engines cut back and rumbled and sputtered. Then they kicked up again, and I did not need to look to know that the yacht was headed my way. I veered left, more sharply toward the island, and sucked in a deep breath when I felt the craft drawing near. I dived under as well as I could, but still the hull knocked me deeper as it passed over. The blast from the inboards tore open my shirt and spun me around under the water. Though the big yacht could not have managed more than fifteen knots in such a short run, the weight of it in the shallow water churned up enough silt and pebbles to score my face.

I flailed under the water for a moment in a panic and then forced myself to keep still until the stale air in my bursting lungs could show me the way to the surface. When I began to rise, I stroked my way to the open air, my lungs feeling brittle, about to crack like glass. I sucked in air and water and coughed and choked as I resumed my swimming to the island. The yacht had turned hard away and now came around for another pass. Once again, I let myself go under. The rush of the boat's displacement pulled me more quickly along in the current, and I soon made the island. As I pulled myself through the cattails near the wrecked pier of the Yacht Club, I turned to see that Lloyd's yacht now circled crazily on the water and appeared to be heading for the bridge. I reached more solid ground, found my feet, and crashed through the cattails onto the grassy slope. Hacking up water and mucus and algae and solid bits of something, I staggered toward the fenced-in parking lot of the Yacht Club and climbed over.

Hardiman's car was still there, surrounded now by a small crowd of well-dressed gawkers, wondering at the damage done to the pier by Lloyd's yacht. They stared at me as I trotted past but said nothing and made no move to stop me. There was no sign of Johnson, so I ran through the lot and past the guardhouse. I made it out to the street, which was dense with tired picnickers. Struggling toward the bridge on jellied legs, I heard shouts of surprise and female screams ahead of me as the yacht came up to the bridge. It was too tall in the water, and I heard metal scraping as the high running lights and the glass windscreen broke off on the underside of the bridge. I pushed through the crowd frantically, bulling my way through throngs pushing back to Belle Isle; the panicked civilians ran crazily from the yacht, as if it might knock down the bridge.

Hands clawed at me and slight fists smacked into me. But I kept on. Over the heads of the swirling crowd, I saw Sherrill come up suddenly over the rail of the bridge, clutching his satchel, pushed up roughly by Rix, who appeared soon after. Sherrill gained his feet and began to limp toward the land end of the bridge. Rix followed and bowled over a colored woman holding a bundled baby in her arms. She fell and fell hard, turning onto her back as she went to cushion the fall for the baby. As I passed her, she was groaning and stamping her feet in pain on the paved surface of the bridge, and the baby was squawking in alarm. The river's strong, slow current and the yacht's rumbling inboards pushed the craft screeching under the bridge, bobbing and crunching on its own wake until it came through to the other side. Then it cruised peacefully, slowly, down the river.

I fought my way forward, careening between groups of blindly lashing young colored men with their dates and families. Over the hump of the bridge, I saw a lone mounted officer trying to control the tumult in the broad, open area along Jefferson at the foot of Grand Boulevard. As I drew closer, I could see the mare's frantic eyes and the tightness of her neck, the bobbing, half-rearing panic. The officer had given up on the crowd and now tried just to calm the horse, to turn her toward the wide boulevard. Rix and the hobbling Sherrill reached the center of the crowd. They pulled the officer from the horse, and he disappeared from my view. A moment later, Sherrill came up onto the saddle, still clutching his satchel somehow, holding it between his legs, hunched over it. He whipped the mare's flanks with his thin cane.

By this time I had ripped off my jacket and my torn shirt, and I plowed bare-chested through the crowd, pale and hairy in the lights of the bridge. I found that people were beginning to get out of my way. Rix stood waiting for me with his feet planted, blood streaming over one side of his face from a gash on his forehead. When he saw me, he smiled and winked, drawing blood into his eye. Even in the riotous crowd, a circle cleared around him.

Before I could reach him, though, a very large Negro came up on Rix's blind side and brought down a big bear's paw to the side of his head. Rix went down but sprang up and onto the larger man, looping wide blows to his head. I ran up and beyond them, wheezing now from the effort, buzzing from draining adrenaline. I saw Sherrill on the horse about fifty yards ahead and continued to plow through the crowd toward him.

Sherrill might have made it past the thickest part of the crowd and out of the mess entirely. Instead he sat high in the saddle and looked around him. He spied a tight group of colored men gathered on the east corner of the boulevard and turned the mare toward them. With a quick twist, he opened the cane and drew out a slender blade and began to slash madly about him as he drove the horse into the group.

Sherrill whipped the silvery blade into the group of colored men. They cringed at first but then drew close as they realized that Sherrill was doing little harm. The horse felt itself closed in and reared up; and as it did, Sherrill dropped from the saddle down into the furious gang. They parted to let the horse go but quickly came together over Sherrill, swinging wildly, kicking and tearing at the frail old man. In a moment, a roar went up as the satchel ripped open, sending a plume of bills into the air.

I took a long look around me. Already, on every side of me, fistfights were breaking out, and small groups rushed past, some heading for the fights, some away. A number of white-suited navy men were rushing up the little hill toward the foot of the bridge, all white men spoiling for a fight. It seemed to happen all at once, flaming up in pockets along every angle of my vision. I bent over and put my hands on my knees and tried to suck in enough air to satisfy myself.

Walking down Jefferson toward the heart of the city, I felt cool for the first time in weeks. I was bare to the waist, and the dirty water of the Detroit River had almost dried from my trousers. Gusts of rioting men and boys blew by me, scrambling in and out of alleys and doorways and racing down the middle of the roadway. None of it seemed to touch me. I wondered idly how a man might go about setting fire to such a great building as the Penobscot. It would take something to get it going.

The only fires I saw burned in upended trashcans, splashing sparks whenever a car whipped by. Rioters seemed to spring up from everywhere and came from all directions. They threw or carried bricks, bats, chains, pipes, whatever they could pick up, like a cleaning crew gone mad, cut loose from everything. The stores and shops close to the street lost their windows, but only the ones at ground level, as if the cost of doing a thorough job meant missing too much action. A car now and then found an open stretch on Jefferson and squealed away, but for the most part the street was blocked by clogs of rioters. Groups of men and a few women huddled together as if to make one bigger animal, taunting and provoking other groups. Squealing, screaming, the low sobs of disbelief from the injured passing by me, blaring car horns, the occasional pop and splash of a shattered window, all of it came together like hissing in my ears.

I was walking, strolling really, down the middle of the westbound side of Jefferson, heading generally toward the real downtown, where the tall buildings made it seem like you were in a kind of hard forest. I knew well that I was steering myself toward the tightest part of Black Bottom, where I surely did not want to be walking. But I kept on, and I began to feel a chill from the wind off the river. I realized that I had lost my eye patch somewhere along the way. I pictured it hooked onto the skull of some unlucky bootlegger at the bottom of the river, fallen through the ice on a winter run to Canada. I didn't miss it, and the coolness made me feel as comfortable as I could ever remember feeling. The bottoms of my bare feet drew some warmth from the pavement.

I thought with a sudden sinking of my heart that it would be good to have my brother Tommy walking along with me, as we had done as boys so long ago. It would be good to have something to lean against. There was so much I wanted to tell him. After a moment of thought, and with a shrug of resignation, I thought that it would be good to have our father along, too. All of us walking abreast down the middle of the street, our own little group; surely we'd pass with no trouble. Maybe Bobby could tag along as well, an overeager mascot, trotting on ahead. *And curse me down to hell,* I thought, *if it wouldn't be nice to have old Toby Thrumm along, too. That poor nigger saved my life.*

My watery chest heaved for breath as I thought of my two dead girls, little sister Eliza and Jane Hardiman. They could not have met in life, but now I pictured them walking hand in hand somewhere, in a world where babies and girls could grow up safe and healthy and happy. With all of us watching over them—my father, my brother, my friends... I wondered briefly if all that kind of thinking meant I was already dead, doomed to walk half-naked for eternity through the streets of the city I'd lived in all my life.

Behind me a car revved and squealed, leaning on the horn so much that its sound had faded to a strangled squawk. When it drew close, I meandered toward the edge of the roadway to give it room to pass. I glanced at the old Negro driver clutching the wheel and then wandered back to my old path after it had passed. The sagging jalopy made it another block in fits and starts, stopping and threatening to stall every few feet. *He doesn't have the sense to turn up from Jefferson and onto a side street,* I thought. *Why doesn't he just get out of this?*

A block ahead of me, the jalopy stopped for good when a swarm of white boys surrounded it and began hitting and kicking at the windows. When the windows were gone, I could see that the punks were trying to drag the colored occupants out the windows. They pulled one out the passenger side, but the old driver stuck tight. They began to rock the car, surging on one side until they could lift it up and over. In all the excitement, the passenger broke free and hightailed it up the street toward Black Bottom. As the car tipped all the way over onto its roof, part of the gang split off and chased after the colored boy.

Though my legs felt numb, I picked up and started to trot after them. I kept to the balls of my feet to keep from slapping on the hard pavement. I passed the gang at the car and saw the runners far ahead of me, still holding to Jefferson. There was no hope of catching them, I knew, until they caught the poor nigger at the front. But I kept on, my legs warming somewhat, loosening up. The air I sucked into my lungs felt humid, heavy with river moisture.

They caught up to the boy and brought him down like a pack of dogs, snarling around him and dragging him to the ground. To my bleary eye, it looked like a fizzy smear on the street. I drew closer, my chest heaving, sharply painful.

I bowled through the boys at the edge of the fray, slamming them from behind with heavy forearms. Then I began to swat away the boys closer in, knocking them silly with quick pokes to the backs of their heads. As I made it to the tight ball of writhing boys at the center, I peeled them off one by one, spinning each away onto the sidewalk and street. Had they been men instead of boys, they might have regrouped and overwhelmed me from behind; but they picked themselves up and stood trembling in fright and anger and disbelief.

When I worked my way down to the last white boy, I found him clutching the colored boy in a desperate hug, trying to ward off the hail of blows that had fallen on him, too. I sank my fingers sharply into the back of the white boy's neck and grabbed one wrist, and then I pried him loose and lifted him, tossed him to one side. We're like animals, there's no denying it; when I had my hands on that last white boy, *I knew that I was touching Alex.* I knew without seeing his face that I was laying hands on someone who shared my own blood.

The colored boy was battered beyond recognition, bloodied and torn up but not yet swollen. His front teeth had been pushed in and hung toward the back of his throat in his open mouth. His knees had been drawn up and now lay out on either side almost to the sidewalk, and his arms lay out from his body like a bird fallen from the nest. I could not tell, with the blood pounding in my temples and in my ears, if he drew breath. His eyes were rolled up in his head, showing just the whites under fluttering lids. A wide swath of blood glistened against the dark brown skin below his smashed-in nose, brilliant red under the streetlight.

I slipped my bad hand gently under the boy's head and searched delicately for a caved-in place on the skull. Finding none, I slipped my hand down around his neck and far enough down his back to get a good grip. With my other arm I gathered up the spindly knees and brought them together. It was like lifting a bundle of cracked sticks, nothing but bones and a bit of soft, loose flesh holding it together. I could not tell if the boy was living or if he had a chance of making it. I looked around to find my bearings and sank with dismay as I realized how far it was to Receiving Hospital.

Some of the gang had moved on, and the rest kept a healthy distance from me, forming a ring around me, not threatening but momentarily shocked into inaction. I flipped the boy's limp arm inward and held him over my chest. Then I started to take a step onto the curb.

Staring out at me from the shadow of a doorway, I saw my only nephew, Alex, crouching with one hand braced on the ground. Though his body was closed tight on itself, his eyes glared so that he might have been a gargoyle. Anger, anger, and beyond it the pale blue terror of the world opening up under his feet. Alex's face began to twist up with the crush of old, old emotion; he seemed about to crack into a leering grimace, teeth gritting, lips quivering.

The colored boy's broken body felt warm against my bare chest. I felt my own bowels shake; I felt my lungs fighting against the still air and felt that I would never again draw an adequate breath. I could not let go of the colored boy, but I would have fallen to my knees, I would have gone down on my belly and pressed my forehead to the cold cement in front of Alex, if only my frozen legs would have let me. There before me was what I had been hoping for all along, the promise of home and family—but I could not attain it. No shred of pride left in me would have prevented me from sobbing and begging Alex to come home; but I could not choose to abandon the colored boy, who deserved his chance at life. I saw something break in Alex, saw it come over his whole body at once: His lips pressed desperately together and his chin twitched as he jerked upright and turned away. Finally I did fall to my knees as the strength in me gave out, and I watched Alex run away toward the black heart of Detroit, disappearing into the night and the smoke.

CHAPTER

20

Sunday, July 11

Someone had been by to cut my lawn, I noticed. Probably the boy next door. He hadn't raked, though, and three weeks' worth of grass lay dry and yellow over the neatly clipped lawn. It was hot, but not so rudely hot as it had been on spring's last day. Someone had brought my car over from the street where we had stopped Hardiman, though I knew the keys were probably at the bottom of the Detroit River. I told the cab driver to wait.

The front door was unlocked, as I had left it, and nothing in the interior seemed out of place except for the pile of letters and bills that had been pushed through the mail slot. Because the windows had been left open, the stale smell of the place had dissipated. Still the place felt strange to me, like I had only seen it before in a dream. I stepped through, feeling as if the house had grown smaller and less substantial. There was nothing in the house that I felt I needed to carry with me. On a shelf at the top of the closet in my room, the box that held my few important papers seemed untouched, as did the shoebox with my small collection of family photographs. When I had satisfied myself that Alex had not somehow hidden himself away there, I walked out of the house and ducked into the cab.

I felt clean in the light new jacket and the crisp shirt I wore. Fresh from the box; I looked down and pressed my hand over the creases on the white cloth. My feet felt smaller in my shoes. I got in the cab and liked it, liked the feel of it, liked the tattered upholstery and the smeared signature on the driver's license in its little case. I liked the crank that let me roll the window down.

I made the driver roll around the city for a while. Cadillac Square, the Campus Martius, where, I had heard, troops had lately been marching. Down Woodward, down Cass Avenue, past the big library, where the trampled lawn told the tale: tents and marches, bored National Guard reserves loafing and smoking. Everything else looked the same, more or less, in the white part of town. We drove down to Jefferson and up to the boulevard, past the bridge to Belle Isle. I saw no sign of the tipped cars, and the spilled blood had washed away or dried and turned to dust by now. The glaziers had been busy; almost all the broken windows I had seen had been replaced. I knew that the riot had been real but felt it might as well have been a nightmare, a common nightmare for everyone that night and into the days that followed. Outwardly everything was the same.

It was a different story in Black Bottom and Paradise Valley. I could see that many of the stores had been looted and trashed, the big windows busted out and covered with boards. Even the places that had heavy grates pulled across their fronts had been cleaned out. Bars, loan shops, hat shops, markets. Except for the liquor, I thought, all that stolen merchandise was probably still around the neighborhood, in closets and cellars. Fire had taken a few small buildings and had charred portions of others, but the riot had not taken everything. I could see how things could keep on going. If Sherrill had hoped to level the city with his fevered scheming, he had failed.

"You were here when it happened?" The cabbie glanced at me in the rearview.

"No," I said.

"They say it started there, at the bridge to Belle Island. A big fight, they say. For what, I don't know. And then everybody was fighting. Just like that."

"It doesn't look so bad now. Just the easy things get broken."

"Oh, there was a lot of things, shooting, fire. Cars burning! It was a bad time. I stayed at home with my gun, that's what I did. My boy wanted to go out, but I kept him in."

"Pull it up here and stop."

"Boss, you don't want to get out around here."

"Stop the cab."

"Okay, you're the boss."

I gave the cabbie a twenty-dollar bill and waved him away. I surveyed the front of the Sally Dee Shop at Illinois and Hastings and wondered if women had looted it or if the men had broken in to lift the dresses and underthings sold there. I walked two more blocks up Hastings and then up a flight of stairs at the side of an old boardinghouse. I recognized the fresh chips in the bricks as bullet holes. The windows had all been replaced with boards or sheets of metal, and the wood of the trim and the stairway had been ripped and splintered. I put my finger into the bright wood where a bullet had torn through and let my palm draw over the smooth gray wood on the top of the rail. When I reached the second floor, I began reading the numbers scratched into the doors. I moved across the narrow porch, removed my hat, and knocked at the third door.

A chain dropped down on the inside and swayed and scratched

over the molding. A heavy bolt drew back and the door opened. "Yes?"

I found my voice stoppered by the clenching of my throat. I coughed and then said, "I'd like to see Officer Walker."

The buxom colored woman eyed me, calm, considering. "Your business?"

"No business," I said. I looked down at the two children who peeked around their mother's skirt. "I just wanted to catch up on old times."

"May I tell him your name?"

"Let him in, Emily. I don't guess he means any harm."

She stepped aside, and I walked into the narrow apartment. Past the entryway and the coat closet, the place opened somewhat to a room that barely held a sofa and two straight-backed chairs. Farther back, Walker stood, filling another narrow hallway. He waved to me to keep coming. We walked through the hallway, past the bathroom, straight through the kitchen, and through a door to the long bedroom. The whole apartment was one long, straight line, with no windows except one at the front and one at the head of the twin bed at the rear, and both of those had been boarded up. Two smaller beds crammed together and a dresser completed the room. Since there was no chair, or space for one, I sat on the edge of one of the small beds.

"Been on a holiday, it looks like, Detective. You picked up some color there."

"I guess so," I said. I rubbed my chin thoughtfully.

"Lost a little weight, maybe, too. Where'd you get that fancy eyeball?"

"Listen, Walker, I don't want to put you out. I know it isn't the time for a white man to come socializing around here."

"Well, I don't plan on feeding you," said Walker. "Say your piece."

"Can you tell me what happened here?" I said. "How was it?"

"Well, you can see how it was. I don't know what you all were doing, but it came to us a little before midnight. I was up to Sunnie Wilson's place, you know, the Forest Club, because I figured that would be the place to be. I was keeping my ear to the ground, like you had asked me to do. Sooner or later, everybody in the Valley shows up there. You know a lot of white folks come in there, too. Then that bug-eyed fool Willie Tompkins came up on the stage, yelling about a riot. We didn't know anything about it. We were all just drinking, you know, folks was dancing and listening to music. Somehow it all just caught on. You could see it happening. It got from where you could see that they didn't want to believe it to where they couldn't help themselves. Willie come up, he grabbed the microphone and hollered out, 'They done throwed a colored woman and her baby off the Belle Isle Bridge!' And that was what did it. Then they all ran out on the street breathing hellfire. You talk about some worried-looking white folks."

"What did you do?"

"I came back here to look after my family, that's what I did."

I looked at him for a long time, then dropped my head and studied the floor for a moment. I looked up at Walker and then realized that my eyes would be pointing in different directions. I lifted my head and said, "That's all right."

"I guess it is," said Walker. "But now there's some talk about my job being on the line. Dereliction of duty. I was here the whole time. How many days? Three days. They were looking for me to come to work. Some fool dropped a brick off the roof and caved in a woman's head down on the street. A woman from the neighborhood with three little ones. Then there was a story that got out, just a lie, that there was a sniper holed up in the building, so the Guard came down here and shot the whole place up to hell. We sat in the bathtub the whole night, all five of us."

"It's a hell of a thing."

"You know," said Walker, "that colored boy of yours is still alive. But the way it is, maybe you'd have done better to let the Lord take him down on the street. If he ever comes to, he won't ever walk again, they say."

"I hardly knew what I was doing," I said.

"His grandfather was killed, you know that?"

"I didn't know."

"So I guess that means you're responsible for that boy now, in a way, don't it? He doesn't have anybody else."

I said nothing. I looked toward the closed-up window and imagined a similar shabby boardinghouse to the rear of Walker's building. My eye went out of focus as I thought things over. "You're a good man, Walker," I said. "Better than me."

"Each man's got to worry about his own life," said Walker. "We're all the same in that way."

I pulled out a folded wad of money from my pocket. I offered it to Walker. "It's a thousand dollars. I happened to come into it, and I figure you could use it as well as I can."

Walker took the money and turned it over in his hand. "There's blood on everything in this world," he said.

"If you can't use it—"

"I can use it," he said. "We can use it."

I stood up. "I'll see if I can put in a word for you with Mitchell."

Walker just nodded and turned away, and I shuffled toward the front door. In the front room, the children and their mother watched me without expression as I passed by. I walked out the door thinking, *I guess I really did lose some weight. The glass eye fits a lot better.*

I had to walk a number of blocks to catch another cab to take me to police headquarters. The place was almost empty, for some reason, as if the criminal element had eased off in honor of the riot or had decided to start honoring the Sabbath. Nobody said anything to me when I breezed in the front door. *It could be,* I thought, *that they don't even recognize me.* I knew that the days of sun had brought out a surprising burst of freckles over my nose and brow, and I had lost enough weight in my face so that the round arch of my teeth seemed to show through my lips and cheeks. I went right for the stairs and made it up to the third floor unaccosted. The door to Mitchell's office was locked and it was dark inside, so I dragged a chair over from the secretarial pool and waited against the wall. The chair wasn't comfortable. I sat straight with my hands on my knees, my new straw hat dangling from a finger. Though it was a Sunday, I knew he'd be in eventually.

A few ladies trickled in and whispered to themselves. They began to clack away at their typewriters and swirled about filing papers in cabinets. After half an hour of it, I heard heavy footsteps on the stairs. Mitchell and another officer rounded the corner and saw me. Mitchell's eyes narrowed a bit, but his mouth, his jaw, and his posture betrayed nothing.

"Sergeant," he said, "I'll need a word with Detective Caudill."

He looked older and smaller than I remembered. The weariness of his features gave him an air of dead calm. We went into the office, and I closed the door after us. I sat before Mitchell's desk and placed my hat carefully on the other chair.

"You've been taking some sun," said Mitchell.

"A little," I said, looking up at him.

"Took a little vacation, then?"

"I had some coming, I guess," I said.

"Lost some weight, too, maybe."

"I guess."

"This is all a little lucky for you, Caudill. The riot took away all the attention you might have been drawing to yourself."

"I don't worry. I'm not sorry for it."

"Have you been up on Hastings Street?"

I nodded. "Just forty-three dead, is that right? I heard four hundred where I was."

"You heard wrong, then," said Mitchell. "That's how things are, rumors all around."

"Sherrill?"

"Dead, we guess. We have a body, but we couldn't find anybody to identify him. Wasn't much left of him. He's still on ice at the morgue if you want to have a look."

"That's all right," I said. "Rix?"

Mitchell shook his head.

"Where could a big redhead like that go and hide?"

"It doesn't matter. It's all over now. Think of it as a little steam letting off. Just forty-three people lost in a city that will have close to two million when the boys come back. Nothing comes for free, Caudill. You know that."

"Steam," I muttered. "That's all." I kept my hands still on the arms of the chair.

Mitchell leaned over and opened the bottom drawer of his desk. He drew out my gun and slid it over the desktop. It made no sound on the polished surface, and the tip of the barrel turned silently toward me when the forward motion stopped.

"Johnson fished it out and cleaned it up for you. I can get you a new badge if you need one."

"That's all right," I said. I thought it over for a moment, squeezing the arms of the chair. "What's all this going to mean for you, Captain?"

Mitchell turned to face me squarely. "In a situation like this," he said, "if you're left standing, and if you've done well under the pressure, there are rewards. If the mayor, say, has had to lean on you and your expertise in a time of crisis, he won't forget about it. This is the way of all politics. If the mayor or the governor has in mind a higher position for me, then I'll take it if I can. I won't deny it."

I looked at him. My breath felt heavy and deep, like I was asleep. I said simply, "Walker's a good man."

Mitchell thought it over for a moment. "I can see what you're saying."

"He's a good enough man to have a break fall his way," I said.

"After the dust settles, I'll see what—"

"You'll put him back on the force and clear his record or we'll see what an embarrassment I can be."

Mitchell sat back and let his posture droop a little. "I never thought that Swope would get—"

"Just cut Walker the break," I said.

"All right," said Mitchell. "You've read the papers?"

I nodded. "You can't trust the papers."

"We're lucky Johnson made it to Lloyd's yacht before anyone else."

I knew that the papers had explained the deaths on the yacht away. For a moment, I wondered when the public had ever been able to deal with the truth of things. When I was a boy, my mother kept a few chickens about the yard. I remembered stepping out with no thought and twisting the head off a plump one whenever she needed it for supper. We had to eat. But now you could just go down to the Kroger's and pick up whatever you wanted, already cleaned and plucked. The good wives of the city had grown away from dirtying their hands in that fashion. I felt regret that something vital seemed to be passing, and wished I could find the words to make it clear to myself how it was wrong. I guessed that Tommy probably could have.

I stood up and pulled my charred badge case from my pocket. I opened it and rubbed my thumb over the silver shield, rubbed until it felt warm. Then I flipped it through the air toward Mitchell, turned abruptly, and left him to catch it or let it smack him in the chest. As I hit the door, I realized I had forgotten my new hat on the chair, but I kept going, kept walking past the secretaries, who stared openly at me. I went down the steps with my hand sliding over the cool handrail.

When I got to the street, I stood for a moment with my thumbs in my pockets and waited. I felt like standing up straight, felt like sucking in a chest full of air and tasting the exhaust from all the cars in my mouth. I couldn't say how long the money would last or exactly what I'd do next or where I'd be tomorrow, but at least I'd found a way to be simple again. *It's easy,* I thought, *it's easy enough.* Funny how the world is so big that almost nobody will miss you if you drop off the face of it. Things keep going, they always do.

There was only one more stop to make before I could get on with living, and I didn't know how it would turn out. Eileen had not heard anything from me since it all had happened, and I could imagine that she had been cut up pretty bad with worry. There was always the chance, I thought, that Alex might have found his way home after seeing what a place the world can be. But I was not optimistic, even though I now found myself alive and almost rid of all the dirty connections. If I could not return her boy to her, at least I could show her that I was still alive and that I was not afraid to give things a try—if she could still bear to have me.

There was no worry. It was as if I had indeed become someone else. I could have hailed a cab or jumped onto the streetcar running up Macomb, but I just started walking, stepping lightly where my feet wanted me to go, through the only city I knew.